Riley, John.
Mutual aid : a novel /

Parma Branch
Jackson District Library

8/18/2016

WITHDRAWN

ACKNOWLEDGEMENTS

I owe a big thanks to Chief Dan Riley of the Pulaski Township Fire and Rescue for checking my firefighting and medical technical facts.

I also need to thank Dale Jordon, retired fireman from the city of Jackson, Michigan, and volunteer for the villages of Hanover and Pulaski. During trips around southern Michigan, he was kind enough to answer my questions, communicate his knowledge of fire and rescue procedures, and share his memories of growing up in the Pulaski area.

A big thank you to my brother, Ralph Riley, for his timely suggestions and for explaining medical procedures in the field.

I need to acknowledge David Shaw, former fire investigator, for his explanation of investigative procedures and methodology. This enabled me to add a whole new dimension to the book.

In summary, I need to thank my wife, Susan, for putting up with my working on the book, being a sounding board for rough chapters, and offering suggestions.

Riley, John.
Mutual aid : a novel /

Parma Branch
Jackson District Library   **8/18/2016**

This is a work of fiction. All of the characters, organizations, locations, and events portrayed in this novel are either the product of the author's wild imagination or are used fictitiously. Any resemblance to characters living or dead is purely coincidental.

Cover photography by Ralph Riley. Cover adaptation by the author.

Mutual Aid

John P. Riley

Chapter One

My cell phone pager went off just before eleven P.M. The wife and I were closing the place up to go to bed. We'd stayed up to watch some chick flick she'd rented from NETFLIX. I don't even recall the name of the movie, just that it wasn't as bad as I had feared.

"Structure fire, 1519 South Stone Road, cross, Stone and Folks," the dispatcher said. I paused on the stairs to listen.

My wife poked her head over the railing of the upstairs balcony. "Is that Pulaski?" she asked.

I was in my stocking feet and had stopped on the second step from the bottom. I nodded my head. "Gotta go," I called back.

"Be careful," she called in a worried voice, still peering down from the balcony.

Thirty-five years of marriage and she was still concerned I might do something foolish. I guess I gave her enough reasons to worry.

"Structure fire. Easy in, easy out," I reassured her, trying to reassure myself.

I sat in a chair to slip into my boots. Central Dispatch repeated the address.

In less than a minute I was out the door, across the porch, and into the early-spring night. Behind me the grandfather clock in the upstairs hall began bonging out the eleven o'clock hour.

The cool air smelled of damp earth and felt heavy with moisture. A lone spring peeper called from somewhere by the pole barn, breaking the heavy silence. In a few weeks the nights in the countryside would be alive with the sound of amorous frogs hopping about and calling to each other.

I grabbed my bunker pants from the floor of my Dodge pickup and slipped them on. The rest of my turn-out gear I left on the floor.

The pager on my smart phone crackled with the voice of our chief responding to the call. He lived within a hundred yards of the fire station in Pulaski and would bring a truck. I'd drive on over to the scene and we'd meet up.

Within moments I was heading down the drive to the road and west on McDonald Road toward Stone, wondering what was going on down on South Stone. I wouldn't have long to speculate as the address wasn't over three miles away. I hit the brakes and my headlights swung around the corner of McDonald and Stone. I half expected to scare up some deer in the high beams. A few farmers had managed to get into the drier fields and the Dodge's lights revealed the freshly turned earth.

Heading south at a pretty good clip, I came to the corner of Stone and Folks Road. Passing the 'Stop Ahead' sign, I spotted the emergency lights of Engine 1 out of Pulaski approaching the corner from the west. As the fire engine rounded the corner and passed through my lights, I could see the chief driving and one other person. They sped southbound on Stone and I followed. A quarter mile down the road I glanced in my rearview mirror and noticed another pair of lights rounding the corner and following me. The rotating strobes cast an eerie glow on the maples lining the country road. We had at least four people showing up.

I didn't need to read the numbers on the mailboxes to find our destination. It was apparent from a hundred yards out. A two-story farmhouse sat back from the road in a grove of trees. The rear of the house was spewing thick smoke that showed up in the yard light and the lights from the fire engine. I followed the engine into the gravel drive and, shifting into four-wheel drive, pulled out of the way, off to the side on the grass.

Seconds later, our tanker truck slowed and eased up the driveway. It carried two thousand gallons of water and had proved itself to be a blessing time and time again around the countryside.

Arriving at a fire was a lot like watching water flow over a dam. At least that's what it made me think me of. Weeds and such slowly approach the dam head, pick up speed, with everything suddenly happening at once, and over the dam they go. That was how things went at a fire scene. Trucks and people came in from all directions, almost like a dream. Then in a burst of activity, lines (fire hoses to civilians) came out, equipment came on, and firemen entered the house.

It was second nature for me to slip on my turn-out gear as I hustled to the smoking house. An orange glow reflected into the night from a window on the far side.

A female, who I took to be the woman of the family, was shouting and hysterically pointing at the house. She wore a loose-fitting jacket over a long nightgown and her blonde-streaked hair was all disheveled. Her feet were in a pair of high muck boots; probably the first thing she found on the way out the door. She clutched a cell phone in her left hand. It probably was the first thing she grabbed when awakened by the fire. I could always pick out the mother at a house fire. She almost always stands in the center of a small knot of people. Some react with hysteria while others are more subdued, with pained looks on their faces, trembling and crying in the arms of neighbors or family members. Neighbors tried to comfort this mom while Nan Spink, the other fireman who had ridden in with the chief, knelt beside a man who I took to be the husband.

A medical kit was open on the ground beside them. Nan had slipped on a pair of medical gloves and was examining the man's arms. She grabbed a plastic bottle with a squeeze spout on it and squeezed a cleansing saline solution on his palms and arms. Nancy, or Nan, as we always called her, was the only female on our rural department. I was glad to see her. She performed miracles with accident victims and hysterical people at fire scenes. She was a large woman, tall and sturdy, but had that special touch that seemed to sooth the fears and pain of the people she came in contact with.

She was good with four-legged patients, too. If anybody in the neighborhood had a sick animal, their first call, before the vet over in Concord, was to Nan.

I walked by as the man grimaced in pain. "The ambulance is on its way," Nan was telling him. "You're going to be okay."

He looked up into her eyes and nodded slightly.

The chief was pulling off a two-and-a-half-inch line from the side of the engine. His assistant chief, John Schultz (Schultzie, to us) had dragged a line from the tanker and was hand threading it to a fitting on the side. Someone started up the generator and the scene lights came on to throw a harsh glow over the area.

Chief Kip handed me a self-contained breathing apparatus and kept one for himself. I slipped mine on as he did the same. Crackling sounds could be heard from the back of the house. Schultzie used a spanner to tighten the fitting on our line.

The Hanover Township tanker slowed on the road, crept up the drive, and eased in beside ours. Twenty-five hundred more gallons. Two men leaped down from the cab.

The hysterical woman broke from the group and came running up to us, getting in the way and shouting, "Richie! Richie's in there!" Her voice quivered with fear and panic as she gestured toward an upstairs window. "My husband tried to get to him but burned his arms. Somebody do something!" She turned and pointed at her husband sitting cross-legged on the ground. He sat is if in a stupor, staring blankly at his arms as Nan finished wrapping them in gauze.

The possibility occurred to me that he could go into shock, but I knew he was in good hands with Nan working on him.

Jabbing her finger at the house, like the

thrust of a sword, the woman wailed again, "Do something! My son is still in there!"

Thick smoke billowed from under the eaves.

"He's only seventeen," a woman, whom I took to be the neighbor, said as she gently wrapped her arms around the now sobbing mom. She slowly worked her friend away from us and back across the lawn toward her husband. Nan had the man's head tilted back and was rinsing the smoke from his eyes.

I hoped this Richie kid had the sense to stay low and make it to a downstairs room.

Kip clenched the hose nozzle in his gloved left hand, and I grabbed ahold about three feet behind him. We both carried flashlights in our right hands. The chief also dragged along an ax. He'd use the handle for sounding the floors, checking for weakness. After running a radio test with Schultzie and Nan, we mounted the steps onto the covered porch. The mom burst from the group of people attempting to comfort her, and came running over to follow us in. The neighbors grabbed her again. She threw her hands over her face and started sobbing. Someone wrapped what looked like an Indian blanket around her shoulders as they led her away.

Kip looked back at Schultzie and nodded his head. Schultzie tapped the valve handle to the line we were dragging to show he was ready.

Another pickup pulled in the drive followed by a Jackson Area Ambulance vehicle. It was a relief to have more personnel on the scene. Nan walked the injured man over to the ambulance and, with a gentle pat on the back and a few kind words, turned him over to the medics. The wife followed at his side, attempting to clutch at his arm, then snatching her hands away before touching his injured limb, not sure what to do. A female EMT put her arm around the woman and led her to the back of the ambulance.

Out on the road, another pickup pulled off to the side as the Concord tanker arrived, lights and sirens going. Two more volunteer firemen hustled through the darkness into the the brightly lit scene. Schultz directed them to their assigned jobs.

Nan and Walt, another fireman, were in full turn-out gear and mounted the steps with another line, prepared to come in when needed. We hadn't been on the scene for more than ten minutes or so.

We entered what appeared to be a living room. Kip first, with me a step behind, clutching the line. Kip started a left-hand search pattern. There was smoke in the room, but not too thick. We remained standing as we dragged the uncharged line in, coordinating our steps so we could pull together. It's hard work dragging fifty feet of line. I was starting to perspire already. Kip would let Schultzie know via the radio when the hose should be charged and it would get even heavier. We might need a third person. Kip thumped the floor with the ax handle as we went, checking for burn-throughs.

We came to an open door providing entry to a small room. Kip trained his light in and around the interior. The smoke was a little thicker. He soundly tapped the floor with the ax handle. We stepped in. There was a bed, dresser, and a small closet. We checked on the bed, under and behind it, and in the closet. Nothing here. The room didn't look used. Guest room maybe. Retreating back out the doorway, I kept the hose looped back out of the way so as to avoid a trip hazard for the chief.

The door to the second room was closed.

Kip approached and placed his hand against it. He turned to me and I could see the concern in his eyes as he juggled the nozzle to remove a glove. He felt the door again and backed away. He looked at me and I nodded knowingly. The sounds of popping and cracking were faint through our headgear, but I couldn't tell from which direction it was coming. I did know from the chief's actions that the room was too hot for us to try and enter. We came to a stairway. Kip radioed out our position and the status of the room. Then we worked our way up the stairs, the thump of the ax handle sounding as we went.

The muted roar of the engines in the yard accompanied us on our climb.

How many times I'd been in a structure fire, I couldn't count. I'd spent my career with the fire department in Muncie, Indiana, retiring only after an injury sustained during a house fire just off Cornbread Road. It was under similar conditions as this fire. The two-story house was going up around us as my partner and I started an organized search, looking for a little boy whose hysterical mother stood in the front yard, shrieking, while neighbors held her back. There was no injured father at that one, though. No burn victim who would have given his life to save his son, like the injured man we found when we showed up at this fire. I imagined this dad would have gone back in with us, if we'd have let him. I know the mom would.

Kip and I arrived at a landing at the top of the stairs. The sound of the fire was louder. A smoke alarm gave off a shrill, but muted scream. The battery was winding down. There was a window to our right where ghostly lights of the emergency vehicles fought their way through the grime and smoke. I knew the rest of the crew would be stringing more lines and monitoring the engines.

We worked our way left to right, and came across another room toward the road side of the house. The smoke was thicker and I followed the chief's lead and dropped to my hands and knees. Entering the room, we crept slowly, the thud of the ax handle ahead of me sounding our way. A search of the closet and around all the stuff in the room revealed nothing. It amazed me how much junk people could pack away in an upstairs room. We worked our way out of the room, keeping contact with the fire hose at all times. Kip retraced our path across the large landing toward yet another room. The door was ajar just a few inches. He eased it open with his flashlight and tapped the floor. I could feel the heat coming up through the boards. We were over the hot room below.

We'd fought a fire one night the past winter in a large farm shop. Crawling across the floor, we were warmed by the heat coming up from the concrete. It had absorbed the energy from the fire and was radiating it back up, into the room. The wood floor in this house was transferring the heat from the fire below, the room that was too hot to enter.

The smoke was like a heavy wool blanket. We couldn't see more than a foot or so ahead of our powerful flashlights. There was no getting below the smoke at this point. It was thick and it was everywhere. We crept in, pulling together on the heavy line.

"This would be a good spot for a body," I said to Kip through my mike. I sure hoped we didn't find one, though. That was the worst part of the job, recovering bodies while the anguished family members looked on. I felt around with my right hand, the one with the flashlight. Directly ahead of me, Kip was doing the same. I could barely make out the bottom of his boots in front of me as the smoke closed in like a suffocating cocoon.

The fire in Muncie came back to me; the smoke thick enough to be cut with a chain saw. I worked my way across the floor behind my buddy, Frank, who opted to take the lead. The frantic mom in the front yard said her little boy was in an upstairs bedroom. At that point I was pretty sure it wasn't going to be a rescue, but a recovery. Thank God for the air tanks strapped to our backs, or they'd have been recovering us, too.

We'd searched the floor, feeling as we went, there in Muncie, too. I don't remember hearing the wood splinter or snap. I just remember feeling the floor dropping away from under us, like some cheap carnival ride. The hose slipped from my grasp as the sounds of the fire enveloped me as we fell. I couldn't see Frank, but I sensed him ahead of me, grasping and clawing at the floorboards as he went through. I landed on my right side with a sickening thud. Something ripped in my shoulder and pain shot through my left elbow as it struck an object buried in the smoke. With a loud "whoosh" the fire erupted around us. Like a patient animal, it had just been waiting for food - fresh oxygen. Now it had Frank and me to go along with it. I felt the heat through my face shield. It had us surrounded. Stunned, I tried to roll over onto my hands and knees, but the pain in my shoulder and elbow made me collapse. There was still a lot of smoke with the occasional lick of flame stabbing through like a hungry tongue. I willed myself to my knees and felt around with my left hand on the floor for the charged line. I knew I had to get some water on us soon or we'd be done for. The fire was beyond popping and cracking now. It roared in my ears and I could feel the heat through my protective gear. Most of the smoke had ignited now and, in the glare, I had trouble seeing anything. Somehow I'd kept my breathing mask on through the fall. I couldn't hear Frank and I shouted his name over the noise as I felt around on the floor. Each team had a radio man, not like now where each person has a radio. He was the one with the radio and I hoped he was calling for help. I found my flashlight. The light still shown weakly through the smoke and flame. It may as well not have been on. Setting it on the floor to shine upward as a feeble beacon, I felt around in the smoke and fire for the hose line, for Frank, for anything. I didn't know it, but the hose was dangling a few short feet above my head. Later, it would be thrown away due to the scorching from the fire.

As I was frantically feeling around with my left hand, and trying to flop my right arm about, a cascade of water rained down on us from the hole above. I heard shouting, but couldn't tell what was being said. The seconds seemed as minutes to me as the flames receded to thick smoke, then the water washed out some of the smoke and I could finally look around. Above me, through a jagged, scorched, hole in the ceiling, two members of my engine company lay on their stomachs, dousing us with water. One of the men had pulled my line back up and was using it to shoot sideways around the room I was in.

Ahead of me lay a soaked form; lifeless, his helmet and breathing mask askew. Someone slogged through the soaked debris and I saw a pair of boots come up beside me.

"You okay?" the person called in a muffled voice. I attempted to look up at the speaker as I fell over.

The tug on the line brought me back to the here and now. I was in Pulaski Township, Michigan, not Muncie, Indiana. A world apart in equipment, personnel, the type of structure situations (not many barn fires in Muncie) but not in dedication. The volunteers in our little community were well trained, the chief saw to that, and eager to serve. They were a good crew to work with.

Ahead of me, Kip eased forward and took another sounding. I could hear the muted radio traffic of the firemen on the porch and in the yard. Suddenly I saw flames shoot up to my right and ahead of me. The floor had opened up and let oxygen in to the downstairs room. Unknown to me, Kip had crept forward, setting his flashlight down with each step and, with a little applied weight, he had put it through the floor. His arm went through clear to his shoulder. With the thick smoke, I couldn't see Kip turn his head, but I heard his voice come back to me in a muffled shout.

"Get out!" he yelled over his left shoulder. With all of the noise and the radio and our protective gear, I still got the message. He didn't have to tell me twice. Dropping the line, I turned and followed it with my right hand back to the doorway and into the hall landing. I sensed Kip crawling along behind me. The landing was now filled with gray and black smoke billowing out the doorway of the room we were escaping. Reaching the banister, I stood and felt Kip's hand on my shoulder. The same shoulder I'd torn up eight years earlier in Muncie.

"Behind you," he said over the radio. I took my first charging step down the stairway and ran smack into a hazy form hidden in the dense smoke.

The kid, I thought. In a split second I knew it wasn't the missing kid, but the first of several firemen who were coming up the stairs. There wasn't supposed to be anybody in the house until the chief called them in. They couldn't have been from our crew. I didn't know who these clowns were, but I had a good idea. In the smoke and confusion my momentum carried me into the figure and on into a second and down a few steps into yet a third. Kip was stumbling along right behind me. On down the stairs we went in a rolling, tumbling, jumble of arms, legs, air tanks, and turn-out coats. We burst through the front doorway in a belching cloud of smoke and collapsed into a scattered heap on the porch.

Kip must have had a death grip on his flashlight and ax as they were still held securely in his right hand. From where I lay I could see the angry look in his eyes. I wondered if he was going to use the ax on the three men who had clogged up the stairs.

Nan was yelling, "I tried to keep them out, Chief!"

"What the hell!" I panted as I stood up and looked around.

Thick smoke billowed out the open door and enveloped us. "Clear the porch!" the chief called. We stumbled down the steps and onto the lawn and into the glare of the scene lights. I saw the "M G" block letters on the fire helmets and turn-out coats of the other men and my suspicions were confirmed. They were from the next township over, Maple Grove. We were on automatic mutual aid and they knew better than to enter the house while a search was being conducted. We all had the same training, but they apparently had gotten too eager. Fortunately no one was hurt. We stood on the front walk sorting ourselves out while Nan stood by us shaking her head in disgust.

"Come on fellas," Chief Kip harshly

addressed the embarrassed trio, "we look like a bunch of monkeys humpin' a football!" He shook his fire ax for emphasis. "Let's get organized with no screw-ups before somebody gets hurt." He looked over at the medics and the family standing near the ambulance down the driveway. The distraught mother was holding her cell phone to her ear, sobbing to someone on the other end. Two county deputies had arrived and were watching expectantly. One, Deputy Flint, was on our fire department and would have been pitching in if he hadn't been on duty. He shook his head knowingly, then turned to talk to the homeowners. He had a notepad and pen in his hand and was jotting down notes.

"Grab the line," Kip called to me as he bent and began pulling the fire hose out of the house. "Lend a hand fellas." The Maple Grove men formed a line and helped out, eager to make amends. I was still feeling wobbly in the knees and from their expressions and silence, I knew the others were shook, too. The chief seemed fine.

The guys from Hanover, Concord, and the rest were in full turn-out gear and ready for action. "Get someone out here to kill the power," The chief told one guy, who nodded and ran to his truck.

"There's a hot room on the left with the door closed, the one I radioed about," Kip said, standing to face Nan. The Maple Grove men and I continued tugging on the canvas hose. "You'll find a hole in the ceiling where I put my arm through the upstairs floor; clear to the armpit. We didn't find the boy, but that doesn't mean he's not in there," he said with another glance over at the stunned parents. "The smoke is just too thick."

Nan nodded knowingly, processing it all in her mind, getting a mental picture. "Where do you need me, Chief?" she asked. Off duty, she addressed him as Kip, like everyone else, but on a fire or rescue scene, it was always as "Chief."

"Take your line around back and pour some water through the window," he instructed. "Go ahead and charge when you're ready."

Nan and Walt, the other fireman, dragged the slack line across the lawn and around the back of the house. As they rounded the corner she nodded to Schultzie, who pulled on the control valve. "We're pouring it on," she called over the radio.

"As soon as the door is opened to that room, it's going to take off, so we'd better stand to one side when we go in," I offered.

Kip nodded in agreement and turned to instruct the Maple Grove men to throw a twenty-eight foot extension ladder against the house, then grab a line and shoot water through the upstairs window. They did so, with the hot glass shattering under the pressure.

We followed our line back into the house, pulling it back down toward us as we went. It was a small miracle that it didn't snag somewhere. The nozzle came tumbling down the stairs and Kip snatched it up. "Charge the line," he called over the radio. The hose immediately swelled with water. He directed the spray onto the door to the side room. We stood to one side and Kip smacked the hot knob with his ax and kicked the door open. We were met with an instant burst of smoke and flame. He directed the spray in through the doorway. Within moments the flames were gone and Kip shot the water around the ceiling and far wall. I could see the spray from Nan's line coming in the shattered window and bouncing around the ceiling and onto our side of the room. A flood of water flowed across the floor and out the door, carrying soot, ash, and charred debris with it. The far wall was black and I could see where the fire had worked its way along the ceiling to the hole that had opened under Kip through the weakened upstairs floor. A shudder went through me as I realized how closely we'd come to a repeat of the Muncie tragedy.

In Muncie, in the little two-story house off Cornbread Road, the fire had been accidentally started by the six-year-old who's small body was later found in the closet of the downstairs room that we had fallen into; the room below where his mother had thought him to be.

The Fire Chief visited me in my room at Ball Memorial Hospital and filled me in. He said it looked like the child was sleeping, curled up in a corner of the closet like a very realistic ventriloquist's dummy. There was not a mark on him. Cause of death was thought to be smoke inhalation. The Delaware County Medical Examiner would let us know for sure. There was a Bic cigarette lighter laying next to his body. Little kids were always fascinated with lighters. Unhappily, this same scenario was played out every day somewhere in the United States. That was also when I was told that Frank didn't make it. My shoulders slumped and the breath went right out of me. I felt bad about the little kid, but even worse about Frank, a man I'd worked with for twelve of my twenty years on the force. We'd joked around, barbecued, and attended weddings and funerals together. I'd attended his kids' graduations, and he, mine. Frank rode a Harley and couldn't understand my fascination with Studebakers. "Just because they were made in Indiana doesn't make them a good car," he claimed. He was as close as I had to a best friend. As close as one of my brothers.

"Cut the line, Nan," the chief spoke into his radio. He'd already turned off the stream at his nozzle. We took a step into the smoldering room. "Let's get a fan set up to clear this smoke, and send a team upstairs. Don't enter the room," he called over the radio to the crew out front. "Hose it down from the doorway."

Thumping the floor with the ax handle, we eased on in the room on our hands and knees swiping away debris as we went. Visibility was improving as the pressure fan came on at the front doorway.

I heard the stairs creaking under heavy boots as another team headed up with a charged line.

A search of the room turned up a charred mess, but no body. The kid wasn't in there. I looked around the room. "This is where it started," I said to Kip.

He looked back at me and nodded. "Yeah, and I'd bet it was set, too," he observed.

"Sure looks like it," I said. Part of my training in Muncie was as a fire investigator. I could see from the burn and smoke pattern that this was where the flames took hold. There was no electrical outlet on the wall where the most burn was, so I didn't suspect an electrical problem. "The bed." I pointed a gloved hand. Kip followed my point and then my gaze to the ceiling where he had almost come through the floor above.

"Someone started a fire there, too," the chief said. The bed showed a large hole in the middle with springs sagging from the heat. The charred and soaking mattress circled the burn-hole and on its outside edges was what was left of black, tattered blankets.

"Somebody tried to burn them out," I said turning to Kip. "This doesn't look like an accident to me."

"Let's search the house again," Kip said in reply. "If the kid's in here, there's got to be something left, but I don't believe he's here."

"Mmm hmm," I said in agreement.

After leaving the house and wiping the sweat from our faces and necks, we reentered and searched the upstairs. Nan and Walt took the basement and downstairs. "The outside wall was going up when we went around to the other side," she said. "I could smell the fuel, probably diesel fuel," she concluded.

Chapter Two

We stood in the gravel drive and talked to the deputies. Fire personnel drifted around, drinking Gatorade or water. The engines had been idled down, so we could actually hear ourselves think.

Our man, Flint, as we like to call the deputy who was also a volunteer on our department, read the notes from his interview with the parents. "The Collins family has an older daughter," he told us, "a senior this year. She was at a sleep-over with some friends from school and showed up here after her mom called her." He paused to review his notes.

"The parents were sure their son was in the house," the other deputy said. "The big sister said he probably snuck out - said he sometimes does that without the parents finding out," he concluded. The deputy was a younger man whom I hadn't met before. He looked like he was still in high school.

They keep getting younger and younger, I thought.

"The parents had no idea the kid was sneaking out," officer Flint said. "He's only seventeen, just turned last month, the mom told me. He's going to be a junior next fall."

"What kind of student is he?" I asked. "Any troubles?"

"Don't know," Flint replied, "but I'll find out on the followup." He wrote a note. "I did get the names of some friends," he said. "Seems he's picked up a few lately that the folks didn't know about."

"Don't tell me," Kip said, "the big sister ratted him out."

"Right," Flint said. "She'll graduate in about a month, and she's concerned about her brother's effort at school."

"From the same high school?" I asked. "With school of choice it's not uncommon to have one kid in Maple Grove and another in Concord or Western."

"There's a lot of school hopping," Kip conceded. "Trying to find the right fit, I guess."

The young deputy spoke up. "Yeah, he goes

to Maple Grove, too. The parents haven't moved him yet. I got a sister who teaches over at Northwest. She told me kids get in trouble in one school, the parents move the little darlings to another school where, guess what? They get in trouble there, too."

"It's always the school's or teacher's fault," Kip stated. "They're in it just for the summers off and the big money. Ain't that right, Flint?" He grinned as he laid a hand on the deputy's shoulder. Flint had taught fourth grade for six years before throwing in the towel.

"Police work is damn well less stressful than teaching, I can tell you," Flint offered with a shake of his head. Then he continued with his notes. "The parents went to bed just before ten o'clock. It had been a long day of yard work and preparing the garden," he said. "They dropped right off to sleep. Richie, the son, was in his downstairs room on his cell phone when they went to bed. Mrs. Collins said his door was open. Their room is upstairs, directly above Richie's. The daughter's room is upstairs, too. The third room up is used as a storeroom," he said, looking up at the group.

"We found the rooms," Kip interrupted, "but there was no sign of the boy's cell phone so he must have taken it with him. His closet was pretty sparse, too," he added.

Our man, Flint looked around cautiously before he spoke. "The little shit probably took it all with him when he cleared out," he said. He continued with the interview report.

"The smoke alarms woke them up about ten thirty. The mom said she must have been sleeping lightly, as she jumped right up. Her husband awoke and ran down to Richie's room, directly below theirs. The door was closed. He burned his hands on the knob, but got the door open. He said there was a fire on the bed and along the baseboard on the far wall, underneath the window. He tried to beat the flames out with a pillow, then realized he couldn't, it was too far gone. That's when he burned his arms." Flint looked at the others.

"Who closed the door?" I asked. "It was closed when we went in." I shuddered in the cold dampness of the night, shrugging my shoulders to increase my blood flow. My right shoulder was aching again.

"Mr. Collins did," Flint said. "Said he wanted to slow down the fire. Good thinking, huh?" He glanced up from his notes. "He didn't see Richie, but it was pretty smoky in there. Also, he and the mom thought maybe their son had gone upstairs to get them and somehow they'd missed him. The wife was afraid he'd become disoriented and overcome with smoke in an upstairs room."

"The only smoke he saw was on his tail as he ran out the door," Kip observed.

"Now, why," I wondered aloud, "would he want to kill his parents?" We looked at each other with sober looks.

"It sure is odd that the older daughter wasn't at home," the young deputy commented. "Think she had anything to do with it?"

"I'm thinking that the school can shed some light on the family dynamics," Flint said.

"There's a girlfriend, too," the young deputy put in. "Nineteen years old."

"Whose?" I asked. "The dad's, mom's, big sister's or the boy's?"

They all looked at me as if I were speaking Farsi.

"The boy's," Flint responded. "This isn't the big city, you know." He shook his head at me and checked his notes. The parents don't approve of her. She's not from the area, and they think she's a dropout."

"Just sayin'," I responded with a shrug, "and, I bet the kid's leaving a trail with that cell phone."

"We're already all over that," Flint stated with a grin. "Sometimes we actually put our training to use, you know. Can't drink coffee and eat doughnuts all the time." The others laughed and looked at me. We gave Flint a lot of ribbing down at the fire barn about his easy police work.

I shrugged it off. "Where did the parents go for the night? The Red Cross find a place?" I asked.

"Staying with the neighbors down the road," the younger deputy said, still smiling.

I thought for a moment. "Anybody search the outbuildings for the missing kid? And if they're good friends with the folks down the road, he might head there and stay in the barn for the night," I offered.

"We did search the sheds here," Flint said. He looked at the younger deputy. "Maybe we'll go down the road to check it out once we get some backup," he said.

"You ever think of being a cop?" the other deputy asked me, obviously impressed that I'd

36

think of something they hadn't.

"You got a name for the girlfriend?" asked Kip. "Maybe someone on the crew has heard of her."

"The parents, especially the mom, had a few names for her that I won't repeat here," Flint answered. "Meagan Grawn. I've never heard of her. Usually trouble sticks its head up and we get familiar with a name," he added.

"I have a feeling trouble just reared its ugly head here tonight," Kip said soberly.

"There's a lot more to this story, that's for sure," I added while looking around the yard.

"Well," the younger deputy ticked off on his fingers, "we have a seventeen-year-old boy who sneaks out at night, has been picking up new friends that the parents don't approve of, has an older girlfriend, and is missing from the home."

"Not to mention secretive," Kip added.

"This has the mark of drugs all over it," I stated emphatically. The others nodded in agreement.

"Well, thanks guys," Kip said with a smile and a nod at the two deputies. "See you at the station," he added with a playful slap on

Flint's shoulder. We turned to give assistance to Nan, Schultzie, Walt, and the other firemen as they rolled up a few lines and stored them back on the trucks. We left one hooked up in case we had to hose down a hot spot.

    The three guys from Maple Grove melted away toward the road, into the darkness, and were gone.

Chapter Three

I stopped by the fire barn about nine the next morning. I had some free time, as my wife and a few of her friends were off to Shipshewana, Indiana, to make the rounds of the quilters' supply stores. They'd be back that evening, loaded down with material, food, and what-nots.

The chief was in his office filling out paperwork. "Morning Tim," Kip greeted me.

"You sleep here last night?" I asked.

"My wife seem to think I do," he replied, not looking up from his computer screen.

"Coffee?" I inquired, sniffing the air.

"On the counter," he waved his hand. "I woke up early and couldn't get back to sleep. You know how that goes," he said. "Figured to get a jump on this paperwork. Never stops, you know."

"I know," I replied, while pouring coffee

into a styrofoam cup. "It gets worse every year." I reached for the container of sugar.

"Any word on the missing kid from last night?" I queried, glancing over my shoulder as I stirred in some powdered milk and a packet of sugar. I took a gulp of the hot beverage.

Kip swiveled his chair around and heaved a sigh while shaking his head. "Nothing," he replied. "Not a thing. Flint sent me an e-mail after his shift last night. He and the twelve-year-old searched the out-buildings at the neighbor's farm. No evidence the kid had been there. County detectives are going up to school today to talk to his friends."

"The twelve-year-old?"

"That new deputy tagging along with Flint at the fire last night," Kip replied. "I swear they're making them younger every year. His mother probably has to help him put on his 'big boy' underwear." He grinned and held up his fingers in quote signs.

"I thought pretty much the same thing last night," I laughed.

Kip picked up his coffee cup, the fire engine red one that said "Hail to the Chief" on it, and took a sip. "I'm thinkin' the kid is long gone," he said. "He was probably crossing into Hillsdale County by the time we showed up at the fire."

"Got to be with someone," I said. I topped off my coffee at the counter, then stepped over to Kip's desk. "According to Flint, there were no vehicles missing," I said. "We know he's not on foot. Kids today don't like to walk anywhere. Somebody was waiting for him. Maybe even showed up to help him. Could've left a car down the road," I concluded with a nod of my head.

"It's the only thing that makes sense," Kip answered. "Flint said he'd be in, mid-morning. I'll huddle with him and see what cooks out," he said.

"Any chance the big sister is involved," I wondered aloud.

"My impression was, no," Kip said. "She seems to think her brother is a total sleaze-bag. I got that from my source inside Maple Grove High this morning," he smiled.

"Been talking to you sister?"

"Could be," he said. His goofy grin confirmed my suspicions. His older sister taught History and Social Studies at Maple Grove and had a hand in just about everything going on at the school. From hearing her stories, I could see why our man, Flint, had gone into a different career.

"I'd like to be there when the cops show up," I said

"There'll be some little bastards crappin' there pants when the note comes from the office," Kip laughed heartily. "Serves them right."

Nan showed up then and helped herself to the coffee. She carried a large cup from the local Gas-N-Go. "Got any Danish?" She looked at Kip. Her hair was still wet from the shower and she smelled faintly of some woman scent. Some perfume that my wife had, too. Must be a favorite among females.

"Good morning to you, too," Kip said.

"Morning, Nan," I said with a tilt of my head.

"Shoulda' brought my own, I guess," she replied. "Good morning Kip, Tim," she said, before raising her cup to her mouth. She took a long swig while leaning against the counter.

"What's up this morning? Any news on the boy?" she asked.

I hung around for a bit while the chief started to retell his story. "If it's safe to leave the two of you alone, I'll head out and actually get something done today," I said.

"Thanks for stopping," Kip said.

"We'll be okay," Nan replied with a devilish grin. "There's not enough room on his desk for both of us, anyway."

Kip blushed and nearly choked on his coffee.

I threw my empty cup into the trash on the way out the door.

Chapter Four

The next few days went by uneventfully on the rescue front. At the farm, I cut another pickup load of firewood from the back lot on our little forty-acres. Sitting in the quiet of the woods after loading my pickup, my mind drifted to the structure fire down on Stone Road. There had been no word on the missing kid, or of his girlfriend. I was sure the parents were frantic, worrying about his safety, and wondering why he'd set the fire and run off.

Later, my neighbor came over with his big Case tractor to work up the fields he rented from me. He'd be planting corn this year.

"Looks like you'll be cutting hay in another couple weeks," he said as he idled the diesel down and stopped in the gravel drive by the house. "By the way," he said, "I ran into your buddy, Hank, over to the M60 Grill. He said to say 'Hi'. Said he'd see you at Farm Days."

Hank McIntyre was a friend I'd gotten to know at local tractor shows. He lived alone on a sixty acre farm west of Pulaski where he kept a few head of Angus cattle and a small flock of laying hens. Ford 8Ns weren't his only hobby. He also had an interest in classic cars, and drove an '86 Chevy four wheel drive. Once, he'd driven one of my Studebakers in a parade while I drove the other.

Another thing we had in common was my being retired from the fire department in Muncie, and Hank from the police department in Chicago. He didn't talk much about his job, just that after fifteen years, he couldn't take the drugs, violence, and the politics anymore. I imagined it being a high pressure job.

Hank was, at six feet, six inches, one of the largest, if not *the* largest, black man I had ever met, and was built like a football player. The man had a disarming smile and a sense of humor which I appreciated. Over the past few years he'd shared that he's a strong Baptist and attends the little church up in

Concord. He leased out his tillable acreage and bought corn and hay on shares from his renter. With everything we had in common, we just seemed to hit it off.

On my own farm, I had kept aside a five acre field of mixed grass hay to sell to the horse people in the area. It was coming along nicely.

"The hay is lookin' good this year," I answered my neighbor. "Yours?"

"Alfalfa's taking right off, for a new planting," he said, adjusting his seed-corn hat. I noticed he was wearing a new one. No stains yet. "The west twenty of mixed grass and clover is just about to the flowering stage. Hope I can get my corn in so I'm not late on the hay," he lamented.

"I'll let you go then," I smiled and waved. "Nice hat," I pointed out.

"Thanks. Cost me five thousand dollars, but I got a bunch of free seed corn with it." He grinned and nodded good-bye as he throttled up the diesel and drove into the first field, the one by the house. The four-bottom plow swung around the corner to follow, its shiny mold-boards reflecting the bright May sunlight.

He'd be back in two days pulling a disc

harrow and followed by his friend John, towing a six-row corn planter behind his John Deere.

I walked back to the house. My wife was kneeling over a flower bed, working at getting some annuals into the ground before they died on her. She looked up as I walked over.

"Thought I heard your phone pager go off," she said.

"When?"

"Just now, as you were talking to Russ," she said.

"Darn, I hope it's not a structure fire," I called as I ran to the front door. My phone was on a small table just inside the door. Usually I wore it on my belt or in a pocket, but I'd been helping with the flower planting, carting junk around with the wheel barrow, and didn't want to damage it.

I entered and snatched up the phone as Central Dispatch was repeating the message.

"Jackson Central to Pulaski Rescue," the woman's voice said. "Trouble breathing at," and she gave an address on North Pulaski Road. It was one of our frequent fliers.

"Won't be long," I called to my wife, and got into my truck. An over-weight, diabetic, asthma sufferer probably was off her medication again and couldn't find her inhaler. This was the typical run for any fire and rescue. We were on a first name basis with a few of our residents who seemed to have 911 on speed dial.

    Schultz's voice came over the radio in my truck. I could hear the rescue's siren in the background as he responded to Jackson Central Dispatch. I drove to the address north of Pulaski and Schultzie met me at the front door, still wearing his purple nitrile gloves.

    "How's Ruthie?" I asked. Ruthie was our gal.

    "Your girlfriend is going to live," Schultzie proclaimed, smiling at his joke. We walked into the living room. The place looked as it always did, like a bunch of wild bikers lived there. There were papers and magazines littered across the end tables and floor. Mixed in were empty diet pop cans and take-out pizza boxes. A Harley-Davidson clock hung on the wall over the couch. I noticed the time was wrong. Probably didn't work. The room smelled faintly of stale cigarettes and some stench I couldn't identify. A big-screen T.V. played silently in the corner. A red-neck couple was fighting on the stage of the Jerry

Springer show.

"I'll be okay now," Ruthie said from her seat on the stained couch. She smiled weakly. "You boys saved my life again," she said. "Sure could use one of you around the house here. Lord knows that piece-of-shit husband of mine isn't no good," she wobbled her fleshy face.

"Good thing he done went and run off," Schultzie offered.

"Ain't that the truth," Ruthie responded.

We looked over to the door as Ruthie's daughter walked in. She was in her mid thirties but looked much older with sun and smoke damaged skin and a bad dye job to her hair. It was some sort of smokey red. Unlike her mother, she was skinny as a rail. I couldn't imagine Ruthie ever being that thin, no matter how hard I tried.

"Hello, Patty," Schultzie said. I nodded my greeting.

"Sorry boys," Patty responded. She had a raspy, smokers voice. Then to her mom. "You wantin' attention again, Ma?"

"Whachu mean, girl?"

"Wasting these fella's time like this. What's this, the third time this month? You should be ashamed." She looked over at us as if we were Exhibit A.

I was edging toward the door.

"Hmmph," her mother responded.

"I'll get her meds and inhaler from the next room," Patty said to us. "I swear, I can't leave you alone for a minute," she directed a verbal jab at her mother. "You get in trouble, why don't you call me. I'm just next door, you crazy old lady." Patty was starting to get revved up now. We'd seen this play out a dozen times over the past year or so.

I threw Schultzie a glance and he cleared his throat. "Well, I guess we'll be packin' up then, if everything's okay," he said. "Be sure to get your mother to the doctor for a follow-up," he said to Patty.

Both women ignored him.

"That's no way to address your momma," Ruthie whined to her daughter. "I gave you life, you know."

Patty snorted in derision. "That's why you live in this pig sty and I live in that hunk-of-junk trailer next door," she replied angrily. "Some life."

Ruthie began to sob and blubber, her whole

body shaking.

    Here it comes, I thought. The water works are about to begin. I took another step toward the door. Schultzie had already picked up a few wrappers and put his blood-pressure cuff back into his medical bag. He stripped off his medical gloves and stuffed them in a pocket and beat me through the doorway as Patty moved to hug her mother.

    "I didn't mean it Ma, you know that," she said tearfully. "I'm sorry!"

    We left the women to sort out their feelings. Several steps away from the house, Patty's voice called out, "See ya Schultzie. See ya Tim."

    "'Til next time," I yelled back.

    Schultz waited by the idling rescue van.

    "Kip mention anything about the fire investigation last week?" he asked.

    "Just that the cops were going up to school to conduct interviews."

    "Put the fear of God into some kids, I heard," he said with a knowing smile. "Also got some more dirt on the girlfriend. Seems she's taking classes at the alternative school, and guess what? Hasn't been in school since the day after the fire when the boy disappeared."

"I could have guessed," I said. "They have to stick there heads up sometime, though. A cell phone trace, a credit card purchase, something will do them in. The cops will find them," I concluded.

"According to Flint, the boy's friends didn't have a lot to say. Didn't know anything," Schultzie replied.

"They know alright," I said. "Somebody does. It's just going to take scaring one enough to get him or her to talk. I've seen this before." With a wave and a nod, I got in my truck and headed home.

Chapter Five

The next day there was a fender-bender at the corner of Victor and Lord Roads. Fender-benders and trouble breathing are the bread and butter of rescue departments. I didn't take the run. Kip and Nan reported with the rescue unit. Schultzie was home and brought Engine 1, in case of a fire, and a few guys from Concord showed up, seeing as how it was close to the township line. Nobody hurt, but according to the story Kip told me later at the station, the driver of a newer Corvette seemed very interested in Nan. He slipped her a business card with his name and number on it. 'Consulting' it said.

Kip said, "The guy was all of five-feet-four, where Nan is a good five-ten. She thanked him," Kip laughed, "then tossed the card in the trash back here at the station." He reached in and pulled the card from his desk drawer to show me, then put it safely away.

"I thought you said she threw it in the trash," I said, somewhat perplexed.

"She did," Kip replied. "I dug it out after she left. This is too good to throw away." He winked knowingly with that dumb grin of his plastered on his face.

I could see where this might come back at the most in-opportune time to bite Nan on the butt.

Walt and Schultzie ran another trouble breathing the next morning. Not Ruthie this time, but someone new, a first-timer.

Later that afternoon, Fred and Kip ran a grass fire. Someone's trash burner got away from them and burned out their back yard. When the guys got there with the grass rig, the homeowner was frantically fighting a losing battle with a garden hose. It was that time of year. Dead grass and leaves were just waiting to ignite. Once the rains came and things greened up some, the fire danger was lowered, but even in late May, we still had a few runs.

That evening we got another fire run. My phone pager sounded as I walked into the house after mowing the first cutting of hay.

"Jackson Central to Pulaski Fire," the dispatcher said. "Kitchen fire at," and she gave the address for a house just down the road; west of the fire barn and across the town's main intersection. I pressed the respond button on my cell phone pager and walked to my truck. Schultzie was responding to the page when I started the truck to turn up the drive.

"Jackson Central, Pulaski Engine 1 in route," his voice came over the radio. He was at the station and would take Engine 1 to the scene.

I got on my phone and called in. I would be in route direct. My windows were down and the heady smell of newly mowed hay filled the cab.

Within five minutes I was pulling up out front of an older, blue, double-wide home. What we called a redneck rancher. Thin, gray smoke came from the back. There was another pickup parked along the road. Walt was just getting out of the cab. Neighbors stood around in the front yard, smoking cigarettes and taking pictures with their cell phones. From their festive mood it seemed more like a carnival than a house fire. In a way, I guess it was. This was more excitement than most of them would see in a year.

Schultz was pulling on his turn-out coat over his bunker pants. Walt rushed over and helped him wiggle on a self contained breathing apparatus. I slipped into my bunker pants and turn-out coat. Walt waived me over. There was already a two-and-a-half inch line hooked up and ready to go. Walt slipped a tank onto me and I shrugged it into place.

A middle-aged woman came over to us and started yelling. "My baby!" she called while pointing to the house. "My baby's in there. Go save him. Hurry up!"

Her bleached-blonde hair was up in big, blue, roller curlers. I didn't know anybody used curlers anymore. She wore cut-off jean shorts and bounced on her skinny legs like they were skinny, white springs. On her feet were a pair of pink flip-flops, the kind kids wear at the pool. "My baby's in there!" She yelled again, while waving a pack of cigarettes for emphasis. Her friends patted her back sympathetically.

"Which room?" I asked.

"I don't know," she wailed. "Somewhere in

there." She waved her cigarettes toward the house again. A few curlers were coming loose from all of the jumping around, and one was bouncing down the side of her face like a blue Yo-Yo.

I grabbed the nozzle of the line and took off across the yard with Schultzie in hot pursuit. We ran a radio check with Walt, he charged the line, and in we went while the woman kept yelling, "My baby. Go get him!"

"I'm going left to right," I told Schultzie over my radio. We began the search pattern. There was very little smoke in the living room and our search turned up nothing. We proceeded to the kitchen and were greeted by a grease fire on the stove and counter. It had nearly burned itself out. The homeowners could have put it out with a proper fire extinguisher or suffocated it with baking soda.

A smoke detector hung from the ceiling near the door, lid open, battery missing. I snatched up the smoking pan of charred bacon, opened the back door, then quickly took it outside and set it in the yard before going back in. Two tomatoes were on the scorched counter, looking a little worse for the wear.

Somebody won't be having BLT for supper today, I thought.

    Off the kitchen was a room with a door slightly ajar. I pushed it on open with my foot and took a peek inside. Laundry room. A battered washer and dryer sat side by side.

    There was an overflowing stack of unsorted laundry taking up most of the floor. I stepped into the room and the stack seemed to explode. A little brown dog, that I took to be a chihuahua-poodle mix, clawed its way from within the dirty clothes and came at me, teeth bared, growling and snapping. I tried to step back, but stumbled against Schultz who had no idea what was happening. Three feet from me, the dog launched itself like a curly-haired missile. It hit me just below the knee and sank its teeth into my bunker pants. Shaking it's head vigorously and growling deep in its throat, the dog hung from my pant leg and tried to bring me down.

    "What the heck!" I exclaimed as I reached down to grab the berserk creature by its neck. "Got me a little dog," I grunted to Schultz who was trying to crowd in beside me to see what was going on. "Damn thing sure is vicious," I said, attempting to pry it loose from my pants. "Strong, too!"

Schultz started laughing.

We backed out of the room with me shaking my leg and spinning in circles. The dog spun out like some kind of crazy ice dancer. Its jaws continued to keep a tight grip on my pant leg, snapping once for a better hold, and snarling all the time. Schultz's laughter filled the house. I gave the crazy mutt a sharp smack on the head and jerked it loose. Thrusting the still snarling dog at Schultz, I said, "Take him, you think this is so funny."

Schultz held the trembling little dog against his chest. Its lips were still curled back revealing black gums and deadly sharp teeth. Its bulging eyes followed my every move. For some unknown reason, that crazy, cursed dog hated me.

We walked back across the living room. "Shut down the water line," I radioed Walt. "We haven't found the baby yet, just some crazy dog." As we walked passed the front door, Schultz set the dog down and it shut up its snarling and dashed outside.

"My baby!" the woman shouted from the front yard. The dog started yipping excitedly and tore across the yard like his tail was on fire. Crying tears of joy, the lady bent over and her baby leaped into her outstretched arms and frantically licked her face, his little tongue working away, tail whipping in delight.

"My poor baby," she cooed, stroking his back. The little dog acted like he didn't have a mean bone in his body.

"Baby, my aunt's girdle," I said to Schultzie. "That dog is a born killer." We went ahead and checked the two bedrooms anyway. Schultzie's laughter following me throughout the house.

Chapter Six

Somewhere off in my sleep, a rapid beeping threatened to pry me awake. I was dreaming about backing my Studebaker Lark into the shop on our little farm. The backup alarm started sounding a shrill warning sound much like those on our fire and rescue vehicles. Somehow, in my happy dream, it all seemed normal. The Studebaker's white paint glistened in the light of my dream. The upholstery was perfect, there was no tarnish on the chrome. The backup alarm continued to beep as I moved the shift lever up into park.

My wife gently shook me by the shoulder. "Your cell phone pager's going off," she said in a sleepy, far-away voice.

I looked around in the car. There was my wife sitting in the back seat. What was she doing back there?

"Tim, wake up," she said. "Your cell phone's going off."

Goodbye shop time. Goodbye dream. Maybe I was finally going to put that four-barrel intake and carburetor on the Studebaker V/8. I'd never know now. I jerked awake and swung my feet onto the floor. The lamp shown brightly on the table by my wife's side of the bed. I blinked in the glare.

"Did you catch the message?" I mumbled, still half asleep.

"Something about a rescue run out on Goose Lake Road," she replied, more awake now.

Goose Lake Road, south-west of Pulaski. I knew the area, and it was very rural. I glanced at the clock. Two-fifteen. Two-fifteen A.M. for gosh sake, in the morning. Some drunk had probably gotten lost on his way home from the bar and missed a curve. The road was gravel and narrow, with only a few isolated houses on it. I'd often thought it was the perfect place to dump a body, or hide a meth lab.

Jackson Central Dispatch repeated the call. A single vehicle crash at a location on Goose Lake Road, cross road, Jordon.

"Almost to the Hillsdale County line," I

thought aloud.

My wife had pulled the covers up over her head. "Mmmph," she replied.

I heard Kip respond to the call. He was already headed to the fire station. That guy never sleeps. I picked up my smart phone and pushed the respond button.

Running down the hall with my pants and a shirt in my hands, I flung myself onto a chair by the door and pulled my clothes on over my boxer-short sleepers. I slipped into my boots, grabbed the truck keys from the peg by the front door and headed into the night. No sound greeted me, not even a dog barking in the distance. It was cold without a light jacket. Right away I wished for a cup of coffee and a long sleeved flannel shirt. Then I remembered the spare shirt behind the seat. The wife had insisted I keep a warm shirt and a change of socks, just in case. After thirty-five years of marriage, she knew what I'd need. I'd have to put the warm shirt on when I reached the crash scene.

Glancing down at the floor in the dark, I was comforted to know my bunker pants were over there if needed for extra warmth or protection. I flipped the the heater control to high.

    I headed west on McDonald, passed Stone, and came to Pulaski Road. I turned south, high beams stabbing ahead, piercing the darkness. There were no cars on the road and no lights in the houses. Only the occasional yard light greeted me as I sped south toward Pulaski. I ran at fifty miles per hour through the reduced speed zone in Pulaski and on south. Not that anybody would have noticed if I blasted through at eighty miles per. The old analog clock in the front window of the general store read two-forty. Had it taken me that long to get going? Or was the clock wrong?

    Passing on through the main intersection, I flashed by the darkened hardware store with its creaky wooden floors and old bins of nails, hinges, nuts, bolts, and hardware of nearly every conceivable kind.

    Old man LaCroix kept it open mainly as a hobby, now. He was well past retirement age, but his sons didn't want to take the store over and be tied down with it. A few old-timers in the area lent a hand as needed. The Oliver Farm Equipment portion of the business had long since closed, shorty after the White buy-out. LaCroix now dealt mainly in parts and a few used implements.

Gunning the engine, I left the sleeping village behind.

Wooden Road appeared two miles south, just before Pulaski Road started a gradual curve to the south-west. Braking hard, I turned and started west-bound on Wooden, toward Jordon Road. I knew that north-south Jordon Road intersected Goose Lake Road close to where I wanted to be.

I got on the phone and called to Jackson Central to let them know where I was and my E.T.A. Kip came on to let us know he was nearing the crash scene with Rescue 1. The rescue truck contained the jaws-of-life along with a couple back boards, medical supplies, air tanks, and a few teddy bears for scared little kids. Walt came on to let us know he was bringing Engine 1 and would be there in about ten minutes. Soon Nan came on. She had left her place south of Pulaski and would meet up with us at the wreck.

The speedometer showed sixty miles per hour as the truck sped down the deserted blacktop. I prayed the deer stayed in the woods and the livestock remained in their fields. Faint pin-points of red tail lights appeared ahead. I was catching up with someone.

The dark shape of an old one-room school house flashed by on the left. The vacant Wooden Road School, on the north-east corner of Goff Road and Wooden. Back in the early nineteen-sixties, the area farm families chose to consolidate with Jonesville, to the south in Hillsdale County.

I backed off the gas as brake lights came on up ahead, then the lights disappeared altogether. Whoever was ahead of me was taking the turn southbound onto Jordon.

Within seconds I braked for the turn south. There was gravel in the intersection and the Dodge broke loose. I wrenched the wheel around and pulled the truck back onto the road. The headlights revealed a low cloud of dust as the pavement ended and gravel took over for the home stretch. I hit the gas and loose stone bounced off the underside of the truck. If I were twenty years old, this would have been fun. At fifty-eight I worried more about wrapping myself around a tree. Let the young guys have their sport, I say.

The Stop Ahead sign appeared and I backed

off the gas and braked. The Dodge hung onto the gravel like it knew what I wanted it to do and we rounded the corner, west-bound, in a bigger spray of gravel than I cared to think about. Up ahead, I could see the strobes of the rescue vehicle. A spot light was shining off to my left, onto something off the road and across a ditch - a white van, laying on its side. I could see the path it had made as it jumped the ditch and gouged up some earth before skidding to a stop in the tall weeds.

Nan's SUV was parked along the road behind the rescue unit. It had been her tail lights I'd followed. I pulled the Dodge in behind Nan's vehicle and got out. I jogged up the gravel while slipping into the long sleeved shirt I'd retrieved from behind the seat. I could see my breath in the flashing rescue lights.

Kip was wading through some weeds, down a slight embankment, and across a shallow ditch, directing a flashlight over the wreck. The van was laying on its side in the glare of the spotlight, its running gear facing the road. A faint wisp of smoke was coming from somewhere inside. Its lights were still on and illuminating the weeds and brush ahead of it.

Nan was carrying her medical kit bag and a flashlight. She waded in behind Kip, bulldozing through groups of cattails growing up from the ditch.

Kip turned to look back up at me. I had gone to the rescue unit for a fire extinguisher.

"Bring an extinguisher!" he yelled. I raised it above my shoulder. "Good man," he called, then turned to the back doors of the van. It was a windowless cargo van, the kind businesses might use for package deliveries... or perverts might use for kidnapping coeds. It was anybody's guess what we'd find tonight.

Kip wrenched at the door handle. Locked. I thought about going back for a crow bar, but decided to see what he wanted to do. He pushed though the waist-high weeds around to the passenger-side door. It was up in the air and he had to jump to grab at it. Nan showed up then and gave him a boost. The door was unlocked and he flung it up and open. I saw a vapor of smoke trailing up from the opening.

"Bring an air tank!" Kip shouted back to me. Still carrying the fire extinguisher, I turned and hurried back through the weeds, up the few steps onto the road, and ran to the compartment on the side of the rescue unit.

This can only be one thing, I thought, while reaching for the compartment door latch. The door popped open and the interior light came on to reveal the rack of four air tanks.

I grabbed two tanks, just in case, dropped the fire extinguisher, picked it back up, and went hurrying back over the road, down to the ditch and through the weeds to the wrecked van.

Kip held out a hand for the air tank and Nan shook her head. She snatched up his turn-out coat that he'd tossed on the front tire and handed it to him. He hurriedly slipped it on. I kept waiting for him to stumble off the over-turned van and come crashing down upon us, but he kept his footing. Next, Nan handed up the air tank assembly. Kip took it and stood to shrug it on.

"Meth lab," she said with a hint of disgust in her voice, confirming my suspicions.

"Here's the extinguisher," I said thrusting it toward her. She took it and turned to the van. Kip had disappeared into the interior. He popped back up through the open doorway and Nan handed him the fire extinguisher. He disappeared again. We could hear his movement through the van, toward the back. The discharging extinguisher made a whooshing noise that we could hear from where we stood outside.

Engine 1 appeared on the road. It pulled over to our side and ground to a stop. The driver's door sprung open and Walt climbed down. He immediately ran to start up the generator. The scene lights sprang to life and the harsh glow lit the area up like it was the second coming. "Need a line?" he yelled over the combined noise of the idling diesel engines and the generator.

"Stand by with the foam," I called up. "I believe he's got it with an extinguisher."

Walt glanced at the open compartment and noticed the missing equipment.

"Don't tell me," he called to us, "meth lab."

"You got that right," Nan yelled back as the back doors of the van popped open. The left side flopped down onto the grass. Kip appeared in his turn-out gear, holding the other door over his head and, in the harsh light, looking like some other-worldly creature just arriving to earth. I half expected him to say, "Take me to your leader!"

Nan had gone to the rescue vehicle and returned with another SCBA. We slipped them on as Walt handed an adjustable rod to Kip for use in propping up the van door. He also brought a back board and it lay in the grass while he returned to the fire engine.

"How many?" I asked.

"Just the one," Kip replied. He gestured inside the van.

Nan produced a cervical collar from her kit.

"I'll get you the back board," I called over my shoulder while stepping away to snatch it up. By now we had a nice path worn though the grass and cattails.

"Here you go Chief," Nan handed the collar to Kip who tore at the wrapper while he ducked back inside the van. Nan followed with her medical bag.

"You read my mind, girl," I heard him tell her.

Up on the road, a pickup slowed and stopped a short distance off. Two men got out and walked our way, appearing as dark forms out of the glow of the headlights. I looked up at the road way. It was Jake LaBlanc, the fire chief from Maple Grove. The other guy was his youngest son; Mark, if I remember right. They walked over into the bright lights and looked down at us.

"You need any help?" Jake called over the noise of the rescue vehicles. His son stood beside him, looking serious.

"Kip and Nan have got it," I said. "Kinda late for you guys to be out and about," I added, wondering what were they doing here in the middle of the night.

"We were up playing cards and having a beer," Jake said. "Heard the call and figured you could use a hand."

Is that kid even old enough to drink? I asked myself.

His son was staring hard into the back of the van where Kip and Nan worked over the injured guy.

I glanced in, making sure that they didn't need anything from me.

Walt walked over and stood beside LaBlanc.

"They got it. Thanks for coming out," he said. "The ambulance is on its way."

A county sheriff's car slowed on the gravel and stopped.

"Catch you later," Jake said, turning with

his son. They walked back to the truck.

An officer got out of the car with a friendly wave to the guys from Maple Grove. Officer Flint, our man, Flint. He greeted Walt, then walked down to the ditch and came across to us.

I turned and handed the back board to Nan.

"What's this, an alien invasion?" Flint joked while looking over the brightly lit scene. He peered into the van where Nan and the Chief were easing the unconscious young man onto the back board. The guy lay with his arms outstretched, one leg pulled up. He didn't move.

"Possible meth lab," Kip yelled out to Flint. "Better stay back. Doesn't look like they were cookin', but there are quite a lot of chemicals spilled around in here." Kip looked up. I stepped in to give them a hand in carrying the injured guy out. Bent over in the confined quarters, it wasn't an easy job getting him out of there and into the open.

"Ah," said our man, Flint. "Those kind of aliens. No one else is dumb enough to screw with this stuff." He sniffed the air and took a step back. "I'm going to get us some help out here." He paused to look back into the interior of the van, then down at the young man laying on the back board in the weeds. "He going to make it?"

"He's pretty beat up," Nan replied. She was busy adjusting a pulse-oxy on the young man's right index finger.

Kip worked at inserting an oral airway into the man's mouth to keep his tongue forward and airway clear. He attached a bag to the end and began rhythmically squeezing.

"By the way," the deputy asked, "what's Big Jake and his pup doing out here? It's the middle of the damn night, after all. Not to mention its the middle of nowhere." He shook his head and glanced over to the roadway.

"Said they heard the call and wanted to lend a hand," Walt answered from the road.

Flint stepped up to the road behind us. He paused to talk to Walt about something, then walked to his patrol car.

An approaching siren signaled the arrival of a Jackson Area Ambulance. It stopped in the middle of the road, next to Flint's patrol car, and two EMTs trotted down to us, carrying their bags and a small oxygen tank.

"Jesus!" the larger of the two muttered when they arrived at the back of the van.

"Not another meth lab! This is the third in the past two weeks," he said. "What's this world coming to?" he asked no one in particular while shaking his head.

His partner, a short, skinny guy looked down at the crash victim, inside the van, then stepped back. "Get him up onto the road and away from this mess so we can work on him, okay?" he said.

"Internal injuries, shallow breathing," Kip said. "I bagged him, but he could use the oxygen."

"Lucky to be alive," the larger man said.

Walt and Flint stood at the edge of the road. Another fire extinguisher sat at the ready in the gravel by Walt's foot, in case he needed to hand it down quickly.

Two more sheriff's cars showed up out of the night, followed by a blue State Police cruiser. It always amazed me how many cops were circulating around during the dead of night. No one would see them, then they seemed to show up in droves for fires and wrecks. Where were they when some moron was driving around with his base-booster cranked up?

We half carried, half slid, the injured

guy over the ditch and up onto the road. We gladly turned him over to the EMTs.

They knelt over him. "Good job prepping him," the skinny guy smiled up at Kip and Nan. "Depending on what's going on internally, he just might make it." He looked down again at the young man, who looked more like a teenager now that we had him out under the lights.

"We're going to take him into Jackson," the larger guy looked up. "It's a level one trauma center. I'll radio in so they'll be expecting us."

"I'll run interference," the state cop stepped forward. He was a large man with closely cropped hair. He didn't look much older that the new county deputy who tagged along with our man, Flint, the night of the house fire where the boy went missing.

The EMTs transferred the man to a gurney. Walt and Flint helped get him up off the road and loaded into the ambulance. The skinny guy was a lot stronger than he looked.

The state cop performed a perfect three-point turn with the cruiser and waited. The bigger EMT asked for someone to ride with his partner in the back, and climbed behind the wheel. Schultz volunteered to work the bag and climbed in the back with the little guy and the crash victim.

"I'll come by and pick you up at Jackson," Kip called to him. "Tim can drive Engine 1 back to the station, then I'll bring him back for his truck."

Flint waved his hand to signal that he'd heard.

The ambulance backed across the road to a farm lane that no one else had seen. It pulled out, lights flashing, siren splitting the night air, then followed the state police car back down Goose Lake Road, passed Jordon to where Goose Lake turned south, then back east to Pulaski Road. The cruiser led the way like a blocker on a well-disciplined football team, its lights and siren going as they disappeared into the night.

Flint and the other deputy were stringing crime scene tape around the van. The deputy in the third car had had enough fun for the night and left. "Who called it in?" Flint asked, looking over at Kip. "Another motorist?"

"We don't know," Kip answered. "There was no one around when we got here."

"Dispatch didn't get a name or a number,"

Flint said. He looked thoughtful. "Call must have been made from a disposable phone," he said. "Unless," and he looked at the van, still bathed in the spot lights from the fire trucks.

"I didn't see a cell phone in there," Kip finished Flint's thought for him.

"I didn't see one either," Nan said, "but one could be lost in the weeds. You know, thrown from the wreck," she added, pausing to think. "But he couldn't have called on it, then, could he?"

"Or," I said, thoughtfully, "Someone else was in the van with the injured man. They made the call to 911 after calling for a ride, then took off."

"That's just what I was thinking," Walt said from his place behind Kip. "If there was another guy, they were getting ready to cook meth and for obvious reasons didn't want to hang around." He'd been quietly following the conversation. The rest of us nodded in agreement.

"I'd been thinking the same thing," the deputy from the other car said. "These guys usually travel in pairs unless they're the odd loner, then they have a little private set-up in the woods somewhere."

"Well," Kip said, "Unless you guys need anything more, I guess we're clear to go."

"Go ahead," Flint said. "We'll hang around 'til the state detectives get here. Wish we had a thermos of coffee," he said, looking around hopefully. Nobody offered to bring any back.

Everyone looked at me. "I'll bring you some when Kip brings me back for my truck," I finally said.

"Thanks man," Flint said and clapped me on the back.

We gave our official statements to Flint and the other deputy, then walked back to Rescue 1. Kip called into Jackson Central Dispatch to let them know we were back in service.

With the equipment stowed, we stood by the rescue and talked.

I said, "Something isn't quite right about LaBlanc and the kid showing up out here. Nobody's that bored in the middle of the night," I added with a look at my watch. The others glancing at their watches.

Kip pulled out his cell phone to check the time. "Four A.M." he said. "You're right, it doesn't make much sense. If it were me, I'd be home in bed with my wife instead of out here with you guys in the middle of God-knows-where." He gave us a big grin.

"You ever notice how young the State Troopers are getting?" Nan asked, changing the subject. "Kinda like that young deputy at the house fire that night," she said.

"I hadn't noticed," I lied.

"They're not really getting younger," Walt offered, deadpan.

Nan threw him a withering glance and walked to her SUV. "I'm not old," she declared as she opened the door, before sliding in behind the wheel.

"We love you, too," Kip called back.

The deputies laughed.

Chapter Seven

It was mid-morning when I pulled into the fire station. Two other vehicles were in the lot. One was the chief's pickup, the other, Nan's black SUV.

I parked next to Kip's Ford and walked through the front door. It was a warm day, and the door stood open. I heard voices and went on into the kitchen meeting room.

"Morning Tim," Kip and Nan looked up and greeted me at the same time. They were sitting in a couple of cheap, blue plastic chairs, looking at a sheet of paper.

"What's up with you this morning?" Nan asked. She didn't seem any worse for the wear after our late-nighter on the van crash.

"On my way to a buddy's house," I replied. "Gonna' help get his 8N Ford ready for the show up in Concord this Saturday."

"Tractors!" Nan shook her head and made a face. "Don't you boys ever have anything else on your mind?" She meant to get a rise out of me.

"Oh," I said, calmly, "I can think of something that's usually not far from our minds."

"Me, too," Kip said with a smirk.

"Heaven help us!" Nan look disgusted and pretended to smack Kip on the head with the paper she was holding.

"We're just going over meeting material," Kip pointed at the paper in Nan's hand. "Got some county guys coming to our Thursday night meeting to discuss the meth problem," he said. "Basically, they want us to be on the look-out for certain things."

"Things like dump sites," Fran read from the paper. "The other stuff, we're already familiar with - propane, Sudafed, carboys, pressure cookers for cooking it down. You get the idea," she said.

"Couldn't come at a better time," I replied. "What'd the EMTs say, 'Third time in two weeks?'"

"Something like that," Kip said.

Nan read more from the paper. "Says here

heroin is also a growing problem as it's getting cheaper," she said.

"Anyway, Thursday at seven," Kip added. "You should have an e-mail. Already sent one to you, Walt, Schultzie, and the rest of the guys," he said.

"Guys?" Nan questioned. She drew back the paper like she was going to nail a fly to his head.

Kip laughed. "Okay, okay," he said. "All the gals got one, too."

"By the way," I butted in on their merriment, "any news on the kid from last nights wreck?"

Kip looked at Nan, then away for a moment. "He didn't make it," he said sadly. "DOA in Jackson."

"Dead on arrival," I said, more to myself than the others. "Figures. He was unresponsive. Maybe we should have sent him to Hillsdale Community," I speculated.

Nan said, "I thought the same thing. It was closer."

"It's not a level one trauma center," Kip said as he shook his head. "We did the best we could. Too many internal injuries. What we saw was just the tip of the iceberg. The way his body was draped over the seat, it looked like he was in the back and shot forward on impact, not to mention being tossed around like a rag doll," he added sadly.

"Flint called this morning and said the kid was full of drugs, too," Nan added. "It's a shame, he being so young and all." She looked as if she were about to cry.

"What about the van?" I asked. "Not the kid's, I take it."

"Stolen, out of Fort Wayne, a month back," Kip said, "and the plates are from a delivery van in Tecumseh."

"These guys get around," I replied.

"The county deputies, state haz-mat team, and Metro Drug Squad were on the scene 'til an hour ago," Kip said. "It turns out the occupants really weren't cooking in the van. Not yet anyway. But from all of the propane, chemicals, carboys, and crap, they were getting ready," he said.

"They?" I questioned.

"The county guys are pretty sure our dead kid wasn't alone," Nan put in. "No driver's license, for one thing. They think there was at least one more, maybe two, in the van."

"Kid?" Another one-word question.

"Marvin Hochstetler," Kip said. "From down Camden way. "He was sixteen, almost seventeen. His parents thought he was staying at a friend's farm to help with hay making."

"Amish?" There I go again with the one-word question.

"Mennonite," Kip replied.

"What's the difference?" Nan asked.

"Mennonites take baths," I replied. We've got them swarming all over northern Indiana. Amish, too. Actually, they're related. The Amish are split off from the Mennonites."

"Well," there are quite a few across Hillsdale County, and several farms between Concord and Pulaski. South of Homer, too," Kip added.

"I don't have any near me, but I hear they make good neighbors," Nan said.

I said, "In Michigan, if there's a big church in a small town, it's probably United Methodist. In northern Indiana, it's going to be Mennonite. The Amish meet in barns or houses," I told them. "They have a reputation for hard work and being good farmers." I had a thought, "You know, maybe we could talk an Amish guy into moving in with Ruthie."

The others laughed.

"She'd need two," Nan stated. We laughed harder.

With that, I said good-by and left for my Dodge truck. Kip had a remodeling job to get to; bathroom, I think. Nan was on her way to her new job as a veterinary technician.

As I was leaving the parking lot, I realized I'd forgotten to ask about the missing kid from the fire on Stone Road. He and the girlfriend had disappeared from the face of the earth. It had been almost two weeks already, and now we've got a dead Mennonite kid who was mixed up in the redneck drug trade. Could they be connected?

I wondered, did Mennonite kids go through rumspringa, like the Amish did? I'd have to Google it later and find out.

Then, there's the stolen van and plates. Apparently these guys weren't just local, but were getting around, or maybe dealing with a wider network. That made sense. Like early Indian tribes having a trading network, the local drug guys were making their connections, too. Now the problem was so bad that county officials were meeting with local fire and police to discuss ways to fight it.

I headed north on Pulaski Road deep in

thought. I didn't even notice the fields of freshly mowed hay at the farms along the way.

Howard Road came up almost before I knew it. I turned left and headed west, shoving my concerns out of my mind. I was going to my buddy's farm for a couple hours of tractor time, and refused to let thoughts of the recent events ruin my fun.

There was no missing Hank standing in the open door of his farm shop when I drove in. He almost had to duck his head in the doorway.

The gravel drive curved around to the left of a nineteen-twenties two-story farm house. A covered porch ran across the front and along the driveway side. Ancient maple trees stood sentinel over the house. To my left was a pasture ringed by a white-painted board fence. A hot wire ran around the inside on yellow insulators. Six fat, Angus steers loafed in the thick grass. There was a small, red barn set back off the road behind the pasture. A door was slid open so the steers could get inside if needed. Behind the house was a red-painted chicken coop with fresh wire netting for the run. A handful of red hens scratched in the bare earth. To the right of the house, dairy-grade alfalfa lay drying in a field.

The gravel drive ended at a cement apron in front of the shop.

Hank smiled and waved in greeting, his beaming face the color of light chocolate.

"Tim Conway! Thanks for coming," his voice boomed as I got out of my truck.

"Henry McIntyre, glad to be here," I responded brightly, using his given name.

"I have everything ready." He pointed in toward a shiny, red and gray Ford 8N. A small work table was dragged over next to the tractor. Tools and parts were neatly spread on a white cloth, reminding me of a banquet table. I noticed the four new spark plugs and breaker point set. A well used Ford manual lay to one side. Hank was a man after my own heart. Well organized and ship-shape. The clean cloth was a new one, though.

"Looks like we're prepped for surgery," I quipped, walking into the shop and pointing at the table. Two lawn chairs sat along the wall and a medium sized cooler rested on the floor between them.

Hank laughed his deep, hearty laugh. "I got the idea from your Studebakers," he said. "The way you drape the fenders and top of the radiator and grill-work with old furniture blankets, reminds me of a surgery."

"That's different," I replied. "Don't want to scratch up the paint on my babies."

"Well, the white cloth makes it easier to locate little parts when I drop them," he said.

I knew what he meant. How many times had I dropped a little part or spring in my shop and searched around for hours? Too often, I'd reckon.

"Where's the radio?" I asked, looking around.

"Got internet radio now," Hank said. "Big band from the thirties and forties." He pointed to his smart phone in his hand, and then to a small speaker box on a shelf. He fiddled with the phone and Count Basie's "Jumpin' at the Woodside" played from the speakers. He set the phone on the work table.

"It's gonna be a hot time in Pulaski Township today!" I exclaimed gleefully.

Just then, Boomer, Hank's old golden retriever, walked into the shop. He sniffed at my hand in a casual greeting, then settled down stiffly under the table. "You still got the dog, eh?"

"He's not dead yet," Hank said, lovingly eyeing his loyal companion.

The first time I'd been out to Hank's place, he'd introduced the dog as Boomer.

"Boomer?" I had asked.

"Ain't every golden retriever named Boomer?" Hank asked. It was more of a statement than a question. I had left it at that.

"Where's Marcel?" I looked around the shop.

"Last I saw the cat, he was on the back porch, taking himself some sun," Hank replied. He'll probably show up later to hand us our wrenches," he laughed.

"Well," I began, looking over the neatly placed tools, "what are we doing today, tune-up? And, I might add, I can use the therapy session."

We called our little work sessions "therapy", especially if either one of us had a stressful previous day. The dead Mennonite kid kept coming to mind no matter how hard I tried to shove the thought away.

"I heard about the run you had last night," Hank said. "That's a rough one."

I looked at him.

"I have my sources." He smiled that broad smile of his. "I don't want to spoil our fun," I said. "How 'bout we have a coffee later and I can bounce some things off you?"

"Whatever works," he said. "Now, let's get a tune-up on this tractor."

We turned to our work. The distributor on the 8N is mounted on the front of the engine. I reached in the narrow gap between the radiator and the engine and pulled off the plug wires, being careful to number them with tape. Then I unclipped and removed the distributor cap. I handed it to Hank. He looked it over and placed it on the cloth on the work bench. He watched for a moment as I worked. Then, picking up a ratchet and spark plug socket, went to work on the spark plugs on top of the engine. The ratchet made fine, clicking noises as he backed the handle, then turned it.

"Already gapped the new plugs," he said.

He started humming along to the music. I could feel the tension start slipping away from my body. It was going to be a good day. A clean shop, the sun shining in the open door, an old dog, big band music playing softly on the shelf, and a kindred spirit to work with.

I pulled off the rotor, then Hank handed me a wrench and I took off the distributor.

Placing it on the cloth covered bench, I grabbed a small screwdriver, one of Hank's special ones that said "Ford" on it in script. Next, I removed the points and condenser from the distributor. Upon close inspection, the points didn't look too bad.

"Seeing as how we've got them out," Hank said, "might as well install the new set. I'll just clean up this old set and keep them as a spare."

"Good idea," I replied. "One never knows when they'll come in handy." Hank must have had a dozen sets of old points and condensers stored in a vintage cigar box up on a shelf. Even with three old Ford 8Ns, he hadn't needed them yet. I opened the cardboard container with the shiny new points.

"I'm sure glad you're here," Hank said. I can't reach in there with these big fingers." He held out his hands. He had large hands and large fingers to go with them.

"You'd drop more parts than you got installed." I smiled at him from where I bent over the work bench, the distributor parts spread out in front of me. I held the new points in place and started the screws, then flipped to the page in the manual for the point gap.

    Hank finished the plug installation as I installed the condenser and gapped the points. He stood there, still holding the shiny ratchet in his large hand.

    "I used to drive my grandfather's 8N when I was a kid," he said with a dreamy, far-away look on his face. "Those were the best days, ever, when I'd visit him on his farm south of Chicago. In the summer, when school was out, my brother and I got to spend two whole weeks with him and Grandma. It was my idea of Heaven. My sister got to spend her own time with Grandma after Harold and I went back home. It was better than any summer camp I could imagine. That man taught us how to handle livestock, and how to drive a tractor, and be safe around equipment."

    I looked at Hank. His face was a mask of pure bliss. He radiated happiness. "I can tell that you had great times on the farm," I said. "He must have been quite a man."

    "That he was. We used to go fishing, evenings, down at the creek," Hank said. "We'd catch pan fish. You know, bluegills and sunfish."

    I nodded.

"Grandma would fry up anything we brought back to the house. Man, that woman could cook! I guess that's why I have this farm," he said, "to capture some of those happy days. I'll never get Grandma and Grandpa back, but in a way, they're all around me, here on this farm," he said.

Here was a side of Hank I'd never seen before. I nodded, understanding exactly what he meant. My own grandparents had lived on an eighty acre farm outside of Cowan, Indiana.

We continued to work quietly, listening to some Glenn Miller music from over on the shelf.

Within minutes I had the distributor back in place. I reached in and finger tightened the bolts. Hank handed me the wrench to snug them down, then I installed the spark plug wires.

"Not too much blood today," I looked at my knuckles. There were a few scrapes on my right hand from getting too close to the sharp radiator fins.

"Success," Hank smiled. I stood back as he checked to make sure the tractor was out of gear, then hit the starter button. The engine turned over once, then purred to life. We listened for a moment and Hank shut it off.

"Put the hood back on... we're ready for the show," he said happily. "Now to celebrate. He turned to the cooler and opened the lid. "Dr. Pepper?" he pulled an icy bottle from the cooler and held it up to me. He bought the glass bottles from some supplier on the internet, said it tasted better from a bottle than a can.

"Thanks," I said, taking the chilled bottle. He handed me a church key and I popped the cap and held out the bottle. Hank did the same and we clinked the bottle necks together.

"To success," he said, tipping the bottle and taking a large gulp. Hank was a tea-totaler, didn't touch alcohol, said it was counter productive. I figured there was a good story behind this. One that he'd tell me when he was ready.

I took a drink. "Bob's your uncle," I said.

Hank snickered while trying to drink. Liquid seeped down his chin and he wiped it away with his free hand. He tipped the bottle down and took a breath, "A stitch in time," he replied.

"A bird in the hand," I replied.

We sat in the lawn chairs and drank our pop and made plans for the tractor show on the coming Saturday. "American Patrol" came on the big band station.

"I'll be bringing the Moline R," I said. We watched as Marcel, the yellow tabby cat, sauntered in on the sunlit concrete. He twitched his tail and rubbed up against Boomer. The old dog opened one eye, but basically ignored him. Walking over to Hank, the cat rubbed against the man's ankles, then flopped down in the sun and began licking his paws.

"You gonna handle waxing the Moline," Hank asked, "or the wife taking care of that for you?" He chuckled at his joke.

"Ha!" I snorted. I shook my head at him and took another sip of pop. I didn't know if he was referring to my tractor or to something else.

Thirty minutes later, we'd put the tools away, tidied up the shop, and I was climbing into my truck and heading home for lunch.

Hank smiled and waved from the door of his shop.

Chapter Eight

My wife met me at the door. She smiled in greeting. "How's Hank today?"

"He's looking well," I responded. "So's his farm. The place looks like it's from one of your home magazines. You know, where rich people rehab hundred-year-old farm houses."

"Umm hmm," she said with a knowing nod.

"He's been busy," I said. "All of the out-buildings are painted barn red, the fences are straight, the house looks neat as a pin..." I shrugged. From the look in her eye, I knew what was coming next.

"We need to find that man a wife," my love responded.

Why some women made it their goal in life to find wives for single men, I'd never figure out.

"Doesn't look like he needs a wife," I responded. "He has Boomer and Marcel for companionship."

"Ha!" she snorted. "Animals, and those tractors you guys are always fooling around with. I'm surprised you don't have me out in the shed, too."

"Well..." I began.

"Don't say it," she interrupted. "Though, I hope you're still in the repair mood." She beckoned me to the next room. "Something's wrong with the quilt machine." She made a pouty face.

"So," I began, "do we play twenty questions, or can you describe the problem for me?"

She gave me that look and said, "Don't toy with me, Buster. It was working fine, then I changed the thread, and now it leaves loops of thread underneath." She pointed at the machine with a half-finished quilt set up on it, a log cabin pattern in greens and browns.

"Sounds like a thread-path problem or maybe incorrect tension," I replied, feeling some tension myself. There was a good chance this was going to take a while. I had important things to do, like getting out in the shop and checking on the hay rake. There was always that one low tire to air up and grease fittings and chains to lube. Then there was the John Deere baler to prepare.

The hay won't bale itself, I thought.

I looked at the pre-tension and the thread routing. "What's different?" I wondered aloud. I picked up the manual and thumbed through to the trouble shooting section. My wife leaned in so see. Why she didn't do this herself, I didn't know.

"Looks like you missed a hole on the pre-tension," I pointed out. The thread path seemed complicated to me. Too complicated, and easy to goof up if care wasn't taken.

My wife pulled the thread back out of the needle and re-ran it on the path. I hoped this would do the trick. If it did, I'd look like a genius. I ran the thread through the needle for her and stood up. She grabbed the controls and started working on the quilt. The machine hummed. She stopped stitching and we knelt to peek underneath. The stitches were tight. Success!

"Thank you, Honey," she said, leaning in to give me a peck on the cheek.

"I was hoping for a little more gratitude," I said, standing up. "Maybe later this evening?" I asked expectantly.

"Dreams are good," she replied. She

smiled, patted me on the butt, and walked out of the room.

I followed her to the kitchen to help prepare lunch. My cell phone pager went off.

"Jackson Central to Pulaski Rescue," the woman's voice said. "Chainsaw accident at..." She gave an address south of Pulaski.

I looked at my wife. "Not a chainsaw!" I felt a shiver run up my spine. This could mean a lot of blood.

The dispatcher repeated the call. Kip came on in response. He must have been working close to the station today and would respond with the rescue van. I knew Nan was at work now, at her new job at the vet's office south of Jackson.

Flint came on the radio. He'd meet the chief at the scene. Two others, Jeff and Fred, called in. Four guys on site, I was off the hook. I sighed in relief.

After lunch, I went to the farm shop, turned on the stereo to an oldies rock station, and started in greasing and checking the hay rake.

I'd barely made any progress when my wife appeared in the doorway of the shop.

What now? I thought. I didn't dare say it

out loud.

"Machine acting up again?" I asked as nicely as possible. Couldn't this wait? I silently asked myself.

"It's fine," she replied. "Don't get yourself all worked up."

The look on my face must have given me away. Thirty-five years of marriage...

"Besides, I'm done with quilting and I'm making zucchini bread now," she said, looking around the shop and then across the rolling fields. "Beautiful spring day, isn't it?" she observed.

She surprised me. I expected her to comment on the smelly and messy condition of my shop.

"Zucchini bread?" I asked, wondering where one gets zucchini this time of year.

"In the freezer from last year. I've got to use it up." She read my mind. This woman never failed to amaze me.

"The reason I came out to interrupt your fun-time is Melissa just called. She's coming up from Angola Friday morning to drive tractor while you bale hay."

My mood brightened. Melissa was our eldest, and always pitched in at haying time.

Either she liked the work, or felt sorry for me. I wasn't sure which.

"She bringing the kids?"

"Yes. They're looking forward to a campout with Grandpa," she said.

"Don't they have school?"

"They have one week left, she's going to collect their work and let them skip Friday. June seventh is their last day, you know."

I didn't know. "Eli can help on the wagon," I said. "He's old enough now. Samara can ride in the cab with her mom, or hang out with you," I said. I wasn't sure about sleeping in the camper after an afternoon of putting up hay.

"Oh, and you got an e-mail from Chief Kip. There's a combined meeting on Thursday evening with Maple Grove and the Pulaski board. You'll have special guest speakers and the whole nine-yards," she said, grinning.

"I was expecting it," I replied. "Thank you."

She blew me a kiss and turned to walk to the house. I wondered if the zucchini bread was my payment for figuring out the quilt machine. I hoped not.

I turned and picked up the grease gun.

"Groovin," by the Rascals came on the radio. This was a song by a white band that Hank would like. He liked Big Band Music, as I did, and old Mo-Town and some black gospel. Didn't have any use for heavy metal or contemporary music. We were in agreement on that. I never could get him to listen to my Cajun or Zydeco C.D.s.

Chainsaw accident. I shuddered and shook my head.

Chapter Nine

The next evening, Wednesday, the wife and I were watching Nature, on PBS. Something about monkeys doing it, I guessed.

I watched while reading a crime novel by Steve Hamilton about a retired policeman living near Paradise, in Michigan's Upper Peninsula.

My animal lover sat on the couch with her puzzle book and caught most of the program. I looked over from my recliner to see if she was getting any good ideas from the frisky primates. No luck.

My cell phone pager went off. I put the book down on the arm of the recliner and listened. On the T.V. two monkeys screamed loudly as they chased each other around through the bushes.

"Jackson Central to Pulaski Rescue, unresponsive male, possible drug overdose." A female dispatcher gave an address in the south-east corner of the township, over near the Maple Grove Township line.

My wife looked up from her puzzle book. "This could be Muncie," she said with a shake of her head.

The message came across again. I stood up and retrieved my phone from the side table next to my chair.

My wife followed me to the door. I kissed her on the cheek, grabbed my truck keys and stepped out into a beautiful late-May evening. The sun was still hanging in the west. June was just around the corner and the days were definitely growing longer. A half moon was just rising faintly through the trees to the east. A waxing moon, it was headed to full within the week. I hoped it would be full, or close to it, when the grandkids were here. It's a beautiful sight, seeing a full moon rising through the trees and over a Michigan hay field as night is settling in.

I got on the phone and called Central Dispatch. Schultz was on his way to the station to pick up Rescue 1. The fire fighter named Fred radioed. He was arriving at the station and would ride in the Rescue with

Schultz.

I figured he must be on vacation or laid-off from his job.

There was more chatter over the radio from Jackson Central and our people responding. Nan's voice came on. She'd meet us at the scene, too. I was glad to hear her. If there was a distraught family, she would handle them better than any of us guys.

Ten minutes later, I reached the address. It was an isolated, ramshackle, two-story place down a narrow, wash-board, gravel road. The perfect place for a drug house. Old blankets were hanging from the windows in place of curtains. One front window had a piece of duct tape covering a diagonal crack.

Rescue 1 was sitting in the driveway with the back doors open, light bar silently flashing. Along to one side was the Maple Grove Chief's pickup It was plainly marked by a decal on the side that said "Fire Chief." There was a light bar on the roof.

"What's he doing here?" I wondered aloud while slowing the Dodge.

Schultzie was carrying a medical bag and Fred was removing the back board from the rear of the rescue unit. I pulled off the road into the front yard. Nan pulled up behind me in her black SUV. For once I'd beaten her to a scene. She hopped out and greeted me.

"I don't see any family members," she said, giving a quick look around the place. There was no one in the front yard.

Schultzie and Fred had entered the house. I heard muffled voices talking. "I don't hear any yelling," I said. "Maybe the guy lives alone."

We hustled across the yard. It wasn't really a lawn, just a motley collection of weeds that needed trimming. "Watch you don't step on anything," I called over my shoulder to Nan. I nearly tripped on an old car wheel and worn-out tire as I said it. There was a small collection of what I took to be engine parts half concealed in the weeds next to the wheel. I paid better attention to my progress.

Down alongside the house sat a couple of older cars - a dirty, gray Toyota, and a dented, black, Pontiac Grand Am.

We leaped up a set of busted-up concrete steps and entered a small foyer. Directly across from the front door, a steep, narrow, stairway led upstairs. The foyer was crowded with Schultz, Fred, myself, and Nan behind me.

The bottle-neck was caused by someone coming down the stairs. It was Jake LaBlanc, the fire chief from Maple Grove. His eldest son, and assistant chief, Mike, was following directly behind him. Mike carried a medical bag in one hand. They were both wearing blue medical gloves. The talk around the county was that the LaBlancs had their own private fire club over in Maple Grove.

"Might as well take your medical bag back out and call for the coroner," Jake said, none too quietly. A skinny girl with stringy, brown hair appeared at the head of the stairs. At Jake's words, she gave a choked sob and ran to a room somewhere above us and off to our right.

"We'll take a look for ourselves," Schultzie said.

"What are you guys doing here?" a voice came from the doorway behind us.

"Good to see you, Chief," Nan turned to greet Kip. She stepped outside to let him in. I squeezed to one side with Fred. Kip came in and he didn't look pleased.

"Anybody call for mutual aid?" Kip asked.

"No, not us," Schultzie replied. The rest of us wagged our heads, "No."

Kip looked up at Jake. "Come on down so my people can do their job," he said.

"Nothing to do. He's dead," Jake said.

"You jumping calls now?" Kip asked with an edge to his voice. "We're still in Pulaski Township. I welcome your help if we call you in, but right now, you men are in our way."

I could tell that Kip was trying to be diplomatic. I would have threatened to have Deputy Flint escort them off the property.

As if on cue, Flint's patrol car showed up. He had the twelve-year-old riding with him again. The two deputies crowded through the door. Flint looked the situation over.

"We having an old fashioned tea?" he asked.

"Trying to get upstairs and do our job," Kip replied curtly.

The younger deputy stepped back outside to relieve the crowding.

"Nothing to do," Jake repeated.

"Jake, Mike," Deputy Flint addressed the men on the stairs, "come on down and let these people up." He stepped back and gestured for Nan to come on in. She edged closer, but remained outside with the young deputy.

The LaBlancs came on down the stairs and

went outside with Deputy Flint. The rest of us snapped on our protective gloves. Schultz and Fred started up the creaky steps.

"Hello?" Schultz called out on the way up.

"Up here," a meek female voice responded.

I followed Fred and the back board up the stairs. Nan was right behind me. We arrived at a good-sized landing. The first thing that struck me was the trash everywhere. To our left was a small room with a stained, faded, pink mattress taking up most of the floor space. There were no blankets on the mattress. The area around it was covered with clothes and trash. Someone had been living in there and not bothering to pick up.

To our right, we could see into a cramped bedroom. The floor and ratty dresser were littered with take-out containers, more trash, and several beer bottles, not all of them empty. There was even a quart carton of chocolate milk. I didn't know if it was empty or not. On the unmade bed lay the lifeless form of a skinny, white male. He was wearing plaid boxer shorts and no shirt and appeared to be in his late teens or early twenties. His eyes were half open. There were scars and red tracks on his tattood arms.

    The skinny girl knelt by his head, stroking his matted, blonde hair and sobbing quietly. LaBlanc was correct. The kid was dead all right. I could tell from where I stood out on the stair landing. I moved some of the trash aside with my foot and looked for evidence of drugs. Nothing.

    The four of us crowded into the room. It smelled of old food, sweaty bodies, pot, and stale cigarettes - all in one powerful, mixed-up stench. I reflexively put my hand to my nose.

    "This place should be condemned," Fred said more to himself than to us. "Makes Ruthie's house look like the Ritz."

    Why are most of our calls to rats' nests and fire traps? I thought. Just once, let it be to a clean, hygienic home.

    Nan murmured from behind me, "I hope these old floorboards hold up.".

    I felt a tense rush as memories of Muncie flashed through my mind. "It's no fun going through the floor," I said to her. I glanced down through the clutter at the old pine boards. They looked sturdy enough.

    "I wouldn't board my dog in this dump,"

Nan added quietly, her voice barely a whisper behind me.

Schultz went directly to the kid on the bed. "How long has he been like this?" he asked the girl.

"I don't know," she said. "Maybe an hour?" She looked around the room at all of us, like maybe we had an answer for her.

"What's he been using?" Schultz asked her. He was looking at the body for evidence of blood pooling.

She took a while to respond. "I don't know. Do you know, Amy?" She looked across the room to a girl sitting cross-legged in a corner, on an old couch cushion. A girl that I hadn't noticed before. She was slumped against the wall and looked as emaciated and disheveled as the skinny girl. She wore a black, loose-fitting top and had an old army blanket spread across her lap.

Amy didn't answer. From the glassy, far-away look in her eyes, I could tell she wasn't with us at the moment.

Papers rustled on the floor as a young man crept into the room. He didn't look much older than the dead kid that Schultz was working on. He wore a dirty, black, Led Zeppelin T-shirt and equally grubby cargo-type shorts. He was barefoot, and carried a cell phone in his hand.

"That's a four hundred-dollar phone," Fred whispered. He'd set the back board down along the bed and went to kneel in the corner, in front of Amy.

"Where'd you come from?" Nan asked. She was the closest to him, and reflexively took a step away.

"Around the corner, in the other room," he said in a dead voice. He was higher than a kite, too.

Schultz looked up from where he was probing the dead kid's neck for a pulse.

"What're you guys on?" he demanded.

"Some good shit," the guy responded with a feeble shrug. He looked around at us, then fixed a vacant stare on the kid on the bed. "He gonna be okay?" he asked.

"No, he's not," Schultz said tersely. I could tell he wanted to slap the snot out of the little stoner.

The skinny girl stroking the dead guy's hair began to sob yet again.

"He's gotta be okay," the boy with the phone said. "I called 911. He's got to be okay," he repeated. The air seemed to come right out of him and his legs sagged.

Nan slipped behind him and I held his right arm. We eased him to the floor. I asked his name as I pulled out my pen light and checked his eyes. The pupils barely responded. Nan was checking his pulse. "Shallow breathing," she reported. "His heart rate is way down, We'd better get him downstairs."

"Steven is my name," the kid responded. "They call me Stevie."

"What's *his* name?" Schultz asked the skinny girl as he nodded to the guy on the bed. She was the only one who seemed to have it together, though not by much. He had switched from trying to find a pulse on the guy to working on chest compression.

I stepped over and began inserting an oral air-way and was preparing to bag him. If the medics got here they could use the paddles, though I doubted it would do any good.

"We just called him Spoons," Skinny girl tearfully replied. "I didn't know him that well. We just came over to party today, that's all."

"How old is he?" Schultz looked up at

114

her.

"I don't know," she said. "Maybe twenty."

Who lives here?" Schultz asked. "Just your friend, here?"

She was silent for a moment. "Stevie stays here sometimes," she finally replied.

"What's your name?" I looked up into her face. With a week's worth of meat-and-potatoes, and a good night's sleep, she could have been pretty. Mascara streaks, or some kind of makeup, trailed down her cheeks in black rivulets.

"Gloria," she replied. Gloria Townsend. She rubbed her eyes with the heals of her hands, smearing her makeup even more. She looked like a scary, stoned clown.

Fred had checked the other girl's eyes. "We need that ambulance," he said in a worried voice. "They should be here by now." He glanced across the room at us.

A noise made us look to the doorway. Jake LaBlanc was standing there, surveying the scene. Skinny Gloria glanced up at him from her place at Spoon's head, then looked down. I saw the fear flash in her eyes. The kid with the cell phone looked visibly shaken when he saw LaBlanc standing there.

What's going on here? I wondered. Did anyone else notice this? I looked around at the others. They were busy working on the girl in the corner and going over the dead kid. Nan had a blood pressure cuff on Stevie. Schultz was still giving chest compression to the guy on the bed while I squeezed the breathing bag. I figured we'd been in the room a little over five minutes.

"Narcan?" Nan asked from her spot on the floor by Stevie, the cell phone kid.

"We're too late, here," Schultz said quietly. "The Medics will probably use it on him and the girl in the corner," he nodded.

Fred said, "She's got shallow breathing and a slow pulse. I can't get much out of her. She tries to say her name, but doesn't respond when I ask her if she knows where she is."

Kip and Flint came up the stairs. "Step back, Jake," Kip said. "My people need to get these kids downstairs." LaBlanc stepped out into the landing area. He kept his eyes on the drug addled group in the room. Deputy Flint moved over next to him.

"Start with him. He's closest to the door," Schultzie nodded at the Stevie kid on the floor. Nan was still crouched at his side, attending to him.

I looked around on the bed and the floor, then opened up the drawers on the battered dresser. There wasn't much in there. A few dirty clothes and some soft-porn magazines that I'd never heard of. There was no evidence of drug use. No syringes, bloody rags, pills, or marijuana. No pipes, chore boys, or baggies. Not even an aspirin. Someone had cleaned up the room, of drugs anyway, before we got there.

Kip and Nan helped Stevie, the cell phone kid, get to his feet. "Can you walk?" Kip asked.

"I think so," he said dreamily as Nan got in front of him. With Kip supporting from behind, and Nan stepping backward, they carefully walked him down the steps. Flint followed them.

"Call for another ambulance," I heard Kip call out to someone in the front yard.

LaBlanc stepped into the room. Amy, the girl against the wall, looked at him and tried to scoot tighter back into the corner. LaBlanc knelt down to give Fred a hand. The girl started to wave her arms and thrash about. She rolled her head and tried to say something.

"Leave her alone," Schultz said over his shoulder to LaBlanc. Fred looked up, eyes wide.

"What's gotten into her?" LaBlanc asked, surprised at her reaction. "Too stoned, I guess," he answered his own question.

The room was getting a little close now, even with Kip, Nan, and Stevie gone.

LaBlanc stood up and stepped away.

With some help from Gloria, Amy gradually calmed down. "It's okay, Amy," Gloria was saying over and over in a soothing voice. "It's okay."

The sound of sirens grew louder and stopped in the front yard. Two EMTs came up the stairs accompanied by Kip and Deputy Flint. I knew one of the ambulance men - Dan Bennett, a good guy to work with. I began to relax. The two men looked around and the shock of the room's condition registered on their faces.

Flint beckoned to Jake LaBlanc, "Come with me," he said. It was a command, rather than a request.

"We were in the area and thought we'd lend

a hand," LaBlanc said as he turned to leave. "Nothin' wrong with helping out, is there?" he asked. "There are Good-Samaritan laws, you know," he added with a glaring look at Kip.

Kip remained stony-faced.

On a hunch, I asked Gloria, "You or your friends ever hang out with Richie Collins? You know, the kid who went to Maple Grove? He's missing and his parents and friends are worried," I said in my best fatherly voice. I touched her arm gently as I spoke and she didn't pull away. She was receptive to talking.

"Yeah, I know Richie." Her voice was sounding a little dreamier. A little more distant.

"Tell me a little about him," I prompted. Again with the friendly voice. I looked down at her arms, at the needle marks.

"We used to party on weekends," she said. "I didn't like his girlfriend, but she's the one who had the stuff. You know, was holding." Her voice had a dream-like quality to it now, with the words strung out.

"Good God!" Schultzie stood up and looked at her. The EMTs were working frantically over Spoons, trying to get his heart started, trying to get a pulse.

Dan Bennett stood and gently reached for Gloria. "Come with me, honey. It's going to be okay. Let's get you down to the ambulance." He glanced at me. The look in his eyes said, "Let's get her the hell outta here."

"Richie ran off with Meagan. Least that's what Mark said," she rattled on dreamily.

Mark, I thought. That's a name that hadn't come up before. "Mark a friend of yours, too?"

She smiled like she was the village idiot, but said nothing.

"How about Marvin Hochstetler? You know him?" I was almost pleading now.

"Marvin?" she asked. "Marvin," she said slowly.

Bennett scooped her up and bodily carried her down the stairs. She couldn't have weighed much more than a new-born calf. A ten-year-old could have carried her.

"Who's Mark?" Fred asked from his spot on the floor in front of Amy. His knees had grown tired from kneeling so, after brushing away the clutter amid the sound of rattling beer cans, he inspected the floor and sat down.

I glanced down at the trash and poked at it with my boot, again hoping to find any evidence of drug use. Nothing there.

"I don't know who Mark is, but I'm gonna find out," I replied, looking over the trashy room, and shaking my head in disgust.

Schultz had moved over by the door to make room for the EMTs. "Did you get the part about Richie and the girl?" he asked. "The kid must still be alive and on the run."

"Yes," I replied, "but on the run from what? Certainly not from his parents. According to the school and the neighbors, he had a good home," I said. "Until he tried to burn out the family, there was no reason to run."

"That we know of, anyway," added Schultzie matter-of-factly.

Bennett returned to the room with Nan. They walked over to Amy, who sat babbling somewhat incoherently.

"Amy. Amy honey," Nan bent over her and gently, softly, called her name. Amy looked up into Nan's face. For a brief instant, her eyes seemed to focus on her.

"We're going to take you to an ambulance,"

Nan spoke softly to her. "This man is going to help us. Can you help by standing up?"

Amy nodded her head.

A good sign.

Fred stood aside as Nan and Bennett gingerly placed their gloved hands under Amy's arms. Amy quivered as she tried to stand. Nan and Bennett gently hoisted her up. The soiled blanket slid from her lap. She was naked from the waist down.

"Oh, no!" Nan drew in a breath.

The girl's spindly legs gleamed dull white with nasty looking sores on them. A faded tattoo of a rose was on her right hip, and a tarnished ring pierced her navel. She looked abound at us with unfocused eyes and didn't seem to notice her predicament.

I turned my head away as Nan snatched up the blanket and hurriedly wrapped it around the girl's waist. She looked at us men and shook her head sadly, her eyes turning misty as she helped Flint lead the girl down the stairs.

Outside, the siren of the first ambulance split the dusk as it sped off on its journey to Jackson.

The other EMT stood beside Spoons,

sprawled lifeless on the bed, and shook his head. He checked his watch. "Anybody else have nine-fifteen?" he asked in a hushed tone, like he didn't want to awaken the dead kid.

Fred checked his watch. "That's what I have," he said.

"Time of death?" I asked. The EMT nodded his head.

I looked at my assistant chief, Schultzie. I realized I didn't know him all that well, even after working with him on the department for two years. "Those girls weren't here just to party," I told him. "They're what we call 'Crack Whores,'" I shook my head, disgusted with the whole concept.

"I know," Schultzie responded with a shrug, and looked around the room. "I don't have an answer to this," he said.

"You got any girls?"

"Yeah, four of them, and one boy," he said. "You?"

"We have two grown girls, a grandson, and two little granddaughters," I felt my breath catch. "I'll kill anyone who tries to get them into the drug scene," I stated coldly.

"I got two girls and two boys at home," Fred spoke up, "and I agree with you. Drug peddlers are a cancer, one that needs to be wiped from the face of the earth."

"Well," the EMT said, "I never get used to seeing this, and we get overdoses frequently around the area. This is classic heroin, this one." He stood with his hands on his hips and looked around the cluttered room with its dingy gray walls that used to be blue. A bare bulb hung on a cord from the ceiling. "The thing is," he continued, "I don't see any evidence of drugs in this room. Do you?"

It was almost a rhetorical question. We glanced around anyway.

He said, "Can't figure out who could have cleaned up the drugs. None of the kids seem capable." He looked at each of us in turn.

"Maybe the girl named Gloria," Fred offered. She was somewhat together when we got here."

Schultz nodded in agreement, "There was that Stevie kid," he said, "the one who made the call. He could have cleaned the drugs up."

"The LaBlancs were here first," Fred observed. "I wonder what they saw." It was almost a question.

There it was. Jake LaBlanc and his oldest

son, Mike, were here first. Policy is that medical mutual aid shows up only when called for. We hadn't called anyone.

"How long had they been here before you showed up?" I questioned. "Did they have time to search the house?"

"That, I don't know," Schultzie replied. "They were upstairs when we got here, Jake and the boy, then they came down the steps. It was almost like they wanted to block us from going up." He got a strange look on his face and looked at me in a new light.

"Who knows?" I answered his unasked question. "They could have had plenty of time to sort through the junk and hide the drugs."

"Where would they put the evidence?" Fred asked. He was standing next to the EMT guy, who was preparing to leave. "I saw you checking the dresser and there's nothing there," he said, looking my way. He gave a slight shrug.

"There's always the other room," I looked at the others. "And we can check the bathroom to see if anything got dropped when they flushed it. It must be downstairs," I said.

At that point, Flint came back up the stairs with the young deputy trailing behind.

They entered the room. As soon as he saw the dead kid, the deputy went pale. He looked like he was going to be sick. Flint snickered and the others looked away.

"You okay?" I asked as I stepped over and put my arm around his shoulders. He was about my size, but solid. Probably worked out a lot.

He nodded his head "yes," but his face told me "no." I looked at the name tag on his shirt. Morgan, it said.

"It takes a while to get used to death, officer Morgan," I told him, giving his shoulder a little squeeze of support. His holstered service revolver, a 9mm Sauer, pressed hard into my left hip. "We've all been through this," I said. "You can't let it get to you or you'll end up a drunk, or worse."

The others nodded and made noises of agreement. Flint stopped his snickering and wiped the stupid grin from his face.

"We've got help coming," he said. "Detectives from the Metro Squad are going to process the place.

That meant that we didn't have to bother with our own search. I was relieved.

"I can't get anything outta' those kids. Maybe tomorrow," Flint said hopefully. "Man this place stinks," he added, with a look around the room. "Somebody puke in the corner?"

Deputy Morgan shuddered and turned away into the landing.

Fred, Schultzie, and I walked down the stairs with the newly baptized Morgan. The EMT guy had left earlier, clutching his medical bag and wishing us luck.

That was it. The LaBlanc boys were carrying a medical bag. They could have picked up the drugs and paraphernalia and carried it all out right under our noses. But why? Why risk careers and jail time? We all knew the kids were using. Why hide it? The thought seemed preposterous, that two respected members of the community would have anything to do with a drug house. I kept my thoughts to myself as we made our way down the stairs and into the yard. I had a lot to sort through in my mind.

The cool, fresh air did wonders to clear our heads and reinvigorate deputy Morgan. A riot of frog noises emanating from a nearby swamp assaulted our ears. They were really going at it tonight. The bright moon was breaking over the trees to the east of the house and heading up into the star-lit sky.

Two state cops stood in the driveway with Kip and Nan. Their blue cruisers idled in the road. Radio traffic and static came from the open windows. Both men appeared to be in their thirties, all fit and tan. One, the blonde one, held a roll of yellow crime scene tape in his hand.

The second ambulance had departed through the dusk, with Amy and Gloria inside. The siren could be faintly heard, tracing its progress down the country roads. Before leaving the yard, the attendants had strapped Amy to a gurney and administered narcon, a drug used to combat the effects of a heroin over-dose.

We stood in a group, talking about the weather, who had their gardens in, and who had Memorial Day plans. Anything to distance us from the senseless death inside.

The blonde cop looked out behind the house. "Man, those frogs are loud," he said, waving the hand that held the yellow tape. "They're enough to wake the dead." He glanced over at the house, realized what he'd just said, then stared down at his feet and was silent.

Flint was still upstairs with the body, waiting for the medical examiner to show up. A blanket was pulled down from where it blocked an upstairs window. Flint appeared, and the sash rattled up. Morgan went in to keep him company. I wouldn't want to stay in that stinking hell-hole instead of coming outside. The dead kid wasn't going anywhere. Chain of custody, I guessed.

Kip looked at me and grinned. "You been cutting any wood lately?" The state cops smiled, having no idea where this was going.

"Saturday afternoon, if the weather holds," I said. "Got the tractor show with Hank in the morning.

"Maybe you could cut a little extra," he led me on. "You know, for the old guy we had the run for yesterday."

"How bad?" I asked. I watched as the state cops cringed. The poor little lambs were starting to figure out what was coming.

"Thirty-three stitches is what I heard," Kip said. "A regular filet-O-leg is what it looked like when we got there. Right in his back yard. Old guy. All the time we were there, his wife kept nagging at him that he was too old to be cutting wood. She wouldn't stop. 'Saw this coming,' she said. It's a wonder he didn't cut his own head off, just to be rid of her."

The state cops looked away. I could see they were getting squirmy.

"Lot of blood?" I joined in the fun.

"Could've started our own blood bank," Kip replied, straight-faced.

I shook my head in amusement. The state cops eased away toward the house. Kip picked up his radio and called in, "Pulaski Rescue to Jackson Central, Rescue 1 clear."

A male dispatcher repeated Kip's call. We turned to go to our vehicles. Oddly, there weren't any neighbors standing around, watching. On a call like this, we nearly always had neighbors come to watch the show. One would come over and say, "You know, I've always thought this could be a drug house," or something along those lines.

It was almost dark now and the place was clearing out.

Another sheriff's car pulled up. Ned Jordon, a deputy we knew from over Maple Grove and Hanover way, got out. He waved to us and walked over to the state cops.

"See you tomorrow night," I called to the

others. I got into my truck, started it, then sat for a moment. The din from the frogs was so bad, I had to run the windows up to be able to think. What the skinny girl had said came to mind, about Richie and the girl friend, Meagan. I wondered about Marvin Hochstetler, the Mennonite kid. I wondered if this Mark person was the common thread.

    I rubbed my right shoulder with my left hand. It was beginning to ache again. Probably from the cool air.

    What was the skinny girl's name? Gloria? Gloria. I paused, checked my mirrors, and put the truck into reverse. I need to look into this Mark guy.

Chapter Ten

My wife agreed to come with me to the combined meeting at the township hall. The members of the Maple Grove Township Board came early. They stood around drinking coffee, sharing wise-cracks, and laughing with the Pulaski Board. A few people from the Hanover and Concord fire boards were there, too.

Kip and his wife walked in. Several of the ladies, whom we referred to as the unofficial auxiliary, brought plates of cookies, cheese dip with assorted tiny crackers, and coffee cake. Things were starting to look up. Kip had them set up a white, plastic, folding table in the back.

Most of our fire personnel were there and didn't waste any time finding their way back to help themselves.

Schultz couldn't make it, though. He was

at work at his job as a foreman in an auto-parts plant, filling in for another foreman for some reason or another. I figured he needed the extra money to feed his wife and all five of those kids. Kip could fill him in later.

Fred was there with his eldest daughter. He introduced her to the Pulaski group. "This is Maureen," he said. Angie is home with the other two," he explained his wife's absence.

"I figure now that Maureen's a junior in school, she's old enough to hear this stuff. Might do her some good," Fred said. Maureen looked like she could be her mother's younger sister. The resemblance was uncanny. We greeted her and laughingly shared a few disparaging comments about her father.

She smiled shyly and took a seat next to where her dad stood, toward the back of the room.

Nancy Spink walked in alone, greeting people and slapping backs as she went. She filled a napkin with cookies, sat down next to Maureen, introduced herself, and immediately struck up a conversation. Probably about Maureen's dad and the goofy guys he hung around with. They both looked up at Fred and giggled. Fred was deep in conversation with a couple of Hanover firemen, and didn't notice.

Walt came in with a few other guys on the department that I usually didn't see much of. Typically they showed up at training sessions and only made it to a few fires. They waved and sat near the front, leaving two rows of seats for the board members. Every plastic chair we had in the place was in the meeting room.

No one from Maple Grove Fire and Rescue had shown up. I wondered if maybe they'd had a rescue run and couldn't make it, then I thought better. We'd have heard the call over our own radios, so that couldn't be it.

A uniformed State Trooper came in and looked around. He smiled broadly, toying with the hat in his hand. Flint came in right behind him. He was on duty and wore his uniform, too. Two others in civilian clothes were with him - a thirty-ish man and a younger female with her hair pulled back like lady cops often did. Kip excused himself and walked over to make introductions. A fourth man walked in and greeted the others. He was of medium build with longish, unkempt, curly hair, and looked like he'd just woken up in an ally. He shook the State Troopers hand and they slapped each others backs in a sort of man-hug way. The trooper whispered something in his ear. The man laughed.

We turned to watch. "Under-cover?" Fred asked.

"Or one of our finer citizens here to make a complaint," one of the other guys added with a chuckle.

Murrey Nichols, our Township Supervisor, walked over to greet the group as they surveyed the room. Kip met him as he approached. They chatted and Kip introduced Murrey to the police personnel. It was nearly seven o'clock. Murrey escorted the group to the front of the room.

I took a seat near the back, behind Fred, Maureen, and Nan. My wife broke off her conversation with Kip's wife and took her seat beside me.

"Oh," she said in a surprised voice, "look who's here!" She pointed to the door.

I expected the group from Maple Grove, but turned to see my tractor buddy, Hank McIntyre, come in from the parking lot. Everyone turned to watch as he entered. After all, in that room, the man stuck out like a sore thumb - a six-foot, six-inch, light-chocolate, sore thumb.

He spotted us, flashed that winning smile, and walked over to shake hands. He greeted Fred, then leaned over, with his hand gently on Fred's shoulder, to greet Maureen and Nan. The girls fairly melted. The man almost glowed with personality and charm.

"Tim Conway!" he turned to me.

"Henry McIntyre!" I returned the greeting, clasping his large hand.

"Mrs. Conway," he took my wife's hand.

"Call me Sue," she gushed.

What's this? I don't think the woman ever gushed for me.

Hank made sure to have some sort of contact with all of the members of the fire crew.

"I have to be nice to them," he said to Maureen, who seemed to be in awe of him, like she was meeting a favorite movie star. "They may have to come out to the farm and put out a fire, or maybe even rescue me someday." He smiled broadly and turned to face the front of the room.

The State Police officer waved him forward.

"Gotta go," Hank said. He turned to

leave, then looked back at me. "Saturday," he said, pointing a finger at me.

"Be there," I said.

We watched him walk along the rows of chairs, introducing himself, and glad-handing all the way.

"That man should be governor," my wife said.

Nan turned to look at her, eyes sparkling. "You ain't kidding," she breathed.

Looking around, I saw the Collins couple, Richie's parents, walk in and quietly take a seat in the back of the room. Their faces were drawn and pale, with dark circles under their eyes. They looked like they weren't doing well and could use a good night's sleep. They sat alone in the back and I made a point of making eye contact and nodding a greeting.

Plastic chairs had been placed at the front of the room for our guests. Flint did a quick head-count and walked over along the wall to get another chair. The assembly slowly quieted as the guests took their seats. Flint remained standing.

A commotion at the side door leading out to the parking lot drew our attention. Flint looked over and the others followed his gaze.

The door opened and Jake LaBlanc walked in, trailed by his two sons and Duke Williams. Duke was a drinking buddy of LaBlanc's and also served on the Maple Grove department.

The group was followed closely by the real attraction of the night. The woman strutted in like she owned the place. Her curves were the first thing I noticed. She wore a frilly, low-cut top that barely contained her ample bosom. Thick, white-blond hair hung almost to her waist and swished when she walked, like the pendulum on a clock. White shorts perfectly contrasted with her well-tanned legs. Her make-up was perfect, her smile dazzling. Bright red toenails peeked from her open-toed, low healed sandals. I couldn't tell you what color her eyes were, or even if she had eyes. I struggled to recall the last time I'd ever seen a female put together quite like this woman.

The breath drained right out of me. Every man in the room, who wasn't dead, surely must have felt the same way.

"You think those things are real?" my wife whispered in my ear.

"Huh?"

She gave me a sharp jab in the ribs with

her elbow.

Nan leaned across Maureen and slapped Fred on the thigh. "Quit that drooling, or I'm gonna tell your wife," she hissed. Maureen giggled.

I quickly scanned the room. Even the ladies were staring at the mysterious woman. The group at the front of the hall got the full benefit of watching her approach.

She followed her entourage toward the front of the room to sit in the chairs behind the Maple Grove board.

Kip turned to look at me from his seat, three rows ahead. "LaBlanc's wife," he mouthed. Then he turned back quickly as his wife pinched his ear. She looked back and gave me a warning glance.

I knew LaBlanc had remarried sometime back, but had never had the opportunity to meet the new bride.

My wife grabbed my right elbow and pulled in close to my side. "She doesn't look much older than the boys," she whispered in a low, disapproving voice.

Nan turned to face us. "She's not. She's his third wife. I don't know where he found her, but she sure doesn't fit in around here," she concluded, wagging her head.

Maureen had also turned in her seat to face us, her eyes wide in amazement. Her father gently directed her attention back to the front of the room.

"Wonder if she even graduated high school?" asked an older woman next to my wife.

"Bet she got all A's from the men teachers," Maureen replied, a little too loudly. Her father gave her a sharp look.

"Men!" harrumphed Nan. She glared at the guys seated around her while the ladies made clucking noises in agreement.

At the front of the room, Deputy Flint cleared his throat, looked away to compose himself, then addressed the small crowd. The murmuring that had started up with the woman's appearance slowly died down again.

"Thank you for coming out tonight," he smiled. "Friends from Maple Grove, we welcome you." He looked at the Maple Grove people, maybe lingering a little too long on the gorgeous blond.

He welcomed the people from Hanover and Concord, then introduced the people seated behind him; the State Trooper who worked with gang work, the male and female plain-clothes detectives from the county Metro Squad, and lastly, the guy we'd pegged for an under-cover cop, Detective Kuhlbaugh. He pronounced it cool-baw.

When the State and County people were introduced, Flint turned to Hank, who actually stood so everybody could get a good look at him.

The plain-clothes county man got up beside Hank and told a little about the work Hank would be doing for them. "He's trained in drug and gang-related crime enforcement," the man said. "He comes to us from the City of Chicago. Their loss is our gain," he said to a smattering of laughter. He nodded to the crowd and sat back down next to the lady cop.

"I'm glad to be here," Hank said. "First, for those who are wondering, I'm exactly two meters tall. You do the math conversion." He smiled and looked out over the group. "I'm retired from the Chicago Police Force, homicide department. I live right here in our community, been here for three years now, so I have a vested interest in our proceedings tonight.

"Our main focus is on the methamphetamine and heroin problem," he said. "I can tell you that these drugs aren't just inner city problems. We had another incident last night, right here in our township, with one overdose death. Three other young people are still in the hospital tonight.

"Each of our panel members will share information with us," he concluded. Then, turning to the State Trooper, he invited him up.

The trooper discussed how drugs are coming into the community on the freeway system, mainly from Detroit and Chicago.

"Our people are making traffic stops every week, only to discover a drug cache," he said. "Sometimes its marijuana, but more and more it's meth and heroin," he said. "The serious dealers are well armed, and we're concerned that it's only a matter of time before someone is injured or even killed." He let that soak into the crowd, then gave a few statistics for arrests, street values, and so forth.

When he was done, the two plain-clothes Metro Squad detectives stepped up. They talked a little about their experiences on the streets, and about the changes in the drug scene over the past five years or so.

"Anyone know the gate-way drug for

heroin?" the lady cop asked. We murmured among ourselves for a moment. I already knew the answer.

"Marijuana?" a middle-aged woman on our township board raised her hand and spoke timidly. Several people nodded in agreement.

"Alcohol?" came a man's voice from the middle of the group. I believe he's a school board member. The police woman nodded and smiled.

"Most people would say marijuana or alcohol," she told the group. She turned to her partner. He nodded seriously and stepped forward.

"It may come as a surprise," he said, "but it's Oxycontin."

Most people in the seats turned to each other and murmured. LaBlanc's group sat quietly.

"Oxy and heroin are chemically quite close he said. As a matter of fact, my own family physician will no longer prescribe Oxycontin. Too many people were having trouble with it. Heroin is also getting cheap, less expensive than prescription drugs. We see it sold on the street in 'tenths' or one-tenth of an ounce at a time." The officer paused for effect as he looked about the room.

I noticed that most of the people were sitting forward, listening intently as he explained the symptoms of heroin use. He ticked them off on his fingers and perfectly described the young people we'd encountered on the previous night's rescue run.

The rough looking under-cover cop stood up and addressed the crowd. "Folks," he began, "it's unfortunate, but rural country roads are the perfect place to dump the refuse from meth labs. We find it happening all around the county. My understanding is there was a car crash involving meth related chemicals just this past week. We have to be vigilante, because the problem isn't going away," he said.

"When out walking or working on your property, be suspicion of garbage bags laying beside the road, especially if they give off a strange odor not normally associated with garbage." His face took on a serious cast. "Be sure to talk to your children about the dangers of playing with trash dumped by the side of the road or in a ditch. Two-liter bottles with a fluid in them should not be opened. Too frequently the fluid is a left-over chemical from meth production. You can always call the police to check it out."

I was glad he didn't say, "Just call the fire department," as that would require even more extensive training for handling dangerous chemicals, and more paperwork. We already had the meth basics during one of our earlier training sessions. The chief had seen to that.

When all was said and done, a few audience members had questions.

"How does a person get started using meth?" someone called from the front.

The female cop answered, "Users can start for reasons that seem logical to them, but silly to us. They may take it to stay awake or get the energy to finish a task," she said, "like an overdue term paper. It may even be taken as a stimulant to lose weight."

Someone asked about the effects of meth use, and how a parent or teacher could spot a user.

Hank stood up to answer that one. "Short term, one might notice a sense of euphoria, moodiness, dilated pupils, and bloodshot eyes. Some weight loss can be expected with continued use. Long term use will result in lack of initiative, sores developing on the skin from the chemicals in the blood stream, and the front teeth may loosen and fall out," he said.

This last detail brought a murmur from the crowd.

"Don't most teenagers exhibit moodiness?" Jake LaBlanc called from his seat. "Surely they all aren't on meth?" The group with him snickered.

"If moodiness equals meth use, then most of the women I know are users," the blond spoke up.

The room went dead silent, waiting for a response.

"The use of methamphetamine isn't a joking matter," Hank responded seriously. He leveled his gaze directly at the two. "Of course, anyone who exhibits one or two symptoms of use shouldn't be suspected of abusing the drug." He held the couple in a steady stare. They shifted uncomfortably in their seats.

"The drug affects various people differently, depending on their genetic makeup," he said. "The pattern of use will bring out symptoms over a period of time." He looked out over the room. "Believe me, you'll know when something is wrong with a loved one. There may be drug paraphernalia, or there may not. You must remain constantly aware," He said.

Kuhlbaugh, the under-cover cop, spoke up. "If you've seen the destroyed lives I've seen, and the deaths your own rescue squad has seen, there wouldn't be anyone making light of the matter." He stood and paced at the front of the room.

Several people in the audience applauded. LaBlanc and his wife blanched at the verbal dressing-down.

There were a few other questions, then the State Policeman thanked the people for coming. The policemen stood, and the crowd stood and stretched. Several people went forward to shake hands and make small talk.

LaBlanc and his group got up and immediately left.

People filed out from the town hall in groups or pairs, some talking animatedly, others deep in thought.

Flint walked up to where Kip, Fred, and I stood near the door. "Wish I had a filly like that to run my race," he said with a smirk.

Kip's wife came over, accompanied by my wife and Maureen, Fred's daughter.

"Gotta get to work," Flint said quickly.

"Catch you all tomorrow." He glanced at the ladies, waved goodbye to us, and scooted out the door.

The Collins couple were talking to Hank McIntyre at the back of the room. Their faces were drawn, as if they were at the end of their ropes. They nodded to Hank, shook hands, then left.

Hank gestured to me. I excused myself and walked over.

He said, "I need to go home and write some notes and look some things up, then I'd like to meet with you, if you have some spare time."

"What's up?"

"The Collin's folks asked if I could lend a hand in locating Richie," he answered. "They're at their wits end, and I can't blame them. After listening to tonight's forum discussion, they're really afraid for their son's safety."

"Maybe we need to meet sooner, rather than later," I told him. "I've got some information that may help you," I said, thinking of what the Gloria girl had told me during the rescue run at the drug house.

"Oh?" He gave an inquiring look.

I told him all about Richie running off

with Meagan Grawn, and about the lack of drug evidence in the house and the mysterious Mark guy. I'd already talked to Flint about it, but Hank was just finding out.

"That's good. That's good," he said. "The police are missing something in not having you as an interviewer."

"Maybe I'll volunteer," I said.

"Oh, no," he replied. That's what I'd like to talk to you about. I want you on my team."

I was going to ask if he was serious, but decided against it. His expression told me he was as serious as a heart attack.

"Let's make some time at the tractor show this Saturday," he said. "I know you've got hay to put up tomorrow."

"That's right," I said. "My eldest daughter is here to drive tractor for me. I raked it this morning, but it's so heavy, I'll flip it tomorrow morning as soon as the dew's off, then bale in the afternoon."

"Come Saturday, you'll need the rest," Hank said. "I hope you won't be too sore to come to the tractor show - guy your age." He grinned broadly, placing a hand on my right shoulder for emphasis.

"I said I'd see you there," I replied, with a smile. "It'll take a lot to keep me away, and besides, I'm not *that* old."

"Well, I've got some digging around to do, or I'd come by tomorrow and lend a hand," he said, giving my shoulder a gentle pat. The shoulder I'd torn up in Muncie. "See you Saturday." He gave the group a wave and walked out.

"What was that all about?" my wife asked as we walked out to the truck.

"I'm not sure," I replied, "but I may have been offered another part-time job."

"Oh, this ought to be good," she said, grinning. "Working on tractors with Hank?"

"The Collins family would like some help tracking down their son, Richie," I said.

"Detective work, then," she said.

"I guess so."

We went home to enjoy an evening of board games and snacks with my daughter and the grandchildren.

Chapter Eleven

The grandkids awakened the whole house at six-thirty A.M. by running down the upstairs hallway, yelling and carrying on like a wolf pack of two. If I had that much energy, I'd be a millionaire. I got up with them so the wife could sleep in.

My daughter walked out into the hallway, saw me with the kids, made a grouchy face and a grunting sound, took her glasses off, then turned around and shuffled back to bed.

The kids and I had a great time fixing a breakfast of pancakes, bacon, eggs, and juice, with coffee for me. The kids begged for coffee, too. I told them coffee would stunt their growth, but gave them a taste anyway.

After we'd cleaned up the kitchen, we got dressed and went out in the hay barn to build forts from last year's hay. The kids romped excitedly in the mow and soaked up the smell of grass hay.

I sat on a bale and watched as the two little kids stumbled and played, and thought of my partner, Frank, and how his grandkids would never know him and what a great guy he had been. His kids had grown up, married, and were raising families. Frank missed it all, or should I say, they missed knowing him. A wave of sadness washed over me. One look at my own grandkids and I was back to laughing and egging them on.

Having the grandchildren visit must have put me in a reflective mood. While target shooting our BB guns, I kept dwelling on the past few weeks. Thinking on the plight of the young people in the drug house two evenings ago, I couldn't get over how disgusting and sick their lives had become, all from chasing the elusive drug high. The dead kid would never have a family, or grandkids, ever. It made me enjoy all the more the precious moments I had with my own innocent, little grandchildren. I called them to me and wrapped my arms around them in a gentle hug, inhaling the smell of their hair, and feeling the warm life in them. They thought I'd lost my mind.

We shot BB guns at pop cans stuck onto the ends of tree limbs in the orchard, quitting around eleven. Nobody shot their eye out.

The dew had finally lifted from the grass. It was time to turn the hay. For safety's sake, the grandchildren went up by the house to stand on the deck with their mom and watch while I turned the hay with the Moline rake hitched to our old CO-OP E3.

The thick hay had been down since Monday afternoon. Three days of sun and breezes, then baling on the fourth day should have it sufficiently dry.

In the afternoon, my daughter drove the White cab-tractor, with Samara riding along. Eli and I stacked on the wagon as the bales came up the chute from the John Deere baler.

We unloaded the first three wagon loads, then left the fourth in the barn for unloading at my leisure. My shoulder was working up a good hurt, anyway. I made a mental note to call the message therapist.

Jackson Central Dispatch called about a child falling from her bicycle. Kip and Nan responded to the call.

After a rest in the shade, the group assisted in hooking up the flatbed trailer and loading the Minneapolis Moline Model R for transport to the show the next morning.

Friday evening was family movie night. Samara and Eli squabbled, as siblings do, over movie titles before finally deciding on a rerun of the original "Shrek." We'd only seen the movie about a hundred times.

I took some Motrin and fell asleep in my recliner chair.

Chapter Twelve

    Saturday dawned warm and bright. Eli rode with me in the Dodge up to Concord for the tractor show.
    We parked the truck and trailer at the school parking lot, unloaded and drove the tractor three blocks to the show. I rode on the broad platform behind the seat as Eli carefully crept along in low gear.
    Downtown, Hanover Street was blocked off from the Farmer's State Bank, at the four corners, east for two blocks. Vintage cars were on display next to the business district, with the tractors located up the street.
    Hank was just setting up his lawn chair as we approached. He snapped open the legs and pushed down on the canvas seat, then placed a small, folding table beside it. He'd saved us a spot in the shade, just across from the hot dog vendor, the perfect location.

I switched places with Eli and backed the little Moline to the curb, then unfastened two lawn chairs that I'd secured under the seat. Eli helped me set them up while Hank placed a little plastic cooler between his chair and mine.

Eli's chair was to my left. He didn't sit in it for very long, but was up and admiring Hank's shiny 8N Ford - the one we'd tuned up in Hank's shop.

Hank addressed him, "Climb up on there, son. You can't hurt it."

Eli looked at me for permission. "Go ahead," I urged.

"This is what shows are all about," Hank declared. "Getting our youth involved. Can't get involved by just looking at 'em," he said.

Eli clambered aboard, grinning in delight.

Hank looked over at me, "Can you use a Dr. Pepper?" he asked.

"Kinda early for the hard stuff," I replied.

"Well, then," he said, "got some bottled water if that will work. It's going to be a nice day, might as well get started right. You know, it's five-o'clock somewhere," he said, laughing heartily.

"I'll take a Dr. Pepper, then, long as you put it that way," I said, grinning.

"Believe I've got a root-beer for Junior, there," he said, pointing his bottle at Eli. "No caffeine, you know."

I nodded in agreement.

Hank fished around in his little cooler and brought out a dripping A&W Root-Beer bottle. Popping the top with his special church key that had 'Ford' embossed on it, he rose to hand the bottle to Eli.

"Thanks!" the boy exclaimed looking over the bottle, then taking a taste.

Hank reclined back in his chair. He took a drink from his own bottle. "Some meeting last Thursday, eh?" he said.

"It seemed to go over pretty good," I said, "at least with most people."

"Something's going on with that big blond," he said, "and I don't mean just what meets the eye." A big grin now.

"How so?" I asked.

"From my seat, I could see things that you couldn't from behind them," he said.

"Bet you could," I replied with a knowing smirk.

"I believe that man is intimidated by the

woman," Hank added.

"How's that?" I asked, incredulous, lowering my voice.

"His body language indicates that he's subservient to her. She's the one who initiated any contact. She's the one who directed them where to sit. Something just doesn't add up," he said.

"Nan says she's his third wife. Says she's not from around here," I said.

"By the way," Hank interrupted, "I had coffee with your friend, Nancy, yesterday. She's quite a girl."

"With Nan Spink? Our Nan Spink?"

"That's right. Right here at the Main Street Cafe." He pointed down the street, toward downtown, with his Dr. Pepper bottle. "I had her over to the the farm to give the new feeder pigs some shots. That woman is very handy around animals. I'd do it myself, but I'm deathly afraid of needles, and not afraid to admit it." He gave a slight shiver.

Nan and Hank. Who'd a thunk it?

"She's from Nevada," Hank said after a pause.

I looked at him. "The blond? Nevada? Like from Las Vegas?"

Hank chuckled and shook his head. "No, not Las Vegas," he said. "From Reno, which is just as bad as far as I'm concerned."

"You ever been to Las Vegas?" I asked.

"Nope, don't have any desire to go. Do they have tractors, old trucks, and green fields in Vegas?" he asked. "Besides, that place is the devil's playground," he added before I could answer his question,

We looked up as Eli brought his empty root beer bottle over. "I'm going to look at the other tractors," he said.

"Don't go far."

"I won't"

We watched him walk over to a row of restored J.I.Case tractors. A man started talking to him and assisted him in climbing up on a shiny model DC.

"Anyway," Hank continued, "the woman is from Reno. She's been to UNLV, and UCLA, and has some experience in the college underworld."

"How on earth did Jake meet her?" I couldn't believe what I was hearing. A college girl didn't seem his type, but I was sure he thought he was *her* type. After all, the man did have an ego.

"Where every modern loser goes to meet his

dream woman, the internet," he answered with a knowing smile. "Your friend, Mr. LaBlanc, must have given her quite a sales pitch to get her here. Either she liked what she saw, or figured she could at least work with it. Anyway, here she is," Hank concluded.

"Huh," I said.

"That's kinda what I thought," he replied.

"How do you know all of this?" I asked. This was getting curiouser and curiouser.

"I have my sources," he said. "When you were over on Tuesday, I wanted to divulge a little of where I was coming from, but I could tell you needed to do some sorting in your own mind."

"You got that right."

"Anyway, I do a little work with the Metro Squad. Nothing big. Just keeping my hand in, you might say."

"Like an Amish Grandfather helping out around the farm," I said.

"Yeah, that's right." A smile and a nod.

"So, you saw the Collins family at the meet-ing, he said. "They're getting no place. Heck, they're even wondering if the kid is still alive," Hank said.

"Richie."

"Yes, Richie," he said.

"I can understand how they feel. What'd you tell them?"

"Just that it looks like he took off with his girlfriend and they could be anyplace. The police have sent out requests that they be picked up, but they've vanished." He paused to reflect.

"They could even be out of state," I observed.

"I'd like you to work with me in locating Richie, and most likely solving who's behind this drug ring in our area," Hank said. He'd turned in his chair to face me.

"Drug ring?" I responded in surprise.

"That's what the State and County guys think, and they've got their finger on the pulse of the scum society," he stated. "The undercover guy at the meeting isn't the only one working out there, you know."

"I didn't think he would be," I said.

"I'll cut to the chase," he said, looking serious. "I'd like for you to come with me on Monday. We'll meet up at the fire station around seven. That's in the morning," he said, grinning over at me.

"Hey, I can get up early," I replied.

Hank said, "A buddy on the Metro Squad has some information for me to pick up. We'll go into Jackson and pick up some papers, then pay some visits around the countryside."

"Any place in particular?"

Hank said, "I know a guy, who knows a guy, who knows a snitch, who says Richie and the girl were seen at a place near Osseo. We won't be going in an official capacity, mind you, only trying to help out Richie's parents." He nodded slightly.

"I see." Though I really didn't see.

"We'll swing by the Sheriff's building in the morning, then be off to Osseo."

"How about we stop in Pittsford for lunch?" I asked. "There's a great little restaurant right across the street from the fire department."

"I think that can be arraigned," he said with a laugh.

I looked down the row of tractors for my grandson. He stood watching a trailer full of operating hit-n-miss engines. One was hooked by a flat belt to an old-fashioned hand pump and was pumping water over and over into a small barrel. The barrel then fed the water back through a black pipe to the hand pump.

Another engine was belted to a corn grinder and was demonstrating how corn meal was made in the early part of the twentieth century.

My wife and daughter showed up with Samara in tow. Hank stood to greet them. "How very nice to meet you," he said to Melissa.

"Glad to meet you, too," she replied. "Dad has told me a lot about you."

Hank looked at me, eyebrows raised.

"All good!" I exclaimed. "I can assure you."

The girls laughed. "We've come to pick up Eli," my wife said. "We'll look around a bit, then they have to get on home."

I hugged my daughter, "Thanks for the help yesterday," I said. "I couldn't have done it without you kids."

"No problem," she replied.

We walked down to catch Eli, who was trying his hand at rope making on an old-fashioned hand crank machine.

"I'll see you back at the house," my wife said with a wave. You boys have fun with your tractor friends."

After hugs all around, they walked off, the grandchildren somewhat reluctantly, and I returned to my chair next to Hank.

"Good kids," he said. "I'm looking forward to having kids around my place."

"You're not getting any younger," I said.

He nodded in agreement. "My brother, Harold, has two boys - twelve and ten years old."

"They like the farm?" I asked, thinking that every boy that age loved a farm.

"They love it," Hank answered. "Harold and his wife have them in 4-H. They show pigs and goats - guess they got the bug from our grandfather. Anyway, my sister-in-law is the swine adviser."

"Grandfather must have been quite a guy," I said.

"He and my grandmother, both," Hank said. "They were wonderful people - had us raising animals, working the garden with them, and tending fruit trees. We swam in the pond and fished in the creek. And," he emphasized, "it was Church every Lord's Day, with a bible study on Wednesdays. That farm was my heaven on earth. My mom is an only child and it was always understood that the farm would go to her." Hank fell silent.

"Didn't she want it?" I asked. Who

wouldn't want a farm, especially one the way Hank described it?

"She was going to retire there with dad, until he died from his heart attack." Hank shook his head sadly.

"I'm sorry," was all I could say. Hank had never mentioned how his father had died, just that he had.

"He was only fifty-six years old. Worked in an auto parts plant in Chicago. He'd worked his way up to foreman on the day shift, and was two years away from thirty and out. That man loved the farm and was looking forward to his retirement there. Mom didn't want to live there alone, and Harold was newly married, so he bought it from the grandparents' living estate. The plan was for the little house to be built for our grandparents. He went ahead with the plan. After the old folks passing on, Mom used the little house as her vacation get-away." Hank leaned back in his chair and gazed down the street where some little kids had gathered around the hit-n-miss display.

"She kept her nursing job in Chicago?" I asked.

"After my father's death, she wouldn't

quit work. Said it kept her going," Hank said. My kid sister, Sarah, came home from Terra Haute with the plan to stay for three months, but went home after one. Mom was glad to have her there, but really didn't need her."

"Sarah have a family?" I asked. This was the most I'd heard Hank talk about his family at one time. It must have been the warm day, the shade of the maple, smell of hot dogs cooking, the tractors, and maybe the heady effect of a cold Dr. Pepper.

"Sarah's a single girl, never been married," he replied. "Married to her job, I guess. She's a professor of English at I.U."

"Huh," I said.

"You know I'm an Irish twin?" Hank changed the subject, and looked at me, a twinkle in his eye.

"No kidding?"

"That's a fact," he smiled. "Harold is Ten months my senior."

"What about Sarah?"

"She came along two years after me," Hank said.

"No more siblings?" I asked.

"Nope. After Sarah, Mom put an end to the 'go forth and multiply' bit."

"I feel sorry for your dad," I said.

"Oh there there was plenty of going forth, I'm sure," Hank said, laughingly. "It's just the multiplying that stopped."

"You tell this in church group?" I asked with a laugh.

"That might be unseemly for a Church Elder," He replied.

"An Elder now?"

"That's right," he said. "You want a direct line to Heaven, come see me, I'll get you in."

"I'm not planning on it right away," I said, shaking my head in amusement.

"Just in case," he said, grinning broadly.

So went our day, until four o'clock, when it was time to present awards, then load up and go home. Hank followed me to the school grounds where we helped each other load and secure our tractors.

Chapter Thirteen

Monday morning; Hank was already waiting in Kip's office when I pulled into the fire station parking lot. His '86 Chevy pickup was parked next to Kip's gray Ford extended cab.

They looked up as I walked in. Kip was working on his computer, his fingers making the keys rattle. He mumbled something under his breath when he hit the wrong one - which was often.

More paperwork, I thought. I went directly for the coffee pot. Kip turned his chair to face me.

"The state boys forwarded a report on the fire on Stone Road. It plays out just like you said it would. I printed a copy for you," he said, pointing at a small stack of papers in the printer tray. "They asked me if you're lookin' for a job."

I took a sip from my coffee cup and glanced over at Hank. "I hope you told them no," I finally said.

"I told them to ask you themselves," Kip replied with a smile.

"The County Fire Chiefs are tossing around the idea of setting up their own investigation squad, and they could use you even more," Hank responded, "but only after your current contract with me is up." He turned to Kip and winked.

"You guys make me feel like the town pump on prom night," I answered laughingly.

Kip howled in delight. Hank grew red and chuckled to himself.

"Come on, Conway," we've got miles to go," Hank said as he slapped Kip on the shoulder and waved his coffee cup at me.

"Before we sleep," I said, hoping I'd remembered the line correctly.

"Good seeing you again, Hank," Kip called as we headed out the door to the parking lot and Hank's Chevy.

We took Pulaski road up passed Swains Lake and on through Concord. We drove by Hanover Street, where we'd been at the tractor show, and on by the Main Street Cafe where Hank had taken Nan for coffee. After passing over the Kalamazoo River dam, with the mill pond stretching to our right, we came to the blinking stop light. Hank turned east on M-60 for the run through farm country and on to Jackson.

In thirty minutes Hank was parking the truck in the lot of a nondescript building a few doors down from the sheriff's office. We got out of the truck and I followed him inside.

Stopping at a directory on the wall by an elevator, Hank searched down the list of names with his index finger. "Here he is," he said. Then we got on and he pushed the button for the second floor.

The elevator doors creaked open and we got off and walked into an office lobby. The place could have been any business or factory office. Behind a wide, white counter were several desks and rows of filing cabinets. Each desk had a laptop or computer screen of some sort. I noticed that the desks were mainly neat and uncluttered. I could never work there.

Behind the counter stood a tall, very attractive, black woman. She wore a well cut dark blue suit with matching, low heeled shoes. The woman walked up to the counter, saw Hank, and did a double take. I noticed right off that she had green eyes. Not contacts, but real, green eyes.

"May I help you?" she asked. I thought she was going to swoon.

"Yes," Hank stammered, obviously quite taken, himself. "Henry McIntyre here to pick up an envelope from John Kuhlbaugh. He said he'd leave it with my name on it. Henry, Hank McIntyre," he repeated.

I noticed how he slipped his name in there a few times so she'd get a chance to learn it.

"His desk is in the back," she said. "I'll go take a look," and the woman actually blushed. She turned to go, glanced over her shoulder at Hank, and with a little head toss, flipped her hair as she walked away. I believe she even put some extra swivel in her hips.

"Good Lord," I said to Hank from the corner of my mouth. That woman is actually flirting with you. Did you catch that?"

"Huh?" Hank responded.

I looked at him. He was staring at the departing female, whose signals evidently hadn't gotten past him.

She brought back a large, brown, envelope. I took a step to the side, not wanting to be part of the circus, but observing.

"Here it is," she gushed, "Hank McIntyre, right here," she pointed. She slid the envelope across the counter, not once taking her eyes off Hank.

I may as well not have been there.

Hank reached for the envelope and she managed to slide her fingers over his. She kept her hand there for a moment too long, I thought.

It was Hank's turn to blush. For a black guy, he could really turn red when he had to.

For the first time, I noticed a name tag clipped to the woman's left breast pocket. "Shonda," it said.

"Hank, meet Shonda," I said. I couldn't believe it. The last time I'd seen behavior this sophomoric was middle school, or down at the fire barn.

Hank babbled something about "Nice day," and broke the trance. Shonda withdrew her hand.

"Just a minute," she said as we turned to leave.

"Yes?"

"There's some important information to add to the envelope." She took the envelope from Hank's outstretched hand and put it on the counter, then hurriedly wrote something on a pink post-it-note, stuck it to the top, then paper-clipped it for good measure. She handed it back to Hank with a flirty smile.

We walked away, Hank reading the new note as we left. Once in the elevator I asked about the information. Hank grinned like an errant school boy getting away with mischief.

"Shonda Miles, (517) 555-4713," he said.

"Oh," I said, "that kind of important information."

"I don't imagine you care to look over the contents of the envelope?" I queried.

"Miles to go," he said, smiling.

I noticed an extra spring in his step.

Chapter Fourteen

We left Jackson, going south on Louis Glick Highway to US-127. Hank had stuck the envelope into a briefcase, which he tucked behind the truck seat.

"Read it later," he said. "Though you're going to want in on this, too. It's some background on the Hochstetler kid that you found injured in the wrecked van, among other things."

"He died later," I replied. "Nothing we could do."

"Ever get stuff like this in Muncie?" Hank asked, glancing over from behind the wheel.

We sped down US-127, between bustling farm fields, toward Hudson, some thirty miles away.

"Occasionally," I said, "we'd have an engine called out to a car crash that involved drugs, or a house fire, but the ambulance service generally handled the 911 calls."

"Hmm," Hank replied with a slight nod of his head.

We stopped for the red light at the intersection of 127 south and US-12, and watched as a small parade of semi trucks thundered by, heading for points east.

Hank gestured at the line of trucks moving east on 12. "How many have something illegal going on?"

I said, "A state cop told me once, that there's more human trafficking coming in by truck than by air or train, and most of it's forced labor, not the sex trade."

"That's what I've been hearing," Hank replied. "Can you imagine?" he shook his head.

Across the corner was a truck stop with a row of semi's parked in the dirt lot. A large, red truck, with an extended sleeper-cab, stirred up a cloud of dust in the lot and entered the highway, west-bound.

"Sure could use some rain," I observed.

The light changed and we sped on south-ward.

Hank asked about my training in Muncie as a fire inspector.

"It isn't as exciting as detective work in

Chicago," I said.

"You mean not as exciting as sitting around for hours watching for someone, or maybe following dead ends over and over, and conducting interviews?"

"I see your point," I said. I guess being a fire inspector wasn't so bad, after all. I'd worked with a mentor for several months who was an ex-fireman. Many inspectors I'd met were ex-firemen or retired State Troopers.

"There were two of us going through training, myself and an ex-cop," I told Hank. "We became quite familiar with Kirk's Fire Investigation Manual."

"Kirk's?" He glanced over at me.

"A reference book supplied by Delaware County, my home county," I said. "We studied metallurgical analysis, melting points of various metals and their components."

"So, by the sag or bending of a metal object, you could tell the location, and how hot the fire was?" Hank asked.

"Exactly. Depending on the composition of the metal object I could get a pretty good idea of how hot the fire was. Also, some metals will bend toward the heat source."

Hank said, "No kidding? I guess it's just

basic physics."

"The metal is softer toward the heat, hard on the other side. The N.F.P.A. gives code information on running an investigation," I said.

"N.F.P.A.?" he asked.
"Nation Fire Protection Association," I said.

"Everybody's got an association," he laughed.

I said, "Code 62 deals with the scientific method. You're probably familiar with that."

"Oh, yes," Hank said with a nod. "Start with a question, gather facts, develop a hypothesis, and then test it."

I said, "I'd take pictures of everything, starting in a particular location, such as an entry door, and work a pattern. There is a test protocol, too. Now, some testing is destructive, and we want to avoid that if possible."

"There's a lot to it," Hank responded, shaking his head. "How would you handle an arson, like the one on Stone Road?" he asked.

"Well," I thought a second, "I'd begin with an electronic sniffer, or a dog, to look for petroleum based accelerates."

"A dog?" Hank looked over at me.

"The one I trained with would sit down when it smelled something," I said.

"Huh," Hank said. "I guess they can find drugs, bombs, and cadavers... so why not chemical accelerates?"

"That's right," I said. "Basically, I'd go about ruling out four possibilities for a fire's cause; mechanical, electrical, natural causes, or in the case down on Stone Road, a match. If I end up in court as an expert witness, I can say that the evidence points to...whatever." I shrugged.

"It's a whole lot like a police investigation," Hank said, shaking his head thoughtfully.

I said, "Well, we also had to document the chain of custody for evidence. There's a form to fill out that states that someone is in possession, not I. Everything is signed and copies are made."

"Yup, it's just like a police investigation," Hank chuckled to himself.

"My mentor had a saying that stuck in my mind," I said. "He'd say somebody was 'stupid in a no stupid zone.' Believe me, I've been to more than a few sites where that proved to be true."

Hank said, "If I burn somebody out, I don't want you on the case." He looked impressed.

"Use rubbing alcohol as an accelerant, and you'll be fine," I replied. "It doesn't leave a trace like petroleum products, even though the burn pattern can show someone poured something to help the fire along."

Hank said, "I'll remember that when the time comes." He smiled and nodded my way.

"My first solo call had been to a combine fire east of Muncie, toward Parker," I continued. "The fire had started at an over-heated bearing that caught the dust and grease on fire. I took pictures and followed the melted wires and hydraulic lines back to the bearing area.

"Sounds interesting," Hank said, with a glance my way.

"It's all in looking for the little details," I said, "mixed with a little common sense."

Hank nodded in agreement.

Before I knew it, we'd arrived at the small city of Hudson. Just past the "Hudson Tigers: State Football Champions, seventy-two wins in a row," sign, we turned west on M-34 for the short drive to the quiet village of Osseo.

Hank looked at the sign, "Seventy-two wins? Man, that's quite a streak."

"Made the national news," I replied, "finally got beat by a team from the U.P. Ishpeming, if I remember right."

Hank said, "Must have been some coach, and lots of talent."

"How about Chicago?" I asked. "You talked about your job as a homicide detective there. Have much to do with the drug culture?"

Hank was quiet, as though thinking hard about something. "I had my interaction with the drug trade," he said. "A few of the murders I helped investigate were connected with drugs. More than a few, I guess. After several cases, it seemed as though the entire human race had descended into one big cesspool. I was completely burned out. Started taking my job home with me." He grew quiet again.

"We had our share of that in Muncie, too," I said. "We made some trips out to wrecks and fires to save some pretty nasty people. There were a few that I almost wished had died on us." I let out a breath and shook my head.

Hank slowed the truck and turned right, passed a Citgo gas station on the corner, and into the quiet burg of Osseo. I watched as he drove us over some abandoned railroad tracks, passed a shuttered feed mill, a closed up store, a clutch of older houses, and on into the countryside to the north of the village.

I said, "Sometimes the EMS guys would share stories about runs they'd been on, and you're right, it sure made me wonder about the condition of my fellow man."

"You know I was married, right?" Hank glanced at me, changing the subject.

"Yeah, you'd mentioned it a few times." I didn't say anymore. He never said much about her. Maybe this was turning into a therapy session, a therapy session without tractors.

"She was a good woman," Hank said, almost sadly. "Still is, I guess. Had a job with the Cook County Health Department. She'd risen up some, to middle management." He paused for a moment and grew quiet again.

The farm fields and woodlots sped by. The day was turning warm, one of those odd previews of a hot summer that we get in southern Michigan during late May. We had the windows cranked down an inch or so for the fresh air.

"Gotta turn here, I think," he said, dropping the conversation, and turning the truck left, up a rutted, dirt road. Small tree branches and tall grasses threatened to rub the side of the truck and maybe even bust up a mirror if Hank wasn't careful. He stuck to the middle of the road, driving slowly enough to keep the ruts from bouncing us off into a ditch.

I asked, "How'd you know where to find this place? Where do you get this stuff?"

Hank gave me a look. I knew what was coming.

"You have your sources," I said, nodding my head before he could open his mouth.

"You could say that," he said. He wasn't going to mention any names. "Google Earth helps a lot, too." He smiled over at me.

I said, "This reminds me a lot of the deserted road when we had the rescue run on the heroin overdose at the drug house. It's pretty isolated here." I was starting to get a bad feeling about this.

"Well," Hank observed, "rats don't like the daylight."

We came to what looked like a farm lane

going off to our right, between trees that arched over-head and formed a leafy tunnel. A battered mail box sat on a leaning, wooden post across from the drive. I couldn't make out an address. Hank drove past it, slowed to a stop, then backed up. "This is it," he said. He actually looked a little nervous.

"The Collins kid was here?" I asked. "He sure wanted to disappear." I rolled down the window and leaned out to get a better look down the lane. "We'd better be careful," I warned, turning to Hank. "This looks like a good place for an ambush." I peered again down the tree-lined lane.

He said, "We'll keep our eyes peeled, always one of us watching our backs."

I said, "I can handle that."

"I'm sure it will be okay, usually is," Hank said, trying to sound positive.

"Never hurts to be cautious," I replied.

"That's why you're here," he said. "An ounce of prevention, you know."

"Stitch in time," I replied.

Hank responded with a chuckle, and I began to relax.

Chapter Fifteen

We drove back the gravel lane, catching a glimpse of a hay field through the trees on the left and following a dim, brushy woods on our right. We came to a thick, rocky hedgerow and drove on through to a large yard. I was mildly surprised to see that the grass had been cut. The house was a small, older, story-and-a-half with a covered porch stuck on the front. There were no railings on the porch. The structure had been painted white at one time. Patches of dull paint had worn away over the ensuing years to bare, dark wood.

There was a newer, but not much newer, two-car garage to our left and set back slightly from the house. Its white paint wasn't in much better condition than that on the house. A full-width, over-head door was in the closed position. The whole place was surrounded by the woods.

Hank rolled his window all the way down to listen. The place was quiet as a graveyard.

"How do we handle this? I asked in a low voice. I hoped it wasn't too late to ask how we handle this.

Hank said, "This is unofficial, remember. We're going to walk up to the front door, nice and pretty." He stared at the house.

"Should've had my Auntie Stella send me some Jehovah Witness brochures," he lamented with a frown. "That would be the perfect cover."

"Clear back here?" I asked, as we got out of the truck.

"Man, those Witness people will go to Hell itself to touch a lost soul," he replied. "I know my dad's sister would." The smile came back to his face.

We got out of the truck and walked from the gravel driveway across the yard to the front porch. The wood floor was made from narrow boards that hadn't seen a coat of paint since the Eisenhower era.

I took the first step up, with Hank behind me. I figured any people in the house would be more likely to open the door to an average looking white guy, than to a big-assed black man, who looked for all the world like a cop.

There was a noise to our left, over at the garage. It sounded like a door opening. I hadn't even had a chance to knock on the house door. Hank trotted around the corner to look. I ran across the porch to keep up with him and jumped down to the yard, hitting the ground at full stride.

Three young people - two male, one female, had just burst out the garage's side door and were making a break down the right side of the yard, between the driveway and the woods. We were after them like hounds to the chase.

Hank is fast, real fast. For an old guy, I'm good at sprinting for a short distance, probably comes from heading off a stray cow or an errant hog, but Hank left me standing still. He raced past the girl, a scraggly, slow girl, and gave her a solid shove on the way by, causing her to belly flop and go skidding on the turf. Within three long strides, he caught the first guy and sent him skidding, too.

The second guy was more athletic, and sprinted on ahead.

By then I was standing over the girl who

was spitting grass from her mouth. Lawn type grass, not the smoking kind, and yelling a bunch of crap about how she wasn't doing anything.

Yeah, right. I reached down and helped her to a sitting position.

Hank was helping the guy to his knees. "Sit on your butt," he said in a voice even I wanted to follow.

"I wasn't doing nuthin' the young man complained. "You didn't have to knock me down!"

"I'll do more than that, you give me any grief," Hank threatened while towering over the kid in a menacing way. I'd never seen this side of Hank before, the cop side of him. Why anybody would give him any lip, I don't know.

I stood there, breathing hard, and wiped my forehead with my sleeve. Hank looked like he'd just strolled through his grandma's garden. Not even breaking a sweat.

He turned to me. "You got a gun?"

"Not on me," I said, shaking my head. I never carried a firearm.

In one smooth motion, Hank produced a pistol from somewhere and tossed it to me.

"Safety's on," he shouted as he turned to chase after the second guy, who was cutting into the woods a short distance away. "Either of these idiots move, shoot 'em!" he yelled over his shoulder as he took off in pursuit.

If I could run like that, I thought, I'd be a millionaire.

I still had ahold of the girl's shoulder, catching my breath. She looked familiar. I'd seen that face somewhere.

I looked at the pistol. The girl looked at me, eyes wide and frightened. She started to whimper, then blubber to herself. Good, I thought. If she's busy doing that, I won't have to answer any questions.

The guy, a young man in his early twenties with long brown hair, started to fidget. He had grass stains on his pants and arms from when Hank knocked him over. I waved the gun in his direction and he settled down.

"What'd we do?" he asked in a demanding voice.

"Shut the hell up," I barked, hoping it would work. He shut up, but he wasn't too happy about it.

"Anybody in the house?" I looked at the girl. Probably get more cooperation from her.

"No," she said, "we're the only ones here."

I decided to keep an eye on it anyway.

Hank reappeared from the woods, empty handed. "Little twerp got away," he called, trotting over to our group. I handed him the gun.

"Are you guys cops?" the guy was feeling brave again.

"That's right," Hank said in a cold voice, "and you don't want to give us any crap. We came out here real nice like, seeking information, and you decided to run. What's that all about, huh?" He produced a leather case and flipped it open in the kid's face. I caught a flash of a badge and a picture I.D.

"We thought you were somebody else, that's all," the guy said. "You didn't identify yourselves. Aren't you supposed to identify yourselves?"

"We would have," Hank replied, "but it's hard to make introductions when somebody takes off like a scared rabbit. And while you're at it," Hank said, "what's your name?"

The young man looked away, refusing to answer.

"When a lawman asks a question, it's best to answer right up, boy," Hank barked. There were little beads of perspiration on his forehead from running into the woods, and he wasn't in any mood to play games with the kid.

"What do you want?" the girl looked up at Hank. She was still sniffing and leaking tears down her face.

"Who's that other guy? Hank asked. "That's what I want right now. Who's the other runner? And what's this clown's name." He pointed at the kid sitting on the grass.

"We don't know anything," the male said, looking up defiantly. He was starting to regain his attitude.

I wanted to give him a crack across the head. To bad I'd given the pistol back to Hank.

I suddenly realized where I'd seen the girl. "You're Amy," I said. You were at the house last Wednesday, where the kid died."

"I don't remember you," she sniffed.

"I was part of the rescue crew that saved your life," I replied forcefully. "I almost didn't recognize you with your pants on."

Hank smirked and threw me a side-ways glance.

"I don't remember anything about that night," she said, looking down at the ground.

Her friend was staring over at her.

"I told you we don't know anything," he repeated. I wasn't even at Spoons' house that night, so I'll just go now." He started to shift to his feet.

The idiot just admitted he knew the guy called Spoons, and where he lived.

"You're not going anywhere, smart boy. Now shut up." Hank gave the kid a solid push in the chest with his foot, sending him sprawling.

The kid started to protest, but this time Hank used his foot to shove him in the face.

"Damn!" the boy exclaimed, picking himself up from the grass. "You don't have to use the rough stuff."

"You don't have to be a wise-ass," Hank replied icily.

I'd never heard Hank swear before. Ever.

Hank snarled, "Things are going to get a lot rougher if I don't start hearing some answers to what I'm asking," To get his point across, he pointed the pistol at the kid's crotch.

The kid flinched.

Hank was making me a little nervous, too.

"Wonder what's going on in the garage?"

Hank asked, looking up. "You kids baking cookies today?" He smiled knowingly at the two sitting on the ground.

Amy sobbed a little louder. "I just got out of the hospital and was only here to visit," she said.

"Shut up!" her friend snapped, throwing her an icy stare.

Hank shuffled his right foot, the kid flinched again, and sat quietly.

I walked over to the garage while Hank stood over the two kids. I could smell it before I even got close, the strong odor of cat piss. Stepping to the side door, I grasped the knob and opened it. The chemical stench of cooking meth and ammonia hit me in the face. I peeked inside. There were two set-ups. One was on a table in the center of the building, another on a work bench against the back wall. Several old car batteries lay against the side wall, like they'd been tossed there after being drained. Papers, fast food boxes, and wrappers were strewn across the floor. Slamming the door, I trotted back to Hank.

"It's a meth lab!" I shouted. They're cooking the crap right now!" I pointed over my shoulder, back toward the garage.

Hank handed me the pistol. "Keep an eye on the girl," he said. "Junior and I are going to the garage and have a little talk."

He reached down with one hand and grabbed the guy by the back of his collar and roughly hoisted him to his feet.

"I'd like to know who the runner is," he said firmly, "and I'd like to know if Richie Collins has been here. His girlfriend, too. While we're at it, we'd like to know what you know about a dead kid named Marvin Hochstetler."

He was lifting the young man high enough that his feet barely touched the ground, and he gave him a little shake to show he was serious.

"And what the hell's your name?"

The kid yelped and said he didn't know nothin'. His line was getting a little old by now.

"Man," Hank said, "it sure would be a shame if there was an accident here at the meth lab. The crazy things are always exploding, you know. Read about it all the time in the papers."

The kid looked at him with dread, then

looked at me, his eyes wide, almost pleading.

I said, "He's pretty good at blowing up meth labs. A person can't even tell it was, shall we say... arraigned." I looked down at the girl and gave her a grim smile.

Hank said, "They're always finding a body or two in burned out meth buildings. Some charred beyond recognition."

The kid's face went white.

Hank marched the guy toward the garage, his feet barely touching the ground, dragging and jerking along like some sort of drunken marionette.

Amy looked up at me and swallowed hard. "It's Mark," she whispered. Her voice was so low I could barely make out what she said.

"Who?" I asked.

"The guy who ran away is Mark," she said a little louder. She cast a fearful look at the guy with Hank, and shuddered.

"Mark?" I asked. There was that name again. The one Gloria had mentioned the night Spoons had died of the heroin overdose.

"Tell me about Mark," I said. "Is he a nice guy?"

"Yes," she replied softly, nodding her head. "He tries to watch out for me. He doesn't make me do anything, you know, for the drugs."

There you have it, a drug dealer with a heart.

"Does Mark have a last name?" I asked as pleasantly as possible. I was hoping my voice wouldn't give away my excitement. I glanced up. Hank was nearing the garage.

"I don't know his last name," Amy replied, wiping tears away with the heel of her hand. "I've only known him for, like, a couple weeks. I think he lives over to Maple Grove."

I froze. Chief LaBlanc's youngest son? His name is Mark. How many guys named Mark could there be in the Maple Grove area? I didn't know the kid, but I'd seen him. He was with his dad the night we found Marvin Hochstetler in the wrecked van out on Goose Lake Road. They'd come out to see if we needed any help. In the middle of the night they'd come out. And, what kind of person knows someone 'for, like, a couple weeks,' and doesn't know their last name? Apparently knowing last names isn't important in this crowd.

Regaining my composure, I said, "You see, Amy, that wasn't so difficult, was it? We just came out here to help, that's all."

Amy looked up and tried to smile. It looked more like a grimace. I wondered what she was on at the moment.

"His name is Ted," she said with a nod toward the kid still firmly held in Hank's grasp. They had reached the over-head door where Hank looked through the narrow windows. Now they were proceeding around the corner to the side door.

"Ted is Spoon's big brother," Amy continued. "He's two years older. Twenty-two, I think."

Man, only twenty-two and throwing his life away. His kid brother overdosing and dying didn't slow him up at all.

"Thank you, Amy," I said kindly. "By the way, I didn't catch how old you are. Are you still in school?" I was hoping the question sounded like a friendly conversation.

She looked at the pistol in my hand. I moved it to my right side, pointed toward the ground.

"I'm seventeen," she replied, looking back up at me.

She looked much older to me. A rough, rode-hard, and put-away-wet, older.

"I had you pegged for twenty-one," I replied, smiling. Then I wondered if she'd be offended by my little joke. Some girls don't want to seem older, even when they're young.

She smiled. Almost a pretty smile. A heart wrenching smile. "When I was in school, people thought I was in the ninth grade, when actually I was going into the eleventh."

"Aren't you in school now?" I asked. I knew she had only a few days until the end of the year.

"Naw, I missed too much, and the truant officer came to the house, so I took off. That was a year ago. I've been living with friends since."

"Where are your parents?

"Dad took off when I was, like, in the sixth grade. Mom has a new boyfriend now and again, but she works a lot and the boyfriends tend to get a little too friendly."

"Oh," I replied. I hoped this wasn't going where I thought it was going.

She said, "One guy, though, I really liked. He'd buy me things and bring home pizza and stuff. We used to smoke dope and get it on when mom was at work, but I think she kinda' knew. Anyway, when I took off, she didn't try to find me. And I ain't going back." She had a calm look of finality about her.

Officer McIntyre and I can get you some help," I said. I couldn't begin to imagine the life she'd led.

"Not juvenile," she said with a shake of her head, meaning the juvenile system.

Foster care or a state home came to mind, though I doubted she'd go for either one.

"There are other options," I said, without knowing what they were, if there really were any.

Hank came back from the garage with Ted. Ted now had a completely different attitude. He was red-faced as Hank, a little more gently now, led him back to us and placed him on the grass, next to Amy.

"Amy," Ted said, "tell them who I am. He doesn't believe me." He tried to fight back his tears, but failed.

"He's Ted," Amy answered. "Ted Kelly, Spoon's brother."

"You got a nick-name, too?" Hank asked.

"They call me Cookie," Ted replied hurriedly.

Hank must have put the fear of God into

the kid.

"Because he knows how to cook up meth," Amy blurted.

Ted said, "That's right."

I noticed there was no glaring at Amy, no reluctance to answer. I couldn't help wondering if Hank had taken him around the corner and kicked him in the family jewels or something.

"What about Richie Collins, and his girlfriend?" Hank pressed.

"Meagan Grawn," Amy replied. "Her name is Meagan Grawn."

"We don't like her," Ted said. "She's a control freak. Always bossing Richie around. She was the one who got us started in cooking, though. Said she had a market for the stuff. She always had the best stuff, too."

The boy was turning into a regular chatter-box.

"What kind of stuff?" I asked.

"Pot, meth, cocaine, heroin, whatever you needed. Strong pain pills. I don't know where she got it all, but it was good quality. She showed me how to cook up a batch of meth without blowing myself up." He looked up at Hank who just smiled and nodded his head in encouragement.

"When were Richie and Meagan, Meagan, right?", I looked at Amy, who nodded her head. "When were Richie and Megan here?" I looked at them both.

"About a week back," Ted answered. He glanced at Amy for support.

"That's right," she said. "They took off a week ago, Saturday. I was here that day."

"They say anything about where they might be headed?" I asked.

Hank nodded in approval at the question. He had remained silent, obviously happy so far with my questioning.

"They were headed to one of Meagan's girlfriend's place," Amy replied. I don't know the girl's name, but she lives south of Hillsdale, somewhere."

Ted picked up the conversation. "If you want to get ahold of them, go to the Hillsdale Auction. Her boyfriend's parents have a produce stand on the south side of the fairgrounds. Meagan talked about how she was hoping they'd get some free food." He glanced up at Hank and me. "It's on Saturdays, you know,"

"Thanks, I'm familiar with it," I replied.

Two kids on the run from who-knows-what, living in flop houses and surviving off begged food. They couldn't get far.

I said, "By the way, what are the two of them driving these days?"

"Some old Ford pickup," Amy replied. "I don't know the year."

"The color?" I prompted.

"It's kinda blue," Amy looked at Ted for help.

"A faded blue," he added for her.

"Describe it," I said. "Any dents or rusted bumpers?"

"No," Ted replied, "just faded paint. Black-wall tires and no hubcaps," he added.

"Back to the boyfriend of Meagan's friend," I said, "does he have a name or an alias?"

"I thought Meagan said once that his name is Mark," she replied. "I don't know his last name."

"You?" I looked at Ted. This was the second guy named Mark to come into the equation

"I didn't even know that," he replied. "Just that Meagan hoped to get food from the parent's stall at the auction. We didn't talk much while they were here. They mostly stayed to themselves. Meagan kept a pretty tight watch on Richie," he shrugged.

"Who owns this place, anyway?" I asked, looking around.

"My grandparents used to live here," Ted answered. Grandpa's dead now, and Grandma's in a care-home in Jackson somewhere."

"You don't know where?" I asked, incredulous.

"My parents know. They visit her," he answered somewhat defensively.

We all looked at Hank, who had pulled out his cell phone. He was still watching us, and gave me a nod and a smile. Pressing some buttons, he held the phone to his ear.

"Where did Richie park the truck while they were here?" I asked. I would check the spot later for any papers and such that might have fallen out.

"They kept it behind the garage," Ted said. "It can't be seen back there."

"It can't be seen anywhere back here." It was Hank speaking. He'd placed the cell phone back into his pocket. "Authorities are on their way," he added. He looked at me. "This just got official," he said.

This brought an instantaneous wail from

Amy. "I thought you'd let me go if I helped you," she said.

"We'll try to get you help, but we can't let you go," Hank responded. "Both of you."

Ted sagged his shoulders. I thought he'd start crying again.

"I can keep you out of the federal pen," Hank told him. "You just keep a positive attitude."

Ted sat with his knees up, arms folded across them, his head down.

"I can't go to jail," Amy sobbed. "I'll do anything. Just name it, okay? Anything." She looked up at us with a tight, frightened smile on her face.

Hank looked over at me with sad eyes. I knew what he was thinking. How much lower could these kids go? I just shook my head and was silent.

We stood there for what seemed an eternity. Amy would beg for a while then go silent. Ted never said a word. Hank stood over them with the gun and a stony stare.

Within five minutes, a Hillsdale County Sheriff's car drove back the lane and emerged from the hedgerow in a swirl of dust. It's light-bar was going, but there was no siren.

Hank had asked for a silent run.

The car pulled to a stop beside Hank's Chevy pickup. A lady deputy got out and walked over. She was middle-aged, and kind of cute in an official kind of way, but she had a hard edge to her.

She gave us all the look over, and sized up the situation.

"Hank McIntyre," Hank nodded toward her. "You bring cuffs?" he re-directed toward the two sitting on the ground.

"There's a third one running through the woods," I said. "Teenage male, with a good head-start. The girl says there's no one in the house, but we haven't had time to check it." Without moving too quickly, I tilted my head toward the old farm house.

She looked at me, then turned to Hank. "Who called it in?" Not a very friendly voice, with no move to get the cuffs. Her hand didn't stray from her holstered gun, her thumb on the snap.

I took a deep breath.

"I did," Hank stepped forward and handed her his I.D. wallet.

"Oh," she said, looking at his I.D. and back up at his face. Handing the leather wallet back to him, she reached behind her and unsnapped a set of hand-cuffs. Stepping forward, she secured Ted's arms behind him.

Ted remained silent. Hank put the gun away.

The deputy produced another set of cuffs and handed them to me. I almost put them on myself. Whatever Hank was showing these people was surely going to get us arrested when the State Police showed up. I hadn't seen the I.D. for myself, but it had to be impressive, and the guy was retired, for Pete's sake.

"Go ahead," Hank was saying. He nodded toward Amy. The deputy gave me a cold stare.

Amy made it easy. She held out her left hand and I snapped the cuff on her thin wrist in a way that I hoped looked professional, then stepped behind her. She placed her arms for me and I secured her right wrist, making sure the cuffs weren't too tight. I'd never done this before, and I wasn't sure if it was like putting a collar on a dog, or slipping on a blood-pressure cuff. Would room for two fingers be okay, or too loose? I didn't know.

"Looks good," Hank said with a big smile. Then, turning to the deputy lady, "We're both retired men, so some things are a little rusty."

I looked away.

The lady deputy relaxed and actually smiled. "More cars are coming," she said pleasantly. "Radio chatter says the State Police are on their way over from Jonesville."

She looked up at Hank and grinned coyly.

How does the man do it?

"I'm going to go peek into the house," she said all perky and nice. "Be right back." She turned and walked across the grass and up onto the porch. We watched as she turned and waved. Hank smiled and waved back. The deputy peeked through the front window, then went to the door. Trying the latch, she shoved the door open and stood aside, then entered. She came back out.

"I'm going to walk through," she called to Hank.

She certainly wasn't calling to me. I realized that I didn't even know her last name. It had to be on her name tag over her left pocket, but I was so concerned about avoiding getting tased, or even shot, that I never bothered to look.

Two more Hillsdale County Deputies showed

up in their cars. We must have had most of their road crew for the day parked right in front of us. A fire engine that had Pittsford-Jefferson painted on the doors rumbled into the yard and over near the garage. The first of the state contingent followed them in. A blue, window-less van brought up the rear.

We turned the kids over to the deputies from Hillsdale County. They led them away, like docile puppies, and put them in separate cars. Then they returned to us, with big grins on their faces.

Hank sent them off to the house to check on the lady deputy.

A man from the state came over. "You McIntyre?" the officer asked.

"That I am," Hank replied shaking the man's hand, "and this is my associate, Tim Conway." He waved a hand my way.

Now I'm an associate.

"Pleased to meet you both," the officer said after we shook.

He looked old for a State Policeman out in the field. As old as myself, nearing retirement. He had a firm hand-shake.

"Don't run into many Federal guys out

here," the State Trooper was saying. He was smiles all around.

"Always a pleasure to work with Michigan's finest," Hank said, all the time grinning like a fool.

This is it. We're going to the Federal Pen in Milan, for sure. How much time is handed down for impersonating an officer, anyway? Make that a Federal officer. Maybe I can use this Ted kid for bartering to keep the rape gangs off me.

"How long you been working this area?" the cop was asking.

"For the last year, off and on," Hank replied.

Adding on an extra five years with that one, I was sure.

"The last two months have been quite active," he added. "As I was telling the lady deputy, both Conway and I are retired men. I had my connections with the U.S. Marshals Service while working homicide in Chicago. That's where I'm from. Mr. Conway is out of Muncie, Indiana." He reached out and placed a large hand on my left shoulder.

I'd noticed he never said anything about me being a civilian. Even though I was a former Muncie Firefighter and Fire Inspector, to the police officials, I was a civilian, not much more than a cub scout.

"We both have small farms up in the Pulaski area." Hank was still spreading it.

He said, "A friend in the Detroit Marshal's office called me about looking into a few things in southern Michigan. Mr. Conway, here, is a former Fire Inspector for Muncie, and has top-quality investigative skills. He keeps me honest."

The State Trooper tossed back his head and laughed, showing deep lines around his eyes.

"I hope I have this much fun when I'm retired," he shook his head in amusement.

I felt the tension melt right out of me. Maybe we wouldn't be cuffed, arrested, and tossed into prison. I looked at Hank. How had he ever come up with this story, anyway? The U.S. Marshals Service?

Two men from the State Police van had put on haz-mat suits and were dragging a couple small, luggage-type carts behind them to the garage. The firemen watched carefully. They'd already strung a few lines and weren't taking any chances.

The older trooper left us and walked over

to the blue patrol cars to talk to three officers. The three troopers came over, two male and a female.

The female asked, "Could you bring us up to speed?" She was a sergeant, but spoke in a friendly, cooperative tone.

Hank and I took a good fifteen minutes to relate who we were looking for, what happened when we showed up, and what the kids had told us. I suggested that after they search the house, they search the area behind the garage where the blue pickup had been parked. The Sergeant lady smiled knowingly and nodded, but she wrote a note.

Hank said, "Work these kids right, and you might get some good snitches."

The sergeant made a noise in agreement and nodded her head. "We'll try working that angle." She smiled pleasantly.

After a pause, where I knew he was doing some thinking, Hank added, "There's a runner in the woods there," he pointed behind us. "We told the County Deputies. I believe they radioed for backup to wait on the next road over and see if he pops out. The kid's got to have a car parked somewhere."

I noticed that he didn't tell them that

Amy had fingered the runner as Mark, maybe Mark LaBlanc.

The State Troopers looked toward the woods and nodded. We'll call for K-9 backup, one of the male troopers said. "I'll get with the County Deputies." He turned and left the group.

When we were finally free to go, I realized I had a lot of questions for Hank as soon as I got him into the pickup.

We climbed into the truck. Hank didn't start the engine. He put his hands on the steering wheel, took a deep breath, and let it out, long and slow.

"Well," he finally said, "that sure was fun." He turned to me and smiled that smile. "I sure could go for an ice-cold Dr. Pepper," he added, running his thick fingers back through his hair.

"U.S. Marshal?" I asked. "I was sure we were going to jail this afternoon!"

He shifted in his seat, reached into his pants pocket, and produced the leather I.D. wallet. Opening it, he handed it over. I took it and looked at the picture. It was Hank McIntyre, alright. It had a complete description under the picture. There was even

211

a contact number for the Federal Marshals Service in Detroit, Michigan. On the other side was an official looking U.S. Marshals badge.

"Is this real?" I asked, both skeptical and amazed that the guy I'd known for two years as a tractor and sometime car-guy, was connected with Federal Law Enforcement. I hoped he'd start the truck and get us out of there before the police became suspicious.

Hank giggled like a school girl. "I'm afraid it's all true," he said, trying to contain his amusement.

The look on my face as I handed back his I.D. must have been priceless.

"All this time you were a Federal Investigator?" I knew a few police officers in Muncie, and there was always Deputy Flint at the fire department, but I had never been to their house for tractor therapy, or sat in their garage drinking Dr. Peppers and solving the worlds' problems.

"It's hard to explain," he said. "I'm retired, just like you, except I sort of let myself get dragged into lending a hand to the Feds."

"Kind of like how I sorta' got dragged

into it, too?" Not that I didn't mind helping out. It was pretty exciting. I watched out the windshield as two State Troopers began searching the area behind the garage where the old Ford pickup had been parked.

"Yes," Hank answered. "My buddy, who shall remain anonymous, asked a favor. I agreed to help out." He spread his hands as though he were revealing something secret in them. "If it helps," he said, "the person drives an eighty-four Avanti."

"No kidding?" I immediately felt my mood improve considerably.

"I knew that would get you," he said with a broad grin. "Yes, it's true. It was her grandfather's. The old guy left it to her in his will. My friend drives it in fair weather only, like you do with your sixty-four Daytona. Her Avanti is red, with fawn leather interior. At least that's how I remember it. It's been a while," he said.

"Okay," I said. "We'll do this for the 'unnamed person' who drives the Avanti." I held my fingers up in quote signs. It just figured that the person is a she. "It *was* kind of fun," I admitted to Hank. Then, "You sure we can't end up in jail for this?"

"Not if we follow the rules," he said.

"Did we break any rules today?" I asked. I was really hoping we hadn't.

"Maybe one or two," he grinned that winning grin.

"Oh brother," I muttered, shaking my head in disbelief. "One other question, what on earth did you do to that Ted kid to get him talking?"

"Oh that," Hank's eyes brightened with delight.

I could tell that this was going to be a good one.

"I took him around the corner of the garage and carefully, in full detail, explained what would happen to him in Federal Prison. I told him I'd do everything in my power to get him sent up, unless he cooperated."

"He bought it?"

"He was a little reluctant at first, 'til I pointed around the corner to the girl. I said the guys in prison would do things to him that he'd never think of doing with the girl. And, when his rectum started bleeding from over-use, they'd start on his esophagus, *if* they didn't start there first. I used all the proper words, no slang, to show him I knew what I was talking about."

I said, "That's a pretty intense pep-talk."

Hank said, "I finished up by telling him that after a few weeks of continuous prison rape, he'd wish we'd have shot him right here. Heck, with the right cell mate, it could be an every night thing."

"Geez," I said, starting to feel a little queezy myself.

"You saw the results," Hank said calmly, "and I'll do what I can to help him if he cooperates."

With that, he turned the key and started the truck. The police officers and firemen looked our way and waved. Hank beeped the truck horn and turned in a circle to head out the drive.

"We need to look into this Mark guy," he said quietly.

"He's the Maple Grove Fire Chief's son, if it's the Mark I'm thinking of," I said. He was there the night of the van wreck where the Hochstetler kid died."

"I know," Hank said. "He was at the combined meeting, too. He was down front with the gang, snickering and playing the fool."

"That figures," I replied.

"We need to know how deep his dad is in all this, if indeed either of them is mixed up in this at all," Hank said.

We rode along in silence for a moment, each in our own thoughts.

"The Hillsdale Auction," Hank finally said, breaking the silence, "you've been there before?"

"A few times," I replied. "Believe me, it's a cultural experience."

"That a fact?"

I related the few details about the auction that I'd picked up over the last several years. Hank seemed interested.

The truck came to the end of the lane, at the gravel road. Hank paused to get his bearings, then turned left, back toward the Osseo Road. Again he drove carefully, avoiding the tree limbs reaching into the path.

"I wouldn't mind going just for the fun of it," Hank said.

"It is fun, but don't say I didn't prepare you," I replied.

Hank nodded his head slowly, "Uh, huh," he said. Then added, "You still up for lunch in Pittsford?"

"I'd just as soon pass, if you don't mind," I said. "We've been so long, that I'd really ought to get on home."

"I hear you there," he said. "Sometime though, we'll go on down. If it's as good as what I've been hearing."

"It is," I replied.

Hank was quiet for a moment, thinking. "You know," he said. "Pittsford isn't far from the Lost Nations Wilderness Area. There's a gun store down there that a friend told me about. I hear the guy's got some collectibles. Maybe we could go get some lunch, then drive on down sometime."

"Your informant friend have an Avanti?"

He looked at me, grinned, and nodded slowly. "You got a gun?" he asked.

I nodded "Yes, a .038."

"CCW permit?"

"I've had it for a few years now," I said, "but I never carry."

"Carry it," Hank said. "You could have used it today."

I sighed, "You're right," I admitted.

"What are you thinking?" Hank asked, looking over at me.

I'm thinking Richie's girlfriend, Meagan,

is involved clear up to her eyebrows. If we can get a lead at the auction grounds this Saturday, it might go a long way in finding him and busting the girl," I said.

"We've already got two dead kids," I continued, "and a couple drug sites, and we've got some guy named Mark, who's name has come up twice now. He supposedly lives over in Maple Grove. I'm telling you, I've got a funny feeling about the LaBlanc family, but I can't prove anything." I turned to Hank and shrugged.

"You sure you've never been a cop?" he grinned.

We talked about guns, tractors, cars, and how to solve the problems in the world, all the way back to Pulaski. Hank dropped me at my truck and I headed for home.

My wife came through to the kitchen to greet me. "How did your play-date go with Hank McIntyre?" she asked.

"I need a nap," I said.

She smiled and reached for my hand.

Thirty-five years of marriage...

Later, I fell asleep wondering what all was in the brown envelope Hank had picked up that morning.

Chapter Sixteen

My cell phone pager beeped. Setting my coffee cup down, I leaned on the kitchen counter and listened. My wife stood at the sink, rinsing the supper dishes that I'd just cleared from the table. The dishwasher door hung open.

"Jackson Central to Pulaski Rescue," a male dispatcher said, "1596 Barryton Road, cross, Church. Unresponsive female. Possible drug overdose."

It had been just a few days since the trip to Osseo with Hank, were we discovered the meth lab. Two weeks since the overdose at the secluded house in the country. Now we had another overdose.

I stood up and picked up the phone. The dispatcher repeated the message.

"Gotta go," I looked at my wife.

"Go on," she said. "I'll see you when you

get back." She smiled and leaned over to kiss me on the cheek.

As I walked out to my truck, I saw her watching through the slider, then turn back to the sink. So much for our quiet Thursday evening at home. We'd gone almost all week with only a few minor calls, one to Ruthie's place. Now this on Thursday night.

The sun was a giant, red ball hanging just above the western horizon. I wondered why drug overdoses seem to always happen at night? What was it that Hank had said about rats not liking the daylight?

I punched the phone icon and called into Jackson Central Dispatch as I got the Dodge rolling to the fire station. Arriving at the parking lot next to the station building, I saw Chief Kip pulling the rescue van from the first bay. He was alone. I parked my truck and hustled over to the passenger side and slid in.

Schultzie had radioed in to say he'd bring Engine 1 as our backup. We usually sent an engine as backup on rescue runs, especially personal injury accidents. Who knew what we'd find tonight? His pickup sped into the parking lot as Kip hit the lights and siren and headed down the street toward Pulaski Road. He paused briefly at the intersection, we looked both ways to check for traffic, then he accelerated and sped on, heading west. In the mirrors, we could see the flashing lights of Engine 1 as Schultzie chased after us.

Two miles west, Kip slowed and turned north on Barryton Road. We were in the one thousand block, the numbers increasing as we headed north. The rescue van sped past the eleven hundred block, the light-bar casting a kaleidoscopic display on the trees as we went.

On and on we drove. Nan's voice came over the radio, talking to the dispatcher. She would meet us on site. Deputy Flint was on duty and would meet us there, too.

We came to the fifteen hundred block of Barryton Road. To the west was a large corn field, forty acres at least. The setting sun bathed the young plants in an orange-red light. On our east side was a wooded area thick with white pines. A driveway appeared, leading back through the trees. A fancy, black-iron mailbox was across the road from the drive.

A young man was standing by the box at the side of the road, waiting for us in the gathering dusk. He was dressed in dark, baggy shorts and a white T-shirt with Micky Mouse on the front. He held a cell phone in his hand.

Kip slowed the rescue, eased the window down, and stuck his head out as the kid waved his arms and ran over to meet us.

"Down here," the kid shouted breathlessly, pointing with his cell phone toward the dark drive that snaked through the pines.

"Is she in the yard?" Kip asked.

"No, in the house!" the kid exclaimed.

"Okay." Kip drove quickly down the drive, the headlights stabbing ahead through the trees. We came to a large clearing.

Off to one side, a few cars were parked on the lawn. Tracks in the grass showed where others had been there, but left. An over-sized log home rested in the center of the clearing - a two-story, with a long, covered porch running across the front. Wooden railings lined the porch, accented by colorful peonies and roses in well tended flower gardens. Accent lights lit up the flowers. The roof was of green metal. There was just enough fading daylight to show a neatly manicured lawn. I was impressed.

"Wow," said Kip. "Some joint, eh?"

"This is the nicest one yet," I replied, thinking of some of the dumps we'd been in.

Kip parked the rescue van in the yard, just off the driveway and close to the house.

I leaped out and grabbed a medical bag. We walked to the porch where several young people had gathered. Two girls were quietly crying, dabbing at their eyes with twisted tissues. The boys with them looked dazed as they tried to comfort the girls.

"In here," a blond guy said as he pointed inside, then led us through the door. The kids on the porch stepped away and stared as we went by.

Schultz stopped Engine 1 next to the rescue van. Running across the yard, he joined us as we went through the door.

A spacious, open room greeted us as we walked in. I guess in the home magazines, it would be called a great room. A massive stone fireplace at the far end anchored the sturdy log walls. Ten feet or so up, a balcony jutted out into space under the cathedral ceiling. The room was as big as my whole house.

A small knot of kids stood looking at something on the floor. They parted to let us through. A girl lay motionless on a large rug decorated with pictures of birch trees and black bears. I looked up. She was directly below the balcony and was laying on her back, dark hair spread to one side. One arm lay across her chest, the other flopped at her side. Her right leg was bent back at the knee. The left was straight, with the shoe missing, revealing a bare foot with shiny, blue-painted toe nails. Kip handed me a pair of blue medical gloves, then slipped some on his hands, too. Schultz was opening the medical kit.

The girl's face was pasty white, lips blue. Her skin had that grayish cast of the dead. I knelt and lay my fingers aside her carotid for a pulse. Nothing there.

Something about the placement of the body didn't fit right with me. I glanced over at Kip.

Schultz and I looked up as a screen door banged somewhere back in the house. Somebody leaving in a hurry?

Kip stood over me. "Who called this in?" he asked the circle of spectators.

Everyone looked behind us. We turned to follow their stares.

"I called." It was the young man who had met us at he road. His face was red and he was breathing hard, probably from running down the driveway, chasing after us.

"What's your name, and how long has she been like this?" Kip asked.

"Seth Randall, and not long," he responded breathlessly. "Half an hour?" He took a guess. He had thick, black, curly hair that came to the bottom of his ears. His deep blue eyes were wide with excitement.

My experience told me the girl was dead for longer than a half-hour, a lot longer.

A few youngsters turned and stepped away.

"What's her name?" Kip demanded. His tone of voice told me that something wasn't adding up for him, either.

"Sandy," Seth said in a nervous voice. He swallowed hard and looked away.

"Tell us what happened," Kip said examining the body, gently lifting an arm, then easing it back down.

Kip, Schultzie, and I knelt beside the girl. While Kip talked to Seth, Schultz began CPR. I looked for evidence of pooling in low points and the extremities.

Seth glanced up at the balcony. "She was

upstairs and must have lost her balance," he said.

"What was she doing upstairs?" Kip asked.

"There's a bathroom up there," he answered as his eyes shifted away. "Maybe she went up to use it, or just wanted to see the view from the balcony." He was fidgeting with his cell phone now.

I figured the view from up there must have been breathtaking, as was the rest of the house. The guy seemed nervous, and not just because he had a dead girl in his great room.

Kip handed me a pen light and I checked the girl's eyes for light reaction. No response.

In my peripheral vision, I was aware of several young people watching quietly from nearby. Looking up, I noticed how well most of them were dressed. Somebody's parents had plenty of money. Most kids were holding cell phones and one girl held a fancy, yuppie-type box of flavored cigarettes.

I thought she didn't even look old enough to have a driver's license, let alone smoke. Doing a quick head-swivel, I noticed pop cans, snack wrappers, a few wine coolers, but no beer or other alcohol containers. Somebody had cleaned up before we got there. I'd have bet the farm we'd find no evidence of drug paraphernalia, either.

"So, you live here?" I asked Seth, looking at him from my position at the girl's side. I already guessed the answer. His parents were away somewhere, and he was just going to have a little party. It's the same old story, only this one didn't have a happy ending.

"Yes," he said, "it's my parent's house. They're on a cruise to the Caribbean."

"So you're here alone, and decided to have a party," I said.

"I guess it kinda' got out of hand," he said, looking fearfully down at the girl. "She gonna be alright? Can you do anything?"

"No," Kip answered. "When the medics get here, they'll do what they can."

Sweat popped on the kid's forehead and upper lip, his face twitched, and he backed away.

He must have known she was dead, but it was still a shock, coming from us.

"What's she been using?" Kip asked.

"I, I don't know," Seth stammered. "She could have taken something before she got here." He shrugged and glanced away.

I saw a glimpse of fear in his eyes.

Voices drew our attention to the door. Deputy Flint and Deputy Ned Jordon had entered the room. They herded a few distraught young people in ahead of them, like border collies bringing in sheep.

Seth let out a low groan.

"Take the back," Flint said to Jordon, who immediately walked through the house to where I supposed the back door was located.

"Could you folks follow Deputy Flint?" Schultzie said.

The party-goers left us to drift off toward Flint, who stood by the front door. He had his notepad out and was taking names and checking IDs. He told a few sobbing girls to take a seat on the couch, the very same girls who'd been crying on the front porch when we arrived. A couple boys sat and put their arms around the girls to comfort them. The Randall kid stayed behind with us, probably feeling responsible for his friend's death.

Schultz waved him away, while Kip took over the chest compression. "Come on Sandy," he said, "breath, damnit!"

I tore open a plastic bag and handed Schultz an oral airway. He tilted the girl's chin and inserted the device. It would open up her airway, while keeping the tongue forward and out of the throat. I thought it a waste of effort, but we had to do something.

"I smell vomit," Schultz stated. He looked at Sandy's blouse collar and pointed to a faint, damp stain. "Been wiped off," he said.

Kip paused for a moment. He was beginning to perspire. Sandy lay still. Seth Randall stood alone, a few feet away, watching in fascination as we fought to save his friend.

Two State Police officers entered and spoke to Flint. One came to us and checked on the girl. He carried a small, black, leather purse in one hand. I assumed it was Sandy's, not his. He was a big guy, and I wasn't about to suggest it was. He fumbled around in the purse and pulled out a driver's license.

"Sandy Wolcott," he said. "She's twenty years old, from Battle Creek. Any of you know her?"

We all shook our heads "No."

Kip stood and I took over the chest compression. "She's a stranger to us," he said.

Schultzie had bagged the girl and was

squeezing in time to my chest compression.

"I see," the officer said. "Well, the ambulance is almost here,"

We nodded our thanks, then returned our attention to working on the girl.

Kip turned the Randall kid over to the officer, who touched his elbow and gestured with a hand to lead him away. I thought the kid was going to faint. The police divided the group and began interviewing people.

Kip knelt beside me. "She's gone," he said in a low tone. "Been gone a long time."

I stopped the chest compression.

"Mmm Hmm," Schultz agreed with an almost imperceptible nod of his head. He was to my right, squatting on his heals, carefully looking the body over. He let go of the bag, and flexed an ankle, then a knee. "Stiff," he said, looking at us. The girl's been dead a lot longer than a half-hour, I'll bet."

"The fall didn't kill her," Kip voiced what I was thinking. "She overdosed on something and vomited," he said.

Schultzie said, "See the pooling under the skin." He was pointing at the body. "The patterns aren't right. Look, if she were on her left side, it would all fit, and her hair's too neat. Someone has staged the body."

We tilted our heads and moved around to better see what he was saying.

"Unless a fall broke her neck and death was instantaneous, there should be bruising and more blood if she were alive when she hit," Kip observed.

I looked at the others and nodded in agreement.

Outside, we heard sirens. The noise stopped out front. Two EMTs came in carrying a couple medical kits and a back board. They nodded in greeting. We stepped aside as they bent over the body and went to work. One guy was new to me - my age, with an old-fashioned crew cut. His partner was the short, skinny guy who worked the wreck out on Goose Lake Road a few weeks back.

Untucking Sandy's blouse, they connected a heart monitor. Schultzie helped untangle the leads as Kip and the older guy stuck electrodes to her body. They then connected the leads and we all looked at the monitor. The display lines were flat.

There were murmurs of disappointment all around.

"Paddles?" asked the older EMT.

The skinny, short guy shook his head. "Waste of time, she's asystole," he said. "Flat-lined, no cardiac activity at all." He leaned over the machine and pressed some buttons. A paper print-out came from a slot in the machine. "C-M-A," he said, snatching the paper and looking around at us to nods and sounds of agreement. He studied the print-out while we jostled to see over his shoulder. He looked up, "Anyone say what happened?"

Kip said, "Kid said she fell from the balcony. It's gotta be close to fifteen feet up." He pointed to the railings above our heads.

"How long ago?"

"He guessed about a half hour before we got here," Kip said. "Ten minutes ago." He checked his cell phone time.

The ambulance guys stared up at the balcony and back down at the body. The skinny guy shook his head in disagreement. "She's been dead for well over an hour, I'd say, otherwise I'd try the paddles."

Kip said, "You read our minds."

"Kinda' hard to fall over that sturdy railing," I said, anticipating their thoughts. I glanced down at the girl, at Sandy, and wished she'd surprise us, like Lazarus from the bible, and let out a gasp and come back to life.

"There's not the swelling and bruising I'd expect to see from a fall," the skinny guy said. "I'm tellin' ya, she was dead before the fall." He stood with his hands on his hips, looking back up at the balcony.

"That's what we all thought," Schultz said quietly.

"Either way, she had some help getting over the railing," I suggested.

Just then Nan walked in. She looked around the room at the police and the young people, then over to our group as we were looking up at the balcony and then back down at the dead girl.

"Not another one!" she exclaimed as she joined us.

"Afraid so," Kip was slowly shaking his head.

"Was she... when you got here, Chief?" Nan asked.

"Dead? Yes, by about a half hour," according to the homeowner's son," Kip replied. "Though we all think it was longer than that."

"I took a wrong turn and headed south," Nan flushed red. "Took me a mile to figure out why the house numbers weren't cooperating."

"Done that," we mumbled in agreement.

The ambulance guy with Mr. Skinny pulled out a cell phone and, scrolling down to a number, pushed the 'send' button. "Calling into Jackson Hospital," he said to the group.

He stepped away and spoke into the phone, occasionally looking toward us standing around the body like it was the centerpiece at a redneck wedding.

"Jackson wants us to work on her and bring her in," the guy said to us, holding his hand over the phone.

"What?!" responded the skinny guy, making a face of disbelief. "The girl's dead, for gosh sake! We need to call the M.E." He looked around, hoping no one had heard him from across the room.

The other guy held out the phone. "You talk to him," he said.

Skinny took the phone. "Yeah," he said, "this is Zimmer. Uh, huh, yes. The girl's dead, asystole. No cardiac activity." He looked at the printout in his hand. "She was dead when Pulaski Rescue got here." He listened for a moment, then looked at us. He pulled the phone away from his head and placed his hand over it. "Idiots!" he mouthed, then placed the phone back to his ear. Whoever had been talking was still there, and apparently still going at it.

"Okay," he replied, wagging his head. "We'll bring her in." He handed the phone back to his partner. "Yes, they want us to work on her and bring her in," he said with a hint of anger. "I guess it's easier this way. No M.E. to bring out, and a lot less reports to fill out, too."

Kip took some quick pictures of the scene, just in case, and the EMT guys loaded up the girl and were gone on the long run to Jackson.

One of the State Policemen came over. "What did Randall tell you guys?" he asked. We related the kid's story about how the girl was upstairs and must have fallen from the balcony.

He looked up, "Yeah, he told us the same story. Seems kind of hard to fall over that railing," he said.

"That's what we thought," Kip said.

"The EMT guys said there was no swelling or bruising from the fall," the cop said.

"Somebody moved the body," I'd bet anything," Schultz said.

"But why?" Nan asked. "Why move the body when your friend is dead?"

"Look at the kids here," the cop said.

We looked over at the cluster of young people. There were only a few left now, waiting their turn to be questioned by the police.

"My guess is the girl died from an overdose of something, and somebody tried to make it look like an accident," he said.

Nan threw up her hands. "That's pretty sick stuff, even for a bunch of stupid teenagers," she said. "What were they thinking?"

"They weren't thinking," I said. "There have been cases where a junkie overdosed and so-called friends took the body out to the countryside and threw it in a swamp or a ditch."

"It's true," said the cop. "I worked a case like that not too long ago."

Kip said, "Schultz is right. I suspect the girl died, and when the kids couldn't revive her, decided to make it look like a fall. The toxicology report will tell us a lot."

I said, "Being her friends, they tidied her up, before calling it in. Somebody straightened her hair, probably one of the girls."

"She regurgitated at some point, probably as she died," Schultzie told the State Trooper. "And her joints are stiffening up," he said.

"When a body dies," Kip interjected, "the blood tends to settle in the low areas. We call it pooling."

"I'm familiar with that," the cop nodded soberly. "So you're telling me, everyone here is sure the girl was dead before the trip down from the balcony?"

"That's right," Kip said. "I'd put money on it."

The group murmured in agreement. Nan excused herself and left for home, but not before walking past Seth Randall and glaring at him.

I looked at the State Policeman, "I heard a back screen door slam just after we entered. I believe someone didn't want to be seen here and bolted.

"Probably more than one," the officer

replied. "Anyone underage and possessing alcohol is cited for minor in possession, or MIP," he said.

"There's going to be a big surprise waiting for the parents when they return from their cruise," I said.

"Detectives are contacting the cruise line now," the cop said. "We're going to be talking to the boy, here, downtown tonight. He's eighteen years old, so we'll handle him as an adult. We feel, like you do, that there's more to this than the kids are saying. Our young Mr. Randall isn't coming clean with us yet, but he will." Looking up at the balcony, he said, "I'll have a look up there before I go." He nodded, gave us a thin smile, and turned away.

I walked across the room where two young girls sat on a couch, sniffing silently. There were only two boys left out of the small group present when we arrived. They sat quietly, staring at the floor.

Seth Randall sat in an over-stuffed chair, looking lost, while a stony-faced State Policeman stood over him.

I walked up to the girls. "I'm very sorry about your friend, Sandy," I said. "This must be quite a shock."

"The cops are calling our parents," a thin girl with dark red curls said.

So much for being concerned about her dead friend.

She wiped at her nose with her shirt sleeve. I reached into my medical kit and handed her a tissue. "Thanks," she said, her voice sounding stuffy from crying.

Her friend smiled wanly. She was an athletic blond, wearing a red flannel shirt, gathered at the waist to show her bare midriff. Both girls looked to be about fourteen. Probably the reason the police were calling their parents.

"Did either of you know many kids here tonight?" I crouched in front of them.

"A lot of them. We know a lot of people," the blonde girl said, nodding her head.

I thought for a moment before asking the next question. "Was Richie Collins or maybe Meagan Grawn hanging out tonight?"

The girls looked at each other, blank faced. They shook their heads. "No," they both answered.

"We don't know them. Where do they go to school?" the curly-haired girl asked.

"I think they go to Western," I lied. "How about Mark LaBlanc? He goes to Maple Grove. Was he here?" I was grasping at straws.

From the look on their faces, I knew I'd struck pay dirt.

"He's so cute," Blondie said blushing.

"He might ask me out," Curly said with a giggle. She playfully twisted a strand of her auburn hair around an index finger.

If he took this girl out, he risked arrest.

"Either of you see him tonight?" I asked.

"Sure," Blondie said. "He went out the back door."

"Right when you guys showed up," Curly added.

There was my pay dirt. He'd been here tonight. Mark LaBlanc. Probably was one of the suppliers. I thanked the girls for their help, and walked away.

The police took down our names and what we'd seen. We then said "Good-night" to the State Police, then told Flint and Jordon what the girls had said. They nodded knowingly. I told them to keep out of trouble, if they could, then Kip, Schultzie and I walked outside.

The stars spread over us in a great canopy of lights. Mars hung like a small moon in the western sky. Night creatures made a cacophony of sound. It was a beautiful night to be alive in south-central Michigan.

"Pulaski Rescue 1, clear," Kip radioed in from the rescue van. The dispatcher echoed his message.

"Pulaski Engine 1, clear." Schultzie waved at us as he let the dispatcher know he was back in service.

"Jackson Central, Pulaski Engine 1, clear, the dispatcher said.

We rode in silence most of the way back to Pulaski. I cleared my throat. Kip looked over in the darkness, the dim lights of the gauges reflecting on his face.

"How well do you know the LaBlanc family?" I asked.

"Not as well as I thought I did," he answered. "Why?"

The name, Mark, has come up on three separate occasions now. I was wondering what kind of activities the LaBlanc kids were in to, other than the fire department, and what kind of family dynamics there were."

"I heard you talking to the little girls, tonight," Kip said. "Jake can be a real jackass, and a pain in the neck, but I always saw him as a hard worker and a good fireman," he added. "Though, with that new wife of his, there's a whole new dynamic introduced into the family."

"Hmm," I said.

Back at the station, I watched as the guys backed the vehicles into their respective bays, then got in my truck and went on home.

Chapter Seventeen

Breakfast with the wife consisted of plenty of hot coffee with pancakes, sausage, and orange juice. After washing down another 800 milligrams of Motrin for my shoulder, I called Hank and filled him in on last night's rescue run.

"I believe Mark LaBlanc was there," I said. "Flint and Jordon know, but maybe we should let the Metro boys know so they can work Seth Randall for information."

"I'll take care of it," he said. "Can you meet at the Fire Station, say, around nine?"

I glanced at the clock. Forty minutes. "See you then," I replied. I finished busing the table and cleaning the cookware.

"You go ahead and play with the boys, the wife said. "I'm going to do a load of laundry and some housework, then work on a quilt."

"I like my shorts starched," I replied,

smiling.

"You've got enough starch in your shorts," she replied with a knowing smile.

We broke into laughter as I picked up my truck keys and went out the door to the Dodge.

Minutes later I was parking the truck beside the fire station. Kip's truck was there, as was Nan's black SUV. The over-head doors were up, letting in the warm June air. June already. Where had the spring gone? I checked the clock in the Dodge, ten minutes 'til nine. I shut the truck off.

A horn honked and Hank's Chevy pickup pulled in beside me. He smiled at me through the window, looking for all the world like the happiest guy on earth. He shut off the Chevrolet and stepped out. "Tim Conway!" he shouted happily, his face bright.

"Henry McIntyre!" I called back. I walked over and shook his hand. His happiness was infectious. He gave me a bear hug and patted me on the back in greeting.

"You're as giddy as a freshman at his first slow dance with a *real* girl," I said. "What gives? You have Nan over to help with the livestock again?" I emphasized livestock.

"Ah, man," Hank said. "She's fifteen

years my junior. I'm old enough to be her young uncle." He shook his head as if not believing how stupid I was.

"Okay, then. What's with all these positive vibes I'm feeling. You get a new, hot, young minister up at the church?"

"You're getting warmer," he said, grinning.

I could hardly stand it anymore. "I know," I almost shouted as I jabbed a finger at his chest, "you got another 8N!"

His dark eyes went wide. "Almost that good, but no." He laughed and, reaching into the cab of his Chevy, brought out a white bag of doughnuts. Reaching back in, he retrieved a brown envelope from the seat. I recognized it as the one he'd picked up at the Metro Squad building.

"I had a nice meal last night with a very beautiful, and intelligent, young lady," he said.

There it was. "Hmm," I said, raising an index finger for emphasis, "This young lady really agreed to have dinner with you?" I tried to sound doubtful. "Did you introduce her to Boomer and Marcel?"

"I didn't take her home yet," he said,

sounding a little put off. "It's a little too soon to meet the family."

"And it wasn't with our Nan?" I asked, looking over at her black SUV. "She's inside, you know."

"No, but you've met the woman not too long ago, yourself," he replied.

I gasped, "You had a dinner date with LaBlanc's wife?"

"Don't be funny. You were there when the girl almost threw herself at me," he said.

"Not the Miles woman!" I suddenly thought him the luckiest guy in the county.

"None other," he replied. "We're going out again Saturday, and I got us a little something in celebration."

"That's tomorrow already, and where'd you find doughnuts in Pulaski?" I asked, eyeing the grease-stained bag.

"Five miles west of me is an Amish bakery," he smiled happily.

"Mmmm," I replied, wishing I hadn't had such a large breakfast.

"You need to start seeing that Miles woman socially a little more often," I said, tapping the bag with my finger.

Hank laughed and slapped me on the back.

"Come on," he said. "We've got work to do, and coffee to drink."

We headed toward the door. "Does she really have green eyes?" I asked, looking sideways at him.

"You noticed," he replied. "Yes, turns out her maternal grandmother was Irish. Go figure," he said with a shrug.

Hank could have red-headed kids, I thought. Wouldn't that be something?

Walking into the kitchen area, we saw Nan standing at the counter, her back to us. She was pouring a cup of coffee.

Kip looked up from the papers he had spread on the table in front of him.

"Doughnuts!" he exclaimed, "Is it your birthday?"

Hank laughed and placed the bag on the table.

"Heard you-all been working too hard," he replied. "I thought you could use a pick-me-up."

"You ain't a kiddin'," Kip said. "It's been an interesting last few weeks around here."

"I'll agree to that," Nan said. She had turned around and was sipping at her coffee.

"Good morning, Hank. Good morning, Tim," she said.

"How are those feeder pigs doing?" she addressed Hank.

"Right as rain, thanks to you," Hank replied brightly.

Nan blushed. "It was nothing," she replied.

"Have a doughnut," Hank said, "or are you sweet enough already?"

Nan reddened again, and plunged her hand into the bag. She pulled out a large, glazed roll, and turned to Kip. "Now this is how to treat a lady," she said to the chief. "You could take some pointers here." She took a bite and smiled.

"I'll write a reflection paper later," Kip replied, reaching in for his own.

Hank and I each poured our own coffee and sat with Kip and Nan.

"Any word on the kids from last night?" I looked at Kip.

"Our man, Flint, said the homeowner's son spilled his guts last night. Turns out, the girl died on a couch in a back room from a heroin overdose. She also aspirated some vomit. A couple geniuses got the bright idea to make it look like an accident, so they cleaned her up, hauled her up to the balcony and shoved her over."

"Lord help us," Hank said softly, with a wag of his head.

"Morons," Nan commented with a twinge of anger. "I thought they all looked like spoiled, little rich kids." She placed her cup on the table and was staring down into the coffee, like it would reveal the solutions to the worlds problems. "How can these people sleep at night, supplying drugs to kids who think they're invincible?" she asked with a catch in her voice.

"We were the same way, I guess," Kip replied. "And, when I think back, there were a few untimely deaths in our group, too."

I replied, "Yeah, but thirty or forty years ago, it was alcohol and cars."

"It's a whole new world out there," Hank said, sipping at his coffee, "and sometimes it ain't very pretty."

"I'm only twenty-seven," Nan said, looking at us guys - us old guys, "but we rarely heard of cocaine or heroin when I was in school. We never heard of meth."

"There's more to it," Kip said. "Flint

said the heroin the girl was injected with was cut with methamphetamine."

We looked at him.

"Not with sugar or flour?" I asked.

"Nope," he replied, "it's hot heroin. The girl didn't stand a chance, the amount she took. She died not long after her friend pulled the needle out."

I looked at Hank. From his expression, I could tell this talk of needles was creeping him out.

"Her friend?" Nan looked bewildered.

"One of the older girls," Kip said. "Then, when she died on them, the whole gang cleaned up the place, and that Seth kid called 911. The dispatcher finally got out of him that it might be an overdose."

"At least he had the smarts enough to do that," Nan replied. She stood up and shoved in her chair. "Gotta get on to the clinic," she said, glancing at the clock above the sink. "Even animals deserve a fighting chance." She paused and looked at us sitting quietly at the table.

"Thanks for the doughnut, Hank," she said, a little more upbeat. She patted his shoulder. "Stay out of trouble, boys." She looked to Kip and me, and was out the door.

"Well," Kip looked at us, "I've got a garage to build down on Mosherville Road." He shuffled his papers together, picked up a small briefcase from the floor by his chair, and put them in it. "Be sure and lock up," he called as he left. He stuck his head back in and looked at Hank. "Happy Birthday!"

Hank wagged his head and waved him away. "See ya," we called.

"There's more to the story," Hank said, after the others had left. He was holding both hands around his coffee cup on the table in front of him.

"The State Police searched the house and the grounds. They found some used syringes and other paraphernalia out in the woods at the edge of the yard where somebody had thrown it," he said. "Several people left as soon as they found out the girl had died. Who knows how many took drugs with them?" He looked up.

"They find out who was mixing and shooting?" I asked.

"They have a name, but haven't made contact," Hank said. "Apparently someone with experience loads the hypo and shoots the kids who are afraid of needles, or are unsure of themselves." He shuddered at the thought.

"We've moved into a new era," he said quietly, reflectively, "from when junkies would shoot themselves up in a back ally or flop house, using a dirty syringe."

"Say hello to influential suburbia," I said.

"I wish every high school kid could see a film of what you guys dealt with last night, and the house where Ted's brother overdosed and died. Trash and all," Hank said.

"That's the worst place I've seen, or smelled," I said. "Ever." I looked around the room, at the bulletin board. There was a flier for Spring Clean-up Day. It gave a date, two weeks away, on a Saturday Morning. The fire personnel always helped out in unloading and sorting out the steel scrap from the actual junk.

Hank set his coffee cup aside and dumped the contents of the large envelope. He held the empty envelope to his face and breathed deeply.

"Still has her smell," he said dreamily. He looked at me, waiting for a reaction.

I shook my head, "You're a sad case," I said.

Hank laughed and handed me a paper. He picked up a copy for himself. "Marvin Hochstetler," he said. "One of six children. Attended Camden-Frontier schools. Well liked, lots of friends."

It was the detectives' report.

"Normal teenager, so far," I said while skimming the paper. "What's this? His parents say he'd dropped some of his old friends at school. He wouldn't participate in FFA or 4-H activities. They didn't see much of his new friends, he would meet them after school or a buddy would give him a ride to meet them."

Hank pointed his finger at the paper in his hand. "His parents say he was getting secretive. It was like they didn't know him anymore."

"Sound familiar?" I asked, looking up.

"Only all too," he replied.

We went back to skimming through the report.

"He was closest to his younger brother James," Hank read. "James had no idea what his brother was up to. It came as a shock to the family. Heck, the whole community was shocked when they learned of his death in the

253

crash."

"There's probably more drug knowledge in the community than anyone cares to let on," I added. In my mind, I could see a meth lab in the basement of every barn, down in farm country.

"Friends at school were worried about him," Hank said, "but only one teacher mentioned noticing anything out of character. Detectives interviewed a few of his friends. One guy said Marvin was hanging around with a school kid from up at Maple Grove."

I looked at the report, then up at Hank. "Did anyone give a name?" I didn't see one mentioned on the page. I took my finger and skimmed again.

"I've read the whole thing several times," Hank said, watching me work the paper. "There's no name mentioned of the Maple Grove connection. Marvin probably kept it a secret." He placed the paper face down on the envelope and picked up a small spiral-bound notebook. Looking at me, he said, "You don't have this one. It's recent notes of my own. I'll make you a copy for your records."

For my records? This was getting rather

254

involved.

He turned a few pages, checking dates and times. "A young man by the name of Samuel Yoder told me that Marvin had met a woman who had become a good friend. An older woman," Hank looked at me.

"Eighteen would have been older," I said.

"Samuel said that the woman wasn't from the area, was blonde, very beautiful, and had a lot of money. Marvin told Samuel that the woman was from somewhere out west, Las Vegas, maybe."

I sat up a little straighter. "Las Vegas? Very beautiful?" I knew exactly who Samuel was talking about, the drop-dead gorgeous Mrs. LaBlanc, herself. The boy had the right state, but wrong city.

"What on earth would a young man have in common with that woman?" I asked. "And what would she see in him?"

"How many gorgeous, blond, Mennonite women have you seen, lately?" Hank asked.

"None, lately," I answered, "but I did see a few in Indiana. Not many blonds, mind you, but a few, over the years."

"Throw that eye candy in with some nose candy, and you've got a combination that's hard to resist. I've got to admit, she turned my head," Hank stated.

"She's the kind of woman who could make a man forget," I said.

"Forget?"

"Forget he has a wife, home, kids, even a job and a mortgage."

"Or, friends, school, and a large, loving family," Hank added sadly. His eyes had a far-away look like he was off and thinking about something. "If she needed some runners for her, should we say... beauty products business, these kids would be perfect. We need to take a closer look at Ms. LaBlanc," he said. "I've got a meeting Monday in Detroit, but we could do some snooping the day after," he said, nodding.

"I'll go over Monday morning and talk to Jake," I said.

Hank raised an eyebrow at me.

"I'm going to ask about the drug scene in their township. Let's just call it friendly networking. He knows we've had several incidents here. I'd like to know what he and his people have seen over there."

"Sounds innocent enough," Hank said. "Do it." He nodded for emphasis.

"Now, about our friend, Ms. LaBlanc," he said, reading from his notebook. "She has no visible means of support, other than her husband's farm income, Fire Chief's salary, and some money from a few LaBlanc family oil wells,"

"Oil wells? I didn't know that," I said, somewhat amazed. "From the old Albion-Scipio field?" This was new information to me. The Albion-Scipio field was a narrow band of oil bearing strata that had first been developed in the late nineteen-fifties. The area in Calhoun, northern Hillsdale, and south-western Jackson counties had provided boom days right up into the nineteen-seventies. Thanks to modern oil recovery methods, a few wells were still hanging on and producing crude, and income, for the fortunate owners.

"The income isn't that much," Hank tapped his notebook with a finger. "Wouldn't even cover most mortgage payments, nowadays."

"So she knows how to stretch a buck," I said, "or she has an independent income that we don't know about."

"Now you're getting the idea," Hank smiled broadly while quietly clasping his hands in front of him. He grinned at me and rubbed them together in anticipation.

"My friend, Tim Conway..." he said, leaning back in his chair and staring up at the ceiling, "I suspect she's got a little enterprise going on the side. Exactly what all it involves, I don't know, but I have my suspicions."

He paused and looked my way.

"The usual?" I asked. "Drugs, prostitution, extortion, theft, cattle rustling?"

"I hadn't thought of extortion or theft," Hank smiled at me. "You're good, buddy. You're good."

I noticed he didn't rule out cattle rustling. In my mind's eye, I could see Mrs. LaBlanc wearing a tight cow-girl outfit while chasing after her neighbor's cattle, twirling her lariat above her head, spurring on a white stallion, blond tresses waving in the breeze.

"You with me here," Hank said. He was waving a hand in front of my face.

"Just thinking," I said, grinning. "Just thinking."

He looked back down at his notebook. "The Hochstetler kid had a scrape with the law a few weeks before he died. Seems someone broke into a neighbor's garage and stole some yard tools," he said. "Chainsaw, leaf blower, rakes, shovels. You get the idea."

"They ever recover the property?" I asked.

"Not yet," Hank replied, "but Marvin and an older friend suddenly had some extra pocket money that no one can explain. Hillsdale detectives interviewed both boys, but didn't learn much. Turns out they were putting a case together and getting ready to pick Marvin up for a lengthier interview," he said, looking my way, "but he died in the crash before they could get him. Officer Flint leaned on the friend, but he isn't talking. Flint's still watching the guy."

I drained my coffee cup and leaned forward, "There have been a rash of auto break-ins over the past month that people are talking about. Mostly over in Hanover and Maple Grove," I said. "Could be connected."

"I wouldn't doubt it," Hank agreed. "Drug culture and crime go hand-in-hand. Drugs cost money, unless you're a hard-up female," he said.

I thought of Gloria and Amy up in the trashy room where Spoons overdosed, and wondered what kind of life they had before getting caught up in the drug culture. Were there a mom and dad, or any friends or relatives around to worry about them?

"Amy told me about her home life and why she ran away," I told Hank, "but druggies are good at telling you what you want to hear," I shrugged. "Was her life really that bad? She seemed sincere." I'd have to ask Flint to look into it. The fleeting feeling came to me that I was missing something. It had to do with the evening up in the room where Amy sat in the corner and Gloria tried to comfort her dead friend. I needed to think about it.

Hank sat stony-faced and listened. He slowly shook his head and got up to refill his coffee cup.

"Remember your old buddy, Spoons Kelly?" Hank asked. "He and his brother, Ted, were up to their armpits in the trade. They were basically street-level, but thought they were big shots."

He stood at the counter and stirred in a pack of sugar and tested the flavor. He always joked that he liked his coffee black and sweet, like his ex wife. He held his cup out toward me, "Just like my first wife," he smiled.

Some things never change. Maybe someday he'd actually talk some more about the woman.

"Look where it got them," I said. "Spoons lived in that disease-ridden dump, and died on a crappy mattress in a crappy room." I shook my head sadly and turned my empty coffee cup in my hands.

"Well, Spoons isn't talking, in his condition, but his brother is," Hank said. He stepped over to the table and sat back down.

"We know Meagan Grawn is, or was, his main contact. Who she reports to, we don't know. We'll figure that out when we nab her."

I nodded in agreement. "It all takes us right back to Maple Grove," I said. "What about tomorrow? Want to meet here or out at your place before heading down to Hillsdale?"

"Let's meet up here," he said. "Seven o'clock okay? I'll drive."

"Good. We'll travel on your nickle," I grinned, reaching into the bag for another doughnut.

Hank poured some more coffee for me. "I almost forgot," he said, placing the coffee pot on the table and shuffling through the paperwork for a smaller, white envelope. He pulled out some pictures and handed them to me.

"Recent photos of Richie Collins and Meagan Grawn," he said.

Richie's face smiled out at me. He was a good looking kid with medium length, light-brown hair, and a broad, happy smile. Meagan had long hair with purple streaks in it. It was fluffed up and back, over her head. She wore too much make-up and had a thin, tight smile. A chrome piercing was in her left eyebrow.

"Good looking girl," I joked.

"Been around the block," Hank said. "She's taken Richie under her wing as a boy-toy or maybe as her assistant. I don't know."

"There's something bothering me," I said, taking a sip. I made a face. The coffee was getting bitter from sitting on the warmer.

Hank wiped some white powder from his lips and looked at me. "Is it the fact that I got the last powdered doughnut?" he asked with a look.

"Get that powder wiped off before Flint shows up and runs you in," I replied.

Hank laughed as he picked up a paper napkin and swiped at his mouth.

"The night we had the rescue run out to the drug house where Spoons died," I said, steering the conversation back on track, "Jake LaBlanc hung around when we didn't need him. Once, he came into the room where we were talking to the kids. They reacted in fear, I'm sure of it. Nobody else seemed to notice. They were all busy with other things, but I'm sure of it, Hank, they were afraid of LaBlanc."

"Makes you wonder what went on before you got there," Hank said reflectively, "and who the real boss is."

"Maybe I can get something out of him next Monday, who knows?" I said.

"Be careful," Hank said. "Don't tip your hand."

"Hold my cards to my chest," I replied with a grin.

Hank laughed again as he rose to shut off the coffee warmer. He emptied the coffee pot into the sink and rinsed it out.

I wiped down the table and tossed the empty doughnut bag into the trash.

"Tomorrow morning," Hank said.

"Bright and early," I replied, as I turned out the lights and flipped the switch on the door lock.

I paused, standing with the door to the

Dodge open. "They had the drugs and stuff in their medical bags, you know."

"I know," Hank replied, getting into his truck. "I know."

Chapter Eighteen

Seven o'clock on Saturday morning, I met Hank right on time.

"I could use another coffee," he said, as I climbed into his truck.

"Don't burn yourself out," I replied, grinning. "Remember your dinner date tonight."

"I'll pace myself," he said, looking over at me. "No way am I missing that!"

Hank drove the Chevy down Pulaski Road, past Mosherville, and on down to US 12 where he turned right, toward Jonesville. He looked longingly down the highway at the McDonald's.

"Go ahead," I said. I could use a cup myself." I was wondering what I was doing there, and not at home in my nice, warm bed. Hank pulled in the lane for the drive-through.

"We'll be making a pit-stop in twenty minutes," I told him as the girl handed the steaming coffee through the window.

Hank grinned and handed me my cup. "One cream, one sugar for you," he said, "and the usual for me."

"Black and sweet," like your fist wife, I laughed.

I had him take the back way through Jonesville, past the Italianate style Grosvenor House Museum, and on through the rolling countryside to the north edge of Hillsdale. We drove through the campus of Hillsdale College. School was out for the summer, but a few students were out walking. Probably working on-campus for the summer, or taking extra classes.

"Look at these houses!" Hank exclaimed as we drove down the main street toward the fair-grounds.

"Somebody had some real money back in the day," I remarked.

Large, old houses, from Queen Anne to Federal style, lined the highway through town. Looking down side streets, we saw more of the same. Most were in very good repair, with a few undergoing some form of renovation.

"That's a lot of dry-wall to hang," Hank marveled when we drove past a columned home with scaffolding along one side and a full dumpster out front.

The fairgrounds appeared on our left. A painted sign on the grandstand said, "The Most Popular Fair On Earth!"

"Wait 'til you see the Grange Hall," I told Hank. "Oldest in the state, I think."

"How long's this place been here?" he marveled.

"Since 1852, if I recall correctly." I directed Hank to a parking area on the east side of the grounds. People were busy unloading trucks and trailers containing hay and straw. Others were examining the different stacks for quality, either comparing with their own at home, or thinking of buying.

A few Amish families wandered the grounds. The older boys and men tended to hang out together, discussing livestock and farming in general.

We walked past one such group who were talking to a few English, probably their hired drivers. The subject was last fall's deer hunting.

"Aaron got his first buck with a shotgun," a younger man was saying to the group.

"How big?" one of the others asked. He

was standing with his hands in his pockets.

"I'm not saying it was small," the first man answered, adjusting back his straw hat, "but it's mother's milk was still on it's lips."

The group exploded and doubled over with laughter. One of the young men reddened. Must be Aaron, I thought. The other man slapped him on the back and said something in German. Hank and I walked on by. I assumed all was forgiven.

I took Hank over to three long rows of goods, all laid out on the ground. In front of us was a cluster of old television sets. Four were the obsolete picture-tube types. One was a flat screen with the back panel removed. The inside circuit boards were exposed to the elements. I didn't see the panel anywhere.

We saw every item imaginable under the sun. A rapidly calling auctioneer was working each row. They were staggered so as not to interfere with the next row over. Several people had purchased long guns and were still standing around watching the sale.

Hank looked at me. "This is slightly nerve-wracking," he said. "People standing around with guns. Shifty looking people. I wonder how many are carrying concealed?"

"Other than yours?" I asked. "Probably dozens." I'd left my own pistol locked in the truck, behind the seat.

We left the sale lines, Hank somewhat reluctantly. He'd never seen anything like it.

"A guy's gotta be quick or they'll sell something and move on," he said with a shake of his head.

"You snooze..." I said.

We came to a line of vegetable vendors. I stopped and looked up and down the row of tables.

"Where do we start? At the end?" I pointed to a stall of flowers and potted plants.

"This way," Hank said, pointing. "We'll stick with just the fruit and vegetable vendors."

We walked over to the first stall that sold veggies and looked around. A stooped, scrawny old man was busy placing peppers in a display box on a folding table. Long, scraggly, white hair stuck out from under his greasy baseball hat. He wore a good two days growth of white stubble on his face. A younger, but not much younger, equally skinny woman in a green, dirt-stained, MSU sweatshirt stood off to one side, smoking a cigarette and talking to another woman. Her friend wore what looked to me like a paisley muumuu. I was sure the second woman had to go at least two-fifty. She was a big girl.

Hank stepped up to the vegetable laden table.

The old man coughed a raspy, phlegm laden cough and attempted to straighten up. I saw Hank stiffen as the man smiled. The old guy had one, just one, green, ragged tooth in the front of his head - on the bottom. He could have used it as a beer opener, except it would surely snap off.

I took a few steps back to watch the show.

"Help you?" It sounded more like "Hilp yee?" He rubbed his gray, stubbly chin with a gnarled hand and eyed Hank curiously.

"Yes, thank you," Hank replied. "I'm looking for the table where a friend works - a young guy, name of Mark, from the shop where we work. I owe him fifty dollars. Wouldn't be here, would he?"

"No, don't know no Mark," the old man said, shifting his eyes to the woman in the dirty sweatshirt. His skinny partner lady came right over and looked up at Hank. I'd noticed her ears perk up when Hank said the magic number, fifty dollars.

"He ain't here right now," she said, "but you can leave the money with us. We'll be sure he gits it." She stared into his face and stuck nicotine stained fingers out, expecting the money.

"No, thank you, ma'am," Hank replied. "I'd better give it to him in person."

"You don't trust me?" the woman said in a shrill, accented voice. I'd have guessed Arkansas.

She took one last mighty drag on her cigarette, exhaled a cloud of blue smoke over her shoulder, and flicked the butt sideways onto the ground, next to the old guy. It continued to send a slight stream of smoke curling up under the table.

I started to snicker. Muumuu woman waddled over to be part of the action. Several other people drifted in to stand around her and watch the fun. An Amish family stopped briefly in the roadway, then the mother softly spoke a few words in dialect and they continued on, the half-dozen little kids reminding me of ducklings trailing after their mother. The younger kids stared back, wide-eyed, at Hank.

Not too many giant, black guys down on the farm, I figured.

"Madam," Hank was trying to explain, "I just feel better paying Mark in person, that's all." He took a step back and turned to look for me. I had walked over to the next booth where I could watch safely from a distance.

A rough looking man dressed head to toe in worn biker leather paused to watch. On his head was a faded skull and crossbones dew rag. He watched for a moment, chuckled, scratched his dark beard, and moved on, which was okay by me. He looked like he'd just as soon cut your throat as look at you. I'd sic the dog on him if he came back my driveway.

"Give the woman her fifty dollars, you big oaf," muumuu lady was saying to Hank, her arms folded across her ample chest.

Hank's eyes locked on mine. "Help!" he mouthed. I turned away and burst into laughter.

The old man bent lower and carefully picked up the smoldering cigarette butt. He placed it to his lips and noisily sucked the life out of it. The spark burned down and singed his fingers. He swore softly and let it drop, then commenced a coughing fit the likes I've never seen. His face reddened and I thought he'd pass out.

"Well?" the muumuu turned to face Hank. "The woman's waiting for her money." She glared at him and tapped one foot impatiently.

"It's not her money," Hank responded evenly. "I'm looking for a friend to give it to, not to someone I don't even know."

"Likely story," said the skinny woman, from behind the vegetables. She was leaning across the table and I thought it might collapse. It would have, under an ordinary person, or the muumuu lady, for sure.

Hank reached into his pocket.

My God, he's going to shoot her! I thought.

He withdrew his I.D. wallet and opened it for the fat lady. He stuck it under her nose. Her new friends crowded in to look, too.

"I'm a Federal Agent, and if you don't want to got to jail today, you'll back off," he said. He turned and showed the skinny woman, who had stepped back away from the table.

Muumuu woman turned gray, reminding me of a dead walrus. Her eyes grew wide, and she hurried away, her audience following along in a protective cluster. She was moving faster than I would have thought possible for a woman her size. Skinny woman fumbled a cigarette from her pack and tried to light it. After flicking her lighter and failing to get a flame, she put the cigarette behind her ear and stared blankly at Hank.

The old man ceased his raspy coughing and walked to the table.

"Free sample?" he gummed a smile and held up a tomato.

"No thanks," Hank said. He folded his wallet and stuffed it back into his pant's pocket and walked away.

I was still snickering when he came over to the next booth, eyes wide. He looked flabbergasted.

"What was that all about?" he asked.

"Told you," I said, grinning like a crazy man. "Cultural experience."

A man, a normal looking man, came over from the next booth, to our right.

"There's a Mark who helps his parents, in the, lets see," he counted down, "in the fourth stall down. They sell bananas and garden produce from Florida. Oranges and such," he said.

A young boy, whom I took to be the man's son, came over, struggling to carry a case of iceberg lettuce. He plunked it down on the table.

"He's down there now," he said, pointing down the rows of vendors.

We followed his pointing finger and saw a twenty-something guy with neat, black hair under a clean John Deere hat, and wearing a blue denim, long-sleeved, work shirt. His shirt sleeves were rolled up above the elbows, revealing muscular arms.

No tattoos, I noticed. Almost a rarity.

A middle-aged couple, whom I took to be his parents, were with him as they waited on customers and moved more produce to their display table.

The young man stood a head taller than his parents. He adjusted his hat and smiled at a teenage Amish girl, who promptly blushed and turned away. Her friends waiting with her covered their mouths and giggled. They left in a clutch, glancing back now and again to sneak a peak at the young man.

"Next, please," the woman was pleasantly saying as we arrived. The heavily loaded table seemed to groan under the load. Most of the veggies wouldn't be picked in Michigan for at least another month or two. The produce looked to be in good shape and busy shoppers were steadily depleting the stock.

Her husband handed a lady a plastic bag with green peppers and plump tomatoes in it. The shopper's little boy clung to a cantaloupe that she'd also purchased. The vendor smiled and thanked them. They smiled in return before turning to walk away.

Hank stepped up. "Hi folks," he said pleasantly.

"Good morning," the woman answered cheerfully. She was solidly built, like I guess a lot of middle age farm wives are. Her long brown hair was touched with flecks of gray. Real gray, the earned kind, not something from a bottle. She wore it tucked under a red kerchief.

"What can I help you with?" she looked up at Hank, then over at me. Her face looked slightly puzzled. Hank's hulking figure must have looked like a cop, or something worse.

He produced his I.D. "Hank McIntyre,

ma'am," he said, showing the identification.

"Oh!" she said, looking over at her husband. He was busy with some people at the other end of the long table and didn't notice.

I cast a quick glance at the son, not wanting to give anything away. He was helping a woman select the perfect Florida-grown watermelon. The family seemed to be friendly, clean-cut people.

"My associate, Mr. Conway, and I would like to have a word with your son, if you don't mind," Hank said. "You may be present, of course. Just a few questions is all."

The woman looked panicky. Glancing at her husband, she interrupted him. "Jeff," she called in a strained voice. "These men want to talk to Mark."

Her husband glanced quickly at us, then back to his customer. "Sure," he said with a wave of his hand.

"Jeff, they're Federal Agents."

Here we go again, I thought. How do I get out of this? I started to look for an escape route.

She had her husband's attention.

"What?" He'd stopped what he was doing and stepped toward us.

"Federal Agents, she said again, "and they want to talk to Mark."

"What about?" He was curious now, and walked over to us. "Gentlemen," he said, looking us over, "what can I do for you?" He didn't offer his hand.

Hank showed him his I.D. Jeff looked at it, then questioningly at his son. His wife looked at her son. The son looked scared. With a sudden leap over the side table, he bolted through the crowd.

"Got the right Mark!" Hank yelled back at me as he took off after the young man.

"We'll explain later," I called to the stunned couple as I hurried after Hank.

The young man was fast, but the crowd of shoppers slowed him down. People struggled to get out of his way as he bulldozed along. He barely avoided crashing into a young Amish family as he headed to the livestock barn.

Careening off a short, solid man with a red, viking-type beard, he staggered, stayed on his feet, then changed course and ran off toward the hay market. The viking halfheartedly gave chase.

Hank was having his own difficulty working through the crowd. While I was sucking air, trying to catch up, he was hurdling over some fool's dog and turning sideways to edge through a cluster of people. He kept yelling "Police!" but that didn't make anyone move any faster. They mainly stood in the way and stared at him, mouths agape.

Why do people insist on bringing their dogs to crowded places? I wondered. And why do they put those stupid neckerchiefs on them?

I ran past the dog. "Good boy," I called as I sprinted by. The dog was an old, gray muzzled, golden lab. He turned to watch me go.

Up ahead, a couple redneck guys tried to chase after Hank. After twenty yards, they'd been left standing to the side, sucking wind. Fishing around in their dirty blue-jeans for cigarettes, they lit up, still bending over, gasping.

I ran on, my lungs crying out for mercy, my legs screaming for me to stop. I saw the kid pumping his arms and angling toward the front gate. Hoping to intercept him, I broke off and cut through the speed barn where race horses are normally kept. There were a few people standing around, talking and drinking coffee from styrofoam cups. I puffed past, ignoring their stares and comments. I could see a lot more people through the open doorway at the end of the building. I popped through into the crowd and looked to my left. Our runner was clearing the end of the merchandise rows and heading for the feeder pigs. I kept moving, not daring to stop, afraid I'd never get started again.

Guys were still standing around with their newly purchased long guns, comparing features. I was afraid they'd get the wrong idea and come to the aid of our runner.

I almost missed the end of the chase when a lady pulling a little red wagon stepped in front of me. I leaped over, snagged my foot on the side, stumbled, and fought to regain my balance.

Looking up, I caught the flash of the black clad biker figure as he burst from behind a stack of hay and launched himself at the fleeing young man. The biker's dew rag flew off to reveal curly, gray hair as he made a clean tackle. The pair rolled over and over on the gravel drive. It was the biker dude I'd seen earlier at the produce booth. He pulled out a pair of handcuffs and, wrenching the kid's arms behind him, slapped them on.

If he were a calf roper at the rodeo, he'd have set a new record. Hank caught up with them at that point. I was still ten long yards away.

"Cool Balls!" Hank laughed while helping the biker to his feet and placing his own huge foot on the runner's back to hold him down.

"A pleasure to see you," Hank said, sounding somewhat winded. He placed a hand on his chest to help catch his breath.

I arrived, bending over and wishing for an oxygen bottle.

"It's Detective Kuhlbaugh," Hank said, still panting slightly. Wrapping his arm around the detective's shoulders, he gave him a squeeze.

Kuhlbaugh smiled and held out his hand. "Good to see you again," he said, breathing hard, but recovering nicely.

I didn't think I'd ever catch my breath.

"How? Why?" I stammered looking at the two men. I shook Kuhlbaugh's hand.

"Heard you guys were coming down," he said. "I was just in the neighborhood, so, well, you know how it is," he shrugged. "I brought a buddy to help out." He pointed to the circle of people who had gathered to watch.

I looked over to see the lady deputy whom we'd met at the Osseo drug house. She was in her brown work uniform.

"Hi there," she smiled brightly.

I nodded and tried to smile. Hank removed his foot from the runner's back and the deputy helped stand him up. He was a little dirty and scraped up, but otherwise unscathed.

"Why you guys chasing me?" he asked between breaths.

I was glad to see I wasn't the only one sucking air after a dash across the auction grounds. I looked at the kid. He had at least thirty years and a twenty-five pound advantage on me. I didn't feel sorry for him.

"Why are we chasing you?" Hank repeated his question. "My question is, why are you running from us? You moron." Hank looked disgusted. I thought he was going to reach out and slap the guy up aside the head.

"I don't want to go to jail," the young man replied.

The lady deputy snickered. Kuhlbaugh shook his head and smiled.

The young man's father showed up then. He looked bewildered. "What's going on?" he demanded. "Why is my son being arrested?"

Hank looked at him. "Sir, he's not being arrested. If you'd allow us all to take a breath and calm down, I think I can explain."

The father looked at his son's hands in cuffs behind him. "Do you need to cuff him?"

"He ran away from a Federal officer. What do you think?" Hank replied, eyeing the man.

"We only wanted to ask him about an acquaintance of his," Kuhlbaugh said.

"Who are you?" The father looked at him with a look of disgust. He obviously didn't care for bikers.

"I'm an undercover agent with the Jackson County Metro Squad," the detective said, "and I truly hope I'm not your worst nightmare." He looked at the young man in cuffs and said, "Though I fear at this point that I am."

The father looked down for a moment, then back up at his son, "What's this all about? Does it have anything to do with those two friends of Alisha's who showed up last week? I knew they were trouble as soon as I saw them." He looked around at us. "Alisha is my son's girlfriend," he explained.

I'd already figured it out.

He was starting to come around, now. I

could see it in his eyes. He'd just realized that this wasn't a case of the authorities picking on his poor little boy.

The lady deputy turned to the crowd of onlookers, "You folks can move along now. The excitement is over," she smiled a friendly, but no nonsense smile. The crowd slowly dissipated, looking back as they left. A little Amish boy took a step forward. He tilted his head back to look up at the deputy with wide, brown eyes. He'd been staring at her service weapon. His head was tilted so far back, I thought his little straw hat would fall off.

An embarrassed young father stepped forward to take the little boy by the hand. "Jacob," he said, pronouncing it Yakob, "come, it's time to go."

The lady deputy held up her hand and knelt in front of the little boy. Any hard edge I'd seen to her earlier had completely melted away. "Yakob," she said, then softly said something in German. She looked up at the young father and spoke to him, too.

The little boy broke into a wide grin and looked up at his father, then glanced shyly at Hank. The young man smiled at the lady officer, and tipped his hat. He actually tipped his hat in a little salute, then walked off with his son.

"Cute kid," the deputy said, standing and turning back to us. We stared at her. "I told him that you're a super policeman, a good guy, stronger than two horses," she smiled up at Hank, who promptly blushed.

The produce vendor was angrily eyeing his own son. "You didn't answer me," he said firmly. "Does this have to do with Alisha's two friends who showed up last week?"

The kid looked away. "Yes," he finally said, glancing quickly at his father. "They're on the run. The guy, Richie, is in trouble at home. He's trying to get away from his parents. His dad roughs him up, and they're always on his case. He has nowhere else to go." He looked around to see if we believed his story.

His father looked at the police personnel standing around. "That can't be it," he said to his son. "The police don't come around chasing people because a kid has run away from home. And what about that girl, Alisha's friend?"

This man was definitely brighter than I

had been willing to give him credit for.

"That's Richie's girlfriend. She's running away with him, 'cause he has no one else."

We all stared at the son like he was a four-year-old caught with his hand in the cookie jar, and couldn't get his story straight. He was digging in, deeper and deeper.

The dad looked at Hank, then at Kuhlbaugh. "What does this have to do with the Jackson, whatever it is?" he asked.

"Jackson County Metro Squad," Kuhlbaugh said. "Drug and gang enforcement. I'm here working with an official Hillsdale County Deputy," he said with a nod toward the deputy.

"Drugs?" the man fairly spit out the word.

I finally thought to look at the name tag above the deputy's left shirt pocket. Troyer, it read. I was starting to get the connection with the Amish.

"I'm not dealing drugs!" his son exclaimed. He twisted away and the lady deputy had to get a grip on his arm again. She turned him back to face his father.

"Look," Hank said to the man. "We have no reason to believe that your son is involved in anything illegal, at this time. We're trying to locate the two kids who showed up here last week. There's much more to it than what your son is saying. I guess you could say it's a completely different story." He looked at the boy and then back at his father.

The man glowered at his son. "We'll get to the bottom of this," he said.

"Maybe we could move on to somewhere not so public and talk," Hank suggested.

"I know the auction manager," Deputy Troyer said. "I bet we can use his office."

She led the son away through the crowd to an office under the grandstand. Our little group tagged along, like school kids on a tour.

The manager was a friendly, middle-aged man who invited us to use a small conference room in the back of the office. Troyer un-cuffed the kid and guided him onto a folding chair. His father sat across the table from him, so he could look into his face. Hank and Kuhlbaugh sat on either side of the man. I sat next to the deputy.

"Okay," the son started right in, without any prompting. I guess the sight of his father and the two cops staring at him from across the table was more than he could take.

I glanced sideways at the deputy. She was wearing Minnie Mouse ear studs. I smiled and looked across the table at Hank. He didn't notice.

"Alisha's friend, Meagan, told Alisha that they were on the run because of Richie's parents," Mark started in again. "She said they didn't want him around. They always favored his older sister because she's a good student."

"This seems kind of drastic, don't you think?" his dad asked, sounding annoyed.

"It's true," the kid said.

Hank cleared his throat, and reached into his pocket and withdrew an envelope. He took out the pictures of the runaways that he'd shown me yesterday.

"Are these the two who showed up last week?" he lay the pictures down on the table.

The son nodded his head. His father turned the photos to get a better look.

"That's them," he said. "Now, what's the story?. Can you tell us?"

Kuhlbaugh looked over at me, "Would you like to begin, Mr. Conway?"

"There was a fire at a farm house in southern Jackson County," I began, wondering exactly how much to tell. "The fire was set. Richie's father was burned on his arms and chest while searching the house, trying to rescue his son. The son, Richie, wasn't there." I pointed at the picture. "I searched the house myself. We suspect he's the one who set the fire to kill the family, then ran off with his girlfriend."

The man looked shocked. His son squirmed in his seat. "Did you know about this?" his father asked.

"No, I swear," the boy answered. "Nothing was said about a fire." The son looked about at us, truly surprised.

I couldn't see the young man's eyes, but from Hank's expression, I felt the kid was telling the truth.

"We have no reason to believe that Richie came from anything but a solid, two-parent, home," Hank said. "According to his parents, he started to change about a year ago. That's around the time he met the Grawn girl," he said.

"Meagan was his introduction into the drug culture," Kuhlbaugh added.

The man looked at his son in silence, stony-faced.

"I had no idea," the son said, holding out his hands in submission.

"Those people were sleeping in our basement," his father said. "Who knows what type of person could have shown up at our home, looking for them."

His son stared down at the table.

"Do you know a guy by the name of Seth Randall, up near Pulaski?" Hank asked Mark. "Have you ever been to a log house up on Barryton Road? A big log house?"

Mark shook his head, "No, I don't know the name."

"It's important," I said, thinking of the screen door slamming, and what the girls said about Mark LaBlanc being there. This Mark was a good looking kid, and if he'd given a false last name... I thought of the possibilities.

"Answer the man," his father demanded forcefully.

"I've never met the guy or been to a log house up on Barryton Road," he said, shaking is head vigorously.

Hank looked at me and nodded almost imperceptibly. The kid was telling the truth.

There was a light knock at the door and it opened slightly. It was the auction manager, and he had Mark's mother with him. "Mrs. Smith," the manager said by way of introduction.

Mrs. Smith stepped into the room. She looked like one frightened, worried woman. Detective Kuhlbaugh stood to offer his seat. He moved around the table and sat next to Mark.

The woman glanced at her son, nestled between the deputy and the detective, then at her husband. Her face was drawn, pale.

"It's okay," her husband responded to her questioning look. "They want to know about Alisha's friends. The kids who showed up last week."

"They slept in our basement last night," she looked at her son accusingly. "You said they'd be staying someplace else."

Her look told us that her husband didn't know.

"I didn't want you to get upset," she turned and looked into her husband's eyes, "or I'd have told you." She looked at us. "We have a walk-out basement with an outside entrance so people can come and go."

The kid shrunk slightly. "It didn't work out," he said defensively.

His father looked betrayed and disgusted.

He tapped his fingers nervously on the table and glared at his son.

Hank and Kuhlbaugh looked at the deputy.

"Are they still there?" the deputy asked.

"They left early this morning, before we did," Mark replied. "They're coming here today," he said, "to get some produce. Then they're heading out." He looked across the table at his parents. They sat staring at him with unbelieving faces.

"They say when they'd be here?" the deputy asked.

"Just sometime this morning," Mark answered.

"How are they supporting themselves?" Kuhlbaugh asked. "They need money to get by."

"Richie worked on a farm last week, baling hay," he said. "I don't know what that Meagan girl does. Not much, I guess. Hangs out at Alisha's place, mostly."

Hank looked around at the others. "Any other questions?" he asked.

"Yes, they say where they're headed, and they still driving the blue Ford pickup?" I spoke up.

Mark looked at me and nodded, "Yeah, Richie drives it. I don't know where they're going."

"They mention any other friends, or relatives they might go see?" I asked.

He thought a moment, "No, not that they said." He shook his head.

That was about it. We looked around at each other. Hank thanked the parents, shaking Jeff's hand. Kuhlbaugh offered his hand. Jeff reluctantly took it, smiled in relief, and shook it. I reached across the table and thanked the parents for their cooperation.

The deputy stood and helped Mark to his feet.

"If you see Richie or Meagan," Kuhlbaugh said, "please don't say a word about this. We'll be around." He handed a business card to Mrs. Smith and patted Mark on the back. "Sorry about the tackle," he added, "but running from the police sure makes you look guilty of something."

Mark smiled shyly and shrugged.

We walked to the door. Mark's father gave him a look. "No more guests in the basement."

"No more," Mark replied, raising his right hand.

The Smith family went back to their produce stall. They thanked the man who was watching it for them, and picked up where they'd left off when we'd shown up an hour earlier. The father kept tossing the occasional look at his son.

We hung around until three o'clock. Richie and Meagan never showed. Either they'd changed their minds and taken off, or we'd been spotted and they fled.

We said good-bye to the deputy and Kuhlbaugh. There were a couple plain clothes Hillsdale detectives who'd showed up. We nodded to them as we climbed into Hank's truck.

We rode in silence. Both of us thinking about what happened, and what didn't happen.

"Bet they were somewhere in the crowd when Mark led us on our merry chase," Hank finally said.

"Makes sense," I said. "They had plenty of time to beat it while we were talking to the family. Boy, I thought we were gonna kill a fat rat with this one," I said.

"Me, too," Hank replied. "Hillsdale has a wants and warrants out on them as we speak," he said. "They'll turn up."

I nodded in agreement.

At the fire station in Pulaski, Hank let the pickup idle. "Sure am hungry for supper," he said with a big grin.

    I wished him luck on his date, got out of the truck, waved my clutch of papers at him through the window, got into my Dodge, and drove home.

Chapter Nineteen

I went home and started a file with the paperwork Hank had given me. I figured I'd throw it out in a month or so.

That evening, halfway through a Star Trek rerun, I remembered that Hank was on his dinner date with the lovely Shonda Miles. I hoped it was going well, and wondered what they could possibly be talking about. Surely not livestock or tractors.

Captain Kirk was slugging it out with an alien bad guy while First Science Officer Spock put another to sleep with a touch to the shoulder.

"You think this is the one?" my wife said suddenly.

I glanced over at her. She was sitting, legs drawn up on the couch, working her puzzle book. She peeked up now and again at the television.

I looked at her, blank faced.

"This Shonda gal," she said. "You think she's the one for Hank? He really needs a wife out at his place."

I could tell she was hoping Shonda was the one, even though she'd never met the woman.

"So, we're back to this again," I commented, turning my attention back to the bridge of the Enterprise.

Something was wrong with the warp drives and Scotty was vigorously complaining to Captain Kirk.

"You men just don't get it," my wife shook her head and gave me that special look, like I was the dumbest guy in the county.

I shrugged, and smiled. Thirty-five years of marriage...

Monday morning, I vacuumed the living room, sorted through some of my stacks of classic car, tractor, and farm magazines, then sat at the kitchen table making notes and thinking about what I'd say to LaBlanc.

I hadn't heard from Hank on how the Hillsdale event turned out. Did the police go looking for the kids at the Smith house and Alicia's place? I was dying to find out. There was nothing mentioned on the radio station out of Hillsdale. I had to assume nothing happened or it was being kept quiet.

I drove over to Maple Grove, my windows down, enjoying the fresh air. We'd had a steady rain most of Sunday, and the Monday mid-morning air had a clean, fresh smell to it.

The landscape was a pattern of fields, scattered farmsteads, and the occasional house stuck in on a chunk of acreage broken off from a farm. Arriving at the village, I went to the building that was a combination fire station/township hall, and drove into the parking lot.

There were no vehicles on the fire garage side. No one around, which wasn't unusual. Like Pulaski, Maple Grove and other small-town fire departments were staffed by volunteers. There could be someone there for maintenance, or Chief Kip's favorite pastime, paperwork. Most of the time, though, the buildings had no one around.

Through a window that looked out from some type of office, I could see a dim light. I got out of the truck and walked over to try the door. Locked. It had the little push button, combination type lock similar to what we had at Pulaski and was used at every other fire garage I'd seen. I was tempted to play with it, but turned away instead. I didn't know what I'd do if I got in. Leave a note, maybe.

It was still mid-morning, just after nine, the time when most people liked to show up and handle paperwork. That's when Kip liked to get his done - while his mind was still fresh, he always said. I didn't know when LaBlanc did his. Maybe midnight. I couldn't guess.

Standing on the blacktop of the parking lot, I looked next door at the township office. There would be someone there, I was sure. They always had a small staff to collect taxes, take complaints, answer questions about ordinances. There would be someone to issue permits for bonfires or building a shed, anything a person might like to do that required government oversight.

A car was parked around the corner. I could see the shiny red of the rear fender and bumper.

I stood in the warming sunlight, trying to decide between getting in my truck and looking up LaBlanc's address and driving out to his farm, or going next door to inquire there, and possibly getting trapped in conversation with the clerk for half an hour.

A man came around the corner. Medium height, fortyish. He saw me, broke into a smile, and waved in greeting. It was Stan Moore, the Maple Grove Township Supervisor. I waved back and waited as he walked over. He had a manila folder tucked under his left arm.

"Morning, Conway," he said, extending his hand.

I smiled and shook it.

"What brings you over here? Not enough fires in Pulaski?" He laughed at his little joke.

"Something like that," I replied. "I was trying to catch up with Jake LaBlanc this morning."

"That makes two of us," Stan said. "Haven't seen him in a day or so, left two messages on his cell, but haven't heard back."

"Hmmm," I shook my head and glanced back at the fire station.

"What did you need to see him about?" he asked, curious.

"Just some checking on what he's seen over here in the township, drug wise. We've had a marked increase in rescue runs for overdoses.

I wondered what's been going on over here."

"Seems like it's all over the county," Stan replied, looking steadily at me. "I guess we've had our share, like everybody else."

"You had a run two night's back," I said, remembering the call I'd heard over the phone pager for Maple Grove Rescue.

"We had to call for mutual aid from Hanover," Stan said. "Only had two guys available. Jake and the boys were out of reach, it seems. Duke Williams and John Tanner made the run."

"How many people on your department?" I asked.

"I think it's eight right now," he said. "We need more people, but I can't get Jake to start a training session. You know how it is with chiefs when they have a farm to run, too darn busy. Rumor has it that he's going to run for township treasurer. How's he going to handle that with all the other irons in the fire?" He shook his head and gave me a smile that was more of a grimace. "And, to top it off, if I had a young wife like that gal of his, I'd never have time to do my work, either. Hell, I'd get fired or run out of office." He chuckled and shook his head.

"I hear you there," I said, laughing.

"Say," Stan said, "you're familiar with that big guy working with the metro squad, aren't you? He lives out your way, big black guy."

"Sure, Hank McIntyre," I said. "What about him?"

Stan looked around, as if checking for spies, and lowered his voice. "The chief mentioned how it seemed odd that a successful black man from Chicago would settle in white, rural, southern Michigan. I guess I never thought about it, myself. But, he's been here for how long now? Two, three years?"

"Three years," I said, wondering where he was going with this.

"Well," Stan continued, "Some of the guys were sitting around the other day, discussing the drug situation in the county. Just killing time, you know."

I nodded. "I know how that works."

"One of the guys, I don't remember who, pointed out that the drug problem around here really took off about one, maybe two years ago."

I hoped this wasn't going where I thought

it was going.

"Jake has been doing some digging, and says that your friend lives in a beautiful home on a nice sixty acre farm. He's also got some fine looking livestock. Registered Angus, if I'm right. That's expensive cattle. The guys say he seems to have some tight Detroit connections, too."

"He likes animals and farming," I said. "I live on a farm, too. But, I'm not selling drugs to pay for it."

"Whoa, don't get me wrong, here," the supervisor said, holding the folder up defensively. "I'm just saying that people are asking questions. They think it's strange, that's all."

"People?" I asked. "Like the LaBlancs?" I didn't share my suspicions of the family, but I sure wanted to. Moore probably wouldn't have believed me anyway.

I stared off over to the tree line to the east. The top leaves were stirring in the morning light.

"Hank McIntyre is a good man," I argued. "We're lucky to have him in the community." I could feel my face redden.

"How well do you really know him?" the

supervisor asked. The breeze kicked up and tousled his sandy hair so it fell over his glasses. He brushed it out of his eyes with his free hand.

"I know him as well as anybody around here, I guess," I replied. "Someone is making a big mistake," I said. Hank and the drug trade? I couldn't, wouldn't, believe it. I stood there, rooted to the pavement, dumbfounded, not quite knowing what to say.

"Food for thought," Stan said. "Well, I won't hold you up," he waved the folder. "I'm sure you've got things to do, too."

"I'm retired, so I've got all the time in the world," I replied, straight-faced, trying to look normal.

Stan gave a polite laugh.

"What's with the folder?" I pointed. "You carrying your work around now, just to stay caught up?"

"Something like that," he said, holding the folder out for emphasis. "I have some receipts I need to look up in the Chief's files. That's why I was trying to reach him. Seems we've got invoices for diesel fuel used in our tanker, and we shouldn't use that much. Must be a mistake in billing. There are a few more bills that I don't have invoices for, too," he said. "Then, there's a complaint from our fire board about reports not getting filed with the state." He tapped the folder for emphasis. "It's probably just an oversite on the chief's part. Anyway, I thought I'd do a little look-see this morning and try to get all our ducks in a row."

I nodded, wished him a good day, and got in my truck. As I left the parking lot, I ran our conversation through my head again. What was it he said, about Hank living here for three years, and the drug problem got worse after he showed up?

I had assumed that Hank had a decent pension check from the Chicago Police Department. That is, if he had started collecting it. Like me, he was still too young for social security, and I knew only too well how much money it took to run a farm. That made the decision easy to rent the land out, all except my little five acre hay field.

Hank leased out his land, too. Seems like he said once that the rent payment paid his property taxes, and a little more. With that income and a decent retirement check, I could see how he could get by. I had no idea if he had money coming in from consulting or a side job.

No, I couldn't see Hank in the drug trade. I'd hung around with him too much to think otherwise.

And what's this about only having eight or so firefighters on the squad? Pulaski had sixteen, maybe eighteen, if I remembered correctly.

The conversation with Stan stuck with me all the way back to Pulaski. There was something he said about Detroit connections. The man works with the Federal Marshals, of course there's a Detroit connection. I guess to those looking for someone to point a finger at, the skimpy evidence would be good enough.

Chapter Twenty

I swung by the fire station before heading home. I needed somebody to unload on. Luck was with me. Kip's truck was sitting off to the side. I parked and walked in.

Kip was in his office, hunched over his computer, filling out yet another on-line form.

"Morning, Chief," I called. I took a seat in the empty chair next to his desk. "No work today?"

Kip stopped what he was doing and looked up. "Just doing more paperwork," he shook his head. "Reports for the state on our training sessions. Waiting on a roofing delivery down on Mosherville Road. Shoulda' been here last Friday." He made a face and shook his head.

He looked at me while taking a gulp from his special chief's coffee cup. "What's with you? You look like you've got a warrant or something."

"Something's come up, and it's bothering me," I replied.

"The wife pregnant?" He grinned.

I didn't laugh.

Kip scooted his chair over. "Sorry," he said. "You're serious. What's going on?"

"I was just over to Maple Grove. Had a talk with the supervisor."

"Stan Moore," Kip said, nodding his head. "Stan-the-man," he threw in jokingly.

"I went looking for Jake LaBlanc, but he wasn't around.

"Jake?" Kip raised his eyebrows.

I decided to lay everything out. "Wanted to ask what they've been seeing in over-dose runs," I said. "Hank McIntyre and I have been talking. We thought maybe I could engage Jake in an innocent conversation and see where it went. Anyway, Stan was walking over to the fire garage to check on some paperwork. We had a little talk out in the parking lot."

"About what?" Kip asked. He reached over and put a pencil on his desk. He'd been playing with it in his fingers, but now gave me his undivided attention.

"Mainly about Hank McIntyre," I said, not

quite knowing where to start.

"Hank? What about him?"

"There seems to be scuttlebutt floating around that Hank's enjoying the good life, the good life that he can't really afford. He may have an unregistered side business, if you get my drift. At least that's the insinuation. Moore didn't give me any hard evidence. Everything was circumstantial."

Kip's eyes grew wide. "You mean...?"

"Stan said folks are wondering if Hank has anything to do with the sudden increase in the illegal drug activity around here," I said.

"That's crazy," Kip responded, wagging his head and waving me off.

I held my hands out in supplication. "That's what I thought, but Moore was serious."

"What exactly did he say?"

"There was mention of Hank's home, and farm - even that small herd of Angus steers. And, they think it's odd that a black man from Chicago would want to live in white, rural Michigan."

"Who wouldn't want to live out here?" Kip replied, incredulous.

"Well," I started, "it isn't for everyone, but, a guy can live wherever he wants, can't he? Stan also said that Jake LaBlanc has been doing some digging and Hank has a Detroit connection. Whatever that means."

"LaBlanc, huh?" Kip made a face. "That guy should be the one being investigated. Flint told me the Metro Squad is doing some snooping, as we speak. And, how many times has LaBlanc, or one of his boys, been at a drug site when they weren't called in?" The chief was really getting warmed up.

"It's been a few. A few too many," I replied. "Remember the wrecked van out on Goose Lake? That was the middle of the night. Yet, there they were."

Kip said, "I'm not buying the story that they were up anyway and decided to come on out." He'd picked the pencil back up and was nervously rolling it between his hands.

"I believe the LaBlanc kid was in the van when it crashed," I said. "Probably was the driver. And, "I pointed a finger for emphasis, "I believe he called his dad for a ride. When Jake showed up, he told the boy to call 911."

It was all starting to make sense, now.

Kip said, "Well, I know Stan Moore. He's a pretty solid guy. I can't see him getting concerned over nothing. And," he wagged the pencil at me, "you're right about Jake and the boys. I've had the same gut feeling you have. So's Flint. At the big meeting, I noticed the younger LaBlanc kid had some bruising on this forehead. I saw it when he walked toward the front of the room and turned to sit down. Kept his hair over most of it," Kip said.

"LaBlanc must be feeding Moore quite a line, then," I said.

"Where's Hank today?" Kip asked. "He around?"

"Not here today," I replied. "He's in Detroit for a meeting." There it was, Detroit. It didn't look good. Didn't help my argument.

"Geez Louise," Kip shook his head.

I thought of something else. "You're always working on paperwork and reports," I said. "Would it be easy to get behind?"

"You know it would," he said, wondering where I was leading him.

"Well, Stan said something about some reports for the state being late."

Kip held up a hand. "That's not too uncommon. If I didn't stay on top of this stuff, I'd be late, too. Murrey and the fire board would be all over me. All of the board members would be getting involved."

"Murrey," I said, "is one township supervisor who would have a coronary if you got behind on paperwork to the state."

Kip nodded in agreement. "You got that right. It takes a while to catch up with us, but someone would notice," he said. "The state is big on losing things, too," he added. "I've had to resend reports more than once. Could be, Jake sent a report over the internet and it fell down a rat hole, never to be seen again."

"I can understand that," I replied thoughtfully. "However, Stan said he didn't know when Jake did his paperwork. I'm led to believe he's not seen him there working on it. You know, like you're here almost every other morning working at your desk."

That brought a big smile from Kip.

"Another thing," I said, "Stan mentioned that there's a problem with the invoicing. Seems there are claims for diesel fuel for a truck that hasn't used it."

That got Kip's attention. He put the pencil back on his desk and sat quietly, looking at me.

"He was going over to look through the files when I talked to him," I said.

Kip looked aside, rubbed his chin thoughtfully, then said, "There's something rotten in Denmark, and it's not the cheese."

"You grew up in the area with him," I stated. "What do you know about LaBlanc?"

"Like I said before, he's a pain in the neck. I didn't hang around with him in school, but I know some of the guys who did. A few of them got into trouble. Nothing serious, but people were somewhat surprised that Jake ended up running the farm and getting the fire chief's job."

"How'd he get the job?" I asked, curious about his credentials.

"His dad was on the department," Kip said. "He got Jake on, too. When the old chief retired, the board wanted someone younger. Jake talked his way into the job. It's been a LaBlanc social club ever since."

"Hmmm," I replied.

"There's something else," Kip said, looking at the floor and absent-mindedly tugging at one ear.

I looked at him with renewed interest.

"This is just between us, you know." He

glanced back up.

"It'll go nowhere," I said.

"Our man, Flint, tells me that a gal from Maple Grove spilled the beans on some missing funds from the woman's auxiliary."

"Maple Grove has an actual auxiliary?" This was news to me.

"Yes," Kip said. He rubbed the back of his neck, as if chasing away tension, then looked at me and sighed. "They have an actual auxiliary. I'm not sure what they do. Help with fundraisers, I guess."

I nodded.

"Anyway, Flint and the twelve-year-old, that Morgan deputy, were down at the Oasis last Saturday. You know the place, on US 12, west of Moscow?"

"I've been by the place," I said. "Lord knows I wouldn't actually go in it."

"I guess Flint was teaching Morgan how to troll the night spots," he said, grinning over at me, "and they were playing Flint's usual game of catch-and-release, when they got talking to this gal."

I nodded for him to go on.

"Apparently the woman had a few too many and, while she was hanging all over Flint, became very talkative. Said there's money missing from the auxiliary's savings account. Guess who's on the account as a back-up?" Kip looked steadily at me.

"Our buddy, Jake LaBlanc?" I took a wild guess.

"You *are* a bright boy," Kip grinned and shook his head. "Stan Moore had an account history printed off. They're missing about three thousand dollars."

"Who signed for it?" I asked. "Somebody had to sign for it." I made a movement with my right hand, like someone holding a pen and signing their name.

"You're right," Kip said. "One check, made out to cash, has LaBlanc's name on it, the other two have the auxiliary's secretary on them."

"Not LaBlanc's wife, then?" I guessed.

"Exactly what I thought," Kip answered, "but, no, she's not on the account. Probably wouldn't be caught dead dealing with the riffraff," he added with a shrug.

"So, Officer Jordon gets involved and talks to the secretary," I suggested.

"Already happened. She denies writing any checks. At least those checks. Names Shelly something or other. Claims it's not her handwriting."

"This just gets better and better," I said.

Kip agreed, throwing a glance as his computer screen.

"I'd better let you go," I said. "Thanks for listening." I started to leave, turned back. "Last Saturday night, you say? Flint gets a day off?"

"Every day is a day off for him," Kip answered.

As I was walking out the door, Ned Jordon from over Hanover and Maple Grove way was coming across the parking lot, dressed in his civilian clothes.

"Undercover?" I asked, looking him over. I knew he worked second shift and was off duty.

"That would be Flint," he said with a wink, laughing and shaking my hand. "Kip inside?" he asked.

"Yeah, I answered, "he's staying on top of his reports. I'll bet he's ready to take a break. Go on in." I grinned happily.

I'd turned the corner onto McDonald Road when my cell phone rang. I could see my driveway a quarter mile down the road. The caller I.D. showed Kip Jones. I'd just left him and wondered what it could be. Pulling into a farm lane that led to a neighbor's soybean field, I answered on the fourth ring.

"Tim, it's Kip," he said, without waiting for me to say "Hello."

"What's up?" I asked curiously.

"Ned Jordon just left," he said.

"I passed him on my way out the door," I replied. "I thought it was kind of odd for him to come visiting. What'd he want?"

"He was here asking questions about Hank McIntyre," Kip said. "He said it couldn't wait until he was on duty this evening, so he came right over, today."

The muscles in my jaw and down my back tightened. "They didn't waste any time," I complained.

"Jordon had the same story you heard from Stan Moore," Kip said. "The good news is, he doesn't believe any of it. He thinks somebody's trying to throw you two under the bus."

"The two of us? You mean I'm included?" I leaned back in the seat and stared out the window, across the countryside. I couldn't believe what I was hearing.

"Jordon asked about your background, is

all," Kip said. "He really seemed disgusted with the whole thing, and kept apologizing for bringing it up."

"I'm a pretty boring guy," I stated.

"I wouldn't say that," he said, "but our buddy, Henry Wadsworth McIntyre has an interesting history..."

"How so," I interrupted. He used Hank's full name. This can't be good. Wadsworth?

"Jordon had a little background on Hank. He tells me that Hank grew up on the edge of Chicago. That much we knew," Kip said. "What we didn't know is that he got a football scholarship to Northwestern University."

"*The* Northwestern University?" I asked. "In Chicago? Football?" I knew Hank played ball, but for some reason, assumed it was just in high school.

"Yeah," Kip answered, "and apparently, he was pretty good, back in the day. I can see why, the guy's as big as a Buick."

"So what's the bad news?" I asked, still feeling a little knot in the pit of my stomach.

"Bad news?" Kip asked gleefully, "There isn't any, other than a few questions being asked. Not only was Hank a superb division one football player, he's also smarter than hell."

"I already knew that," I said. "All it takes is to have a conversation with the man."

Kip said, "He has a brother, Harold, who still lives in Illinois on the grandparent's old farm, not too far from the Chicago area. Guess you could say he 'bought the farm,'" he joked. "There's also a younger sister, Sarah, who lives in Terra Haute.

"Hank speaks fondly of spending time on the farm when he was a kid," I said.

"Well, the place is still there," Kip said, "and Harold lives there. By the way, brother Harold is a successful corporate attorney in Chicago."

"Now it makes sense," I said. "Harold ended up with the grandparent's farm, so Hank buys a substitute here in Southern Michigan. Those happy times must have made quite an impression, 'cause he sure loves his farm."

"There's more," Kip said. "Hank had a spotless career with the Chicago Police Department. Up until five years ago, he was moving up in rank, earning the respect of the brass."

"What happened?" I asked.

Kip said, "He went through a burn-out. Started drinking, got a divorce. Got dried out and moved to Michigan. Somewhere in there he returned to his Baptist roots and found the Lord. His ex-wife is a psychologist for Cook County. She remarried two years back."

I sat silently, thinking. "She's missing out on a good man," I finally replied. "But, I guess the wonderful country life isn't for everybody."

"Especially a city bred and educated woman," Kip said.

"Oh yeah," he said, "one more thing. Hank inherited two hundred grand from the sale of his grandfather's farm to his brother, Harold. The place must really be worth some money, eh?"

"So that's all Jordon wanted? To basically warn us that somebody's started a smear campaign against us?"

"Yeah, that's about it," Kip agreed, "but he also wanted to let us all know that Hank is really the great guy he's always seemed. He has his own financial independence. Doesn't need any easy money."

"Okay, thanks for the call," I said. I knew what he meant by 'easy money.' "I'll see you at the station sometime, if not in the middle of the night, somewhere," I said.

"Sure, see ya," Kip replied.

"One more thing."

"Yeah?" Kip asked

"Wadsworth?"

Laughter on the other end, then Kip was gone.

I sat in the truck and worked over in my mind the talk with Stan Moore, and now with Kip. Before backing the Dodge out onto the road, I looked up Hank's home number and pressed the send button.

I didn't think he was home, yet, but I'd leave a message. His answering machine picked up on the third ring. Hank's voice came on,

"Hi, this is Hank. I can't come to the phone right now, but please leave a name, number, and message. I'll call you back as soon as I can. Oh, and did I say leave a number?" followed by Hank snickering.

"Hank, it's me, Conway. Give me a call when you get in. I should be at the house. Thanks."

I left my cell number and the house landline number, even though I knew he had them both. Then I thought how I had Hank's home number, but not his cell number. He'd never offered and I hadn't asked.

I drove on home. There was another line of thunderstorms working their way across Lake Michigan, and I wanted to put away some lawn furniture before the rain hit in the evening.

Hank called me back just after supper. I was standing on the patio, watching the dark clouds roll in from the west. The wind had picked up some and was whipping the tree limbs.

My wife waved me into the house, the portable phone in her hand. "Hank," she said.

"Hello, Hank."

"Tim Conway," he greeted me happily, but sounding tired. "What's going on?"

I told him about the meeting with Stan in the parking lot of the Maple Grove fire station. Then the phone conversation with Kip, while parked in the farm lane on the way home.

Hank listened silently. Once I even wondered if he was still there. I finished my story.

"Well," he began, "the good news is, we've got a friend over at Maple Grove. Jordon sounds like a good man."

"I've always thought he was," I said.

"Kip's known him most of his life. Since high school anyway," I added.

"Well I had a fascinating day at the Federal Building in Detroit," Hank said.

I could hear the weariness in his voice.

"It seems somebody in Jackson has heard some concerns about me, and shoved it up the line. My contacts in Detroit knew about it before I got there," he said.

"What?" I exclaimed, looking back at my wife. She stood in the kitchen doorway, coffee cup in hand, eavesdropping. Her face wore a puzzled expression.

Hank laughed, "They got a lot of miles out of it, joking around and being funny at my expense," he said, perking up slightly.

I breathed a sigh of relief.

"What is it they say about Mondays being rough days?" he asked. "We'll get together this week and go over things," he said. "I've got some research to do, and some notes to write."

"Speaking of miles," I said, "how did your dinner date go with the lovely Shonda Miles?"

Hank laughed. "That restaurant in Pittsford is as good as you claimed," he said. "Shonda said the house salad was to die for.

I had the baked spaghetti. It was a real nice time. The waitress treated us like royalty. Probably don't get many black folk at a little country restaurant like that," he said.

I could almost see him smiling.

"Especially one with green eyes," I said.

"The waitress mentioned that. Shonda explained how her maternal grandmother was Irish. Even the woman cooking came out front to meet her."

"I know who the *real* royalty is, then," I replied.

"You got that right, brother."

I thanked Hank for the call-back and hung up, my spirits lifted.

Outside, the rain came in a sudden downpour.

I had to relate the entire phone conversation to my inquisitive spouse.

"That man needs a good wife," was her only response.

Chapter Twenty-one

We had an uneventful week on the farm. I sold some hay to a nice couple who raised horses. I had the easy job of tossing it out of the barn, down into their pickup. The next day I threw down a pickup load for a girl in 4H. She needed it to feed two goats and a few steers she planned to show at the fair next fall.

Friday afternoon came, sunny and bright. Large, puffy, cumulus clouds sailed slowly overhead like some kind of vaporous galleons. I'd just finished mowing the lawn and had poured a couple glasses of lemonade. One for the wife, one for myself. We sat in the shade of a towering maple tree, in some antique metal lawn chairs that the wife had bought at a yard sale. I'd repainted them in bright pastels and we had them parked where we could sit and admire the flower gardens. Peonies, irises, and purple and white lilacs ringed the yard in a riot of colors. The tulips and daffodils had already faded and passed on.

From across the yard, a fountain in the fish pond bubbled soothingly away.

"This is the life," my little gardener, and love of my life, said. She sipped her cool drink, then hoisted the frosted glass toward the lilacs, the ice cubes clinking in the glass. "This is a good year for lilacs," she said. "I can smell them from here."

We sat in silence, listening to the burbling fountain and the lazy sounds of summer, and sipped our lemonade. I placed my glass on the little red table between us.

"All we need is an in-ground pool," I said. "That would be the icing on the ol' banana."

"What would you do with an in-ground pool?" she asked, looking bewildered. "You'd have to be out here all the time doing maintenance."

"I'd invite the young neighbor ladies back for a refreshing swim," I answered with a loving smile.

"You don't need a heart attack in a swimming pool," she said. "You could drown."

Thirty-five years of marriage...

My cell phone pager went off. The tone for Hanover sounded, and the dispatcher said "Jackson Central to Hanover Rescue, single vehicle crash on Wellington, cross, Maple Grove."

"Just over the line in Hanover Township," I said, looking over at the wife.

The call repeated on my phone.

Her eyes met mine, "Your friends over at Hanover can handle it," she smiled coyly and had that look in her eye. "You're going to be busy with your own rescue."

Oh boy, a beautiful June day is going to get even better. I felt a surge of optimism as I put the concerns of the past week out of my head. I smiled contentedly.

My wife reached across the table and took my fingers in her hand. We sat for a few minutes, quietly enjoying the view.

"Jackson Central to Pulaski Rescue, mutual aid requested by Hanover Rescue, single vehicle crash on Wellington, cross, Maple Grove."

I looked sadly at the wife. "Maybe somebody else will call in," I said hopefully.

"Everybody's at work, or in the fields,"

she answered. "You said Kip was finally finishing that garage down on Mosherville Road. Better respond." She pointed at the cell, still laying on the table.

The dispatcher repeated the call for mutual aid.

I called in. The wife kissed me on the cheek. "There's always tonight," she said sweetly.

Harrumph!" I exclaimed, then smiled brightly. "Be back before you know it," I said, heading for the Dodge.

As I drove away in the truck, I heard Schultzie call in. Hanover had a rescue unit on site. Schultz would bring Engine 1 in case of a fire.

It took me a few minutes to work my way over to Maple Grove Road that ran on south, down into the village of Maple Grove. I turned and headed south toward Wellington, a narrow, paved road that ran east off Maple Grove, just inside Hanover Township.

I beeped my horn and pulled out around a lumbering John Deere tractor. The guy was pulling a load of round bales stacked two-high on a flatbed wagon. The driver smiled and waved. I waved back as the Dodge flashed by.

Coming to Wellington, I was met by Schultzie, in Engine 1, coming up from the south on Maple Grove. He'd taken the road east, out of Pulaski, then headed north.

I waved him on and followed the fire engine down the patched and potholed road.

The brake lights came on and Schultz slowed the big International and stopped. I pulled up a few yards behind and shut off the Dodge.

Schultzie grabbed a medical bag and trotted up the road with me. There was no traffic, and we went up the middle of the pavement to avoid tripping in the worst of the potholes and maybe breaking out necks. Hanover Rescue was ahead, sitting in the road. There was a drop-off to the right that led to a copse of box elder and scrub, wild cherry.

Then I saw it, Jake LaBlanc's pickup facing us from the other side of the road. It was a good ten yards down from the Hanover Rescue unit. Nobody was in it or around it.

"See that," I said to Schultzie, "What's he doing here?"

We walked over to the edge of the slope and took a look.

Wrapped around a good-sized box elder at

the bottom of the steep slope was a John Deere Gator. At least that's what it was before it went down into the trees. Now it was a tangle of green metal. The machine lay on its side. The canvas roof was missing and the battered dump box was wrenched to one side, clinging to the frame by one pivot point. I could see the path it had taken down the steep hillside to the trees. It must have been twenty feet down there.

A guy from Hanover was bent over the Gator, looking at something. He stood and looked up as we approached. His expression didn't look good. LaBlanc and his assistant chief, his son, Mike, appeared from behind the wreck. The son made the motion of handing something to his father. A medical device? A wrapper? I couldn't tell for sure, if it was anything at all.

"He has a pulse," the Hanover guy said.

"Do you need a back board?" I called down.

"Right side, back door on the van," he called up to me.

The sound of a car pulling up drew my attention to the roadway. A sheriff's car.

Schultz was already to the van, retrieving the back board.

Jake LaBlanc began struggling up the steep incline, grasping at bushes and tree roots to help him along. I stepped aside to let him by.

"Jake," I nodded politely.

"Conway," he said, walking past me. "How's it going?"

I thought of my wife waiting at home for me. "Couldn't be better," I said. "Who's in the wreck?" My grandkids called this type of vehicle a side-by-side, due to the seating arrangement.

"Young guy," Jake turned to face me. "Looks like he lost control and wrapped it around a tree."

That much was obvious to me.

A fresh-faced, deputy sheriff walked over and stood looking down at the wreck. Schultz was skidding on his butt down the slope with the back board trailing behind.

"How ya doing, Norm?" he greeted the Hanover man. Schultz seemed to know everybody.

LaBlanc walked over to his pickup, opened the door and leaned in. I wondered what he'd gone to get. Closing the door, he walked back over, hands empty. He saw me watching him, and stared back until I looked away.

"He's pretty beat up," he said to the deputy, and nodded toward the embankment.

"Young guy?" the deputy asked. He stood with his hands on his hips, staring down at the wreck.

"Yeah," LaBlanc replied. "Going too fast, I guess." He shrugged and shook his head.

I returned to Engine 1 and dug out a fifty foot length of sturdy manilla rope. Tying off one end to a guard post beside the road, I gently played out the rope, easing myself over the lip of the embankment.

Up on the road, two more sheriff's cars pulled up. With all of the light bars flashing, I was glad I wasn't prone to epilepsy.

A car backed out of a driveway about fifty yards east of us, then proceeded our way. One of the deputies went over to talk to the driver. Two teenagers stared wide-eyed out the side windows.

I used the rope to skid down to the crash scene. Without it, I was sure I'd have gone tumbling down into the group below, like some kind of human bowling ball.

Schultzie and Norm, from Hanover, helped position the back board so I could secure the rope. Mike LaBlanc stood and watched.

I put on a pair of medical gloves and pulled an extra pair out of my pocket for Schultz. He'd snagged his while moving some debris to get at the crash victim.

The young man, not much older than a middle school student, was wearing a cervical collar that Hanover Rescue had placed on him. Schultzie and Norm had already secured him to the orange back board. His face was pretty beat up. One eye was swollen over and oozing, his lips puffy and bleeding.

Norm had put a pulse-oxy sensor on the kid's right index finger and had a blood pressure cuff on his left arm. The victim had been silent, but now let out a low, painful, bubbly moan between his bloody lips.

Internal injuries, not a good sign.

"How do you want to do this?" I asked Norm, while nodding at the rope leading up the slope.

"Have a couple deputies pull on the line and we'll go alongside to help ease him up," he said.

"Hey fellas, give us a hand, will you?" I called up to the deputies. Two grabbed the line. One actually had gloves on to protect his hands.

"Yell when you're ready and we'll take it easy," the younger one shouted down.

I looked around at Schultzie, Norm, and Mike LaBlanc. Norm nodded.

"Okay, ease us on up," I called. The rope tightened as the deputies began pulling. I bent over and tugged at the back board, attempting to back up the hill. Schultz and Norm pushed from the side and from behind.

Mike LaBlanc was searching for something in the weeds around the wrecked Gator.

Slipping and sliding, we struggled a few feet up the slope over the trampled weeds and a few scrubby little bushes.

Up on the shoulder of the road, the deputies were straining and grunting under the load. The older one called to the third deputy to return and lend a hand. He walked over, and the people he'd been talking to drove around the rescue vehicles and left. I wondered what had happened to Jake LaBlanc.

It was all we could do from below to haul ourselves up, let alone shove the now moaning crash victim strapped to the back board. I grabbed a small bush for balance and leverage. It came out by the roots and I began sliding. Schultzie was behind me and stopped my downward motion. We all came to a halt.

"This is nuts!" I exclaimed in frustration.

"I'll go up and help the deputies," Schultzie said, working his way around me and scrambling up the incline. Little clumps of dirt and stone slid down behind every footstep he took.

We waited, sweating like plow horses and catching our breath, until Schultz was with the deputies. I wiped my forehead with my sleeve. It *would* have to be the hottest day of the year.

A voice called out to us from the road, and a figure appeared. It was our man, Flint. He wore civilian clothes and had on a pair of leather work gloves. After greeting the other deputies, he snatched up the end of the rope. With the five men hauling away, we soon made progress. I dug in my heels and backed up the slope, gripping the back board with my right hand and guiding it around the larger shrubs, while bracing my left against the slope to balance myself. Norm, from Hanover, gave up on pushing and scrambled alongside, attempting to keep an eye on the crash victim.

An ambulance arrived as we worked, and two

EMTs peered down. When we reached the roadside, they somewhat gently slid the backboard up onto a gurney. The kid let out a louder moan and tried to shift around. The restraining straps kept him in place.

I wiped the sweat from my brow. "I was beginning to wonder if you guys were gonna be able to pull me up," I complained as I untied the rope. "You were pulling me along with the victim."

"That's why I kept my hand on the back board," said Norm. "I couldn't climb up without help."

"That explains why the kid was so damned heavy," one of the deputies complained.

The EMT guys chuckled at us and loaded the young man into the ambulance, then off they went. Two of the county cars followed in hot pursuit.

"They'll want to talk to the victim when he's stabilized at the hospital," Flint told us.

Mike LaBlanc had hiked down a way where the slope wasn't so steep. Now he came walking along the road to stand by his father. Jake stood silently off to one side, hands on his hips, watching.

Flint had started to coil the rope into tight loops, and glanced down the road.

LaBlanc and his son were walking off toward their pickup.

"I didn't smell any alcohol on the victim," I said, while watching them go.

"I don't believe he'd been drinking," Norm said. "He was just going too fast and lost it. Some of these potholes are pretty deep. Anybody would have trouble, if they're going too fast."

Flint stopped working with the rope. He turned to the other deputy, the older one that he seemed to know. "What say we go down and take a look," he said. It wasn't a question, and the deputy picked up on it.

"I believe we should," the deputy said.

Flint tied off the rope to the same post I'd used earlier, and tossed the coil down the slope.

"We'll need this to get up and down," he explained to the deputy. "Breaking our necks going down and clawing our way back up is for dumb farmers," he grinned at Schultzie and me.

"Dumb farmers smeared your butt on the football field, if you care to remember," Schultz sounded offended.

I just shook my head. "I thought I saw Mike hand something to his dad, just as Schultz and I got here," I said to the deputies.

"Did you see what it was?" asked the one on duty.

"No, couldn't tell. May not have been anything," I replied. "But I was sure LaBlanc put something in his truck. Otherwise why go over to the truck and walk back empty handed?" I looked at Schultz, "You see anything?"

"No, I was trying to see what Norm, here, was doing," he shook his head. "You've met Norm?" he asked me, tilting his head at the Hanover man.

I smiled and shook Norm's hand.

"Second cousin, twice removed, on my mother's side, or something like that," Norm said with a nod at Schultzie.

I didn't see any resemblance.

"At first I thought the kid had to be dead," Schultzie said. I was mighty glad when Norm said he'd found a pulse."

The deputies prepared to go down. "Flint, one moment," I said. He stopped and turned my way. "What was LaBlanc doing here, anyway? The call was for mutual aid from

Pulaski. There were enough personnel here, especially with the three on-duty deputies."

The old-timers always said that Pulaski and Hanover go way back, so it was only natural for us to respond.

"Maybe I can find a clue when we go down there," he said, pointing at the wreck.

"When the kid comes around in the hospital, we'll find out more," the other deputy said.

"You guys can clear out when you're ready," the deputy added. "I'll consider the scene transferred."

"Not much more I can do," Norm said. He gave his name and a description of what he saw to the deputy and Flint. The deputy wrote everything down on his note pad. Norm thanked us and climbed into the Hanover rescue unit and left.

Schultz and I watched as Flint and the deputy descended the slope and began to inspect the wrecked Gator. "Don't move anything until an investigator gets here with a camera," the deputy told Flint.

"Thanks," Flint said, "this is my first time, you know."

"Sorry."

They kept searching around the area and went back over the slope leading down to the wreck.

"Nothing," the deputy said, looking around. He stood with his arms wide, indicating the area around him.

Flint knelt by the wrecked machine and peered underneath. He grabbed a handy stick and poked around under it.

"Rattlesnake?" I jokingly asked from up on the road.

"Better," Flint said. With a flourish, he popped out a baggie stuffed full of marijuana. Holding the discovery high for all to see, he called up to us. "I'd say this fell from the Gator when it tipped up against the tree."

The deputy walked over to examine the find. "We need a dog out here," he said, turning to come up the slope. He grabbed the rope and walked himself up, then went to his car to call in.

Schultz shouted out a goodbye to Flint down below, then walked to Engine 1 and called Jackson Central. "Pulaski Engine 1, clear," he said.
The dispatcher repeated his call back to him. Schultz waved to me, and drove off.

The deputy tossed Flint a roll of yellow crime scene tape.

I walked to my truck and drove back home.

What did LaBlanc put in his truck? The question haunted me all the way back. The kid getting busted for pot wouldn't be the end of the world, so what did LaBlanc pick up? And his kid, Mike, why was he standing around down there, while we worked on the crash victim? Was he looking for the baggie of pot? Who knew? I'd have to run this all by Hank next time I saw him.

Arriving at home I immediately sat down at the kitchen table, pen and yellow legal pad in hand.

I wrote down all that had happened and followed up by jotting down a few questions.

The clock chimed in the upstairs hallway.

"Six o'clock, time for us to think about supper," I tiredly told the wife. The rescue run had taken more out of me than I realized. My wife sat across the table, asking questions and picking my brain, helping make my list better.

"Supper can wait," she said, smiling. "Right now you have another rescue." She took my hand.

Chapter Twenty-two

The next morning, Saturday, the wife and I took my Dodge and went up to Concord for a lazy breakfast. We lingered for over an hour, drinking coffee and talking to some friends I'd just met. My wife says I'll talk to anybody. We finally left the restaurant and headed across the street to the old IHC dealership. A row of hundred-year-old, two-story, brick buildings lined the block on the east side of the street. The dealership anchored the north end. It's ancient, wooden floors creaked and groaned when walked on. The ceiling was of ornate tin-work. It was like shopping in a historical museum.

I needed some Cub Cadet parts for the relic from the nineteen sixties resting in the back of my farm shop. Hank said he'd help get it running if I'd buy the parts. I walked past the plumbing supplies, pulled out my list, and stepped to the parts counter. The wife wandered the isles in the housewares section.

It was past mid morning before we headed back home, following the road back south around the east side of Swains Lake and then on to Pulaski. As I drove past the entrance to the county park at Swains, my cell phone pager went off.

"Jackson Central to Pulaski Rescue, injured man in road, possible burn victim. Two-thousand block of Staley Road, cross, Jordon."

No mention of a vehicle. I looked across at the wife.

"What was that?" she asked, raising an eyebrow. "No car? Just a man in the road, burned?"

The dispatcher repeated the message.

"That's out past Hank's place, then north-west," I told her, "almost to the county line, if not *at* the county line."

"This ought to be good," my wife said.

We listened to the radio traffic. Kip called in, on his way to the station to pick up the rescue van.

"Drop you at home?" I looked at the wife.

"Sure. It'll give me time to finish your to-do list," she laughed.

I called in to Central Dispatch and told the operator I'd be on my way in five minutes.

After dropping off the wife, I headed back north to Howard Road, then sped on west, honking the horn as I passed Hank's farm, just in case he was home. Two miles on, I came to Jordon and turned north toward Staley. Staley went west from Jordon, toward the Calhoun County line.

Several miles through farm country I found the rescue unit parked in the road, lights flashing. There wasn't a house in sight. A farmer had parked his tractor and hay rake on the other side of the rocky fence row and was lending Kip a hand. Towering, old maples lined the road and sheltered us from the sun.

Kip and the farmer had a man laying on a blanket in the middle of the deserted road. The man was burned all right. He cried out and kept moving his arms and legs about on the blanket. Kip was attempting to cut away his burned, tattered, shirt.

I rushed up, slipping on my medical gloves. I notice the farmer had on a pair, too. He stood as I approached and let me kneel beside the victim.

Kip looked over, "Good to see you, Tim." Looking up; "This is Matt English. Lives just over the hill," he said, nodding to the west, down the tree lined road.

I glanced up and nodded in greeting to Matt, "Good to meet you," I said. We didn't bother shaking hands.

"I checked his mouth," Kip said, glancing my way. "No flash burns."

"Ah," I said, "he's lucky, I guess." That meant no lung damage leading to edema. I looked down at the burn victim who didn't look so lucky at the moment.

Matt crouched by the injured man's head. Second degree burns were on his cheeks and forehead, and his eyebrows had been singed off. "What can I do?" he asked us.

Kip was reaching for his saline bottles for rinsing the victim's burned arms and chest. He handed the farmer two large plastic packets. "Tear open the packets and use the sterile pads to hold his shoulders down," he said.

Matt started ripping at the top of the packets.

"What's your name?" Kip asked the victim.

"We're going to cut your burned clothing off and do something about your pain."

The young man didn't answer, just groaned and nodded his head.

I felt his pockets but found no identification, then grabbed some scissors and began cutting at the singed pant legs.

"Lord," Kip said softly as he reached for a roll of gauze.

I looked up, the skin was sloughing off the burned man's arms and upper chest. Third degree burns, this was not gonna be good.

From behind us, an ambulance siren sounded louder as it approached from the east. The burned man was whimpering in agony.

"It's going to be okay," Kip said. "Take it easy. You're safe with us."

"Where's Nan when you need her?" I asked.

Casting aside the man's pant legs, I grabbed a plastic bottle of saline, double checked the label, and rinsed his reddened thighs. From the pattern on his skin, I could see the burns were a hot flash on the front of his body, mainly the upper chest, neck and face. Something blew up in his face. I thought I knew what that something was.

The ambulance guys trotted over. They had

a gurney and a medical kit. One was our buddy, Dan Bennett. He took one look at the burn victim and took a deep breath.

"Okay, buddy," he said, kneeling next to the burned man, "It's going to be okay now. We'll get you into Jackson." He opened up his medical kit. "It's going to be okay," he repeated.

Bennett pulled out a flashlight and looked in the man's mouth and up his nose. "Didn't suck it in, apparently," he said, looking over at the rest of us.

We nodded in agreement.

The farmer, Matt, stood and stepped away. I could tell from the look in his eyes, he'd be seeing this in his mind for a long time; probably over and over the first night. I knew I would if I were he.

I stood and walked over to him. "You the one who called it in?" I asked.

He nodded. "Saw him stumbling down the road, calling out for help. Drove my tractor over and called in on my cell phone." He nodded toward the big International tractor idling under a tree on the other side of the tumbled down fence.

"Must have looked like the walking dead,

like a zombie," I said. "He give a name?"

"No, just kept calling out for help. I got him to sit down. Actually when he saw me, he more or less fell down," the farmer said, shaking his head and looking back down at the man.

The EMT guys had eased him onto the gurney, and were trying to talk to him as Bennett started an I.V. They weren't wasting any time in loading him up for the trip to Jackson.

"Where could he have come from?" I asked looking out across the fields. I saw no evidence of a fire.

"There's a wooded area just over the county line," Matt said pointing to the west. "He could've walked from there."

I looked to the west and back down at the burned guy. "He did a lot of walking," I said, shaking my head.

We turned when a siren sounded from the direction Matt had just pointed. A brown and white police cruiser appeared over the slight rise and was rapidly approaching.

The car stopped in the middle of the road and a lady deputy got out. Calhoun County Sheriff's Department, it said on the door.

The deputy walked over. "How's he doing?" she asked, nodding toward the burn victim.

"Second and third degree on face, arms, chest, and thighs," I said.

The doors slammed on the ambulance and we watched as an EMT jumped behind the wheel. They took off, back down Staley Road, to work their way over to Pulaski Road, and the trip into the hospital.

Kip walked over, accompanied by the farmer. "Deputy," he nodded a greeting, "what brings you over our way?"

"An unknown fire in the woods," she quoted a dispatcher. "Turns out a meth lab in an old travel trailer exploded. We found a guy laying in the leaves, near the trailer. He said his friend had gone for help." She gave us a tight smile and shook her head.

"That's over a mile away," Matt said. "That old trailer is used as a hunting lodge."

"Badly burned?" I asked.

"Mainly second degree on hands, neck and face," the deputy said.

The farmer, Matt, listened in fascination as the Calhoun deputy gave a description of the burn victim.

"Sounds like our guy, here," Kip said.

"Where'd you take yours?"

"Into Marshall," she replied. "Then he'll probably go on to Battle Creek."

"What were they doing?" Matt asked, lookin a little guilty for interrupting.

The deputy looked at him and smiled, "Shake, bake, and boom!" she grinned, making an upward exploding motion with her hands. "They were cooking up meth using a newer technique. A two liter bottle and explosive chemicals to break down sudefed." She cast a quick look at the scattered rags on the roadway where we'd cut the man's clothes from him. "Doesn't seem worth it, does it?" she asked.

It was more of a commentary than a question.

"It's crazy, that's what it is," Matt said. He gave his statement to the deputy, wished us a good day, and returned to his tractor. He was still wearing the medical gloves that Kip had given him. Stripping them off, he waved and stuffed them in his pant's pocket.

"He's got something to tell the wife tonight over supper," I said.

"We all do," said the deputy. "I'm

married to a civilian, and he thinks I make some of this stuff up. Nobody can make this up," she stated with a shake of her head.

"Do you see much of this in your county?" I asked.

"We're seeing more meth in the rural areas and in a few certain neighborhoods of the larger towns," she said. "Used to be, it was rare," she said soberly. "Now it's not uncommon at all."

"We've had an increase over the last year or so, with a big spike in meth and heroin incidents just over the past month or two," Kip said.

The deputy nodded. "We have identification from the guy over at the trailer," she said. I'll get back and fill everyone in on your victim. The fire department was still there when I left."

"Tell them we said 'Hello,'" Kip said.

The deputy got into her cruiser, turned around in a farm lane, and headed back to the west. She was on her radio as the car disappeared over the rise.

A blue State Police car approached from the east. We talked to the trooper, pointed in the direction of the Calhoun County deputy's route, and nodded good-bye as he climbed back in the cruiser and took off.

I grabbed a trash bag and Kip helped me pick up the rags and wrappers from the roadway.

He leaned against the open door of the rescue unit. "The kid in the Gator wreck is coming around, and Flint says he's singing like a canary," he said. "Metro squad detectives are questioning him more today."

"Anybody talk to the parents?" I asked, curious.

"Yes," Kip said, "the Gator was his father's. They used it to haul wood and stuff around the place. They live about a mile away from the crash scene.

Matt went by on his tractor, making another round inward on the field, hustling to get the hay in.

Rain wasn't predicted for another three days. With farming, everything depended on weather and equipment breakdowns.

"Was he supposed to be using it?" I asked about the Gator.

"That's just it," Kip replied. "The kid was using it without his father's knowledge. This was the only way to get around, unless a friend or parent took him somewhere."

"Did he say where he was going?" This was starting to sound like so many other young people that we'd come across lately.

"He was making a delivery, and it wasn't pizza," Kip shook his head and chuckled.

"Let me guess," I said. "Pot-luck to a sick friend.

"Something like that," Kip replied. "The baggie of pot was for a friend down the road, and there was another baggie, too."

"Meth or heroin?" I looked at him.

"Meth," Kip said. "Any guesses where it went?"

"Nobody ever found it, right?" I asked, thinking of the LaBlanc boys poking around at the wreck. The kid could have died while Jake and Mike were searching for the drugs.

"I still don't get it," I said. "Why the hell would Jake risk everything to steal some kid's meth? It just doesn't make sense."

Kip leaned in the rescue unit to make sure the mike wasn't keyed, then got a serious look on his face. "Flint says the Metro boys are looking at LaBlanc as the supplier. I don't know where he's getting the stuff if he is. Could his boys be cooking it up? There's also a question of the wife's involvement."

"That woman could get away with murder," I replied. "One look and a jury would never convict her."

"A jury of men wouldn't," Kip laughed. "That woman oozes pheromones."

We both laughed. Kip reached in to grab the mike and call in to Central Dispatch.

"It's not the middle of the night, but good to see you anyway," he said with a wave as I walked back to my truck.

Chapter Twenty-three

According to our man, Flint, it was just a simple traffic stop on Moscow Road, south of Hanover. He and deputy Jordon were sitting with a group of us around the break table at the fire barn, drinking coffee and discussing the run on yesterday's burn victim out on Staley Road.

Flint listened closely to our story before changing the subject. "You two will find this interesting," he said, looking at Hank and me.

Jordon nodded in agreement.

Kip looked down at his special chief's cup. "Be nice if Hank had a dinner date with that Miles woman," he said, glancing around at our smiling faces. We nodded our enthusiastic agreement, while looking over at Hank.

Hank just shook his head and signaled for Flint to continue.

No Amish made doughnuts today.

The way Flint told it, two black males were in a white Toyota Celica. The sheriff's deputy working traffic that day normally wouldn't have thought anything of it. They weren't speeding, but as they went by, he noticed the right tail light lens was cracked, with a piece missing. He decided to let them know about the broken light and send them on their way.

He lit them up, and they braked to pull over. The right brake light didn't work.

He called in the plate, no problems, then walked up to the driver's side, checking out the backseat as he went. Stopping just behind the driver seat, at the B post, the officer leaned forward slightly and greeted the driver.

"You have a broken right - rear, tail light lens," he said, "and your brake-light bulb isn't working. Just something you should know, so you can get it fixed."

"I, I didn't know, officer. I'll be sure to get it taken care of." The driver nervously looked behind him, as if to check the broken light from inside the car, or maybe to look for witnesses.

The passenger seemed jumpy, squirming in

the seat and looking around, not meeting the officer's eyes.

The officer instinctively reached into his right pocket, where he kept his emergency .380 pistol.

"May I see your driver's license and registration, please," the officer asked in a friendly manner, trying to put the driver at ease.

"Sure," came the response. The driver dug around in the console and sorted through a mess of papers. He found the vehicle's registration. The insurance card was paper clipped to it.

"Thanks," the officer responded, taking the papers in his left hand. "Not many people have their papers organized like this. I appreciate it."

"No problem," the driver said, throwing a quick glance at his passenger beside him.

The vehicle was registered to Antoine Green, of Romulus, Michigan. The officer compared the driver to the photo on the license. It was a match.

"And your name?" he looked at the passenger.

"Lamont. Lamont Brown." The passenger

still wouldn't look directly at him.

"If you gentlemen would keep your hands on the dash and on top of the wheel, it'd make me feel a lot better," the officer pointed with the paperwork in his left hand. "Thanks, guys. I tend to get nervous."

"We wouldn't want that," the driver said, with a forced smile.

"Be right back, then we'll get you on your way," the smiling officer said. He stepped away from the car and walked backwards to the county patrol unit. He could see the two individuals as they sat in the car, talking animatedly, and glancing in the rear view mirrors to watch him.

It was a relief to know that his vehicle's dash cam was getting everything, just in case trouble developed.

Placing the paperwork on the seat, he grabbed up the mike and called for back-up and a K9 unit. "I have some nervous individuals in the front of a car," he said. "There's also the strong smell of marijuana and something else that I can't place."

The dispatcher had two units on the way before he hung up the mike. The K9 unit was currently on 127 south, on the way to a demonstration at a school somewhere, but would swing around and cut over to them.

The officer ran wants and warrants on the driver. No outstanding warrants. He waited a few minutes, but not so long that the guys would get jumpy, then walked back to the car, keeping his hand in his right pocket.

"Things check out," he told the driver. "Where are you guys off to, anyway?"

"Umm," the driver's eyes got big and he shifted a look at the passenger. "I've got a friend over by Maple Grove," he finally said.

"The reason I asked," said the officer, "is that there's a garage over there that could replace that light bulb for you, then all you'd have to do is get the tail light lens when you get home."

The driver nodded nervously, licked at his lips, and shifted his eyes away. "My friend has parts in his garage. I'll bet he can replace it," he said.

"Who's your friend?" the officer asked. "I know quite a few people over to Maple Grove Township. Maybe I know him." Still smiling and acting friendly.

"Who's my friend?" the driver repeated, stalling for time. "Joe. Joe Williams, he said. "No, I don't think you know him. He's new in the area. Just moved in a week or so ago," he said, looking down the road, "from Detroit."

"We gotta get going," the passenger mumbled under his breath. His hands had slipped from the dash and were in his lap. There was something under his left thigh, by the center console. It looked like the butt of a gun.

The officer swiftly pulled his hand out of his pocket. It held the .380 pistol, his back-up.

"Keep your hands on the dash, above the glove box," he told the passenger sternly, holding the pistol alongside the open window so the men could see it. Their mouths hung open in surprise. They got the message.

"What's going on? What'd we do?" the driver questioned.

To the driver; "Put your hands on the steering wheel. Your passenger has something hidden under his left thigh. I told you men that I get nervous. We're going to keep me from getting nervous."

"I ain't got nothin'" the passenger protested defiantly, holding his hands in the air.

"I said, on the dash," the officer demanded a little more forcefully. "We're going to sit here nice and easy-like for a few minutes."

A second county patrol car pulled up behind his, with a blue State Police car driving by and angling in to block the Toyota from the front. The trooper got out, hand on his service weapon.

"Passenger has something under his left thigh," the deputy said.

The State Trooper pulled his weapon and trained it on the passenger. "Take the driver first," he said to the deputy.

"Slowly turn and step out of the car," the deputy said, taking a step back.

The driver shook his head wearily. "It's all a mistake, man," he said. "We don't want any trouble."

"Neither do I," the officer said. "For all of our protection, I'm going to place you in cuffs while I check this out. Nobody's under arrest right now. If there's nothing in the car, would you mind if I have a look?"

The driver let out a sigh, "Yeah, go ahead, man."

The deputy directed the man to face toward the front of the car, hands in the air. "Walk back toward me," he told the driver. "Now, go to your knees. That's good. Now lay flat on your stomach and put your hands behind your back." He cuffed the driver and turned the man over to the arriving county deputy who stood off, watching.

The passenger slumped in his seat, but kept his hands on the dash.

The State Trooper stood back so he could see clearly and ordered the passenger out of the car.

"I ain't got nothin', man," the passenger screwed up his face like he was being wronged, and didn't move.

The state man pulled out his taser and aimed it at the passenger.

"I'm coming out," the man said hurriedly.

The trooper repeated the process that the county deputy had used on the driver. Both men were cuffed and lay face-down on the shoulder of the road.

Two cars went by, heading north. The occupants staring at the scene on the side of the road.

The state cop leaned in over the

passenger's seat and pulled out a hand gun. "Looks like a forty caliber," he said. He pulled out the magazine, "Loaded, with one in the chamber." He pointed the gun into the ditch and racked the slide, then placed the weapon on the hood of the Celica.

The first deputy shivered at the thought of what could have happened.

The policemen looked up as a black suburban pulled alongside. The window eased down. "Still need me?" the officer said.

"Work the car for us?" the state man asked.

The suburban pulled ahead of the state car and parked. He opened up the back and brought the dog out of his cage. They walked to the Toyota, and the trooper spoke to the dog.

The others watched as the dog, a German Shepherd, worked his way around the car, sniffing eagerly, tail wagging.

The first county deputy brought the keys from the front and popped open the trunk.

The dog stopped at the trunk and put its paws up on the lip and whined. He looked nervously back at the deputy.

"Good boy," his handler said.

The others peered in over the dog to look

at a black duffle bag and a kid's Spider Man back pack

"Well, well. Look what we have here," the dog handler said, lifting out the duffle bag.

The dog became agitated and kept looking at the handler, then back to the bag.

The officer gingerly zipped opened the bag. It was full of plastic baggies containing something. He had slipped on a pair of medical exam gloves and reached in to pick up a sample.

"Meth, I'd bet," he said, "and heroin, too." The others nodded in agreement. The officer standing over the car's occupants looked down at them and shook his head.

The handler picked up the back pack. Spider Man was shooting a web from his hand, out toward the viewer.

The dog sniffed the pack, now sitting on the gravel behind the car, and started in whining again. The cop opened it up. It was stuffed full of money. Fifties and twenties, mainly. There was a small baggie of pot in with the cash.

"This your personal stash?" the State Trooper said to the men on the ground.

"We don't know nuthin' about that," the

driver said. "It ain't ours. This is a borrowed car."

"How come it's registered to you over in Romulus?" the state cop asked. "Or, did you have your memory erased coming through the neutral zone?"

One of the county deputies, the oldest one, snickered.

"Huh?" the driver looked up, confused.

"The Romulan Neutral Zone," the state cop answered. "Everybody knows about that."

"Huh?" the man said again, scrunching up his face. His passenger looked bewildered.

The others looked at the State Trooper like he had just gone crazy.

He said, "Star Trek," you guys. "You know, Spock and Kirk." He paused, looking at their blank faces. "Scotty and the rest. The neutral zone was the boundary between the United Federation of Planets and the Romulan Empire. What kind of childhood did you guys have, anyway?"

The officers all laughed. The tension of the arrest was broken. They went on to search the car.

There was more pot hidden under the front seat, along with a loaded pearl-handled revolver directly under the driver's side. The dog had a hit in the back seat. The county deputies pulled the seat to find a brick of brown heroin.

"I didn't know that was in there," the passenger protested. He'd lifted his head a few inches off the gravel road-side. Bits of dirt and gravel clung to the side of his face and his hair. "I was just getting a ride... that's all," he complained.

"What about the gun?" the first county deputy asked, still feeling a little excited about the find.

"That's not my gun. It's his," he nodded toward the driver, laying a few feet away.

"No, man," the driver said. "I'm not going down for your gun, you fool!"

The passenger looked up at the officers, "The gun was on the seat when I got in the car. I just slid it over, to make room. I've never seen it before in my life."

"We'll know whose gun it is when we run the serial number," the state man said. He reached down and plucked the passenger's wallet from his pant's pocket and waved the driver's license at him. "Lamont Brown of Detroit. The gun going to be registered to you?"

"I told you, it's not mine," said an exasperated Lamont. "It's his. So's all this dope. I had no idea it was in the car."

"You lyin' bastard!" shouted the driver. "I get outta these cuffs and you're dead!"

"Okay, okay, men," the State Trooper said, "we'll get this sorted out back in Jackson. Right now, Mr. Green, you're under arrest for possession of a concealed weapon, and drug smuggling. Mr. Brown, the deputies tell me that you're a felon, so you're being charged with drug smuggling, and felon in possession of a firearm."

Both men shook their heads and lay quietly, the fight taken out of them.

A pickup, with a light bar on the roof, approached from the north and slowed. The deputies turned to watch. The truck stopped behind the last deputy's car. Jake LaBlanc got out and walked up to the county deputies.

"Hello, LaBlanc," the first deputy said, recognizing him. "What can we do for you?" He turned to the others, "We're kinda' busy right now."

"I heard the call on my scanner, decided I should come over," LaBlanc said.

"Do you know these men?" the State Trooper asked, glancing down at the two cuffed suspects.

"No, I don't, but I think I know someone who does," LaBlanc said. "Has either Hank McIntyre or Tim Conway been here to talk to these men?" he said with a serious nod at the two.

"Who?" the state man asked. "Nobody's been here. What are you talking about?"

"Hank McIntyre is a former Chicago resident. Big black guy, lives the high life out west of Pulaski. Tim Conway is from Muncie and he has a nice place north-east of Pulaski. They're both in the same township and have no visible means of support. I just thought there might be a connection between these guys from the Detroit area and two men from Muncie and Chicago, both high crime cities."

The police looked at each other, baffled.

"I've heard the McIntyre name," said the first deputy, "but not in a watch-list sense. I thought he was working with the Metro Squad."

"That's what I heard," said the second deputy, shaking his head. "I've never met either man, but it would be news to me if they're involved in this." He gave a look in the general direction of the Toyota.

"We don't know no McIntyre or Conway!" the driver exclaimed from his spot on the ground. He threw a bewildered look at his passenger, who shook his head in agreement.

"The state cop pulled out an ink pen and note pad. He wrote down the names. "I'm not familiar with either person," he said with a shrug, "but it never hurts to look. Stranger things have happened." He tapped his pen for emphasis on the page with the two names, then put them in his shirt pocket.

The first deputy looked incredulous. "LaBlanc, I've not met either man," he said. "But I know I've heard the name McIntyre connected with the Metro Squad. You don't thing he's gone bad, do you?"

"There's a lot of money to be had," said LaBlanc. "It sure wouldn't surprise me. Why, just the other day, a kid crashed a Gator out in Hanover Township. There's a chance that some marijuana was planted on the wreck. I suspect Tim Conway. He was there. My son saw him poking around the wrecked Gator. He could have planted it," he said forcefully.

The state cop looked down at the two men

in cuffs. "Who were you meeting over at Maple Grove?" he asked.

"I told the other guy... my old friend from Detroit. He lives alone, out in the country," the driver replied.

"Black guy?" asked the trooper.

"Yeah," said the driver with a nod.

The second deputy said, "Yeah, that's right, and we're going to look your friend up. What'd you say his name is?"

"Joe Williams," the driver answered.

Turning to LaBlanc, "You know anybody in your township who just moved in from Detroit, or the Detroit area? A black man? Goes by the name of Joe Williams?" he asked, looking down again at the two men on the ground.

"No, but I would bet my life either McIntyre or Conway know him," LaBlanc answered, gazing steadily into the deputies eyes. "Maybe if I talked to these guys, I could find out if they're connected."

The State Trooper stepped forward. "There's no need for that," he said in a serious tone. "It would be best if you leave now. These men are going to the post in Jackson."

Another State Police car pulled up and the

two men were separated and placed in the vehicles. The State Troopers thanked the K9 officer, who tossed a chew toy for the dog, then loaded him into the suburban.

"I'm a little late, but I've got a great story to tell the kids this morning," he said, closing the rear doors on the vehicle.

He drove away to keep his school appointment just as a truck with a roll-off bed came to pick up the Toyota.

LaBlanc walked back to his truck and stood watching for a minute, then got in and left.

The two county deputies approached the State Trooper who looked on as the tow truck driver hooked a cable to the front of the Toyota and eased it up the tilted truck bed.

"What do you think that was about?" asked the deputy who knew LaBlanc. "Should we report this to administration?"

"Put it in your report," the trooper said. "I'll make sure it's reported on my end, too. It may be nothing, but it's got to be checked out."

The deputies thanked him and got in their cars.

Chapter Twenty-four

I looked around the table as Flint and Jordon finished up their story. Hank sat across the long table from me, next to Flint. He listened intently, nodding occasionally.

Kip sat next to me. Deputy Jordon anchored the end of the table, looking at all of us. He and Flint were off duty, and wore civilian clothes.

Nan was at her job at the vet's office and missed the update. Schultzie was at the auto-parts plant.

"As I said, that was yesterday morning," Flint said, looking at us seated around the table. "I know the deputies who were on the scene. They can be trusted to give a pretty accurate report. The arrested men have been transferred to Jackson and are still in custody at the county jail," he said.

"By the way," Jordon added, "Flint and I

explained to the other deputies that there's nothing to LaBlanc's story. Who knows what kind of trouble he's stirred up?"

"I appreciate that," Hank said, looking at Jordon. "It's nice to know we have some friends out there."

"It's interesting that he's thrown my name in there, too," I said. "If his intention is to tie up resources investigating Hank and me, then I guess maybe he's done that."

Hank cleared his throat. "The Metro Squad is getting closer to Mr. LaBlanc, and I believe he's feeling the heat," he said. "We have a reliable mole in the Maple Grove Fire Department, and we're building a case with the prosecutor's office."

I said, "A mole? I thought moles were only in international espionage; like a Russian mole in the pentagon, or the state department."

"Surely, not one of the boys?" Kip looked up. He'd been silently toying with his special chief's coffee cup and now he slid it away to concentrate on Hank.

"I can't say at this time," Hank answered Kip, "but believe me, you'll be the first to know when all of this comes down. And...

don't call me Shirley." He grinned at Kip and then around the table at the rest of us as we laughed.

Then he turned serious, "My concern is that once this drug ring is busted, someone else will move in to fill the void. Nature abhors a vacuum," he said.

"By the way, what happened to the kid in Hillsdale," Kip asked, changing the subject. He picked up his cup to drink.

"The one Tim and I went looking for, or the one we had to chase down?" Hank asked.

"Both," Jordon answered for Kip.

"Start with the Collins kid," Kip said. "Have there been any leads at all? He sipped from his cup, made a face, then set it down. "Cold," he said, looking up at us.

"I got it," Flint said, and got up to make a fresh pot. He turned and faced Hank. "Shouldn't we be eating special 'hot date' doughnuts today?" I could tell he'd been saving this up.

Hank shook his head and waved a hand as the rest of us chuckled. He'd been seeing the lovely Shonda Miles on a regular basis.

"That was a one-time deal," Hank laughed, "too bad you missed out. Maybe it's your turn now." He turned to grin at Flint.

"I'm not about to get tied down," Flint responded while pouring water into the coffee maker.

"That's not what I heard," Deputy Jordon interrupted. "I heard you were tied down last Tuesday!" He looked around the table for a response.

He wasn't disappointed. The group erupted, and we all nodded knowingly. Flint deserved it, he'd cultivated a reputation as a Casanova.

Flint said, "You've gotta get your story straight. That was tied up, not tied down. There's a big difference, you jokers." He was wiping down the counter with a damp paper towel, and turned to grin devilishly at the group. "And," he added gleefully, "if I brought in doughnuts every time that happened, I'd have to quit the fire department. It would get too expensive."

He was met with hoots and derisive laughter.

"Okay, okay, you guys," Hank raised his hands for silence. "There will be no doughnuts today, so get over it. I swear, firemen." He looked at us all with a exasperated look. "Cops, too," he looked at Jordon, who just laughed.

"Now, about Richie Collins," he said, finally getting us back on track. "Shortly before Tim and I left the Hillsdale Fairgrounds last Saturday, Hillsdale County Deputies, backed up by State Troopers out of Jonesville, raided both the Smith farm and that Alisha girl's place."

We looked on expectantly. Hank wagged his head. "They came up empty." He held out his hands, palms up. "No Richie, and no Meagan." He looked around at us. "Right now, my money is riding on Meagan Grawn being the most valuable target," he said.

"I have a feeling that Meagan reports to..." I paused to correct myself, "or used to report to, Jake LaBlanc and his wife, the charming Mrs. LaBlanc."

Flint brought the coffee pot over and worked around the table, filling our cups.

Hank reached over to grab the little bowl containing packets of sugar and creamer. He placed them in the middle of the table.

Kip said, "We've talked about this, and I have to agree with you." He looked up from his coffee as he stirred in some sugar.

"Thanks, Honey," he grinned over a Flint.

Flint waved him off and placed the coffee pot back on the warmer.

I said, "It's just a gut feeling I have, after being out on those rescue runs and up he pops, like the devil or something."

"You're not the only one, is all I can say," Flint said, nodding his head.

Hank said, "The kid we chased across the flea marked turned out sadder but wiser. He's clean."

"No more guests in the basement?" I laughed.

Hank smiled across at me.

"Any word on the burn victim?" I asked. "You know, the guy from the meth lab?" I looked around the table. "I heard on the news that he'd been air-flighted out to the University of Michigan's burn unit."

"Still hanging in there," Flint said. "I'm not even sure the detectives have talked to him. He's pretty messed up. Those meth chemicals are nasty business. I'm telling you, more people, especially the teenagers, should see what happens when they explode."

"Well," Hank said, getting us back on the Richie Collins subject, "the blue pickup wasn't found, either. My hunch is that they moved on to safer pastures. Maybe even left the state. Indiana is close by."

"So's Ohio," Jordon added. From Hillsdale, they could be in Pioneer in a matter of minutes. It's practically a stroll down M99 to the border," he said.

"What about the kids you interviewed who mentioned the rich, blond woman?" I asked.

"They've picked out Mrs. LaBlanc's photo as the woman they met," Hank said, looking across the table at me. "That, plus the background I told you about and what I saw at the big meeting, makes me believe she's more involved than what we'd like to believe."

"So, she's the brains of the outfit," I said, "and the boys work for her."

"Could Jake be bright enough to put together an organization and keep it running?" Hank asked Flint.

"I don't see him keeping it together after a few tragedies," Flint said. He'd taken a seat next to Hank and was sipping his coffee from a ceramic cup with a yellow Tweetie Bird on it. "If the kids were producing for him, he has to be having a hard time supplying the goods, what with them dying off and all," he

said.

Kip said, "The gang, if it's really a gang, sure seems to be accident prone."

We nodded in agreement.

"That's where our guys from Romulus and Detroit come in," Jordon said. "Turns out, they had been scheduled two weeks ago for a delivery to Maple Grove. They were to meet a girl and her boyfriend. They claim they didn't know their names, if you can believe that - just going to meet them at the parking lot of the Gas-N-Go at Maple Grove."

"In a blue Ford pickup?" I asked.

"You got it," Jordon answered with a nod.

"What were they doing with all the money if they were coming here to sell?" Kip asked.

"They'd already made deliveries in Ann Arbor and Jackson," Flint put in. "They're busy boys, apparently."

"Motivated self starters," Jordon said, grinning.

Hank said, "They're off the street, but someone else will step in to take their place, the money is just too good. The guys higher up are who we really want, but they're practically invisible, unless we can get someone to talk."

It was Jordon's turn to speak. "Mr. Brown and Mr. Green tell us that our little group in Maple Grove used to be meth exporters. They were doing so well, they would swap for heroin. Somebody had a nice little import-export business going," he said.

"Mr. Brown, Mr. Green. I suppose LaBlanc plays the part of Mr. White," Flint joked.

The group laughed.

"Jeez," Kip said, "It's a whole sub culture out there that we never knew about."

"To sum it up," Jordon said, "if he's really involved, I believe LaBlanc's in over his head.

Nobody really wants to believe he's into the drug business, I thought.

"How deep are the boys in with him?" Kip asked. "They've been on site, too. Where LaBlanc shows up, one of the boys is almost always with him," he added.

"Like the John Deere Gator crash over in Hanover," I said, feeling my blood-pressure go up a notch. "You know, the one where I planted the pot under the wreck."

"Yeah, and I'm the one who recovered it," Flint said. "I guess we're both guilty of collusion."

Hank said, "The story is that the boys are with their father in official positions, one as the assistant chief, the other as a fire fighter."

"Hard to argue with that, now tell me more about planting the pot under the Gator wreck," Jordon said, looking dead pan.

We looked at him.

"You conducting an investigation?" Kip asked.

For a brief moment, I wondered the same.

"Just want to be loaded with ammo when the questions start about you two," Jordon answered, a devilish grin appearing on his lips.

"That's right," Flint added, barely containing his laughter, "you never know when somebody from internal affairs is going to come poking around. They have to follow up, you know." He looked at Jordon.

"My guess is that there's already rumblings at the state level," Hank said quietly. "How far it'll go, I can't say."

"I was just kidding," Jordon interjected.

We all gave him 'the look.'

I said, "I noticed LaBlanc's son standing around the crash site. He didn't render aid or help remove the victim, just stood around poking through the weeds."

"I thought that was odd at the time," Flint spoke up. "After I found the pot, I knew what he'd been looking for."

I said, "We all did."

"It's now evidence in the on-going investigation being conducted by the Metro Squad," Hank said. "Remember, men, you didn't hear anything here." He glanced around at us.

We made noises of agreement and grew quiet.

"How'd the injured kid turn out, anyway?" Kip asked.

"He's pretty well busted up," Flint said, "but he's going to pull through. Detectives talked to him the next day. He's changing his story ever time he tells it. First, the pot was for a friend down the road. Next time, he's sticking to the story that he'd been going to visit a friend, and didn't know the pot was there."

"Maybe we arrest his father," Hank said, reflectively. "It was his Gator."

"Any guesses as to who showed up to visit?" Jordon asked. "Mark LaBlanc," he said, not waiting for us to answer.

"He's connected, somehow," Kip said.

Flint said, "Getting back to the crash scene, the other deputy told me that Tim went down the slope to help pull up the kid. That's it. He wasn't even near the Gator, that he saw. And, when I showed up, the thing was laying up on it's side, against a tree, all smashed to hell. Schultzie and Norm, from Hanover, already had the victim loaded on the sled and Tim was on the slope helping to pull him up."

"That's the way it happened," I said, shaking my head in agreement.

"And another thing," Flint continued, getting on a roll, his voice rising, "the only reason I went back down there to double check the wreck was because the LaBlancs were acting so weird. Deputy Rakowski was with me. He didn't put the pot there, and neither did I. Tim didn't. Nobody did," he said, jabbing his finger emphatically.

"That's a pretty strong denial," Kip said. "You sure you didn't do it?"

Flint looked like he could strangle somebody.

Kip wiped the smirk from his face.

"That leaves Schultzie," Jordon said.

"I'd never believe that one either."

"I was there when he went down to assist Norm," I said. "At no time did he reach under, or poke anything under the wreck. Neither guy did. They were too busy saving the boy. They didn't do it, and the LaBlancs were standing right there, watching." I shook my head.

"Well, LaBlanc's pointing the finger at you two," Jordon looked at Hank and me. "I think it might be time Flint and I paid him a friendly visit."

"Might not be a bad idea," Hank said. "Listen to his story, see if it changes any. Turn the heat up, so to speak."

I nodded in agreement. Whatever was going on, we were now mixed up in it, up to our eyeballs. It looked more and more like LaBlanc was involved in some kind of funny business. Funny business that resulted in at least three dead kids, and several injuries. The problem was that no one had caught any of them with drugs on them, and getting someone to talk was proving difficult. I wasn't really sure where his wife fit in, but felt she was a major player, too.

I went to the bathroom to get rid of my

coffee. When I got back, the others had stood and were tidying up the table.

Chapter Twenty-five

Hank and I said good-bye to Jordon, Flint, and Kip.

He asked me, "You got time to take a look at your Cub Cadet?"

"Sure," I said, "It's already on blocks and the engine is on the bench." I was thinking maybe we could talk some more.

We got in our trucks, and I led the way out of the parking lot and back toward my place. It was another sunny, warm, early June day. The earth was wide awake and humming after a long winter of cold and snow. My first cutting of hay was in the barn and, except for this LaBlanc mystery, all was right with the world. I powered the windows down to take in some fresh air. Hank followed me the few blocks over to Pulaski Road and we turned right. On the way through Pulaski, I noticed a silver Jaguar convertible parked in front of the general store. A newer one, with a black top, something you don't see every day in our little town.

The general store's front door opened and a man and woman came out of the building and stood in the shade of the covered, concrete porch. Both carried a bottle of orange Nehi pop. I recognized the woman's long, blond hair right away; LaBlanc's wife. Her hair actually shimmered in the sun. She wore a sleeveless red top and black shorts. Again, I couldn't tell you if she had eyes or not. Kip had been right. The woman fairly oozed pheromones.

Instinctively backing off the gas, I slowed to take a better look, hoping Hank wouldn't rear-end the Dodge. I took a quick glance in the mirror. He had backed off, too, and was looking at the car. Probably had already checked out the lovely Mrs. LaBlanc.

That man with her, I knew him from somewhere. Younger guy. Mid thirties, maybe. I drove on by. I wasn't going to stop in the middle of Pulaski Road and stare. The speedometer needle rested on twenty. I hit the gas and drove away.

In the rearview mirror, Hank had flipped

on his turn signal and turned right, onto a side street. I slowed and pulled to the side of the road and watched.

Hank's truck came back out and made a left turn back in front of the general store. I watched as he pulled in next to the Jag.

He got out and stood by the truck door for a moment, then began walking toward the store. The man and woman were now walking across the parking lot, laughing about something. From her reaction, I could tell Mrs. LaBlanc recognized Hank. I couldn't see her expression, but she and the guy stopped and said something to him. He said something, nodded, and walked on into the store. The couple got into the Jag, Mrs. LaBlanc driving, and backed out onto Pulaski Road, then headed south-bound.

Hank came out of the store, returned to his truck, and stared after them. He started the truck and backed out to follow me.

We drove out north of town, with my Dodge leading the way down McDonald Road. I parked and got out of the truck, then waited for Hank to walk over. "You pull in to get a good look at Mrs. LaBlanc?" I asked.

Hank grinned. "I wanted to get a better

look at that Jaguar convertible," he said. "It's an XK8. About a 2012 or so. Even as a used car, it's pricey."

"She does know how to stretch a buck," I said.

Hank laughed. "Probably makes the payments out of her baby-sitting money."

"The guy looks familiar," I said, thinking back to where I'd seen him. "Duke Williams," I said, snapping my fingers and pointing at Hank. "He's on the Maple Grove Fire Department. One of LaBlanc's drinking buddies."

"Looks like he's moved up to a better class of buddy," Hank said, grinning at me.

We walked over to the work shop and I raised the overhead door. "I've got the parts on the workbench over there," I said, nodding. I took a couple of denim shop aprons from a peg. We slipped them on.

I looked at Hank, "Looks like I got the big one," I said, pointing at the aprons. The aprons were really the same size, but Hank's looked more like a postage stamp on him.

I pushed the power button on the C.D. player and some early Motown came on for background music.

"This'll do," Hank smiled.

I pointed to the combination starter-generator that lay on the bench, a clean cloth under it. "Needs these new contact brushes installed," I said, handing Hank a plastic parts bag.

"This is nice," he said, looking over the layout. "You've got the parts all clean and the case is repainted. It'll be like new when I get done." He looked around and grabbed a stool to sit on. It had a red, wooden top.

A few feet away was a yellow-topped stool, Minneapolis-Moline colors. I sat down and went to work on installing a points set on the eight-horse Kohler engine.

"What'd LaBlanc's wife say to you?" I asked as Smokey Robinson finished singing about "My Girl."

"Wouldn't you like to know," he replied, not looking up from the equipment he was working on.

I could see him smirking to himself.

"Actually, I said I liked her car," he said. "She thanked me and complimented my truck. Said she liked old trucks. Her friend told me his dad once had one like it."

"Hmmm," I said. "So, you offer her a ride

in your cool, old truck?"

"Ha!" he replied, "I know someone who would raise an objection to that." He stopped what he was doing and pointed a screwdriver in my direction.

"Well," I said. "The lovely Ms. Miles would certainly understand if you had to pump Ms. LaBlanc for information." I turned on the work stool and faced him, to see his reaction.

Hank grinned, "I think your friend Duke Williams is already doing that."

"No way!" I let my imagination go for a moment.

"Hey," he said, "They were very familiar with each other. I just added two and two, and got four."

"You think Duke's involved in their little side business?" The possibility hadn't occurred to me before.

"Remember the big meeting?"

"Yes," I answered, "where Mrs. LaBlanc had her big coming out." I raised my fingers in quotation marks.

Hank nodded. "Duke sat next to her, on her right. Jake sat on her left. I told you, there's more going on with that woman than meets the eye," he said.

"Jake will kill him," I said, returning to my work. Over on the shelf, The Supremes were singing something about stopping in the name of love.

"I have a feeling the woman is a bit of a *cocotte*," Hank replied.

"Sounds French," I said. "Isn't that a type of bagel or something?" I'd finished setting the gap on the points and put the feeler gauge down.

Hank laughed. "It's French alright. A fashionable woman of, shall we say, loose morals," he said.

"Where was she when I was in high school?" I lamented.

Hank said, "I knew a few like her in my wild, younger days, back before I met my wife." He shook his head, almost sadly. "You knew I was married once?"

"You mentioned it," I said. "She must have been a special girl."

"I'd still be married to her if I weren't such an moron," he said.

I looked at him, blank faced.

He said, "She was a smart girl. Her dad, my ex-father-in-law, is a pastor in a little church in the suburbs of Chicago."

"Baptist?" I prodded.

"One would think. But, no, they were Lutheran. Lot of Germans in the area. They settled in the area back in the eighteen hundreds."

"How did you meet her?" I put my tools down and turned to face him.

"At college. I was playing football at the time. She was in one of my psych classes and I invited her to watch a game. We dated for a year and a half." He shook his head slowly and his shoulders slumped.

I didn't know what to say, so I didn't say anything.

"We lived in Chicago, where I was working my way up through the police department. I'd made it to detective." He looked at me. "You think some of the stuff going on around here is bad, you should have been with me in Chicago," he said. "There were even little kids involved. Some of them ended up dead. Celia and I were thinking of having our own kids, for crying out loud."

Celia, I thought. Finally a name to go with the person.

Hank continued, "The long hours and the situations started to get to me. I couldn't let it go. I broke from my roots and started drinking. At first it was a cold beer after my shift with a buddy on the force. Then it was the hard booze. I didn't have time for my friends, or family. My brother, Harold, didn't know about it. He'd have tried to kick my butt, if he did."

I couldn't imagine too many guys kicking Hank's butt for him, or even trying, for that matter. I picked up a head gasket and tried to act busy fitting it to the engine.

"Celia took my crap for about two years," he said. "Mind you, I wasn't a lush the whole time. I'd have a good month or two, then fall off the wagon. When she finally left me, I'd hit rock bottom."

"What'd you do?" I couldn't help asking.

"There was a little baptist church in the neighborhood of our precinct headquarters. I'd worked there with the kids and knew the pastor. About five or six of the men and a few of the sisters came to see me. I guess you'd call it an intervention. Believe me, they knew all about drunks and ruined lives. Most of them had been through it."

He sat facing me on the work stool, his hands in his lap.

I just nodded.

"They got me into the meetings, kinda like AA. I started going to bible study on Wednesday nights."

"Did it help?" I asked. I felt I had to say something.

"Yes, some. I'd go for a while then drop out. Then go back again. Then I realized I had to break my ties with my job and acquaintances. I took some time off from the force and went down to the farm."

"No chance of reconciliation?" I asked.

"I tried, but she'd heard it too often by that time. My father-in-law wanted us to get back together. That man is a saint. I still send him an e-mail or a card every so often." He let out a sigh.

"How'd your mom take it?" I took a chance.

"She was devastated. Dad wasn't much better. I thought they'd disown me. They even ratted me out to my brother and sister. It took me a while before I could look Harold in the eye. Good thing my sister, Sarah, was in Terra Haute. I felt like an oriental son who'd brought dishonor on the family."

"What happened?" I asked.

"Mom came down to the farm and took charge. I don't know what Harold and the family thought about it. He's got a wife and two kids, you know. Well, Mom hit that place like a hurricane. Harold put us up in the little house where Grandma lived before she passed away.

Mom made me her special project. A Marine Corps Drill Sargent has nothing on my momma. I tell you, Conway, she had me working in the barn, cutting wood, and attending church about a dozen times a week." He grinned and shook his head.

I stared at him, waiting for more. This was too good to miss.

"If that woman couldn't scare the devil out of someone, she'd sure try to work him out," he said. "I looked on it like it was my punishment for driving off the woman I loved."

I had to laugh in spite of myself, and wasn't sure if I wanted to ever meet Hank's mom.

"Dad seemed okay about Mom coming down to work me over," he said. "I guess he needed the break." Hank laughed along with me.

"You know, in a way, Shonda sort of reminds me of Celia. They share a few mannerisms, both are organized, and have a great sense of humor. Good looking, too," he concluded.

"Shonda know about any of this?" I asked.

"Some," he said, "just the general details. I'm sure it'll all come out." He picked up a wrench and turned back to the work bench. He started humming along to the music on the C.D. player.

I grinned at him from the other end of the bench.

We worked for another hour or so. Much to Hank's delight, my wife surprised us with a couple of cold Dr. Peppers. She brought them out with a plate of bagels for a snack.

"Cocotte," Hank said, holding one up.

"What?" my wife replied, curiously looking at me. I burst into laughter. She stared at us like we were the village idiots, shook her head, and walked out.

Chapter Twenty-six

I woke up early the next morning with that old ache in my right shoulder. Must have aggravated it wrenching on the lawn tractor engine. In the half-light of dawn, I fumbled in the bathroom for some Motrin, downed a couple, and headed downstairs to the kitchen to make a pot of coffee.

I nearly jumped when the cell phone rang. It was Hank.

"Hope I didn't wake you," he said.

"No, I'm just dumping water into the coffee maker," I replied sleepily.

"Dump it back out," he said, "I'm buying breakfast. Pick you up at your place?"

"What?" I rubbed my eyes with my free hand.

"I had a call from Flint last night," he explained. "He and Ned Jordon paid a little social call to LaBlanc yesterday evening, before going on duty."

"They sure didn't wast any time," I replied, looking out the window at the brightening sunrise.

"They couldn't lay out too much to him without tipping their hand about the Metro Squad investigation," Hank said. "We'll talk over breakfast."

"Well, if you're buying, how can I say no? Let me take a quick shower and I'll be ready," I said, glancing up at the kitchen clock. Five-thirty. The clock up in the hallway chimed once for the half-hour.

I grabbed a pencil from the holder on the counter and wrote a note for the wife, then jumped in the shower.

Twenty minutes later, Hank's truck came in the drive. I checked the door lock, then stepped out the back door, off the deck, and into the yard.

Hank looked tired, almost worn out, but he greeted me with a big smile on his face as I climbed into the truck.

"I really need a cup of coffee," he said, steering the truck out my driveway.

"You look like you've been rode hard and put away wet," I said, giving him a good look-over. I wondered if he'd been up all night working with the Metro Squad.

He was silent for a moment. "Well, rode hard would be one way to describe it," he said, staring over at me through bleary eyes.

"Actually, ridden for miles, late into the night, is more like it." He managed a feeble grin.

"What kind of miles?" I asked, starting to catch on. "Would this have anything to do with the lovely Shonda Miles?"

His look told me all I needed to know.

"This is our secret," he said. "Don't say a word to the boys. I'll never hear the end of it. Especially from Flint."

I smiled and nodded knowingly.

"Besides," he said, "I'm a little confused over this. I didn't plan it. It just happened. We went out for dinner, went back to my place for T.V. Next thing you know..." he shrugged and glanced over at me.

"Where'd you go for dinner?" I asked. That was the only detail I felt safe asking about.

"The Finish Line, down in Hillsdale," he answered. "*You* would wonder about the food, jeez."

I shrugged and raised my eyebrows.

"I don't know what the pastor will say," he continued. "Hey, maybe I can use this as confession," he said, looking over at me.

"So how come you're up so early? I asked. Anything to change the subject.

"Girl had to get up for a meeting or something or other," he replied.

"Oh," I said.

We'd turned north on Pulaski Road, toward Concord, and rode on in silence for a few minutes.

"First time for a sleep-over?" I pried.

"First time," he said in a tired, but contented voice.

I didn't know what to say. "Don't kill yourself over it," I finally said. That drew an evil chuckle from Hank.

We drove north, around Swains Lake, and on into the slumbering village of Concord. It looked like the place was deserted, then I remembered it was Saturday. Instead of everyone heading out to M60 in their cars, like water draining from a bathtub, they were still sleeping in. We soon arrived at the Main Street Cafe, Hank parked the truck and we walked in.

Several men sat around the liar's table at the center of the restaurant, laughing and arguing over something. Soon the smart phones came out and they started researching on-line to support their arguments. They had barely looked up as we entered. A few nodded and said "Good Morning," then went back to their research.

We took our seats at a table along one wall. Hank claimed the gunslinger's seat and sat down where he could watch the door.

A waitress brought coffee cups and a carafe. She poured us each a cup of coffee, left some silverware, and walked away.

"LaBlanc has changed his tune," Hank said.

"How so?" I stirred in a packet of sugar and some creamer.

"Flint and Jordon cornered him at the Gas-N-Go. He now seems to think he may have been mistaken about the pot under the wrecked Gator. Also, he's back-tracking on the accusations about me having a side business to support my farm. Flint and Jordon brought up the subject about that little problem with the checks from the woman's auxiliary. That got his attention."

I raised my eyebrows and looked at him

across the table. "So it's true?"

"It's true. Flint said that Jake tried to shift the blame to Duke Williams. He claims Williams has debt problems. Gambling or something."

"Spending money on that hot blond, Jake's wife?" I asked.

"That's a possibility," Hank replied, looking up from the menu that the waitress had dropped off. "The State Police have been called in by the township supervisor."

"Stan Moore," I said, thinking back to the accidental meeting with him in the parking lot of the Maple Grove Fire Department. The meeting that really got the ball rolling on all this mess.

"Yeah, Stan Moore," he said. "A handwriting analysis expert will clear up the little matter about the checks," Hank said.

I had a thought. "Suppose the signatures don't match Jake LaBlanc's. I think the best bet is to look at Mrs. LaBlanc."

Hank shook his head. "We might think so, but the county guys seem to think LaBlanc's the mastermind in all of this, with a little help from his unwitting sons, of course."

"I believe they're wrong," I said. "As

I've said before, I have a gut feeling the lovely Mrs. LaBlanc's involved, if not the brains, and the rest are caught up in varying degrees."

"You'll get no argument from me," Hank shrugged and spread his hands.

The waitress arrived, expectantly holding her pencil and order pad up in front of her.

We placed our orders and she went away, but not before smiling sweetly at Hank.

I looked at him and shook my head.

He grinned back at me. "Williams doesn't seem to need the money," he said, setting his coffee cup down. "I can tell you that he isn't involved in the manufacturing or the distribution of the meth."

"How did you come to know this?" I asked. "Don't tell me..."

He nodded, "I've got my sources."

We talked a little more and listened in on the conversation at the liar's table. They were discussing the upcoming fortunes of the local high school basketball team, the Yellowjackets.

The waitress brought our breakfast platters and set them down. "Anything else?" she smiled.

"We're good, thank you," Hank said.

We dove into our meal.

Twenty minutes later, Hank paid the tab, then gave me a ride back home.

"Remember, you heard it here first," I said before closing the pickup door, "It's Mrs. LaBlanc." Even though I didn't really want to believe it.

I thanked him for the breakfast, and watched him drive off, headed back to his place for a well-earned nap.

I snoozed on the couch while the wife played in her quilt room.

Around ten o'clock my cell phone rang. It was Kip. "Thought you'd like to know," he said, "Duke William's wife has reported him missing. He didn't come home last night, nor this morning, either," he said.

"Doesn't he have to be missing for twenty-four hours before the police get involved?"

"Something like that," Kip said. "His wife called Ned Jordon directly this morning. Ned called Flint and Flint made a few calls."

"Has anyone thought to contact LaBlanc's wife?" I asked.

"What?" He sounded surprised.

"Hank and I saw them come out of the

Pulaski General Store yesterday. She was driving a silver Jaguar convertible.

"No kidding?" Kip asked, unbelieving.

"Wouldn't it be wild if they both were missing?" I asked.

"That'd be something, all right," Kip said. "Well, I'll let you go. Just thought you'd like to know, is all."

I thanked him for keeping me up to date and hung up.

What an interesting development. Jake's drinking buddy comes up missing. Maybe he'd turn up today, but again, maybe he and the gorgeous Mrs. LaBlanc had split for parts unknown. Split in that silver Jag.

Chapter Twenty-seven

I dropped in at the fire station on Monday morning. Kip's truck was out front as well as Nan's black SUV. Fred's truck was there, too. It was still early, so they were probably on their way to work. Kip had finished the garage down on Mosherville Road and had started construction on a carport over in Hanover.

They were sitting around Kip's desk, drinking coffee. He had slid his lap top aside to make room for a plate of homemade cookies.

"What's the occasion?" I asked Nan.

"I didn't make them," she said. "Fred brought them in." She pointed with her coffee mug.

"Maureen made them to celebrate my new job," he said, with a broad smile. "I start tomorrow at Highway Trucking down in

Hillsdale. I'll be running the truck repair garage. Help yourself, Tim. They're sugar cookies." He pointed at the plate.

I reached for one, then turned to the coffee machine on the shelf behind Kip's desk.

"I can't wait for my daughter to get old enough to bake," Kip said, waving the cookie he was eating. He held it out and inspected it like it was a fine work of art.

"Why don't you guys learn to bake your own?" Nan complained. "Why is it always the female who has to do the cooking, baking, and cleaning?"

"Don't you have someplace to go?" Kip gave her a grin.

"I'm serious," she said. "I'd like to meet a guy who can cook and knows how to run a vacuum and do laundry."

Kip reached into his desk drawer and produced the card - the business card he'd been saving for just such an occasion.

"Here," he said, handing the card to Nan, "I hear this guy's been to cooking school and does all his own house work. Plus, he drives a Corvette."

Nan looked at the card and made a face like she was going to snap.

"Men!" she declared, ripping the card in half and throwing it in the trash container by Kip's desk.

Fred laughed, while I turned away so she couldn't see me smile. Kip grinned like a fool.

Nan glanced at the clock on the wall above Kip's desk. "I've got to get going anyway," she said, giving Kip a sour look. "Dogs and cats are a whole lot better behaved than some people I know."

She picked up her coffee cup. "I came in to find out about Duke Williams," she said. "Think you could fill me in before I go?"

"No news yet," Kip said, turning serious. "He's still missing. Mrs. LaBlanc isn't, though," he said looking at me.

"Shoots that theory," I said, before sipping my coffee.

Nan looked at me curiously.

"When I heard that Williams was missing, I thought maybe he and the lovely Mrs. LaBlanc had disappeared together," I said.

"What's behind that?" Nan asked.

"They were seen together in her car," I said, not wanting to get into the complete story.

"Probably innocent enough," Nan said. "After all, they're both adults married to other people, and hang out in the same crowd."

"The county deputies are looking into it this morning," Kip said.

"Where's his truck?" Fred asked. "Anybody seen it?" He leaned forward and took another cookie.

"Flint tells me it's missing, too," Kip replied. "There's still a chance he'll come crawling back to his wife, all hung over and asking forgiveness."

"I'd change the locks," Nan said. She stood up and prepared to leave. "Tell Maureen thanks for the cookies," she said to Fred.

"Have a good day," Kip said as she left.

She waved and was out the door.

Kip looked at me. "You think it can be taped up?" He pointed toward the trash can.

Fred and I laughed with him.

Kip said, "The word on the street is that a state forensic accountant is meeting today with LaBlanc."

"That can't be good," I said.

"What's a forensic accountant do?" Fred looked at us.

"That's a person who looks at your income

and life-style," I said. "They'll look into tax returns, credit card receipts, purchases, and compare it all to your cash flow."

"Uh, oh," Kip said, "think they'll find that silver Jag?"

I shrugged. "Who knows? I don't know that much about it. I believe the LaBlancs are in for some seat squirming, though."

"I'd have no trouble with the state accountants," Fred said. "I don't have any assets, to speak of."

"You've got a daughter who can bake cookies," Kip laughed.

Fred smiled and nodded in agreement.

"Hank was concerned that they'd be coming after us," I said, "after LaBlanc shot his mouth off with the State Trooper at that traffic stop on Moscow Road."

"Jordon, and our man, Flint, took care of that," Kip said, looking at me. "Hank's buddies in Detroit put in a good word, too."

Our cell phone pagers beeped at once. A male dispatcher called; "Pulaski Rescue, man in the water, pond in nine-hundred block of Odem Road, cross, Anderson."

We looked at each other. "That's down in the south-east corner of the township," Fred said. "Kind of deserted out there."

"That's a swampy area," Kip said, "lots of holes to fall into." He picked up his phone and called in.

We stood and walked to the rescue van. Kip ran to his truck and got out his dive gear. "Who knows?" he asked, in answer to our looks.

"I'll follow in my truck," I said, turning for the parking lot.

Kip and Fred got in Rescue 1. The lights and siren came on and out the door and down the road they went.

I jumped in the Dodge and followed. We went east to Anderson and turned south. At Odem we turned east again. A woman stood in the front yard of a house, smoking a cigarette and watching us go by. Two little kids were chasing a yellow kitten around in the yard behind her,

A mile on down, a county sheriff's car was parked on the right side of the road, lights flashing. The officer waved us down and pointed back a trail to our right. We pulled up. The cop was our buddy, Ned Jordon. Kip leaned out the window.

"A body floating in the pond, about a quarter mile back," Ned said. "The trail goes through some fields, then cuts left through some trees. I had my car back there. It's firm enough for your rescue unit, but I wouldn't get too close to the pond."

"Who called it in?" Kip asked, turning the wheel.

"Some kids were back playing around," Jordon said. "They saw something floating in the water, about fifty to sixty feet or so off shore, and ran to the house and told their dad. He's the one who called."

I followed the rescue van back the trail, the long grasses brushing against the side of the trucks. Jordon followed behind me in his police car. We traveled along a soybean field on the right, went through a tree line, then along another bean field.

The trail bent left through a small group of trees and sumac, the branches rubbing the side of the rescue and grabbing at the mirrors of my Dodge.

We pulled into an open area and slowed. There was another sheriff's car already there. The deputy, a man I didn't know, stood at the edge of the pond with two elementary-age boys. When he saw us coming in, he ran to his patrol car and pulled it ahead, out of our way.

I parked the Dodge to one side. Jordon stopped his patrol car behind me. We got out and walked through the matted down grass to the edge of the pond. I guessed it to be about an acre or so in size, and probably not too deep. There were a couple muskrat houses on the far side, rising like little, brown-matted islands. A pair of mallards had built their nest on top of one.

The ground under-foot was firm on our side, but looked marshy across the water, on the far shore. Pond lilies grew in clusters and cattails sprouted at the water's edge.

The boys turned to face us as we walked up. "Out there," one of them said, pointing.

We could plainly see something floating in the water, most of it just under the surface. It was definitely a body. A man's body. He was face down, dressed in a short-sleeved, white shirt and dark pants. I could see dark stains on the shirt. His brown hair floated around his head like a lazy, wavy halo.

"The M.E. coming?" Kip turned to the deputies who stood next to us. Jordon introduced us to officer Isaac.

"He's on his way," Isaac said. "The kids' dad called it in. I was the first one here and talked to the dad. He's gone up to the house to get his boat, but will be right back. Looks like we're gonna need that boat." He turned to look out at the pond.

"Probably," Kip said, "unless we can snag him with a hook and line."

I looked at Kip. "You know you're going in the water," I told him. "We don't know what other items are on the bottom of the pond." I waved an arm toward the water for emphasis. Flint asked, "Should we call in the rest of the county dive team to help out?"

Kip sighed. "No, not yet. Let me go in first." He glanced at us, then back out at the floater. "I'll get my gear out of the back," he said, turning to the rescue unit. "I'm not going in with just my underwear on." He gave a quick look over his shoulder at the smiling deputies.

"Never stopped you before," Fred said, laughing.

I wondered what the story was behind that. Next chance I got, I'd have to ask.

Fred said, "I'll give you a hand with the gear." The two walked to the van and got in the back.

I stood on the shore with Jordon, Isaac,

and the two boys. "Is it really a man?" the taller boy asked Deputy Isaac." I took the kid to be the older brother, they looked so much alike. They both were sandy haired, freckled, skinny, but all muscle, like a lot of little farm kids.

"Afraid so," Deputy Isaac replied.

"What was he doing in our pond?" his little brother asked, wide eyed. "There aren't any big fish. Just frogs, turtles and polliwogs."

"Maybe he was trapping muskrats," his older brother said. "I seen one yesterday, over in the weeds by the shore." He pointed toward the far side.

I felt the presence of someone walking through the tree line and turned as a man approached. I'd expected the boys' father, but was greeted by our man, Flint.

He called the deputies by name, and nodded to me. "I parked over by the field," he said. "Figured it'd be crowded over here." He smiled at the boys as he stepped over to stand next to me.

"Bets?" he asked in a low voice.

"That's our guy all right," I said in a voice just above a whisper. "It's Duke. I can feel it in my bones."

"I got a steak dinner says you're right," he answered.

"No sign of his truck," I said, pointing at the ground. "No tracks."

"It'll turn up," he mumbled. He looked around at the other officers, who were standing back, talking quietly among themselves.

The kids had wandered along the shoreline and were crouched down in the weeds, looking at something at the water's edge. It jumped in with a splash and was gone. The older boy threw a stick in after it and laughed.

"Wonder when Jake's going to show up," Flint said.

Isn't today his meeting with the state accounting expert?" I asked.

"Should be done by now," he said. "Could be he already knows what we're going to find here." He looked around as though expecting to see LaBlanc pop out of the weeds at any moment.

Kip and Fred returned from the rescue van. Kip had put on his black wetsuit and was lugging a single air tank. Fred carried his swim fins for him.

A tractor pulling a flatbed hay wagon came

through the trees from the bean field. There was a small row boat rattling along, upside down, on the wagon.

"Dad!" The boys went running over to the tractor. Their father pointed at them and they stopped at a safe distance. He idled the diesel and climbed down from the seat.

The deputies went over to help unload the boat. They carried it over and slid it, bow first, into the pond. A set of oars were bungied inside. The farmer leaned over and held on to the edge so Fred and I could climb in.

The boys crowded up, expecting to climb aboard, too. Their father told them to get out of the way.

"Yes sir," they replied. They must have been used to following directions, as they immediately stepped back, all the time intently watching us.

Kip slipped on his swim fins and waded into the water. It was up to his knees. "A little muddy," he said, looking up at us. He grabbed the side of the boat for stability, causing it to rock. I thought he'd dump us in the muddy water.

"I don't want to get wet!" Fred exclaimed.

The deputies laughed at us. Kip ignored them and took another step. "I'm almost to my knees in mud," he said, sounding concerned. The water was stirred up, thick and smelling like rotted vegetation.

"Shift your weight," I told Fred, as I leaned away from Kip's side. "Now, Kip, pull yourself up using the side of the boat for leverage. Remember, Fred doesn't want to get wet."

"You got that right," Fred said, scooting to the other side. He held a coiled line attached to an orange float and a black body-bag in his hands.

Kip leveraged himself out of the mud while I grabbed up an oar. Leaning alongside, I drove the oar into the muddy bottom and shoved us out into deeper water.

"I can swim now," Kip said, letting go of the boat and causing us to tip precariously before sliding into the middle and leveling out. The boat's flat bottom slapped against the water as it righted itself. Up in front, Fred was hanging on for dear life.

Kip put his mouth piece in, pulled down his swim mask, slipped under the water, and swam the last twenty yards out to the body. I crouched on my knees and used the oar like a canoe paddle to work us closer. The water appeared to be about six or eight feet deep. There were a few weeds and lily pads, but otherwise I could see clear to the dark bottom.

The male duck had been watching our floundering about from the far side of the pond. He stepped off the muskrat house and swam in circles, the better to keep an eye on us, just daring us to come closer. His little brown mate hunkered down on the nest. I thought I could see tiny yellow duck bills and bright eyes peering from beneath her wings.

Kip surfaced next to the body, treading water, and looking our way. Fred leaned out and handed him a small anchor on the line attached to the orange buoy. Kip took it and dropped it beneath him.

"How deep?" Fred asked.

"Right here? About eight feet," Kip said, confirming my earlier guess.

"There's a hole farther out that might be a spring. I don't know if this pond has a drain channel or not," he said. "Though it must, if it's spring fed."

"Anything on the bottom?" I asked, trying

to see down beneath the body.

"Nothing I can see," he answered. I'll get the county dive team out here to give it a good going-over. He looked at the floater, then back at us in the boat. "I think he was put in here after he died," Kip said, gripping the bow and guiding the boat a little closer to the body.

Fred had on a pair of blue, medical gloves. He leaned out over the front to help pull the corpse into the boat and onto the open black bag that he'd spread out on the bottom. Because of the boat's small size, the bag was draped up and over the middle seat and almost to the back. We soon had the victim flopped over the seats, too.

I gasped as I stared into the lifeless face of Duke Williams. Kip was right. He hadn't drowned. We looked him over. The small, matted hole in the back of his head told me he was dead before he hit the water. There were two small holes in the back of his shirt, too, surrounded by a dark stain of dried blood that hadn't yet been soaked away by the water. The fabric near the wounds looked like it'd been tie-dyed.

My eyes met Fred's. He shook his head.

"Lord have mercy," he said quietly.

"He must have known his killer," I told Fred, "to let him get that close behind him."

I hated to think Duke had been murdered by one of his friends. I hated even more to think on my other theory, that he'd been overpowered by at least two other people. Armed and dangerous people. They'd killed him execution style, then dumped his body. I didn't mention those disturbing thoughts to Fred. He was already upset enough to see a fellow fireman, dead, with a hole in his head.

"I'll bet the autopsy will show no water in the lungs," Kip said over the side of the boat. He hung on with one hand. I picked up the oar. With Kip kicking along in the water, I worked the oar on the other side and we thumped and splashed along, guiding the boat back toward shore.

A plain, black car pulled through the gap in the trees and parked next to the farm tractor.

Hank McIntyre got out of the passenger's side while Detective Kuhlbaugh slid from behind the wheel. Kuhlbaugh looked almost normal; clean-shaven, with blue-jeans, red golf shirt and baseball hat.

They walked to the bank, shaded their eyes to look out at us, then said something to the deputies, who nodded and stepped closer to help pull the boat in.

Kip held onto the side and pulled himself along to the shoreline. The mud from the bottom was still stirred up and stinking. The farmer stood on the hay wagon with his sons, watching in fascination. Hank reached out and helped Kip over the slippery weeds and onto solid ground. Fred and I crouched low over the body in the bottom as the deputies lifted and slid the prow of the boat up onto the bank.

"Tim Conway," Hank nodded and held out his hand.

"Hank McIntyre," I replied, "good to see you." I took his hand and stepped up and out of the boat.

Flint stepped forward and helped Fred over the gunwale and onto solid ground.

We turned to the boat and slid it up over the grass and onto the ground. I glanced over to make sure the boys were still standing with their dad.

Hank and Kuhlbaugh were looking at the body. "I never thought it'd come to this,"

Hank said, staring down at Duke's lifeless form in the bottom of the boat.

I felt numb, seeing him like that. Sure, he wasn't a friend, but he was a fellow fireman, and I'd seen him around the area and at a few training sessions over the years.

It came to me. I looked at Hank, then at Kuhlbaugh. "He was your mole," I said.

"How'd you know that?" Kuhlbaugh asked.

"I told you he was a bright boy," Hank said, glancing at Kuhlbaugh.

"Do you think this had anything to do with Jake's wife?" I asked.

"That, or LaBlanc's little enterprise," Kuhlbaugh said with a nod. "Look at his skin. He hasn't been in there more than a day, if that."

Hank and I nodded in agreement.

"Somebody's getting desperate," Hank said.

A minivan pulled in through the trees and drove up behind the rescue unit. The M.E. got out. Flint and the other deputies greeted him.

They pointed over at the boys, and went through the story of how the kids found the body. Kip pointed at the orange float out in the pond.

I gave a deputy my name and told him what

I saw, then walked over to the farmer and the boys to say good-bye. Kip had slipped out of his swim fins and gingerly walked along with me. We stood by the wagon, looking up at the man and his sons.

"By the way," Kip said to the boys, "there are fish in there. I saw several sunfish, and I scared up a bass about ten inches long." He held out his hands to indicate the length. "Where there's one, there's got to be more," he said, grinning up at the boys.

The brothers looked at each other in amazement. We'll come back later with our fish poles," the older one said. Their dad laughed and reached out and messed up their hair.

I left them and got in my truck to leave.

Chapter Twenty-eight

Two days after we pulled Duke Williams' body out of the pond, his truck turned up. The Steuben County, Indiana, Fire Department had gotten a call about a vehicle fire and discovered the pickup in a wooded area. The cab was fully engulfed when they arrived, the front tires burned to the ground, nobody around. The plates were missing, but the Sheriff's Department had traced the truck through the VIN number and called Jackson.

Jackson County Sheriff's detectives were en-route to rural Angola, Indiana.

I was helping the wife change the sheets on the bed, and was having a hard time getting my side tucked in to her liking. It sure seemed okay to me, being a fitted sheet, after all.

After a few tries at getting the corners right, she was happy. "I'm telling your therapist about this sheet fetish," I said.

She said, "Thirty-five years of marriage to you, and I still can't get good help making the bed." She looked over at me, eyes bright, lips smiling. She snatched up a spray dispenser from the dresser and began spraying some smelly chemical stuff on the pillows and sheets.

"What are you doing?" I asked somewhat aghast.

"Spraying on lavender scent," she said, sucking in a deep breath. "Doesn't it smell clean and fresh?"

"You're kidding, right?" I asked. "That stuff is pure chemicals. It's no wonder all my joints ache," and I rubbed my right shoulder. The same shoulder I'd messed up during the fire in Muncie.

"This isn't making your joints hurt," she snapped.

She looked angry, but I saw a little smile sneak through.

She said, "Falling through a floor might make them ache a little, but not this stuff." She waved the bottle at me.

I made an attempt to steer the subject down a different path. "Hmm, clean sheets," I said, running my hand over the bed, "You know what this means?"

"Dreams are good, she said, turning to pick up the laundry basket.

My phone rang. I picked it up off the dresser and answered on the second ring. Hank was on the other end.

"You sitting down?" he asked.

I glanced at the bed.

"Duke Williams' pickup turned up yesterday morning outside of Angola, Indiana."

"What?!"

"You said it'd turn up," he said, "and it did."

I sat down on the bed as Hank filled me in on the discovery of Duke's truck.

I looked over at my wife. She stood in the bedroom doorway and listened in on my end of the conversation. I patted the bed and smiled. She shook her head and left.

"A farmer called in the fire early yesterday morning," Hank said. "The guy was getting up to do his morning chores and noticed the glow in a group of trees on the back of his farm. His place is out east of Angola, south of Highway 20. The Steuben deputies have the truck cordoned off with crime scene tape, waiting for the Michigan people," he said, finishing his update.

"Was there a body in the truck?" I asked. I was thinking this might be a good time for Richie Collins or Meagan Grawn to turn up. Maybe both.

"Haven't heard either way," Hank said. "Kuhlbaugh is on his way down there this morning. I'm sure he'll give us a call."

"It might take a while to get there," I said, "especially if it's off the beaten path. I wouldn't mind going down myself, just to check out the truck."

Hank said, "I was just thinking the same thing."

"They could have taken one of a hundred routes to get there," I pondered out loud, thinking of how Duke's truck could have shown up in Indiana. "The most direct is M-49 south, out of Hillsdale County and into northwest Ohio, to U.S.20. Then, go west to Steuben County, in Indiana."

"Maybe, or maybe they took back roads all the way down," Hank replied. "That is, if they know the countryside."

"I guess my point is, somebody must have seen the truck," I said, "somewhere."

"I hear it was a red Ford crew-cab," Hank said.

I noticed he used the word "was."

"That's right," I said, "an F250, four-wheel drive. He took good care of it. No dents and always washed and waxed."

"Did it have a light bar?" Hank asked.

I thought back to the few times I'd seen the truck, when Duke had driven to training or to a fire, like the one out on South Stone Road. "Yes, I believe it did," I answered.

"You feel up for a ride today?" Hank asked.

"I'm ready to go," I told him.

I put my hand over the phone, checked with the wife, and got the all-clear.

"Good," Hank said. "I'll pick you up in fifteen minutes."

Before I could get out the door, I had to bring the wife up to speed on the new developments.

"Be careful," is all she had to say, before kissing me on the cheek.

"I'll help with the clean sheets later," I smirked.

"Get out!" She laughed.

Hank's truck was just pulling up to the

parking area behind the house as I walked off the deck. I climbed in.

"M-49 south?" he raised his eyebrows questioningly.

"We could do that," I nodded. "That, or go over to I-69, south to US-20 and cut back east," I said.

"Let's assume these people are keeping their heads down," Hank said. "What would they do?"

"They'd go down M-49 through Camden and on into Ohio," I replied. When they hit US-20, it would be a short drive toward Indiana and all that empty farmland.

Hank was quiet for a moment, thinking.

"Why go all the way to Indiana?" he asked. "We've got enough empty farmland around here, and a lot more woods to hide a vehicle in than they have in Indiana. And," he continued, "why burn it? I'd just wipe it down and dump the thing." He shook his head, unbelieving. "Doesn't make a lot of sense, does it?" he asked.

"Maybe they used the truck to transport something, or somebody," I said, thinking hard. "Or, maybe they used it to go pick somebody up in Indiana. Somebody with a broken down truck," I said. A funny feeling came over me.

"Maybe two somebodies," Hank responded. He reached over and tapped me on the shoulder. "I bet we find a body when we get down there," he said, eyes bright with excitement.

"A body, or two bodies, that they aren't telling us about!" I exclaimed suddenly.

"Indiana, here we come!" Hank hollered, raising a hand to give me a high-five.

We drove on south to Jonesville, as excited as school kids, then over on US-12 to south-bound M-49 on the east side of Allen.

Hank drove us through the farming villages of Reading and Camden, and into Ohio. We came to U.S. Route 20 and headed west, toward Indiana. Off to our left, over the corn fields, we could see the tops of big trucks on I-90, the Ohio turnpike. Once across the state line, I-90 became the Indiana toll road. Into the Hoosier state, US-20 crossed under the toll road and we were well on our way toward Angola.

We rode along between corn and soybean fields for another half-hour. The miles seemed to melt away as we talked, only stopping once for a coffee and bathroom break on the whole trip.

    Just before Indiana Route 1 crossed Highway 20, we saw an Indiana State Highway Patrol car at the side of the road. It blocked a narrow lane going south to a small woodlot. Hank slowed to a stop and poked his head out the window. A young, black, Indiana State Trooper climbed out of the car, put on a Smokey Bear hat, and walked over. He was a big guy, almost as big as Hank, and he didn't look too friendly.

    "U.S. Marshals Service, pleased to meet you." Hank held out his official identification wallet with the photo and badge.

    The trooper took it, looked at Hank, then at me. A little suspiciously at me, I thought. With this guy, I was wishing I had a badge, too.

    "This is my associate, Tim Conway," Hank said, grinning at the stony-faced trooper. "Formerly of the Muncie, Indiana Fire Department," he added.

    I had that old feeling that he was going to get me arrested. I shuddered at the thought of spending time in the State Reformatory down at Pendleton. I'd gone on a tour of the place as a senior in high school. The whole auto-shop class went, and it scared the hell out of us. The auto-shop teacher must have thought his class full of rambunctious, teenage boys needed the experience.

"Right this way, sir," the trooper handed the wallet back to Hank and walked to his patrol car. The man never smiled. Not once.

He backed his car away from the trail and pointed.

We smiled and waved as we turned in. He didn't wave back.

"That went well," Hank said. "Hope I used my turn indicator when I turned. That guy would run us in for sure."

"He was probably voted Mr. Personality in Trooper School," I said.

Hank turned to me and grinned while reaching down to put the truck into four-wheel drive.

We drove slowly back the graveled, bumpy lane between knee-high corn fields that seemed to never end. I could imagine getting out of the truck and wandering off through a mature corn field, never to be seen again. After what seemed like forever, but was probably only about five minutes or so, we arrived at a small woodlot of about three or four acres.

The trail led into the trees and opened into a large, circular clearing. Somebody's camp ground, I thought.

Behind a band of yellow crime scene tape, in the middle of a scorched circle of grass, rested the charred hulk of an extended-cab pickup truck. The first thing I noticed, other than the paint being burned off, was that the tires were burned away to wire cords and the vehicle rested on the steel rims. The window glass was gone, either broken or melted away.

"Look at the light bar," Hank pointed as he slowed his pickup. The plastic had all melted down, either finally burning up, or pooling in black globs on the cab roof.

Kuhlbaugh's black sedan was parked to one side, next to a Michigan State Police cruiser. There were two Indiana police vehicles parked there, too.

Only two men in uniform were there to greet us. The rest wore civilian clothes. They looked up as we drove in.

Kuhlbaugh was standing beside the blue Michigan car, talking to an Indiana State Trooper, one of the two in uniform. He said something to the trooper and turned to walk our way. Another man walked with him.

Hank and I got out of the truck.

"Hank, Tim," Kuhlbaugh greeted us. "This is Jack Armstrong, a fire inspector for the State of Indiana."

Jack Armstrong, the All-American Boy, I immediately thought. He kind of looked the part. A little taller than I. Neat, sandy hair. An easy smile. I'd have bet he got a lot of comments about his name.

The man smiled and held out his hand. I shook it, then Hank did, too.

"Detective Kuhlbaugh already filled me in," he said. "I'm glad to meet you guys."

Filled him in? What was my role in all this? I looked at Hank.

"Fire inspector, eh?" Hank said to the All-American Boy. "Do you know Conway, here? He's from the City of Muncie fire department." Hank laughed.

"Can't say as I do," Jack Armstrong responded, looking at me.

"It's been a while," I said, shrugging.

"Back when horses pulled the fire pumps," Hank added.

The men enjoyed a good laugh at my expense, then turned serious.

"We've already examined the body at the morgue in Angola," Kuhlbaugh said. "We'd just got done going over the truck when you showed up."

Aha! The body. I nodded knowingly to Hank. "Only one body?" I asked.

The Indiana man looked at me. "Yes, were you expecting more?"

"Two actually," Hank replied. "One male, one female."

"This was a female," the fire inspector said. "No identification on her. From the morgue in Angola, she'll go to the crime lab in Fort Wayne."

"You know the story about how the fire was discovered?" Armstrong asked. "The farmer and all?"

We nodded.

"What time did the call come in?" I asked, as Kuhlbaugh led the way across the clearing. He lifted the yellow crime tape so we could walk under and then led us to the truck. I recognized pin oak, sugar maple, and sycamore trees towering around us.

"Just before five-thirty," Armstrong answered.

The two uniformed troopers leaned against

the side of one of the Indiana State patrol cars, watching us. They seemed bored. We were probably just the last in a whole string of visitors.

"Somebody drove in under cover of darkness and lit it up. Probably had the site picked out," I speculated.

"That's what we think," Kuhlbaugh answered.

Two plain clothes cops met us at the burned out truck and introduced themselves as Michigan State Police Detectives.

They both were middle-aged, and seemed friendly enough.

"Captain Hard-Ass still out at the road?" the taller detective asked.

"Still there," I replied.

"Thought he was gonna strip-search us," his partner said. "Sure takes his job seriously."

"You'll get no argument from us," Hank stated, shaking his head in agreement.

"Zack Barnes," Jack Armstrong said, "he's not so bad once you get to know him."

"It's just getting to know him," Hank laughed.

We inspected the truck. The driver's door

was ajar. Hank and I looked at each other.

"Was the door open when the fire department arrived?" I asked the Indiana inspector.

"No, it was closed," Jack said. "The county coroner team opened it to extract the body. There was no I.D. on her.

"No I.D. That figures," I said, shaking my head. I glanced at the burned out cab. "Any prints on the door are long gone, burned away." I turned to the others. "They give any idea on age? We're looking for a girl in her late teens, early twenties."

The Michigan men stood watching and listening. I had a feeling they'd already suspected what Hank and I were thinking. That the dead girl was Megan Grawn.

"Tom, Jerry," Jack called to the Indiana troopers. They looked up. He waved them over.

I looked at Hank and caught his smile. Tom and Jerry? I wondered when Laurel and Hardy would show up.

The troopers walked over, casting glances at the burned-out truck.

"Officer Jones was on the original call yesterday morning when the body was discovered," Armstrong said.

"Arnie Jones." The trooper extended his hand. "This is Jerry Garcia." He jerked a thumb at his partner. "Everyone calls us Tom and Jerry."

I nodded. Tom Jones and Jerry Garcia. The boys back home in Pulaski would have a blast with this.

"I came in after the fire was out, with the coroner's team," the trooper called Tom said. "Once things had cooled down, we pried open the door and took her out. She was pretty badly burned. Somebody used a good accelerant."

I held my nose against the smell of burned tires, foam rubber, and flesh, and peered through the missing drivers-side window into the interior of the truck. I noticed that the passenger's door was closed. Except for a small spot of scorched material on the passenger side, where the body must have been, the front seats were gone, burned down to the wire framing. Bits of melted foam clung to the seat springs. That's where she sat, I thought. I could actually tell what the material was on the passenger side. The back seat was completely burned away.

I stepped back and looked around. The

grass by the driver's door was burned down to charred, bare earth where someone had slopped fuel onto the ground. The burn pattern spread outward and ended in a ragged circle around the truck.

I looked back up, "You pulled the body from the passenger side?" I asked Tom. Or was it Jerry? Glancing at the name tag on his pocket, I saw Jones. It was Tom I was talking to.

"Yes, a guy from the coroner's office leaned in from the driver's side to help ease her out." He nodded to the truck. "A fireman must have closed the door on the passenger's side. It was closed when I got here, before we pulled her out," he said.

"Did you get a good look at the body?" I asked.

"I helped get her out of the truck," Tom said. "Yeah, I guess I got a pretty good look at it."

"The reason I ask," I explained, "did it look like she was killed by a small caliber gun. Something like a .22?" I thought of the wounds we saw on Duke when we pulled him out of the pond.

The policeman looked at me in surprise,

"That's what one of the coroner's people thought," he said. "Shot in the back of the head."

"So," I said, "somebody drove out here with a dead body next to them, or in the back, doused the truck, then torched it." I pointed back, toward the truck bed.

"We found what's left of a tarp in the back," Jack Armstrong said. "We're gonna send it to the lab and look for DNA, just in case they wrapped her in it for transport."

"How about tattoos?" Hank asked. "Could you tell if she had any?"

"Looked like she had one on the back of her neck," Tom said, "and a tramp stamp of some sort. That's all we could see directly. Everything else was, well, you know. We'll use that along with her dental records to get a positive I.D."

We nodded our heads knowingly.

"There was an eyebrow piercing," Armstrong said.

I thought of the picture Hank had shown me. "Meagan had a chrome stud through one eyebrow," I said.

"Yes," Kuhlbaugh said, nodding. "The Coroner has it in Angola."

442

"Did the body show evidence of restraint?" I asked, looking at Officer Jones. "Were her hands behind her back like they'd been secured, or her feet bound?"

"No," Jones relied. "There was no evidence of her being bound by anything. Her arms were at her side. Why do you ask?"

"Meagan, if it is Meagan, wasn't overpowered, then," I said. "She was probably surprised by the killers or was with them and comfortable. Does that make sense?" I turned to Hank.

He nodded his head, "I believe you're right," he said. "She was probably with them willingly when things went south."

"We found fresh cigarette butts in the grass over there, where somebody stood around," Jerry Garcia pointed back toward the trail. There was a small, numbered, plastic tripod on the ground. "They're on the way to the lab, too."

It was all starting to come together for me. The killer or killers lured her into meeting them, killed her somehow, more than likely with a .22 caliber pistol, transported her out here in Duke Williams' pickup, soaked her down, lit her up, then got away in another car. Or, they lured her out here in the middle of the night, killed her here, then lit her up and left in another car. Either way, she must have felt safe with them, at ease and comfortable, until someone shot her. I'd have bet she didn't even see it coming.

I walked to the pickup bed and looked in. The front was burned clean of paint, but the burn pattern stopped roughly at the wheel wells. There was still some red paint in the back, by the tail-gate. A remnant of a green tarp lay there. The killers didn't soak down the bed as much as the interior of the cab.

"Hank," I called, "look at this." I pointed to what was left of the tarp.

Hank looked down, over the side of the truck bed. "They had her wrapped in the tarp," he stated. She was dead before they got out here, I'll bet."

"If she wasn't in the tarp," I observed, "It probably would have blown out of the bed on the way here. Her weight kept it in. Then they moved her up front and torched her."

Kuhlbaugh stepped up beside Hank and pointed, "If you look closely in the fold there, it looks like a blood stain."

"It could be," Hank agreed.

"If this is Meagan Grawn, and I'm pretty sure it is, she felt safe meeting someone in Duke's truck," I added.

"Sure looks like it," Hank replied, looking around at us. "I'm with you on this one, Conway, it was someone she knew, or otherwise felt okay meeting with."

"One question," I said, looking at the group, "Where the hell is Richie Collins?"

Chapter Twenty-nine

Hank and I said good-bye to the Michigan men and thanked the Indiana investigators for their help.

We got in his truck and drove out to the road. Officer Barnes was outside his car, leaning against the door. Hank and I smiled and waved as we turned east-bound on Highway 20. Barns crossed his arms and nodded his Smokey Bear hat. I guess that's all we were going to get out of him.

About five miles east, Hank's phone rang. He fumbled around looking for it until I picked it up off the seat and handed it to him.

"Thanks, man," he nodded to me and took the phone. "Hank," he answered. "Um hmm," he listened. "No kidding?" he glanced over at me and nodded his head. "How 'bout Mrs. LaBlanc?"

He listened for a moment, "Yeah, that

figures. Okay, thanks for the info. Sure, I'll tell him. See ya," and he hung up.

"That was Flint," he said in answer to my inquiring look. "Jake LaBlanc just passed a lie detector test on Duke Williams' murder."

"No kidding?" I said. "I was sure Jake was somehow involved."

"You're starting to sound like me," Hank said.

"Flint said LaBlanc seemed genuinely shook by Williams' death," he added.

"You mean he doesn't know about Duke and the lovely Mrs. LaBlanc?" I asked.

"He does now," Hank answered. "That was part of the questioning. Jake didn't know anything about it. Anyway, at this point, it's mainly conjecture."

"I was kinda' rooting for Duke," I said, grinning.

Hank shook his head. "You're a sad case, Conway."

I asked, "What about Jake's wife? Did they give her a polygraph?"

"Temporarily missing. They're looking for her," Hank said. "Jake told the cops that she's out of town on business, whatever that means."

"It means this doesn't look good for the alluring Mrs. LaBlanc," I said, feigning sadness.

"Could be nothing, but I wonder if she's somewhere in Indiana as we speak," Hank said reflectively. "I've got a funny feeling." He rubbed his hand over his chin, thinking.

"Could be," I said, "and I'll bet somebody's going to tip her off. Somebody who just past a lie detector."

"Hmm," Hank said, thoughtfully. He slowed and pulled the truck into the gravel parking lot of a road-side market.

"What's up?" I asked.

"Gotta call Flint back." He picked up the phone from the seat and scrolled through the numbers, before punching the send button.

"Hey, it's me," he said. "Yes, Conway and I are still in Indiana, and still on our way back to Michigan." He shook his head and grinned. "Listen, has anyone put a trace on Mrs. LaBlanc's cell phone?"

He looked at me and winked.

"If she had anything to do with Duke's murder, or the Grawn girl's murder, she could still be in Indiana, or maybe on the run. Conway thinks someone might try to tip her off. Yeah, that's who we think was in Duke's burned-out truck." He nodded at me.

Hank held his hand over the phone, "They have a trace on Jake's phone, but not the wife's."

"Fools," I said. "I'm telling you, she's the one. I've felt it all along. Well, at least since Angola, twenty minutes ago."

Hank grinned over at me and nodded in agreement. "Yeah, I'm back," he spoke into the phone. "How long has the wife been gone? Well, maybe you guys could ask around. No need to be polite, now. We've got a couple murders on our hands. Call me if anything pops up. Sure, I'll tell him. Bye." He pushed the end button and waved the phone at me.

"Flint said he owes you a steak dinner. How do I get in on this?"

"If this pans out, I'll buy you a meal," I said.

Hank smiled. "I must be getting hungry."

We rode on, talking and weighing all the possible scenarios. Before I knew it, we'd passed under the toll road and arrived at the junction where Route 49 came in from the south to join Highway 20. A few miles further on,

Hank turned the truck onto Route 49 north. It wasn't long before we were back home in Michigan and passing through Camden. I started looking for a restaurant. There had to be one, but if there was, neither Hank nor I could spot it. One didn't appear until we hit the south side of Reading. The Frying Pan, the sign said. Hank pulled in. There were several pickups nosed in along the south side of the building, lined up like baby pigs on their momma. Hank pulled into the gravel lot and parked next to the truck on the far end.

We got out. Stretching, glad to be out of the truck, I looked around the lot, then froze. "Hank," I said, my voice low. "Look out back. Whose car is that?"

"Holy!..." Hank said, looking at the silver Jaguar convertible with the black top. "It's the XK8," he said in a low voice.

The car was parked out behind the restaurant, backed in against a dingy, brown, wooden privacy fence.

We stood in the parking lot next to Hank's truck. I wondered what to do next. Call the authorities?

"I'll buy you another steak dinner if it

isn't who I think it is," Hank said.

"Let me walk in and see if she's here," I said. "She'll recognize you." I couldn't think what else to do.

"I'll make myself scarce," Hank said. He walked away, back around to the driver's door, and got in.

I stepped to the entrance door and walked into the restaurant. The first thing I noticed was the frying pan motif. Fry pans of every size and description hung from the ceiling and were attached to the walls in what I guessed were artistic displays. A bunch of angry, Friday-night drunks would have a blast in this place.

A few farmers were sitting in booths along the walls, drinking coffee and talking. Then I saw them. It was Mrs. LaBlanc alright, looking stunning as usual. Nobody could hide those curves, or that hair. She was in the back, in a corner booth, sitting across the table from a teenage boy. She faced away from me, toward her companion, and wore a black baseball cap over her long, blond hair. The boy looked familiar, like I should know him from somewhere. Men in the booths closest to the woman were unable to help themselves and kept throwing glances her way.

A waitress started to approach me. She carried some menus in the crook of one arm. I waved her off and went back out the door.

I tried to walk calmly, fighting the urge to run back to the truck as my pulse quickened.

"She's here," I said excitedly as I climbed into Hank's truck. "She's with a teenage boy. You still got that picture of Richie Collins?"

"Sure, right here." Hank turned and dug behind the seat for the brown envelope. The same brown envelope he'd gotten from the lovely Shonda Miles.

Reaching in, he pulled out the smaller, white envelope and took out a picture.

"This the kid?" he asked, handing me the photo.

Richie Collins stared out at me. The same Richie Collins who was in the restaurant with Mrs. LaBlanc.

"That's the guy!" I exclaimed, tapping the picture. "It's Richie, alright."

Hank let out a long breath. "Okay," he said. "First we call the State Police. Then we call Flint. Finally..." he looked at me, bewildered, thinking of what to say next.

"I don't believe it," I said.

Hank said, "We chase all over southern Michigan looking for this kid, and end up tripping over him here at The Frying Pan. How lucky can we get? And what's he doing with the LaBlanc woman?" He gave me an incredulous stare.

I looked out at the restaurant and shook my head. "We've got to get you and your truck out of here," I finally said. I could feel my pulse picking up again.

"You got your gun?" Hank asked.

"No, I wasn't going to take it into Ohio and Indiana," I said.

He grunted something, "Good thinking," he replied.

Hank started the Chevy and backed out of the row of trucks.

"We'll go down the street a way," he pointed south, "so we can still watch the place."

"Good idea," I said. I really couldn't think of much else to do.

"Hey!" I exclaimed, "maybe we could disable her car." Though I really didn't know how we'd do that.

"What'll we do, sneak back and let the air out of a tire?" he asked as he drove us away from the building.

"We could," I said, wishing I'd thought of it first.

"That wouldn't make anybody suspicious, would it?" he asked, raising his eyebrows.

"Just sayin'," I replied, folding my arms.

Hank grinned and shook his head.

He drove south a block, pulled a u-turn, and slipped the pickup into a parallel parking spot right in front of the Methodist Church. Pointing north, we could look across the lawn of the church and have a clear view of the Jaguar in the restaurant's back parking lot.

The day was warm, and we sat there with the windows down, listening to the noises of summer. A lawn mower sounded from a few blocks over. Somewhere a dog barked.

Hank got on the phone and called a number. "Hank McIntyre," he said. "We've got them, Mrs. LaBlanc and Richie Collins. They're in the Frying Pan Restaurant on M-49 in, in..." he looked at me.

"In Reading," I said.

"In Reading. South side." Yes, I'm armed. No, they don't know we've spotted them," he looked over at me again.

I shook my head, no.

He hung up. "That was the State Police liaison with the Jackson County Metro Squad," he said. "He's going to get things started."

"Should we call Kuhlbaugh?" I asked.

In the street ahead, three young guys wearing Reading Ranger T-shirts walked across, laughing and playfully jostling each other as they went into the restaurant.

"Good idea!" Hank said. He was fairly giddy at this point.

Scrolling down his phone list, he found the right number and pushed the button.

"It's ringing," he looked at me. "Come on Cool-balls, answer the phone." He nervously tapped his fingers on the steering wheel and stared down the street at the restaurant.

The silver Jag was still parked out back, no other cars around.

"He's probably eating a late lunch somewhere," Hank said, looking down at the phone.

"There's a great deli on the square in Angola," I said. "They have the best Philly Cheesesteak sandwich I've ever had."

"And we're missing lunch," he said, putting the phone back near his ear.

His eyes lit up. "Hey, guess what?" he said into the phone while glancing at me. "I'm in Reading, Michigan, looking at Ms. LaBlanc's silver Jag, that's what."

Hank's face looked like he'd just gotten the best Christmas present, ever.

"Conway spotted it when we pulled in to eat," he said. He listened a moment. "I already did. He's getting the ball rolling. Where the heck are you?" Hank glanced back over at me, excitement written all over him. He was really enjoying this.

"Route 49, heading north? Oh, man, this is great," he said, looking at me and grinning.

"He's crossing into Michigan right now," Hank said to me.

"Well, put the lights on and get up here," he said into the phone. "She's not going to hang around all night, you know." He told Kuhlbaugh to drive safely, then hung up.

"Our body is Meagan Grawn," Hank said. "She was shot twice with a small caliber weapon. Probably a 22."

"We were pretty sure of that," I said.

"Well, somebody saw the truck two days back, pulling out of a farm south of Ray, wherever that is."

"They didn't waste any time putting Duke's truck to good use," I said, "and the Indiana-Michigan border runs east-west right through the center of Ray. There's not much there. Just a wide spot in the road."

"Like Pulaski?"

"Smaller," I said. "Not even a store or gas station. There are a lot of small run-down farms in the area. Good place to hide out, I guess"

Hank stared at me, "How do you know this?" he asked.

I didn't miss a beat, "I have my sources," I said, dead-pan.

Hank laughed. "Got me there."

We went back to watching the restaurant. The minutes ticked by. An older man wearing a faded, gray T-shirt that matched the color of his unkempt hair, drove past on a rusty Ford 8N tractor. We watched as he pulled into a gas station up the street, north of The Frying Pan.

"Hank laughed and said, "This is my kind of town."

"Probably ripe with old Ford tractors," I teased.

We went back to watching the silver Jaguar

in the parking lot.

"Uh, oh." Hank pointed out the window.

"I see them," I answered.

Mrs. LaBlanc and Richie had left the restaurant and were walking to the car.

Hank picked up his phone. We watched as the woman took out her key fob and pushed the button to unlock the car doors. Richie stood on the passenger side, his arm out, waiting to pull the door latch. They got in the car and LaBlanc started it. Nothing happened for a while. They sat in the car, talking. I could see Richie fiddling with the dash controls in front of them. Probably adjusting the air conditioning.

Finally, the Jaguar started moving.

"A coffee says north," I said.

"You're on," Hank replied, never taking his eyes off the car.

The Jag slipped out of the parking lot, hesitated, then turned south, coming right at us.

Hank slumped in his seat. "Oh boy!" he muttered.

I crowded against the door to give him room. "Told you we should have disabled her car," I said.

Mrs. LaBlanc was looking at the young man next to her, waving a hand while she talked. The gorgeous car, with the beautiful Mrs. LaBlanc driving, went on by with no sign of recognition.

"That was a close one," Hank said, shaking his head.

"Rats!" I exclaimed. "I owe you a coffee."

Hank grinned over at me, started the truck and swung another U-turn. He picked up his phone from where he'd dropped it on the seat, and punched in a number. "Hank again," he said. "We're following a Jaguar convertible, black over silver. LaBlanc and Richie are in it heading south out of Reading" He paused a moment, "Do me a favor, get ahold of the locals, tell them to keep off. Don't let them ruin this. Kuhlbaugh is coming up from the south. I'll have him find a narrow spot and block the road." He listened for a moment. "We got this," he said, nodding his head. "Sure could use a State Police back-up, though. See ya," and he hung up.

"All we need is a local cop try to make a name for himself," he said.

We were following at a distance, out of

Reading, toward Camden.

Hank thumbed his phone again, and hit the green call button. "Kuhlbaugh? Yeah, Hank. Listen, I don't know if you've heard, but LaBlanc and Richie are heading south on M-49 in the silver Jag convertible. Yeah, the one with the black top," he grinned at me.

How many Jaguars heading south from Reading, Michigan? I wondered.

Hank glanced at me and said, "They're north of Camden, coming with grill lights on."

"There's a creek north of Dimmers Road," I said. "It's just south of Frank Road. It's marshy and the roadway should be narrow there, no chance to leave the road and escape."

I looked at the cab ceiling and thought hard, trying to see the road map in my mind. With my daughter's family living near Angola, I'd driven these back roads dozens of times over the years. Now I wish I'd payed better attention.

"Where are you now?" Hank asked into the phone. He listened, then looked at me.

"They've crossed Montgomery Road and are coming up on Dimmers." he reported.

"We've just gone by Lilac Road," I announced. "Get them to block the road at the

460

ditch and we'll seal them in from the rear," I said. "If they don't make the ditch, and see them coming, block the road at the best spot available and we'll get them from behind." I was really getting into the chase now.

I looked over at the speedometer. Hank was doing fifty-five, keeping back a good quarter mile. We met very little traffic. The occasional semitruck rumbled by, heading north.

A mile or so further down the road, the Jaguar slowed and the right turn signal came on.

"She's turning west, onto Frank Road," I said, trying not to sound excited.

Hank spoke into the phone. "Kuhlbaugh, she's turning west on Frank. She's turning west on Frank."

"Ask him if he's passed Dimmers," I instructed.

Hank asked and reported back, "They're just now coming to it," he said.

"Have them take Dimmers west-bound," I said. "It's a straight shot. Now, if Kuhlbaugh can get on his secret radio and get someone to block the intersection of Abbott and Frank Road, we'll be in like Flint," I

said.

"In, like our man, Flint," Hank snickered.

"This is a gravel road," I said. "Why drive a shiny Jaguar down this thing if you don't have to? You think she's turning to avoid Kuhlbaugh?" I asked. "Or, could she be going down Frank Road anyway?"

"Could have a police scanner in the Jag," Hank said, thoughtfully. "I guess we'll find out."

The speaker in Hank's phone rattled. Kuhlbaugh was saying something. Hank put the phone to his ear. "What?" he asked.

He listened for a moment, then glanced at me. "The State Police are coming down Abbott Road. Kuhlbaugh will block from the south. We'll keep going here, on Frank. Jonesville post is sending out some more backup."

The Jaguar was still a quarter mile ahead. Evidently, the occupants were too engaged in conversation to notice the pickup truck tailing behind them. They took an S curve to the south-west, then right, back west again.

We trailed along without incident for about a mile. "We've got company," Hank said. "Looks like the cavalry has finally showed up."

I leaned forward and peeked into the

outside rearview mirror mounted on my door. A blue State Police car had pulled within twenty yards of us. It slowed and kept pace, the trooper running with no lights or siren.

We passed between marshland on either side of the road. A ditch appeared up ahead and ran through a culvert beneath us.

Past the ditch, a farmstead was located back off the road on our right, the house partially obscured by a planting of pine trees that lined the long driveway.

We had a clear view of the intersection dead ahead, where Frank Road ended at Abbott. There was nobody there.

"Where's she going to go?" Hank asked himself.

"Bets?" I asked.

"With my luck, she'll pull a u-turn and come back on us," Hank replied.

"There he is," I pointed. A second State Police cruiser had just appeared over a slight rise to the north on Abbott Road, and was barreling down on the intersection.

The Jaguar's brake lights came on and the car slowed to a crawl. It turned right, into the farm lane that led to the house and out-buildings.

Hank slowed the Chevy pickup and stopped in the road a ways back. We watched the silver Jag creep up the lane, appearing now and again between the pine trees. The occupants seemed oblivious to the vehicles in the road.

Hank looked at me, like he was looking for ideas, then spoke to Kuhlbaugh. "We're in front of a farm on Frank Road," he said. "I'm going to follow her up the lane. There's a State Police car behind me. I'll have them follow me in." He listened a moment, then put the phone down. "He's coming up Abbott Road, nearly to the intersection. Brace yourself, we're going in." He pulled ahead, turned the truck, and drove up the driveway, not bothering to be too careful.

The police cruiser followed behind us, kicking up a cloud of dust. The Chevy burst into the farmyard and stopped behind the Jaguar. I could see the LaBlanc woman's alarmed face looking at us in the rearview mirror of the idling Jaguar. Richie Collins opened his door and peeked out.

The State car pulled around us and blocked the Jag from the front. A female officer jumped out, her gun drawn.

Hank looked at me, "Be right back," he said, and was out of the truck before I knew it, gun in hand.

As a civilian, he didn't want to place me in any danger. I was okay with that.

"Driver, keep your hands where I can see them!" the lady trooper shouted as she approached the front of the convertible.

Hank trotted up to the back of the Jag and around to the passenger's side. The lady trooper stepped off to the side and covered the driver.

Richie stared in disbelief, but offered no resistance as Hank rushed in, grabbed him by an arm and dragged him from the car.

He had Richie laying prone on the grass as the State Trooper ordered LaBlanc to shut off the car, then open the door. Hank watched the woman through the open passenger's door, gun trained on her.

The State Police car, that we'd seen racing down Abbott Road, burst into the yard, followed closely by Kuhlbaugh's black four-door. Kuhlbaugh stopped at the entrance to the yard, effectively blocking escape out the drive.

"What's going on?" LaBlanc demanded. "I'm

visiting friends with my son. Why are you doing this?" she protested.

"The lady trooper ordered her out of the car at gunpoint and led her around behind, in front of the truck where I sat watching. She instructed her to lean forward, against the trunk of the Jag, and proceeded to pat down the lovely Mrs. LaBlanc.

Hank got my attention and waved me out of the truck. I walked past the cop and LaBlanc and up to Hank, all the while keeping a wary eye on the house and barns. "Keep an eye on the kid," he said, handing me his pistol. I got a feeling of deja vu all over again.

Kuhlbaugh and a male State Trooper walked up, guns drawn, and stood off to watch the police lady question the loudly protesting LaBlanc.

Hank reached in and poked around under the seat of the Jag. He picked up Mrs. LaBlanc's purse and walked it back to the lady cop.

"You're being detained for questioning in the murders of Duke Williams and Meagan Grawn," the police woman said.

"I don't know anything about that," Mrs. LaBlanc answered, obviously nervous and growing more so by the minute.

The lady cop opened the purse and peered inside. She glanced up at us, then reached in to pull out a hand gun. "You got a permit for this?" she asked LaBlanc.

The woman remained silent.

"Who are you?" Richie asked me, "and what's she saying about Meagan Grawn being murdered?" He lay on his stomach, arms stretched forward, head turned toward me.

"I'm Tim Conway," I answered. "I'm one of the people who could have been killed searching your parent's house the night of the fire. The fire you set before fleeing with Meagan Grawn. And, yes," I nodded for emphasis, "yesterday, Meagan's body was pulled from a burned-out pickup truck, just east of Angola." I didn't care if he was shocked or not.

"What?!" Richie exclaimed. "She went to Angola to look for a job. That's what Claudette told me."

"Claudette?"

"Mrs. LaBlanc," Richie said. "She told me Meagan was going to Angola to apply for a job. We were going to get married, someday." He scrunched up his face and looked like he was going to burst into tears.

"Who took her?" I asked.

467

"Some friends of Claudette's," he answered. "We've been staying here the last few days. Claudette called Meagan on her cell. She said some friends would be by to pick her up. I told her not to trust her." He looked down and tried to stifle a sob.

"Why didn't you go with them?" I asked.

"They said I was needed here. I was being paid to watch the place, and I needed the money."

I looked around at the typical two-story, white, wood-framed farm house. There was a sagging, red, gambrel roofed barn out back. A rusty Farmall H tractor sat in front of the large double doors. Off to one side, in a growth of saplings, rested an ancient chicken coop, its windows still covered in rusted chicken wire. Ahead and to our right, across the drive from the house, was a red pole barn with a slider door.

Claudette, I thought. What a hot name. It sure fits her.

"My lawyer will have me on the street in a few hours," I heard the lovely, but apparently deadly, Claudette remark to the State Police lady.

Richie looked up at me again. He hadn't

been cuffed, and he used his hands to wipe his eyes. "Meagan owed Claudette some money," he said in a low voice, looking back at the woman.

"How much?" I asked, intrigued. "Would she have her killed over it?"

"I don't know exactly how much," he said, "maybe ten thousand dollars. Meagan said she took it off the top of drug sales. Claudette didn't pay her enough, so she kept some. I can't believe she'd be killed for it. Hell, she was going to pay it back someday. That's what she told me. We just wanted to go away and start over someplace."

Hank stood by, listening. He glanced over at Mrs. LaBlanc. I could see the disgust written on his face.

"Tell me about the people who picked Meagan up. What kind of vehicle were they driving?"

He said, "A guy and a woman. They were driving Duke's Ford pickup. Said they borrowed it."

"You sure it was Duke's?

"I know his pickup," Richie said. I saw it over at LaBlanc's house. They were friends. It was red. A four-door, and it had a light bar on top. Duke's on the Maple Grove Fire Department. It was his truck all right."

Another blue State Police Car appeared in the lane. Kuhlbaugh had to trot back and move his car to let them in. The trooper standing next to him started looking in the windows of the Jag.

"You'll need a warrant!" shouted Claudette LaBlanc. "You'll need one to search my purse, too!"

"We've got it," the cop replied.

"Probable cause," the lady cop said.

I said to Richie, "The truck was found burned to a hulk outside of Angola early yesterday morning. I'm sorry to tell you, but Meagan's body was in it."

"Did she, did she die in the fire?" Richie asked, weeping openly now. Hank leaned forward and helped him to a sitting position.

I thought a moment before answering, "No," I said, "she was dead before the fire. She didn't feel it." Like that was any consolation to Richie. His girlfriend was dead.

The State Troopers were leading a handcuffed Mrs. LaBlanc to the back of the first cruiser. The woman complained and threatened all the way to the car. She paused before getting in. "You!" she glared at Hank, a hateful look on her face.

"Yes, Mrs. LaBlanc," Hank nodded and replied in a firm voice, "it is I."

The police helped their prisoner into the back of the car and shut the door.

"Mr. Conway," Richie said softly. "We were supposed to meet the people out here, the people who gave Meagan a ride to Angola." He looked around nervously at the out-buildings.

"Claudette took me to lunch up to Camden. She wanted to talk about me working for her, then we were coming back here to meet up with the man and woman who took Meagan to Angola." He paused to take a deep breath. "Meagan was supposed to be with them," he sobbed.

Hank looked at me, concern on his face.

I nodded and waved at the red pole barn.

"Guys," he called to the troopers. "There may be somebody here. Two somebodies. Cover the house for me, would you. Kuhlbaugh and I are going to check out the pole barn. Then we'll go through the house.

The officers nodded in agreement and drawing their weapons again, trained them on the house.

"You got a spare piece I can borrow?" Hank asked the troopers. "Conway has mine." He nodded in my direction.

The lady trooper looked at him for a moment, then reached in her pocket and pulled out a .380, nearly identical to mine. She handed it to Hank. He looked at it. It looked like a toy in his hand.

Kuhlbaugh was already on his way to the pole barn. Hank caught up with him in about five strides.

Two more State Police vehicles pulled into the yard and stopped. The place was swarming with them. The officers got out and looked at the other troopers watching the house with guns drawn, looked over at me standing over Richie with Hank's gun, then at Hank and Kuhlbaugh creeping up to the side door of the red pole barn. They looked momentarily confused, drew their service weapons, and walked over to the other troopers.

"What in the Sam Hill is going on?" one asked the other two.

The lady trooper glanced my way and, in a low voice, began explaining all that had happened. I don't know how she explained me.

They fanned out and advanced on the house.

Suddenly, shouts and sounds of car doors slamming came from the pole barn. Hank and Kuhlbaugh had disappeared inside. The big door slid open and a man and woman came out, hands in the air, followed by Hank and Kuhlbaugh who had a grip on the back of their belts.

"Got any cuffs?" Hank called. "Caught these two hiding in the back of a van."

"And they weren't in there making out," Kuhlbaugh said with a grin.

"Those are the two who took Meagan in Duke's truck," Richie said in a shaky voice. "They killed her."

"Take it easy," I told him. "The police will take care of them."

Two of the troopers rushed over with hand-cuffs.

Hank looked over at Richie and me. "Are these the two?" he asked.

"Yes!" Richie shouted. "They killed Meagan!" he screamed. "They killed Meagan," he said more to himself and put his hands over his face and sobbed softly.

I almost felt sorry for him, until I thought again of the house fire - his father sitting in the yard, arms and hands burned,

Nan working over him, and Kip and I going into the burning house where Kip nearly went through the floor.

I looked at him sitting on the ground, crying. He had gotten in over his head and this is what it had led to.

Hank and Kuhlbaugh turned the pair over to the State Police, who turned their pockets, patted them down, then put them in separate cars.

"There are a few guns in the van," Hank said to the other officers. "One is a .22 pistol." He glanced at Richie. "I didn't touch anything, so the crime scene crew can dust for prints."

"They're on the way," one of the cops said. He was holding a roll of yellow crime scene tape.

Two troopers approached the house, while the lady cop covered them.

"What's the layout of the house?" I asked Richie.

"Living room in front, then a dining room leading to a kitchen in the back," he said.

"There's a bedroom off to the left. A stairway in the living room goes to two bedrooms up."

"The bathroom and basement?" Hank asked.

"Bathroom is off the dining room and the basement door is in the kitchen," Richie replied, wiping tears away with his arm.

Hank looked over to a State Policeman who had walked up by the cars. "You get that?" he asked.

The cop nodded and hustled off to inform the other officers. Withing minutes they had the house checked out. Sweeping across the back yard, they moved on to the barn.

Kuhlbaugh and one officer cleared the hen house. An policeman returned from the barn to report finding Richie's pickup truck.

A blue van pulled in the drive. The crime scene crew. The lady cop directed them toward the pole barn.

She walked over to where Hank and I stood over Richie. "No drugs in the house," she said. "Got any hidden?"

"No," Richie said. "Meagan wanted to go straight. "She just had some pot on her when she,..when she," and he broke down again.

"You'll find drugs in the van," Hank told the trooper. "There's a small baggie of pot laying on the front passenger's seat, some meth and a pipe in a clear bag in the back.

The two didn't have any on their person when we surprised them."

Hank and I turned Richie over to the police, gave our statements to the lady trooper and left the police to finish up their work. Kuhlbaugh came over to shake our hands and say good-bye.

We got in Hank's truck and he maneuvered it around and through the cluster of police vehicles. Two Hillsdale deputies had arrived and were being briefed by the lady trooper.

Hank drove back to M-49 and headed north, through Reading. He drove past The Frying Pan restaurant and on to Jonesville, where we grabbed a quick burger at a small mom-and-pop place on the west side.

The sun was hanging far to the west when Hank dropped me off at home. "This has been a productive day," he said, smiling. He left with a promise to keep me updated on any new developments.

My wife met me at the door. I gave her a long hug. "It's been quite a day," I told her. "We found Richie Collins with Claudette LaBlanc down in the Reading area. His girlfriend ended up dead in Duke Williams' burned out truck in Indiana."

We sat at the kitchen table and I relayed to my wife all that had happened since leaving with Hank that morning. She shook her head in disbelief.

"What an awful ending for those kids," she said. "They didn't know what they were getting in to."

I got up to pour a cup of coffee.

"By the way," she said. "Did you have some hay sold to someone in a white pickup truck?"

I thought for a moment, "No, I don't recall anyone scheduling a load," I said. "Why?"

"This afternoon a white pickup came in the driveway. It sat for a moment, then backed out."

"Anyone get out?" I asked.

"No. Maybe they had the wrong house," she said. "And before you ask, I didn't see what they looked like."

I grinned and shook my head. "Maybe they'll be back."

Chapter Thirty

I woke up early and lay in bed, half dozing and trying to force myself back to sleep. Finally I reached over and shut off the alarm before it could come on and wake the wife. Getting out of bed, I went down to the kitchen, started the coffee, then sat by the slider doors overlooking the deck and side yard. I watched as the night slowly faded away to dim daylight and the world came to life. My favorite time of the day.

On the kitchen counter, the coffee machine burbled away, working on that wonderful first pot of the morning. I poured coffee into my Studebaker mug that the wife had ordered from the Studebaker National Museum in South Bend, then I walked over and checked the outdoor temperature. Sixty-two degrees at six o'clock. It was going to be a warm one. Radio Hillsdale said to expect a high of eighty-five. Picking up my note pad, I slid open the glass patio door and walked to a chair on the deck. The deck boards were dry on my bare feet. The dew point must have been low last night.

Birds were beginning to stir in the bushes, a few started in singing their lungs out. A dog barked somewhere down the road, no doubt the same place where some horses whinnied. Out on the road a car went by, probably taking some poor stiff to work. I leaned back and sipped my coffee while going over the notes I'd jotted on my yellow legal pad, then added a few more.

The sound of the door sliding open caught my attention. I turned my head to see my wife coming through. She was still in her pajamas, her hands wrapped around a steaming cup of coffee. She shoved the sliding door closed with her foot and walked over, sipped her coffee, and smiled at me.

"You're up early," I said.

"Heard you get up and couldn't get back to sleep," she said. She stood there, looking down, both hands gripping her coffee cup, warming her fingers.

"Hank going to meet with you today?" she

asked.

"I think so. I've been going over some things, and had a few questions and comments." I pointed at the note pad on the little table beside me.

"You really think that girl, Meagan, was killed because she was skimming?" she asked.

"I believe so. Or, could be she knew too much and was going to rat them all out," I said.

I was silent for a moment, eyeing my notes and thinking. "I believe Richie Cummings was the next in line," I said. "He was being taken to his killers by Claudette LaBlanc when we caught up with them."

"In other words, you guys saved his life, and he doesn't even know it," my wife said. She took another sip from her cup, her eyes watching me from over the rim.

"I believe so," I replied, looking off across the yard. A doe and fawn were walking tentatively along the edge of the grass. The spotted fawn was about the size of a border collie.

"Jake LaBlanc's youngest was in the van wreck out on Goose Lake Road," I said. "I know I've told you before, but I really believe it. He was the driver and survived pretty much unscathed while the Mennonite kid was killed."

"Another argument for seat belts," my wife said.

"I can't be absolutely certain, but I believe the LaBlancs were the suppliers for the kids where the boy over-dosed and died, and at the party out at the log house. They were paying kids to cook up meth and distributing that, too."

"How did Duke Williams fit into this?" my wife asked. "Wasn't he a, as you say... a drinking buddy of Jake LaBlanc's?" She pulled a deck chair over to sit next to me, trying not to spill her coffee onto the planks.

"He was," I replied. "According to Hank, Williams figured out what was going on and approached the police. Actually, he contacted Ned Jordon, and offered to supply evidence of the goings-on. Jordon put him in touch with the metro squad."

"That's why he was killed?"

"That's why he was killed," I said. "Trouble is, according to Flint, Jake LaBlanc didn't have anything to do with it. He didn't know about the murder until he was called in for questioning."

"So, who did it?" she asked.

"My money is on Jake's wife, Claudette," I replied. "She had him killed by the same people who killed the Grawn girl. You know, Hank and I saw her with Duke Williams coming out of the Pulaski General Store. I'm wondering how friendly they really were. Maybe Duke said something that tipped his hand."

My wife smiled at me. "Pillow talk can cause a lot of trouble," she said. "That woman obviously could have persuasive powers."

"You called that one right," I said, grinning. "And, I know I sound like a broken record, but I'm gonna say it again, I really believe she arraigned for Meagan Grawn's murder for skimming the drug money. She was going to have Richie killed, too, just to get rid of him."

"So, Jake didn't even know about the people his wife was working with?"

"I wouldn't be surprised," I replied.

We sat looking over the lawn, lost in our own thoughts. The doe and fawn had wandered off between the lilacs and disappeared.

"How about breakfast?" my wife asked,

turning to me.

I nodded and got up from my chair. Picking up my pen and note pad, I followed her into the kitchen.

Mid-morning, Hank called. The wife and I were finally cleaning out that closet in the spare bedroom, the one that was full of extra quilting material and clothes that were too small to wear.

I picked up the phone, "Good morning," I said, "What's up?"

"It's a beautiful Friday, that's what," came Hank's friendly voice. "Any plans for dinner tonight?" he asked.

I looked at the wife, who had put down a small box of quilt scraps and was beginning to sort through them. "Dinner tonight with Hank?" I asked.

"Sure," she said, "as long as I don't have to cook. What time?" She pulled out a piece of flannel, looked it over, then set it aside.

"What time?" I asked Hank.

"I was thinking around five-thirty, at that pizza place right on Main Street in Homer," he said, "I've been doing some thinking on the LaBlanc case and thought we could hash some things out over dinner.

I looked at the wife and relayed the time and place.

"Like I said, as long as I don't have to cook," she replied.

"We're on," I told Hank. "By the way, the wife and I got up early and talked over some ideas, too."

"Good," he said. "I'll fill you in on what the police have learned from Claudette LaBlanc and the two who were hiding in the pole barn."

"They were going to kill Richie, weren't they?" I asked, too eager to wait.

"I'm afraid so. Anyway, pick you folks up around five so we can be there by five-thirty?"

"See you then," I said.

"Oh, I'll be bringing Shonda Miles with me," Hank said in an upbeat tone.

I smiled over at my wife. "Looking forward to it," I told Hank.

I hung up and I filled the wife in on the conversation.

"Shonda Miles, huh?" she said. "They're getting to be quite a couple."

"Don't schedule the reception hall yet," I said. "He's in no hurry to tie the knot."

We finished reorganizing the closet and I

carried the discards out to the van for a trip to the recycling center.

The day warmed up considerably, as I'd expected. We sat under an awning that covered part of the deck, listening to the fountain bubble in the fish pond, and enjoying our lunch. I'd made a pitcher of lemonade and the wife had made cold-cut sandwiches with a light salad to go along.

"Good day to relax and read a book," she said. "I got a few murder mysteries from the library - Steve Hamilton."

"Can they top what I've been living over the past few weeks?" I asked, grinning.

"Probably not," she laughed. She got up and gathered the dishes together. I started to get up, too, but she waved me away.

I slid over into a reclining chair, leaned back, and closed my eyes. The perfect summer day. Nothing to do, and nowhere to be, until Hank showed up at five o'clock. A gentle breeze rustled the trees and washed across my body. I heard my wife come back and sit down. She opened a book.

I must have dozed. The phone woke me. I looked over. My wife was gone. Reaching to the small table beside me, I grabbed the phone and answered. I didn't know how many times it had rung.

"Hello?"

"Tim, Hank." His voice sounded drawn, tight, like he was in trouble.

I sat up. My phone vibrated. A rescue call came over the app.

"Hank," I said. "I'm getting a rescue call."

"It's for me," he said. "I've been shot." His voice trailed off.

"What?!" I jumped up and ran into the house. "Where are you? How bad?"

"In my yard," he said. His voice sounded odd, distant, like he was getting weak, under stress. It didn't sound good.

"I'm on my way," I said excitedly, trying not to sound excited. "Keep talking Hank. Where are you hit?" I grabbed my keys from the peg by the door and raced for the truck. I didn't get an answer from Hank.

"Where are you off to in such a hurry?" my wife asked from across the yard. She was moving some pots of flowers around under the shade of a maple tree.

"Hank's been shot!" I yelled to her from across the lawn. "Gotta go."

"What!?" she exclaimed, standing there with her mouth hanging open.

I started the truck and slammed it into drive. "Stay on the phone," I called to Hank. "Are you alone?" My question was met with silence from the other end. I raced out the driveway and west on McDonald, past Stone Road, and on to Pulaski Road. I wondered who was bringing the rescue van from the station. In my rush, I'd forgotten all about responding to the page.

I wrenched the Dodge left, around the corner of McDonald and Pulaski and headed south at a high rate of speed. My tool box slid around in the bed of the truck, slamming into the right side.

Picking up my phone, I responded to the call, then concentrated on my driving. One mile south, Howard Road came in from the west. I braked hard, turned right, and floored it. The tool box slid back into the left side of the truck bed. Ordinarily I'd have pulled over and secured it.

After trying to get Hank back on the line, I gave up and threw my phone down on the seat.

I headed west, racing past fields and farms. The same farms that Kip and I had driven by on our way to the log house where the dead girl awaited us. Even farther out, near the county line, was the turn north to Staley Road where the farmer discovered the burned kid wandering in the road, walking away from the meth lab explosion.

    Rescue 1 appeared in my mirror, coming up fast. Kip must have had that diesel wound out to the max.

    Hank's farm burst into view and I slowed for the left turn into the drive. A motionless form lay in the grass over by the barnyard's wooden fence. Hank. A white, five gallon bucket lay on its side next to him, spilling it's contents of grain. Boomer, the old golden retriever, lay on the grass snuggled in close to Hank, head down on his paws. I'd kept my phone on all the way out and hadn't heard anything new, and feared the worst.

    As I drove over the lawn and stopped near his crumpled form, he moved his right hand, the one with the phone. I was out of the Dodge in an instant and ran to his side.

    Boomer wagged his tail and looked up with worried eyes. Hank groaned and turned his head. I couldn't see where he'd been hit.

"Where?" I asked, looking him over, "Where're you hit?" He was wearing a blue work shirt and jeans. I slipped my left hand under his upper back and felt something warm and sticky. I pulled my hand away and looked at it, stained with blood - Hank's blood. "I need some medical gloves," I said to Hank and Boomer, just to say something, trying to be helpful. There were some in my truck, but I didn't want to leave Hank. I noticed his cell phone laying in the grass, still showing my number. He'd scrolled down to another number and it was highlighted. I picked up the phone with my right hand, pushed the red disconnect button and shoved it into my pant's pocket.

The rescue van had followed me across the lawn, leaving heavy tire tracks in the grass. Kip was driving, with Walt in the passenger's seat. They stopped next to my truck and the guys hopped out.

Kip looked at me, standing there staring at Hank's blood on my left hand, and dug into his medical bag. He tossed me a saline bottle, some bleach wipes, and some gloves.

"Looks like the back," I said, rinsing my hand.

Walt knelt next to Hank and Kip dropped to

one knee to help ease him over onto his side.

Walt grabbed some surgical scissors from the kit and began cutting off Hank's shirt.

I slipped on a pair of medical gloves and held his head off the ground while trying to get him to talk to me. Kip slipped a blood-pressure cuff on Hanks left arm and pumped it up. He told the results to Walt, then ran to the rescue van and returned with a pillow.

"Take it easy, buddy," I said. "Here's a pillow. I'm going to lift your head a little and we'll slip it under."

I felt Hank lift his head with me. He'd heard me, and had some strength left. That was good.

Kip eased the pillow under Hank's head. "Gotta watch for hypoxia," he said, looking up at me.

He carefully probed at Hank's back and shook his head. "Two holes," he said, "small caliber, I'd say."

"I thought the same thing, small caliber," Walt agreed. "I wouldn't be surprised if they used a .22."

Kip looked toward the road. "Where's that ambulance? His left lung is bound to be damaged and is going to be filling with blood."

I looked at the oozing, black holes with coagulated blood and puckered skin around them. It looked like someone had used an ice pick on Hank's back. "We've seen this before, I said to the guys. "First Duke Williams and then the Grawn girl down near Angola. Both killed with a .22 caliber gun."

Kip used a stethoscope to listen to Hank's breathing. I picked up a hand and looked at his nail beds. His hand felt warm. His circulation was good. Walt put a pulse-oxy on Hank's right index finger.

"What's your name?" I asked.

"Hank," he mumbled, opening his eyes.

"What's today?" I asked.

"Friday, you dolt," Hank sounded a little irritated. I guess that was to be expected.

"Still lucid," I said, looking at Kip.

"We have some lung sounds," Kip said. He pulled the stethoscope from his ears, let it fall to his shoulders, and shook his head slightly.

Out on the road, a State Police car slowed and pulled into the driveway. Just seconds behind was Flint in his personal car.

The men fairly leaped from their vehicles and came running over. We nodded a tense greeting.

Boomer wagged his tail and whined. He kept looking at Hank and then at each of us in turn, like he expected one of us to miraculously make Hank well again. I reached out and patted him on the head. "Good boy, Boomer, we'll do our best for him."

The Angus cattle crowded the fence and lowed mournfully. Obviously, Hank and Boomer were going out to grain the steers when he was shot.

Walt had set the grain bucket upright and out of the way. Flint snatched it up, took it over to the steer lot, and dumped the contents over the fence into a feeder.

The coming siren signaled the arrival of a Jackson Area Ambulance.

"White," Hank mumbled.

We stared down at him. "What's that?" I asked.

"Are you trying to tell us something?" Kip asked.

"White pickup," he said, slowly, deliberately. "Ford. Extended cab. Shot me from the road." He seemed to grab some strength from somewhere. "Two young white guys. Saw them when I fell," he said.

We all turned to look toward the road as though expecting a white Ford extended cab pickup to suddenly appear.

"Newer model, or older?" I asked.

"Eighties," Hank replied.

Then it hit me. Hit me like a ton of hay. "Two guys in a white Ford extended cab!" I exclaimed, jumping up. "They were at my house while Hank and I were at the crime-scene down at Angola," I told the others. "My wife saw them sitting in our drive."

"Holy Shit!" Flint exclaimed. "They were probably looking for you. Call your wife. Now! I'll head over. You stay with Hank." He was off at a sprint to his car.

I took out my phone and stepped away as I called home. The phone rang several times. I listened impatiently as it kept ringing and had taken the first steps toward my truck when my wife finally answered. I'd expected my call to go to voice mail.

"Yes?" she asked. "How's Hank?"

"Where were you?" I stammered.

"What?"

"Sorry," I said, "I'm a little excited. Hank's going to be okay. The guys are here and the ambulance is here," I said. I realized I wasn't making a whole lot of sense and tried again. "Listen, that white Ford you told me about, the one that pulled into the driveway?"

"Yes," she said, her tone a little worried from the concern she heard in my voice. I couldn't hide it.

"This may be nothing," I tried to sound calm, "but Hank spotted a white Ford pickup in the road as he was shot." I cringed, hoping I wasn't causing her undue alarm.

"Also, Flint's on his way over, just in case."

"You think that's necessary?" she asked. "I've got my .38 here if I need it."

"Good idea, just don't accidentally shoot Flint. I'd never hear the end of it from the guys," I said nervously, hoping to break the tension.

She gave a little laugh, "Like *I* wouldn't?" she questioned.

"You want me to come home?" I asked.

"No need," she said. "You go with Hank. Call me from the hospital. I'll come in there if you want."

"Thanks Honey. I owe you," I said.

"You always owe me," she replied. "Now,

go save Hank. I love you."

"Love you, too," I said. I hung up and turned back to crouch next to Kip and Walt on the lawn next to Hank.

The ambulance crew arrived. The driver was our friend, Dan Bennett. He had a young lady riding with him. I relaxed some, but not much. I stood and let them attend to Hank.

"Which way was the truck going?" the State Policeman asked.

"East," Hank replied with a feeble wave of his hand. I thought his breathing seemed labored.

Walt was already in the road, looking for clues - shell casings or who knows what.

I joined him, just to have something to do, walking along in the gravel at the side of the road and looking down in the grass and on the shoulder of the road. We walked past Hank's yard, then stepped onto the asphalt and searched back, giving us a different perspective and inspecting the roadway, too. We found nothing.

The State Cop joined us, searching the other side of the road.

I walked back across the yard to where Hank was being loaded into the ambulance. Kip and Walt stood with me, worried looks on their faces. They looked like I felt.

Two more police cars arrived, parking on the front lawn.

The ambulance guys had started an I.V. for Hank and had given him an oxygen mask.

Hank reached up and tugged the mask aside.

He looked up, "They didn't shoot my old dog, did they?"

I had to laugh. "No, they didn't shoot Boomer," I said. "The livestock's okay, too."

"Good," he said, pausing to catch his breath. "Do me a favor?"

"Sure, Hank." I looked up at the others.

"Call Shonda," he said. "Dinner tonight."

"You won't be making it," Kip said. "Better take a rain check."

Hank smiled weakly. "Call the pastor?" he asked.

"We'll handle it," Kip answered.

"Once I get to the hospital, I'll be right as rain," Hank said.

"Easy in, easy out," I said, "Bob's your uncle." I forced a smile down at him.

"You riding?" Dan Bennett asked me.

"Sure, I'll go along," I said without hesitation, and climbed into the back. The lady medic got behind the wheel.

"Meet you in there," Kip called as he closed the door.

We were off, speeding down the road to the sound of the siren, lights flashing.

Attendants met us at the E.R. entrance and rushed Hank right in. Kuhlbaugh met us in the hall. Flint showed up with my wife just as we were following Hank down the hall, escorted to surgery by a team of doctors. Through the open doors, we saw them slide him onto a table, then the doors closed and we were left standing in the hallway. We looked at each other, wondering what to do next. My wife held my hand and tried not to look like she was going to cry. Once she started, then I surely would, too.

A volunteer came along and led us to a waiting room containing chairs, couches, a little hutch with a coffee pot, and some teeny water bottles.

"I called Hank's pastor," Flint said. "He said he'd be in shortly."

I nodded numbly. I'd forgotten all about the pastor and Shonda. "Kip said he'd call, too," I said. "The pastor is going to think it's the end of the line for Hank."

I took my phone out, excused myself, and stepped into the hallway to call Shonda. My wife followed me. "I don't know her number," I said, looking around for help. Then I remembered Hank's phone in my other pocket. I pulled it out, turned it on and, with the wife's help, looked up his phone list. There she was, under Miles, Shonda. I highlighted the number and pressed send. The phone rang a few times while we stood in the hallway, looking lost.

"Hi Baby," she answered in a silky smooth voice that made my heart flop around in my chest. I looked at my wife for support.

"Shonda? Ms. Miles?" I stammered. "This is Tim Conway. I'm a friend of Hank's." I tried to sound normal. Something in my voice must have given me away.

"What's wrong?" she asked in alarm. "Is Hank okay?"

"I'm at Jackson Hospital," I said, "with Hank. Well, not *with* Hank. He's in with the doctors." I didn't know how to say he'd been taken to surgery with gunshot wounds.

"Let me have that phone," my wife said, taking it from my hand. I gladly let her have it.

"Shonda? We've not met," my wife said, "but I'm Tim Conway's wife, Sue. Hank's going to be okay. Nothing life threatening, it seems, but he's been shot. The ambulance brought him in about fifteen minutes ago."

She listened for a moment. "Come in through E.R.," she said into the phone. "We're on the second floor, east wing. That's right," she said, "surgery. I'll meet you at the nurses' station." She listened for a moment more, "Okay then, see you in a few."

She turned to me, handed the phone back, and said, "One would think this was your first rescue."

"The first for a friend when I wasn't all busted up and in the hospital, myself," I said.

She put an arm around me and forced a smile. "Sorry," she said. "I can see it's really getting to you guys, that's all."

An aide came to the room and said the doctors expected Hank to be in surgery for another hour or so. They were removing the bullets now.

"Any damage?" Kuhlbaugh asked. "Lung or rib damage?"

"The doctor will fill you in when he's all done," she said. "I can't really say much at this time, just that he's doing well."

We all breathed a sigh of relief.

Kip showed up then with Walt alongside him. They wanted to know what was going on, too, so the aide had to repeat her report.

"Any internal damage?" Kip asked when she finished. She smiled as we burst into laughter. Kip looked bewildered.

"A doctor will fill you in after Mr. McIntyre's out of surgery," she grinned at him.

I decided to go to the cafeteria. Kuhlbaugh said he'd come along. My wife said she'd walk with us as far as the nurses' station. The others decided to hang around the waiting room for a while.

We walked down the hall. "I'm meeting Shonda here," my wife said. "You guys go on ahead."

I kissed her on the cheek and left with Kuhlbaugh.

We grabbed some coffees and sandwiches at the cafeteria and took a seat near a window. Kuhlbaugh ate a few bites of his sandwich, then looked across the table at me. "Jake LaBlanc was relieved of his duties as fire chief of Maple Grove Township last night", he said.

There go his plans to run for Township Treasurer," I said, shaking my head.

"Apparently there were, or are, irregularities in state reports, receipts, supplies, and missing funds from the woman's auxiliary." He looked at me. "Training and certifications hadn't been kept up, despite fire board prodding." Kuhlbaugh paused to take a drink of coffee, then continued.

"Jake and his sons are being picked up today for questioning in the death of the kid in the meth van," he said. "The boys are being questioned for their role as runners for their step-mother. They supplied the heroin to the kid known as Spoons. Mark LaBlanc was the one who supplied the heroin that killed the girl out on Barryton Road."

"At the log home," I nodded. "What better marketing strategy than to have a high-school kid dealing. What about the kid in the Gator wreck over in Hanover Township?" I asked, thinking that this was just getting better and better.

"He was making a delivery of meth and weed down the road at the time. We figure he hit a pot hole, lost control, and ended up wrecking his dad's Gator," Kuhlbaugh said. "The irony of the situation is that he was making enough money, dealing for Mrs. LaBlanc, to buy his own Gator."

"Hmm," I answered between bites of my sandwich. I relived the scene in my mind. The wrecked Gator down the embankment, and the LaBlancs standing around watching. "We never found any meth," I said.

"The kid said he had it," Kuhlbaugh said.

I swallowed a bite of sandwich. "How was the traffic stop on Moscow Road connected?" I asked.

"The men were scheduled to meet Meagan Grawn in the parking lot of the Gas-N-Go," the detective said.

"That much I knew," I said, taking a drink.

"Turns out, Meagan was a street coordinator for Claudette LaBlanc," Kuhlbaugh said. "She kept the street-level dealers in line and supplied. Pretty good business for a nineteen-year-old."

"I'll say," I replied, "and she didn't even have a high-school diploma."

"She was a natural as an independent contractor," Kuhlbaugh chuckled. "That is, until she got greedy."

"I take it she ran off with Richie Collins to get away from the LaBlancs," I said.

"You hit the nail on the head," the detective said. "Richie told investigators that she talked him into running away with her. She had some money squirreled away and needed a companion to share it with. Apparently it was the money she'd skimmed from her street sales."

"So," I said, "he really wasn't running to get away from abusive parents? Like anybody'd believe it."

"That was their cover story," the detective said. "Richie's older sister was getting on him for hanging out with Meagan and the drug scene. She threatened to tell the parents. The girl, Meagan, talked Richie into setting the fire to keep the parents from tracking him. With them and the sister out of the way, he'd be free as a bird." He finished the last bite of his sandwich and placed his napkin on the red, plastic tray.

"They didn't think it out very well," I said.

"You got that right," Kuhlbaugh said. "They seldom do."

We got up and took our trays to the return

station, then walked down the hall to the surgery waiting room.

"They killed Duke Williams because he'd been talking to the police," I commented, looking at the detective.

"Yes, that's what it looks like. Claudette LaBlanc lured him into an affair, then had him killed, is the way we figure it right now," he said.

"Now we need to find the guys who tried to kill Hank," I said.

Kuhlbaugh looked at me, "We'll get them," he said. "Sooner or later, we'll get them."

We walked into the waiting room.

My wife was there, seated on a couch, talking to a red eyed, worried looking, Shonda Miles. Both women clutched tissues in their hands.

We greeted them and I sat down next to my wife.

"He's out of surgery all ready," my wife said. "They have him in recovery and expect him to be in a room later tonight."

I looked at the women. They sat knee to knee, my wife holding Shonda's hand. Shonda still had those captivating green eyes, albeit a little tearful right now.

I remembered her as being a good looking woman, but I hadn't noticed until now that her hair and complexion had a slightly European look to them. It wasn't hard to see why Hank was smitten with her.

A female nurse, dressed in surgical scrubs, entered the room and looked around. "Shonda Miles?" she asked pleasantly.

"Here." Shonda stood up, trying to smile.

"Mr. McIntyre is asking to see you," the nurse said.

Shonda smiled and looked around the room, somewhat embarrassed to be singled out.

"Tell him we're praying for him," my wife said. She patted Shonda's hand.

Shonda left with the nurse.

We sat and made small talk for about ten minutes. Kip and Kuhlbaugh checked their cell phone messages, excused themselves, and stepped into the hall to make their calls.

Fifteen minutes later, Shonda returned. We all looked up as she entered the room.

"How is he?" I asked.

"He's pretty loopy," she said. "He's resting now, but wants to talk to Detective Kuhlbaugh in a little while. "He said he's sorry about not making dinner tonight - wanted me to say 'Hello' to everyone." She looked around the room, then at the wife and me.

"They're be plenty of other times," I said, "and please tell him that I'll take care of the chores and check on Boomer and Marcel."

"Thank you," she replied, "I'm sure he appreciates it. I'm going to stay here for a while, myself," she said.

"Is there anything we can bring you? Would you like company?" my wife asked.

"No, thanks anyway," Shonda said with a thin smile. "I've come prepared. I'll read a book while I'm waiting." She pointed to her bag on the floor.

We said good-by, and left Kuhlbaugh, Flint, and Shonda alone in the room. Kip and Walt followed us out.

A few policemen stood in the hallway, looking lost, and talking among themselves.

"That's the woman for Hank," my wife said after we'd cleared the hallway.

"Looks like it," I said absentmindedly. I was tossing around in my mind everything Kuhlbaugh had told me. Apparently the Maple Grove Township Supervisor, Stan Moore, was correct in being suspicious of LaBlanc's book keeping, after all. Things were really heating up. LaBlanc's wife had been arrested with two of her henchmen, or one henchman and a henchwoman.

We'd found Richie Collins, probably saving his life in the process, and pretty much figured out how the ring was being run.

Meagan Grawn was the street-level boss until she got greedy and ended up dead. Duke Williams was dead because he knew too much and was talking. Somebody was still out there, though. Hank was shot and recuperating in the hospital, and I was sure the shooters had been to my house. They probably had left because they got cold feet, or didn't see me around.

Chapter Thirty-one

Early the next morning, my wife and I rode in her mini van into Jackson Hospital to check on Hank. There weren't many cars in the visitor parking lot at that early hour. Schultzie met us on the sidewalk and we walked in together. After checking at the information desk for Hank's room number, we took the elevator up.

He was sleeping when we walked in. We sat down and looked at each other, trying to decide what to do next. Finally, we went back to the nurses' station and got a cup of coffee. Schultzie knew one of the nurses, a former baby-sitter or something, and stayed to catch up.

"I'm going down to the cafeteria," my wife said. "I could use some more coffee and some of those rubber scrambled eggs."

One of the nurses was going on break and

went along with her. They walked down the hallway chatting like old friends. And she says *I'll* talk to anyone.

I went back to Hank's room alone and sat in a chair and sipped my coffee, listening to his breathing. He had a monitor hooked to him and an I.V. port on the back of his right hand. An I.V. drip bag hung on a stand next to the head of the bed. Probably antibiotics. There were two pillows jammed under his left side to take some of the pressure off his wounds. I couldn't figure out how he could sleep like that, but then assumed they'd given him something to put him out. The place smelled like antiseptic and medicine of some type. It gave me the creeps.

Schultzie walked in and sat down. "Kid used to baby-sit for us when the kids were little," he said.

I nodded. Hank stirred and moaned in his sleep, then lay quietly. Schultz and I sat there looking at each other. I glanced around the room searching for some reading material.

Hank stirred again, and his eyelids fluttered. He cleared his throat. "Good morning," he said, his voice a little raspy from the tube they'd run down his throat during surgery.

He cleared his throat and tried again.

"Thanks for coming," he croaked. He looked at Schultzie and me. We leaned forward to hear him better.

He said, straight-faced, "When I first woke up, I thought maybe I'd died and gone directly to Hell. Couldn't make up my mind which of you was Old Scratch, come to greet me." He laughed hoarsely and winced in pain.

"Serves you right," I said, snickering to myself. "Old Scratch, my Aunt Tilly's corset!"

Schultzie laughed low, not wanting to make a scene.

Flint walked in then, all smiles and fresh-faced.

"Speak of the Devil," I said to Hank and Schultzie.

Flint looked at us questioningly. I told him about Hank waking up.

"Good one, Hank," he said. "I'll have to remember that one, just in case I ever find myself shot all to hell and laying in the hospital." He pulled up an extra chair and sat down next to the bed.

"We went back out to your place," he told Hank. "Searched back over the road and found nothing." He turned his empty hands palms up. "The State boys threw up a cordon around your place, while the ambulance was hauling you in, but no white pickup turned up. Of course," he said, "there are a lot of back roads and farm lanes in the area. Jordon came over and we started searching barns and out-buildings. Whoever it was, they got away." He shook his head.

"Any more details on the truck?" I glanced over at Hank.

"There's a dent in the box, and a bent bumper on the right-rear," Flint said, "and Michigan plates. That's all Hank could remember."

"It happened so fast," Hank croaked. "I was walking across the lawn with my old dog, Boomer, and heard the truck approaching out on the road. I didn't think anything of it. Traffic goes by now and then, even out my way. When they slowed down, I looked over and saw the white truck," he said. "Two white guys in it - younger guys. I never saw a gun." He paused to rest a moment. "Hurts to talk," he said with a pained smile.

I stepped over next to Flint and held a styrofoam cup and straw up to Hank's lips. He took a long sip.

"Thanks," He whispered.

"The ribs?" I asked. I sat back down, still holding the styrofoam cup.

He nodded slightly. "That and my throat." He swallowed and continued. "The guys were young, late teens, early twenties. I told the state guys yesterday," he said. "The truck didn't stop, so I turned to go on over to the feed lot. That's when the shot's hit. One went by my head, then the two in my back."

I stood and held the cup of water so Hank could have another sip from the straw.

"My Lord," Schultz said, "how bad did it hurt, getting shot like that?"

"That's the funny thing," Hank said. "I felt the rounds hit, like getting punched, then stinging. Then the truck accelerated and took off, heading east."

"Stinging?" I asked.

"Yeah, a bad, burning sting," Hank replied. "Then it started to hurt. The doctors tell me one of the rounds deflected off the back of a rib. The other went into a lobe of my left lung and hit the back of a front rib. They took both slugs out in the surgery."

".22 caliber," Flint said. "The doctor gave us a report last night. The state police have the bullets."

Hank closed his eyes and rested a bit, still all doped up. "Conway," he finally said, "Shonda tells me you're taking care of the chores. Thank you."

"Glad to do it," I replied.

Hank said, "Now, think you could slip these pillows out from under me? I need to shift position."

I looked at Schultz and Flint. "Sure," I said to Hank. I set the cup down on the little hospital table and walked around to the side of the bed. I wasn't sure if I was breaking a hospital rule, if I was supposed to be assisting patients. Schultzie came to help. Hank lifted his body, with some help from us, and we pulled the flattened pillows out. He eased himself down on his back, made a face, then relaxed.

"That's better," he said.

"Doesn't it hurt now?" Schultz asked.

"Some," Hank replied, "but they've got me on pain meds."

"If it gets too bad," Flint said, grinning, "maybe we can get some street stuff in here. I hear it dulls pain."

We all laughed at that one. Even Hank.

Someone stepped into the room. Nan Spink. Evidently she was on her way to work, as she was wearing her veterinarian outfit.

"Good morning, Hank," she said cheerfully. "Morning boys." She looked around the room and nodded a greeting. We stepped back so she could stand next to the bed. "I can only stay a minute," she said. "Got puppies to save, you know." She smiled down at Hank.

My wife walked in then and greeted Nan.

Flint excused himself and left with a promise to come back later in the day.

Nan asked Hank how he was feeling, promised to check on the feeder pigs, chatted for a few minutes, gave his hand a little squeeze and was on her way, too.

We sat and talked to Hank for a while. We did most of the talking while he grunted or put in the occasional word. Around eight o'clock Shonda Miles came in. She carried a bag and looked prepared to spend the day.

The wife, Schultzie, and I excused ourselves and went back down to the cafeteria.

A half hour went by and we returned to the room to join Shonda in a semicircle of chairs around Hank's bed. A nurse came in and checked with Hank about some breakfast. He begged off for the time being. She looked over his I.V. port, smiled at us and left.

Hank drifted off to sleep and we talked low among ourselves.

A disturbance in the hallway drew our attention. An older, black woman, maybe sixty something, walked in the door. Or should I say, blew in the door like an arriving storm. She was slim, well dressed, and wore a string of white pearls, reminding me of a black June Cleaver. A foreign doctor followed at her heals, white coat flapping. A young nurse trotted along behind the doctor.

The woman gave us all a quick look, "Hmmph," she said, then turned to examine the I.V. bags, labels, tubing, and the port on Hank's hand. She pulled back his flimsy sheet to probe at his bandages.

"Oh, Mom," Hank groaned from his bed, wide awake now.

The doctor, a young, middle-eastern man, stepped forward, "Who are you, Madam?" He asked in his accented English.

I didn't know what went on out in the hallway, but he had the look of someone who'd had his feathers ruffled and didn't like it. The nurse stood by, smugly clutching an electronic clipboard to her chest. She was putting her money on the doctor.

"I'm his Momma. That's who I am," the woman answered curtly, giving the man an icy stare. "When I heard he'd been shot, I dropped everything and drove up from Chicago. Now, who might *you* be?"

"I'm Doctor Kazan, his attending physician," the doctor replied firmly. "I wasn't aware that Mr. McIntyre had relatives near."

"Didn't you hear me?" Hank's mother asked. "I drove up from Chicago." She crossed her arms and gave us all a steady look like she was dealing with a room full of idiots.

The nurse took a step back.

"Somebody's got to make sure my little boy's being taken care of," Hank's mother said, "and I'm here, now." She nodded her head for emphasis.

I found it hard to imagine Hank ever being her little boy, even though I knew he once was.

"Well," replied the doctor, somewhat taken aback, "unauthorized people shouldn't be checking his I.V. It takes a trained professional to attend the I.V.s." He looked around the room at the rest of us. We looked down, or away. This was his battle.

"I've been playing the nursing game since before you were in diapers," she responded firmly, giving the nurse a hard glance, then fixing her gaze steadily on the doctor. "Chicago General, if you feel the need to check."

So this is Hank's mother. How was it he described her? Like a hurricane? His earlier description didn't do her justice.

The doctor seemed to deflate some. Shonda and my wife looked at each other, not sure what to think. I was wishing I'd stayed in the cafeteria.

"By the way doctor," Hank's mother said, raising her index finger to command his attention, "whoever hung the I.V. knows what they're about." She gestured at the drip tubes. "I couldn't have done a better job myself. I can see that the Lord has put my Henry in good hands." She broke into a broad smile.

We sat in our chairs and looked at each other with relief. Hank groaned, "Oh, Mom."

"You may leave now," Hank's mom said to the doctor. "We're okay here." She glanced at the door.

We all looked toward the door. The nurse and the doctor looked toward the door, then the doctor turned to leave with the nurse trailing behind like she was connected by a string. The doctor made a sudden stop and turned around.

"Madam?"

"Yes?"

"Are you available for marriage?"

"Honey, you wouldn't last through the first night." She stood, hands on her hips. Her eyes softened, and she giggled like a school girl.

The doctor grinned broadly, waved to us, and left the room.

"Oh, Mom!" Hank moaned from his bed.

"Now Henry, you just rest easy," she said, bending over him to straighten his sheets.

"Your brother, Harold, and sissy, Sarah, send their love."

So went our introduction to Hank's mother. She had the confidence and disposition of a veteran school teacher, and certainly wasn't one to be trifled with.

She more or less lined us up and gave us all the once over. "And you must be Shonda," she said as she came to Shonda and grasped her hands. "From Henry's description, I'd know you anywhere."

"Yes, Shonda Miles," Shonda answered, "a friend of Hank's."

"The way he talks about you, I'd hope you're more than just a friend." She threw her arms around Shonda and gave her a warm hug. "It's so nice to finally meet you," she said. "You really do have beautiful eyes."

Shonda blushed deeply.

I wondered what, specifically, Hank had told his mother. Or, more than likely, what she'd brow-beat out of him.

When we left, Shonda and Hank's mother were nestled in the room talking like life-long friends. I knew Hank was doomed. I figured the wedding invitations would be coming in the spring.

Schultzie walked out with us, wished us a good day, and left in his truck.

We got in the wife's mini-van. She didn't waste any time. "I thought Hank's mom would measure Shonda's hips for birthing babies," she snickered.

"That's kind of sexist," I replied.

"Somebody once told me that the truth is never sexist," she said, smirking.

She had me there. I laughed. "I guess the hunt is over. You ladies can move on to the next target."

She gave me that look women give to men when they can't believe how stupid they are.

Chapter Thirty-two

I stopped over at the fire garage the next morning before heading in to visit Hank. Kip's truck was in its usual spot next to the building. He almost always came in on Sunday mornings for a few minutes. I walked past his pickup and could hear the pinging noises of the engine cooling off. He hadn't been there long.

I walked in. He was in his office, working over his computer. He looked up, "Good morning, Tim," he smiled.

"Kip," I replied. "You going in to see Hank?" I glanced over at the coffee pot on the shelf. Empty.

"Saw him last night. I'll go in with the wife and Nan this evening." He waved his hand at the coffee maker. "Go ahead," he said. "Run a pot. I could drink a cup, just got here, myself."

I filled the coffee reservoir with cold water, added eight spoonfuls of coffee to a fresh filter, put it all in the basket and turned it on.

Kip had returned to filling out a form on his computer. "Leaving a paper trail for the fire trucks on the Fourth," he said over his shoulder.

There was a calender on the wall above Kip's desk, between the windows, right below the clock. It was turned to July, and featured an antique Seagrave fire engine. A dalmatian was sitting behind the wheel, wearing a miniature fireman's hat. I noticed the Fourth of July was circled in red.

"Holy cow!" I exclaimed, "That's next week."

"I know," Kip said. "Three days. Kinda' crept up on us, didn't it? Flint would tell you that summer's almost on the down-hill side, might as well get out the snow shovels." He grinned at me.

"How's your sister feel about it?" I asked. "The one who teaches at Maple Grove."

Kip shook his head. "She feels the same way. After the July Fourth Holiday, it's all down hill to September. Kind of depressing, ain't it? Must be something they put in the water at all the schools," he said.

"I don't doubt it," I laughed. "Anyway, you driving a truck in the parade over in Hanover?"

"Engine 1," Kip replied. "Schultzie and some of his kids are taking the tanker. You want to drive the rescue van or the grass rig?"

"Not I," I said. "I'll be taking a Studebaker to the parade. Hank was planning on driving one of his 8Ns."

"Maybe next year," Kip replied sadly, glancing down at his keyboard. "By the way, when's he going to be released?" He said it like Hank was in prison, not a hospital.

The doctor thinks he's in for at least four or five days," I replied, "maybe longer. Knowing Hank, he'll be wanting to go home sooner, like yesterday."

"Well, it's been two days, now," Kip replied. "He's probably searching for his clothes as we speak."

"You got that right," I said. "He can be a persistent old cuss." I poured coffee for the both of us, drank a cup while we talked some more, then said good-bye to the chief, and drove on to Jackson Hospital.

Hank was awake and talking to an aide who was taking away his breakfast tray. He looked up as I walked in.

"Hey, Tim Conway," he grinned. "Good to see you, as usual."

"Hank McIntyre," I answered, "you're looking chipper. How's the food?" I pointed at the red plastic tray, with the plastic dishes, that the aide held in his hands.

"You help me get out of here, we'll go out to the Wooden Spoon, in Spring Arbor, and have us a real omelet," he answered. "That's how it is."

The aide shook his head in amusement and left.

"Sorry buddy, not until the doctor says so," I said.

Hank folded his arms over his chest and inclined his head to give me a stare. "Some friend," he commented.

"Making me feel guilty won't work," I replied. "The way you're looking, it won't be long anyway. You're mom will be up, taking you home."

"You put it that way," he said, grinning, "maybe I'd rather stay here."

I said, "I talked to her yesterday when I

went over to feed the cattle and those feeder pigs. She insisted on taking care of the laying hens, said it makes her feel like a kid again. She's fallen for Marcel, you know."

"That old tom-cat sure knows how to steal a girl's heart," he laughed. He looked around the room and tried to peek out the door to the hallway. I thought he was fixin' to ask me to help him escape again.

"I have a confession," he said in a low voice. "Don't say anything to my mother or to Shonda."

I couldn't imagine what could be so serious. "One of the female nurses give you a special sponge bath?" I asked straight-faced.

"No," he waved a hand at me. "When I was shot, and that truck took off, I said the firetruck word. Out loud."

"Not *the* firetruck word?!" I couldn't hide my surprise.

"Afraid so," Hank responded dejectedly. "I wanted to snap some little red-neck legs, and it just came out."

"I think it's understandable, considering the special occasion," I explained. "You talk to the pastor about it?"

Hank grinned, somewhat embarrassed. "No,

you know how that goes," he said. "His ears would probably ignite, a real conflagration. He's a good man, though. Been in to see me twice now... even met Shonda."

"Met your mom?"

"She thinks he's a saint," Hank replied. "They hit it off like old school mates."

"It helps that he's a Baptist," I said, grinning.

"And his grandfather's from Chicago," Hank added with a laugh. "You really think I should talk to him?"

"No, no need, I said. "You told me, and I'm not breathing a word. That ought to be good enough. You were shot in the back, for cryin'-out-loud."

"Thanks, man," he said, looking relieved.

I turned serious. "Any complications?" I asked. "No fluid on the lungs or the thorax?"

"No," Hank replied shaking his head. "I'm a lucky guy. Doc says the bullet nicked the lower lobe of my left lung. I've got a cracked rib in the back, but I'm going to heal," he said.

He glanced out the open doorway into the hall again, then back at me. "When I get out of here," he said in a serious tone, "you and

I are going dumb-ass hunting, if you'll pardon the expression."

"I'm with you," I said. "By the way, any word on the drug-bust front?"

"Mrs. LaBlanc made bail," Hank said, shaking his head in disbelief. "The two we found in the pole barn are still being held. Richie Collins has been cooling his heals in juvenile. His parents have visited him a few times, but his big sister refuses to see him. 'Least that's the word I got," he said.

"That's too bad," I responded. "He really needs to make amends with the whole family. I'm betting sister will come around after a while. She just needs to sort some things out."

Hank nodded in agreement. "What's that you got there?" He pointed to the laptop under my arm and the plastic bag I had carried in and placed on a chair.

"Your laptop from home," I answered. "Also, I brought a blue-tooth receiver and speaker kit."

Hank looked at me, puzzled.

"I'll set this up so you can stream the internet radio through the speakers. Tonight's Sunday, and there's a program of big band music on at eight 'til midnight. It's out of Fordham University in New York City."

"Big band music?" Hank asked with interest.

"Called 'The Big Broadcast'," I said. "Music from the twenties and thirties. I know you like more of the forties stuff, but this will get you your fix, I'm sure."

"Hey, thanks, brother," he replied happily as I plugged in his laptop and hooked up the speaker bar for him. We did a quick run through of how to find the station, then I had him do it. He seemed to perk up considerably.

We talked a while longer, with me filling him in on how the animals were doing back on the the farm. "The feeder pigs miss you," I said, "but they're still getting fat."

That was met with a knowing smile and head nod. "You driving a Stude in the Fourth of July Parade over to Hanover?" he asked.

"You bet," I responded with a nod. "You know it's this Wednesday, right?"

"Wish I could be there, but doesn't look like I'm making it this year, even if they let me out of here," he added, looking as sad as I'd ever seen him look.

The man loved parades, especially parades

with old tractors and classic cars.

"Mom will have me chained to a bedpost, if I know her," he said.

I lingered a while, then said my good-bye and left just as Dr. Kazan came in to check on Hank. He was still being followed by the nurse clutching an electronic clipboard. She glanced around the room as if expecting Hank's mom to pop out of the closet or something.

On my way to the truck, my cell phone pager went off. "Jackson Central to Pulaski Rescue. Woman having difficulty breathing." The dispatcher gave the address on the north side of Pulaski. Ruthie's address. I paused and listened to the call come back from Pulaski. Kip was arriving at the station and would be driving Rescue 1 to the scene. Fred called in and was in route direct to Ruthie's house where he'd meet up with Kip.

I got in my truck and started the drive home, listening to the radio traffic out of Central Dispatch. Half-way through Jackson, Kip's voice came on, calling for an ambulance. He was at Ruthie's house and reported in;

"Unresponsive female, age sixty-three. No pulse and no circulation," he said.

I could visualize Kip and Fred working

over Ruthie as she lay in a heap on her stained couch in the middle of a sea of litter, the television silently playing in the corner. The Jerry Springer show came to mind.

Over the radio, I could hear Fred's garbled voice calling from the background, "Still no pulse, Chief," and I knew he was working on her, not giving up.

At this time in the morning, Ruthie's daughter, Patty, would be at home. She was still working her second shift job at the party store up in Concord. One of the firemen had seen her there last week.

I could imagine skinny Patty storming in, ready to light into her mother again, only to find her laying motionless on the couch, or maybe the floor, while Kip and Fred stood around nervously waiting for the police and ambulance to show up. I found out later that Patty *was* home, saw the rescue unit, and came running over to lay into her mother, only to discover she was dead. Kip told me she didn't break down into hysterics like he expected.

"I told her this would happen," she said tearfully to Kip and Fred. "To tell the truth, I've been expecting it."

Kip said she sat on the couch next to her

dead mother and held her lifeless hand while waiting for the authorities to show up.

Deputy Jordon arrived and stood talking quietly with Kip and Fred.

Central Dispatch alerted an ambulance crew that was stopped for lunch in Concord. Within minutes it was on the scene. Shorty, I heard Kip report to Central Dispatch, "Pulaski Rescue 1, clear," he said in a subdued voice.

The ambulance crew had loaded Ruthie up and taken her to Jackson Hospital, where she was pronounced dead.

I drove on home, out M-60 through Spring Arbor and on through the countryside to Concord, then south to my little farm. It's a scenic drive, but I was deep in thought about old Ruthie. I'd been to her house a half-dozen times over the last couple of years. Kip, the same, along with Schultzie, and we'd learned a lot about the family, more than I wanted to know. I wondered if Patti would end up moving into the house and renting out the trailer. Maybe she'd sell the place and move away.

I parked the truck and walked into the house. My wife was busy at the kitchen counter. She turned and smiled, "How's Hank today?"

"He's really doing well, ready to go home," I said.

"Then what's wrong?" she asked.

The look on my face must have given me away. Thirty-five years of marriage...

"Ruthie died while I was in town," I said sadly. "Kip and Fred had the run. I expected the usual, they check her out, give her a lecture about taking her meds, have a talk with Patti, then leave."

"Oh, no," my wife said. "I'm so sorry." She stood at the counter, facing me, a wooden spoon in her hand. She'd been to Ruthie's, once, delivering a Christmas bundle for the Church. Patti had cleaned the place up some so the church ladies didn't experience the house in all its glory.

"I guess we should have expected it," I said. "She suffered from cardiopulmonary disease among a variety of other ailments.

"Well, it's too bad, anyway. She'll be missed," my wife replied sympathetically, turning back to whatever she was working on.

I went out on the deck, leaned against the railing, and pulled out my cell phone to call Kip.

Chapter Thirty-three

The phone rang in my hand. It was Kip.

"Yes, Kip?"

"I've just left Ruthie's house," Kip started in.

"I heard it on the phone, and the truck radio while I was in town," I said. "Kind of depressing, isn't it?" I gazed off across the lush, rolling fields of my farm.

Each July Fourth, Ruthie's daughter, Patty, would load her into her worn out car and take her to the parade in Hanover. I made it a point to look for them while driving by in my Studebaker. Ruthie loved old cars.

"Yes, it is, but that's not why I called," he replied. "Schultzie and I were out by the road, seeing the ambulance off, when a white Ford pickup went by, heading south."

"Extended cab?" I asked. He had my rapt attention.

"Yes," he replied, "I radioed in to Central and a cop is on the way."

"So am I," I said. I slid open the patio door and called to the wife, "I'll be right back. Gotta check out a pickup truck, if I can find it."

She turned to look at me. "You be careful."

I was already off the deck and heading toward the Dodge. I still had Kip on the phone and asked him to call Central Dispatch and tell them the truck is suspected to have been used in a shooting and a witness is coming out to I.D. it.

"A witness?" Kip sounded doubtful.

"Well, what else can we tell them that can get me near the truck?" I asked.

"How about we had an arson and the truck was seen leaving the area. I'm sending out a fire investigator to take a look," Kip said.

"Wish I'd thought of that," I replied.

"Call you back," he said.

I headed south through Pulaski, past the four corners and the general store. A few cars and a pickup truck were parked out front. Across the side street, the hardware had a closed sign in the dusty front window.

Without knowing where I was going, I headed south on Pulaski Road. The white pickup could have turned off anywhere. It could be behind me now, for all I knew.

My cell rang again - Kip calling me back. "Hillsdale County Deputies have a white Ford pickup truck pulled over on Mosherville Road in Mosherville. Right there by the lake," he said, "near where we drafted water last year for that barn fire."

"I know the place," I said. "Any word on the driver?"

"None so far. Sounded like only one person in the truck, though," he replied.

I thanked him for the information and hung up with a promise to call him with an update. Goose Lake Road appeared. It was the last road before the Pulaski Road curved to the west, bent back south, and entered Hillsdale County to become Concord Road.

Goose Lake Road, the wreck of the white van came to mind as I drove on south through the quiet countryside the few miles to Mosherville Road.

I turned west and skirted the south side of the hamlet that used to be known as Mosherville Station, but now was known to everyone simply as Mosherville, the railroad tracks having been pulled up long ago. The road began a slow curve around a small, lovely lake, shining like a fine jewel in the warm July sun under a nearly cloudless sky of deep blue. It didn't take much to imagine I could see the bass and bluegill hiding in the shade under the lily pads.

Up ahead, red and blue lights flashing from two brown Hillsdale County patrol cars, along with the red bubble of a blue State Police cruiser, told me I'd found the spot. They had boxed in a white Ford pickup, extended cab, but not the one I was looking for. I saw no dent in the back bumper or evidence of a caved-in right rear fender. There was a scrape in the paint on the left rear, above the wheel well, that Hank hadn't mentioned.

The elderly driver looked shaken as he leaned back against one of the brown sheriff's cars. He picked his dusty Farm-all hat off his head and wiped his forehead with his arm.

A lady deputy leaned alongside him, talking.

Stopping behind the squad cars, I got out of my truck. The officers looked up. I was in luck. The lady deputy looked familiar, must have seen her somewhere around Hillsdale. The state man was one I'd seen somewhere, too. Maybe at the meth-lab bust outside of Osseo.

"Mr. Conway," he greeted me as I walked up, "Detective Kuhlbaugh told me to expect you." He gave me a friendly wave.

"Gentlemen, Ma'am," I nodded at the lady deputy.

"You're the investigator from the auction grounds," she said, smiling in recognition.

"Yes Ma'am," I grinned back at her. "You're Deputy Troyer," I checked her name tag, "the one who speaks in dialect to the Amish kids," I said.

She grinned, "Yes, and you're the one who chases suspects half-way across town."

"You're thinking of McIntyre," I replied. "I was just trying to catch up."

"The runner made a move to the Speed Barn just when you popped out," she said. "That turned him back toward Kuhlbaugh and me behind the hay bales."

I grinned some more, glad that somebody thought I'd had something to contribute. In-vestigator. How about that for a title? I'd have to remember to tell my wife this.

"Well," I said, "I'm afraid this isn't the truck we're looking for."

"I suspected as much," the State Trooper said. "Mr. Dancer, here, doesn't appear the type to be driving the truck you're looking for." He nodded at the old man, who smiled meekly and nodded his head. He was dressed in faded denim work pants, a white T-shirt that hadn't really been white in years, and oil stained work boots.

"I've been to the I.H. dealer up in Concord," he said. "Needed some parts for my baler. I must say you folks startled me out of ten years growth."

He didn't look to me like he had ten years to spare, so I just smiled and extended my hand. "Thank you for your patience, Mr. Dancer," I said. "Your truck somewhat resembles one were looking for, one that was involved in an earlier incident," I said.

"Involved in a shooting," the state cop interrupted, apparently not buying the story Kip told Kuhlbaugh, or Kuhlbaugh didn't pass it on.

The old farmer looked shocked. "A shooting, you say." He lifted his dusty cap from his head, wiped his brow again with his arm, and nervously repositioned the cap. "Anybody dead?" he asked, looking at me, then to the state trooper.

"No," the trooper replied, "but a man was shot in the back."

"A good man," the lady deputy added.

"He's a friend of mine," I said, "and he was badly injured."

"I hope you find the shooter," the old guy said, looking at all of us. "Come to think of it, somebody over Litchfield way has a truck like mine. I was over to the I.H. dealer on the north side, on M-49, and one of the mechanics said something about me getting the dent fixed on my truck. Said it must have been a quick job, seeing as how it was dented up just the day before. 'The right-rear fender,' he said. I was in a hurry to get back to the farm and didn't have time to stop and straighten him out."

I nodded in encouragement. "The equipment dealership on the north side of town, you say?"

"Yup, I guess there's somebody driving around the area in a white Ford like mine." He shook his head slowly. "Maybe that's something you fellows could check out. Oh, you too, Ma'am," he said, shyly looking at the lady deputy.

"Did the mechanic say where he saw the truck?" Deputy Troyer asked.

"No, but I took it that it was there at the dealership," the farmer said. "Last Monday, if I recall correctly. I was there on Tuesday, the next day," he added.

"Well, thanks again," I said. "Good luck with your haying." I turned and stepped back, watching him walk over to his pickup cab and open the door.

The State Trooper got in his blue cruiser and pulled it ahead, out of the way. The Hillsdale officers stepped back with me and watched the truck leave.

"Litchfield area?" The trooper looked at me. He'd gotten out of his cruiser and walked back to us.

"Sounds like it," I said. "Maybe the people at the equipment dealership know the person."

"I'll relay the information to our detectives," the State Trooper said.

I thanked the officers for their time and got in my Dodge and left. Glancing at the clock above the radio, I saw that it was getting on toward one o'clock. The thought crossed my mind to turn west and drive over to Litchfield, then I remembered that today was Sunday, the implement dealership would be closed. A trip would have to wait until tomorrow.

I drove to Pulaski and pulled into the Fire Station, hoping to find Kip's truck there. It wasn't. I parked by the office, pulled out my cell, and called Kip. He answered on the third ring. The sound of a little kid yelling and running around in the background came over his phone. His little girl. I let him know about the possible Litchfield connection, if there really was one.

"I'll give Kuhlbaugh a call, if it's okay with you," he said.

"Sure," I replied. "He might like to go along. In fact, he'll probably insist on it," I said. "It would be nice to have someone from law enforcement with me." If I couldn't have Hank along to lend an air of authority, Kuhlbaugh would do.

"If he can't go, our man, Flint, might go along," Kip said.

We talked a while more, then I hung up and resumed my drive home.

Chapter Thirty-four

The next morning, around nine, Kuhlbaugh stood on my rain-soaked deck and tapped on the glass. He was sipping from a take-out cup of coffee, and was dressed in blue jeans, a denim work shirt, and a John Deere hat. The rain had come in about midnight, then moved on an hour before he'd shown up.

I kissed the wife and, grabbing my to-go cup, joined him on the deck. Off to the west, patches of blue in the sky hinted at the return of fair weather.

"Good to see you this morning, Conway," he said, smiling and shaking my hand. "I've got a good feeling about today." He took another sip of his coffee.

"Let's hope so," I replied, looking around the yard and down the damp gravel driveway. Kuhlbaugh's black four-door rested off to one side, in the wet grass.

"Flint's going to meet us in Pulaski," he said in answer to my inquiring look.

"Okay then," I said, with a nod, "let's get on the road." Per our conversation of the night before, it was decided to take my truck as it would fit in the best. Flint wanted to come along in case we needed him, and would follow in an unmarked car.

We talked and sipped our coffee as I drove west on McDonald to Pulaski Road, then south. Kuhlbaugh asked how I wanted to handle it, once we got to the farm equipment dealership.

I thought of the time Hank and I went to the Hillsdale auction and he used the story of owing some guy money. "I'll owe a guy one-hundred dollars," I said. "People give up information if it will help a friend get money, especially if it's one hundred bucks. At least that's what Hank claims."

"I've used that one, myself," Kuhlbaugh said, grinning. "We'll play it by ear."

"Mmm," I replied with a nod while taking a swallow of coffee. We drove south, through Pulaski, and into the rich, rolling, farm country dotted with scattered farmsteads. A mile south, a silver Chevy two-door pulled up close behind, dropped back fifty yards, then followed. "Our man, Flint, has decided to join us," I said with a nod to the mirror.

We drove on into Hillsdale County and came to West Litchfield Road. I turned right. It was now a straight shot across northern Hillsdale County to the town of Litchfield.

We were there in fifteen minutes, coming into downtown just south of where M-49 joins M-99. I drove north through town on M-99. A large Case-IH sign stood up ahead, on our right. I turned into the gravel lot, driving through puddles, past rows of gleaming red tractors, and huge implements that my grand-father would have killed for.

"Looks like they got more rain here than we did," Kuhlbaugh remarked as I pulled up to a parking place by a door that had "Parts and Service" painted above it on the block wall.

The silver Chevy drove on by to the far end of the lot and entered a drive that led to the used farm equipment. As Kuhlbaugh and I walked to the parts department door, I saw Flint get out of his car and walk over to a used International 1066 tractor. He pretended to look it over.

"Can I help you gentlemen," a friendly, older parts man asked as we neared the counter. He was a tall, thin man with a receding hair line and twinkling blue eyes.

"Good morning," I said, smiling my best smile, and tilted my seed-corn hat back on my head. "A friend of mine was in here last Tuesday," I began, hoping I sounded sincere, "buying parts for his tractor. While he was here, he said one of the mechanics got his truck confused with one that had a dent in the right rear fender and the bumper. It's a white, extended cab, four-wheel drive Ford. That's the guy I'm trying to find."

"You guys cops?" asked the parts man suspiciously. "Somebody in trouble?" He leaned over the counter and looked at our scuffed work boots.

"No, we're not cops," Kuhlbaugh half lied. "You think we'd be riding around in some crummy Dodge pickup if we were?"

I shot him a quick glance. Crummy Dodge?

"Nothing like that," I said to the counter man. I owe the guy with the dented pickup a hundred dollars, that's all.

The man raised his eyebrows in surprise. "A hundred bucks! That's a lot of money!"

"We were at the Hillsdale Auction last week," I started in, hoping my story sounded good. "I bought a .30-06 Springfield rifle from the guy. I sold it later and more than doubled my money. I told him at the sale yard that I'd pay him extra if I made big money off it. Well, that's what I did. I don't think he believed me, as we got to talking guns and I didn't get much out of him about where he lived, other than around Litchfield. I did see his truck, though."

"It's a damn good gun," Kuhlbaugh stepped forward. I'm the one who found the collector to buy it. The man at the sale yard got took if my friend here can't find him to pay the extra money. It's only the right thing to do," he said, his voice dripping with sincerity.

"You're one honest man," the counter man said to me. The name above his pocket said Dave. "Not many people would put forth the effort."

"He seemed like a nice guy and, to tell the truth, looked like he could use the cash," I said. "I would look for him at the sale barn, but I work most every Saturday and can't be there."

"Hmm," the man said. He turned to an open door leading into a room stocked with shelves overflowing with parts. "Hey, Carl, you back there?" he called through the door. "Carl?!"

"I'm coming," a voice called from somewhere in the back. A young man appeared in the doorway. He was wearing a standard shop uniform of a white short-sleeved shirt, with his name above the pocket, and blue work pants with leather work boots. He had a shaved head and a silver stud earring in his right ear. Tattoos of a bird that somewhat resembled a peacock covered both forearms. "Yeah?" He eyed us suspiciously.

"You see a dented up white Ford pickup in here last week?" the counterman asked.

"Somebody in trouble?" Carl asked, his eyes narrowing on us.

"No," nothing like that." I repeated my story about the auction.

"Yeah, I saw it, a four-wheel drive Ford. A white one," he said grudgingly, not too eager to help. "I thought it was in here the next day. An old man was driving. It had been repaired, but had a new scrape on the left fender."

"Did you see the driver on Monday?" I asked. Kuhlbaugh was browsing through a bin of assorted draw pins and didn't seem to be paying attention.

"Two younger guys, I think," Carl answered. They were buying baler parts for a round baler. I had to order one part from our warehouse."

My ears perked up. Two younger guys. Kuhlbaugh stiffened and glanced my way.

"So they'll have to come and pick it up later?"

"Yeah, it came in last Friday. The office called and left a message but they haven't come in to pick it up yet," he said.

"Guess it couldn't be too important," I said. "But, if you've got a number, I could call the guy. Bet he could use the money to pay for that part," I added.

Kuhlbaugh eased up behind me, evesdropping.

"Hell, I can do better than that," Carl answered. He went to a computer and typed in something. He looked up. "Here it is," he said, turning the monitor on its swivel base so I could see it.

Bingo! I had a name and an address. I started to reach in my pocket for my pen and paper that I always carried, but a pen and note pad appeared over my right shoulder from

Kuhlbaugh. I took them and copied down the name, address, and phone number. If this was really our guy, he lived south-east of Homer, in the middle of nowhere.

I handed the pen and pad back to Kuhlbaugh. We thanked the men for their help and turned to leave.

"You sure you're not cops?" Carl asked.

I laughed and waved as we walked out the open door.

"Nice story back there," Kuhlbaugh said when we reached the parking lot. "The gun angle really pulled then in."

"I didn't think it would work at first," I said, shaking my head.

We got into the truck. "Tony Marshall, on 28 Mile Road," Kuhlbaugh read my note. He looked at me. "Feel like going for a drive?"

"Let's go," I said, looking into the side mirror as Flint's car crept through the machinery row toward us. He pulled up next to Kuhlbaugh's side of my truck.

"We got an address," the detective said. "Care to follow us up to Homer?"

"Lead the way," Flint said.

I backed the truck up and left the parking lot, headed north on M-99. At West Mosherville Road, I turned east and drove through the open countryside to Adams Road and headed north. Adams would turn into 28 Mile at the county line.

Kuhlbaugh got out his smart phone and was looking up the address of the farm. "Should be up here on the right," he said, "about a mile past South County Line Road."

I nodded. An aging, two story, farm house came into view. Two little kids were playing on an old swing set in the front yard, sheltered under an aging maple tree.

There was a small, gambrel-roof barn that was in bad need of paint, resting just behind the house. Next to the barn, a skinny, chestnut-colored horse stuck it's head over a wooden fence. In front of the barn sat a white extended cab pickup with a dent in the right-rear fender and a bent bumper. A Dodge pickup.

I looked at Kuhlbaugh. "Looks like another crummy Dodge," I said.

He smiled back at me. "Maybe Hank got it wrong," he said.

"So'd the guy at the parts counter," I said, "but he was probably smokin' crack."

I slowed the truck and Flint went around

us, driving slowly past the farm. Down the road a way, I saw his brake lights come on.

"Pull in," Kuhlbaugh said. "We've got to check it out anyway."

I pulled into the drive. Now that the sun was out, most of the rain had dried up. The little kids, a boy and a girl, ran up onto the porch and silently watched us. A young woman came to the door and stood behind the screen.

Kuhlbaugh got out first and I trailed along behind, wondering how this was going to play out.

"Good morning," Kuhlbaugh called out. "We've just come from the Case-IH dealer in town. They have a part on order for a round baler and it's in. Carl, at the parts counter, said the office called, but no one has been in to pick it up." He smiled broadly at the young woman.

She opened the door and stepped onto the porch, but didn't say anything. The little kids crowded close to her and clung to her legs. "Must be Tony's dad's," she finally said. "They're over to his farm now, fixin' to use the neighbor's baler, once the hay dries." She had a guarded look to her.

We stood in the yard, looking up at her,

and I could see we weren't getting anywhere.

"I told Carl I was coming this way and would swing by to let you know the part was in," Kuhlbaugh said, still smiling. I noticed he was glancing around the place as he spoke.

I kept an eye on the barn and the side of the house. "That your horse?" I asked the woman.

"Yeah, she's not much to look at, but she's a good ol' gal," she replied, relaxing a little.

"Got some standard bred in her," I said.

The woman's face lit up. "That's right," she said, taking a step closer on the porch. "I used to ride her in competition at the fair when I was in 4H. That's been a while."

"Nothing like a good horse," I said. "She looks to go about fifteen hands. Mind if I go look at her?"

Kuhlbaugh was giving me a stunned look.

"Sure," the woman said, easing her guard. "Come on, kids. Let's go see Josie." The kids took off like calves released from a pen. In an instant they were off the porch, around the house and standing at the fence, petting Josie's muzzle.

We walked along behind. I noticed the

woman's clothes were worn, but neat and clean. There were well tended flowers planted along the house and a few tomato plants in a raised garden off to the side. I decided that the family didn't have a lot of money but, by the looks of the place, the young woman was a hard worker.

I stepped up beside her and stuck my hand out. "Ma'am, I'm Tim Conway, from over Pulaski way," I said. "I'm on the fire and rescue department over there. We've been to Litchfield trying to find parts for my buddy's hay rake." I nodded at Kuhlbaugh.

"I'm Darcy," she smiled back as we walked up to the fence. This is Aiden, and his little sister, Heather. The kids looked up at us with bright eyes, smiled, and returned their attention to the horse's head hanging over the fence.

"And this is Josie," she said. The horse's eyes lit up in recognition and she gave a little wicker of welcome.

"Nice to meet you, Darcy," I said, while reaching out to let Josie smell my palm.

Kuhlbaugh stood there, looking incredulous.

I stroked the horse's graying muzzle and

talked sweet talk to her.

"You're a horse lover. I can tell," Darcy said. My husband, Tony, couldn't care either way."

"Doesn't know what he's missing," I replied.

The little kids had disappeared into the barn and came running back out with fists full of grass hay which they promptly thrust at Josie. "Can we go for a ride?" asked the little boy, who I took to be around four years old.

"Later, after supper and chores are done," his mother answered.

The little kids hung their heads momentarily, but soon perked right up. They were two busy experiencing life to be depressed.

The horse noisily munched its hay.

I turned to face Kuhlbaugh, who'd hung back. If I didn't know better I'd have thought he was afraid of horses. I felt the fireman come out of me. "Hey Delmont," I called, "don't you think this is a friendly horse?" I patted Josie's muzzle. Kuhlbaugh's real name is John, but I couldn't help having some fun with him.

"It's a nice horse," he agreed, not coming

any closer.

"I think she wants you to pet her," I said waving him forward.

"That's okay," he said, nervously looking around.

That's when I knew it. He was afraid of the horse. The guy who'd tackle suspects, gets in physical fights with drug dealers, and had, according to legend, been in at least one shoot-out, was afraid of a little, old, horse. And I mean old. The poor girl had to be at least twenty-five.

"Guess what, kids," I said. "My buddy Delmont, here, used to be a real cowboy. From Montana, big-sky country." I was really warming up now. The kids turned and stared up at Kuhlbaugh with wide, admiring eyes.

"Say," I said to Darcy, "that your husband's Dodge truck? Some people don't care for Dodge's, isn't that right, Delmont?" I looked at Kuhlbaugh.

He shook his head at me and rolled his eyes. I wished Hank, Kip, and the gang were here to experience the fun.

"That's my truck," Darcy said. "Tony's the one who put the dent in it, though. Backed into the hay elevator. It's hard to see the far corner of the truck when you try to get close to something."

I thought of the two times I'd smashed the right-rear, tail light lens on my own truck, trying to get close to something to either load or unload.

"I know how that goes," I replied. "He dent the bumper, too?"

"No, I'm afraid I did that," Darcy answered, laughingly. "Did it down at the feed mill in Homer."

I chuckled along with her. "The guy at the Case-IH dealer thought your truck was a Ford. He got it mixed up with a friend's Ford. They're both white, all-wheel drive, extended cabs, so I guess I can see how he'd do it."

"Hmm," Darcy said, "maybe what he saw was Tony's friend's truck. It's a Ford extended cab. White, like mine," she said.

My eyes met Kuhlbaugh's. This is it, I thought. "Dented fender?" I asked.

"No, that's the thing. It isn't dented up, just rusty," she replied.

"Oh," I said, trying not to sound disappointed.

"Tony took my truck to order parts last

week, 'cause it was low on gas. He was going to fill it up in Litchfield. His buddy, Jeff, followed him in, then went on home from there."

"I guess the guys at the store could have seen both trucks and gotten them confused," I said. "It happens."

"I guess so," she shrugged.

"Well," I said, "thanks for your time. Be sure to tell Tony his baler part is in. Nice kids, too," I said with a wave to the little ones, hoping I'd covered all bases.

"Nice meeting you, Mr. Conway," Darcy smiled brightly. "You too, Delmont," she said, giving Kuhlbaugh a friendly smile.

We got in the truck. The little boy and girl started to run down the drive after us, yelling "Goodbye Delmont!" until their mother called them off. They stood on the porch smiling and waving like we were long lost relatives.

"I almost wanted to give the girl the hundred bucks," I said, pulling out the gravel drive.

"Huh?" Kuhlbaugh looked at me.

"You know, for the gun," I said, grinning. "She could sure use it."

We'd left the farm behind. Flint's car

came up behind and followed us.

"Delmont?" Kuhlbaugh gave me a look.

"Hey, it all fit, didn't it?" I said. "You're lucky I didn't tell her you had the hundred dollars for her husband," I added with a snort.

"Firemen," he stated, "I'll never figure you guys out."

"So," I said, "you think that's the truck or a dead end?"

"Dead end," the detective said. "We're back to square one.

Glancing over at him, I said, "Put a hot tail on the lovely Mrs. LaBlanc and I bet you'll find your shooter. No pun intended."

He shook his head. "You're a sick boy, Conway," he said with a grin. "We've already got that going on. She, her husband, and the boys."

"Something's going to pop loose," I said. "I can feel it in my bones."

"We've rattles some cages," Kuhlbaugh admitted. "You and McIntyre especially so."

He punched in a number on his smart phone and called Flint. He relayed the story of the white Dodge. I noticed he left out the parts about the horse, and Delmont.

Chapter Thirty-five

July 4th. I'd been looking forward to my eldest granddaughter, Evelyn, coming up from Yorktown, Indiana, to ride in the parade with us. Something had come up, and she couldn't make it. Band, or some sort of play practice the next day, my wife said. So the wife and I loaded up the '62 Studebaker Lark with folding chairs, cold drinks, and quilts for the show, then drove over to Hanover. I followed the signs to the east side and the elementary school parking lot, where we sat in a short line of classic cars to register for the parade.

After receiving the registration forms, I parked the Studebaker and unloaded the quilt supplies. The wife and I lugged them to the area where *the quilt ladies*, as I call them, displayed their projects. I helped her put her quilts on a display rack, chatted up a few old ladies, and then we returned to the car.

Popping the trunk, I got out a folding chair, and my wife sat down to read a book while I checked out the other classic cars. Most were from the mid fifties on up - Chevrolets and Fords, mainly. One old fellow had an ancient REO touring car. I stopped to look it over and we talked for some twenty minutes.

I walked back to the Lark.

"I see you met a new friend," my wife said.

"You know me," I said, "no strangers, only friends I haven't met yet."

She closed her book, another mystery of some sort, and put it into her bag. "Let's go look at the horses," she said, getting up from the chair. I popped the trunk again and she put the bag in on top of the folding chair.

Horses and antique tractors were grouped separately in a mowed field to the south of the school.

We walked past the line waiting for the porta potty and down the row of a dozen or so horse trailers. There must have been every type of horse imaginable tied off to the sides of the trailers, eating hay, calling out to other horses, or simply just standing there looking bored. 4H kids and adults fussed over several, getting them decorated for the parade.

Off to my right, the sounds of old tractor engines popping, barking, and rumbling, called to me.

"Go ahead," my wife said in response to my pleading look. "I'll be along shortly."

I had already turned and walked away.

Several rows of tractors were lined up, not for the parade, but for the tractor pulls afterward. I looked over the major brands as I made a bee line for a Minneapolis-Moline ZB. There were a few Molines, with only two actually entered in the parade. As usual, the John Deere club was well represented as were the IHC collectors.

I was drawn to a lone Ford 8N, sitting in the bright sunlight like a shrine to Dearborn, all painted up better than what the factory would have done.

Hank would have been proud. I'd talked to him earlier that morning and he expected to leave the hospital the next day, the fifth.

"I'm still working on the Doctor," he said. "He knows mom now, and feels safe letting me go home under her care."

I smiled at the thought of Hank's mother whipping him into shape.

Walking on, I came to the ZB Moline and walked slowly around it, looking at little details as I went. I stopped and checked out the wiring on the voltage regulator. My model R Moline didn't have stock wiring and I was curious about how any others were wired. The Moline regulator mounts on top of the generator and I peered in behind it to check out the wire connections.

"How's it going today?" a friendly voice called.

I looked up. A man about my age, or a few years older, was walking over, holding a styrofoam cup in one hand. He sipped from it, then nodded at the tractor.

"Any questions about Minni-Molines?" he asked.

"I have a model R and the voltage regulator is mounted with the connections facing out," I said. "Several, like yours, have the regulator turned 180 degrees."

"The factory shipped them with the regulator mounted like this one," he said, pointing.

"Hmm." I took out my phone and took a

picture. We started talking Molines and tractors in general. He told me about an informal gathering the retired tractor guys had each weekday morning for coffee and doughnuts, and invited me to show up.

"By the way," I said, looking into the man's smiling face, "anyone in this area have a white Ford pickup, an extended cab? I was talking to a young man who drove that truck and wanted to buy some spare truck parts I have," I explained. "I didn't get his name, but sure would like to catch up with him."

He thought a minute, "No, I don't know anyone who has a truck like that." He shook his head. "Guess I'm not much help."

"That's okay," I replied. "I'll catch up with him later." We'll catch up to him all right, I thought.

All to soon, the wife walked up. I shook the man's hand, thanked him for his time, and left.

"No problem. I enjoyed the talk." He smiled and nodded.

"Make another new friend?" my wife asked.

"Yes," I answered, "and I got invited to coffee at the Dead Pecker Society."

"The what?" she stopped walking and turned

to stare at me.

"You've heard of the Dead Poets Society, right?" I asked with a straight-face.

"Yes, but I can't imagine you tractor guys discussing poetry."

"This is a loose group of old tractor collectors who meet for coffee and doughnuts each weekday morning in a guy's pole barn," I said. "Hank's mentioned them. I'll have to go with him sometime when he's out of the hospital, if his mother will let him go."

"Old, retired guys, huh?" my wife said grinning, with a thoughtful look on her face. "I get the club name now."

"It isn't a club," I reminded her. We started walking again, back to the Lark.

"It's very informal" I said. "Guys show up when they want to. They talk tractors and solve the world's problems. Kick in a buck or two for coffee and rolls and you're all set."

"Just old guys?"

"Yes, no ladies allowed, I'm afraid."

"Then, it's a club," she stated firmly.

I looked at her, and smiled. Thirty-five years...

We walked back past the horses and arrived at the car. A young man and lady came around and picked up the information card that I'd filled out for the Lark. We were car number twenty-six. There were a good dozen after us. Up ahead, on a side street, the police cars, veteran color guard, and community business floats started the parade. Slowly, the different parade elements moved out and took up their positions. Harried looking volunteers, wearing official Hanover Fourth of July T-shirts, ran around and directed them.

I saw Schultzie drive our tanker around a far corner. He had his kids with him and they were already tossing candy to other little kids along the route. Kip and his family followed in Engine 1. Next came Nan with Fred's oldest daughter, Maureen, in the grass rig.

After fifteen minutes, the first classic cars fell in line, followed by the tractors. Horses followed the tractors with volunteers wielding shovels and a wheel barrow bringing up the rear. The last car in the parade was Officer Jordon's squad car.

Up ahead, we could see boy and girl scouts walking along, as were various church groups. Local politicians worked the crowd along the route, handing out candy and pamphlets.

"Slide the sunroof back?" I asked the wife as we paused momentarily.

"I don't think it will be too warm," she replied.

I reached up and, turning the unlocking handle, slid the folding sunroof back a foot or so. Studebaker called their sunroofed cars "skytops" and they were a rarity. Heck, having a Studebaker was a rarity. We welcomed the sunlight and fresh air from the open roof. I liked to stick my hand up through it and wave to little kids and old people along the street. They seemed to like it the most.

As we crept along the parade route, I watched behind the crowds and along the side streets where vehicles were parked, hoping to get a glimpse of a white Ford pickup. I had a few false sightings, but didn't see the one I was looking for.

Forty minutes later, we'd finished the parade and drove back a side street to the staging area. I parked the Lark and we got out. The tantalizing smell of the Hanover Township Fireman's chicken barbecue drifted over to us. Hungry parade watchers stood in the line snaking around the grounds as firemen and their wives scurried about serving up chicken dinners in styrofoam boxes.

"There are the girls!" my wife yelled out as she waved and called to several of her friends. The ladies were making their way to the chicken line.

"You go ahead," I said. "You gals have a good time with the quilt show, and I'll meet you back home."

"Don't worry about me, Janet's going to drop me off around five," she said, referring to one of the gray-haired ladies in their group.

I got back into the car. She stuck her head in the window. I kissed her, then put the car in drive. It took a few minutes to negotiate the side streets clogged with cars, tractors, and horses; not to mention the swarm of pedestrians shoving strollers and leading excited little kids.

I came to Hanover Road. Traffic lightened considerably and I turned right to head west, out of town. I thought I'd take the scenic route toward Luttenton Road, then head north toward home, jogging over to Stone and up to McDonald.

Leaving the village, the road entered a gentle curve that dipped down by a shallow lake. The wind and sunlight came through the open sky-top and windows. Driving along at a leisurely forty-five miles per hour, I enjoyed the trip through the wooded country. The road climbed a gentle hill on the other side of the lake and the woods gave way to open fields and pasture. Old maple and wild-cherry trees lined the country road and the sunlight filtered down through the roof, flickering around the inside of the car.

Listening to the purr of the little Studebaker six, my mind drifted back to the events of the past two months or so.

I thought about the dead kids and the murdered fireman, Duke. His wife had packed up and put the house up for sale. The story was that she and the little kids were moving back in with her parents.

There had been a memorial for Megan Grawn, Richie's murdered girlfriend. Her parents were devastated, but her father admitted he'd always feared this is how it would end.

Claudette LaBlanc was still out on bail, and her husband, Jake, and the boys had been questioned several times by police detectives, and released. They had good lawyers. The authorities had questioned every one of the

Maple Grove Township firemen and the township and village officials as well. The village was in an uproar with speculation as to who was involved and who knew what. My new buddy, Kuhlbaugh, was rather tight-lipped about the case. So was our man, Flint. We figured, because he was a county deputy, he wasn't in the insider loop of need-to-know, anyway.

I checked my mirror to make sure I wasn't holding up traffic. The road behind me was clear.

I passed a large farm house where several cars were parked in the yard in the shade of a gnarled, old oak. A couple charcoal grills sat off to one side, smoke leaking from under their lids. Little kids kicked around a soccer ball. A tiny, mixed-breed dog chased between them, yapping loudly. Some adults were tossing horse shoes with some older kids. Red, white, and blue bunting hung from the porch of the farm house. All across America, this scene was being repeated in some form or another as the nation celebrated Independence Day.

I slowed and, sticking my arm out the open sunroof to wave, tooted the horn. The kids yelled in greeting and waved back. A few adults pointed, their faces breaking into broad grins, having never seen a Studebaker Lark before.

Accelerating back to forty-five or so, I drove on. My mind turned to Ruthie dying on Kip and Schultzie. I felt guilty not having been there to lend support, and letting the guys deal with it. Ruthie had been part of our community for a long time.

"Born and raised here," Schultzie had said. We'd held a memorial for her at the local Free Methodist Church. She had a brother and a sister that no one knew about. They showed up looking self conscious in clothes that they must have thought looked dressed up, until they saw the firemen in suits and ties. Most of our wives came along, too, to offer support to Patty and her two adult kids who lived out of the area. We'd met them once or twice over the last few years. Ruthie's ex husband lives in Jackson, but didn't show up. I wondered if he was as big an ass as she'd always claimed. The Free Methodist ladies put on a nice memorial meal in the church basement, and that was it.

I shoved the events of the past few months from my mind and tried to focus on the beautiful July day as the countryside rolled by. I couldn't have asked for a better day for a country drive. There was hardly a wisp of clouds in the sky. Clusters of farm buildings, with cattle or sheep in verdant pastures, passed by and into my rearview mirror. It was a good day to be alive in south-central Michigan. I wished the wife was with me to enjoy it.

Chapter Thirty-six

I glanced in the mirror to get another look at an old, stone smokehouse in the yard of a centennial farm, when I noticed it. A white truck was coming up rapidly from behind. A white Ford truck. I instinctively edged a few inches to the right to give the driver more room to pass. The truck pulled up behind for a moment. To close for my comfort, but I was used to people wanting to get close. They liked to check out the Studebaker name on the trunk lip.

There were two young men in the truck. They pulled around the car and came up beside me. When they didn't pass, I glanced over. The passenger motioned for me to pull over. It was then I saw the dent in the rear fender of the truck. Trying to remain calm, I looked at him questioningly. I found myself looking at a pistol in the guy's hand. He didn't point it at me, but wagged the barrel for me to pull over. That's when all hell broke loose.

I jammed on the brakes and the truck flashed by. There was the dented rear bumper that I expected to see. The brake lights came on and the Ford skidded to a stop twenty yards ahead, crossing the road, and effectively blocking my way.

"What the ...!" I exclaimed, reaching toward the glove box to retrieve the .380 I'd placed in there that morning. Hank and Flint had really been laying it on me about not being armed, so I was trying to be prepared.

Two young men got out of the truck. Leaving the doors open, they began walking my way. Strutting was more like it. The dark haired passenger still carried the pistol.

Snatching up the .380, I sat back up and pulled the shift lever down from drive into reverse. The old Borg-Warner automatics had reverse gear down where modern trannies have drive. In my panic, I was glad I remembered to pull the shift lever down and not up, into park.

The Studebaker shot backward, at least for the little six cylinder, it shot.

The guy with the pistol sneered and raised his arm to point it at me. He was going to shoot at my Studebaker!

Stomping on the brakes, I threw the shift lever up into park and dove out the driver's door, pointing my pistol at the pair. They stopped and looked at each other with confusion, not knowing what to do next. I figured their prior victims hadn't had a firearm to defend themselves.

I used the indecision on their part to scoot around the back of the Lark and into the ditch. Creeping along through the weeds and dead leaves in the ditch and up alongside the car, I paused where I could peek out from behind the right-front tire.

The men took a step forward and stopped again. They didn't have that cocky, smart-ass look on their faces now.

"Come any closer and I'll shoot," I bellowed at them, hoping I sounded a lot tougher than I felt.

"You won't shoot us," the driver said, not sounding too sure of himself. "We just want to talk." He was a thin, white male, about six feet tall, with lighter colored hair. I noticed he was wearing a baggy Pistons basketball jersey and equally baggy shorts. His red, high-top basketball shoes were untied, the long white laces flopping as he walked. A wanna-be gang banger.

The guy with the pistol still held it pointed in my direction, but not directly at me.

"Lower your weapon," I shouted.

"We just want to talk," the diver repeated as his friend kept the gun trained my way.

I detected some nervousness in his voice and now wondered how this was going to play out. Would I have to fire off a round to let them know I was serious?

"Lower your weapon," I called again. "I don't even know you guys. What is it that you want to talk about?" Keep them talking. I had a pretty good idea what they wanted, but sure wasn't going to let those idiots know.

"You need to back off your investigating Claudette," the one with the pistol called out. "She has nothing to do with you."

"You need to talk to the police about that," I shouted back. "Now get back in your truck and keep moving." I sighted in on his chest with my weapon, my heart pounding in my ears. With my luck, this would be the perfect time to have a heart attack.

"We're not going anywhere," the pistol guy said. He looked up, past my Lark, and down the road behind me. I could hear a car approaching at high speed.

I cringed and got a sinking feeling inside. Don't let this be some of their punk friends. The image of Duke William's body floating face-down in the pond popped into my head. I didn't want to end up the same way, or maybe being burned up in my little Lark in a woodlot somewhere. I was sure glad my wife had stayed behind with her friends and wasn't with me – even more glad my little granddaughter couldn't make it this year.

The two turned tail and ran toward their truck.

I glanced back in time to see a Jackson County Sheriff's car come racing up behind me, then whip out to go around the Studebaker. Flint! Man, was I glad to see him! He'd barely stopped when the guy with the pistol opened up on his car from behind the truck bed. Flint's door popped open and he tumbled out, service weapon firing as he came. The police car was parked at an angle across the road, maybe ten yards ahead of me. I heard rounds zipping through the air and ducked back behind the Lark's front tire.

The pickup driver had retrieved a rifle from behind the truck seat and pointed it at Flint's car. I heard the crack! crack! crack! as he jerked the trigger, causing the rounds to go high. It sounded like a .22 caliber semi-automatic.

Flint worked his way to the back fender of his patrol car and crouched behind the rear tire.

"Drop your weapons!" he shouted. His call was met with a barrage of rounds that shattered the side windows of his cruiser.

"Damn!" he shouted to no one in particular as shards of glass flew. Duck-walking to the open driver's door, he attempted to reach in for the radio mike. More shots forced him to back out. He scooted himself back to safety behind the rear tire. His eyes met mine.

"You okay?" he called to me.

"Yeah. Just a little shook up," I called back.

He nodded. The firing had stopped. Flint peeked under his car. I could see glimpses of the guys behind the truck. They were talking excitedly about something.

"You want me to give some support?" I asked Flint.

"Not now," he said, glancing my way. "There should be help coming along soon." He said it loud enough for the gunmen to overhear.

The skinny guy with the rifle popped up and fired off a round that ricocheted off the pavement under the squad car.

Flint sprung up over the trunk and squeezed off three quick shots before emptying his magazine. He dropped down, fumbling for his spare magazine and had it slip from his grasp and clatter to the pavement. Frantically looking around, he spotted it laying in the road, near where he'd tumbled out of his car.

"Damn!" he exclaimed again.

I followed his gaze, then looked back at him, meeting his eyes. He shook his head in disgust. I spotted the shotgun mounted in front of the seat and wished I had it now.

Crab-walking down the ditch behind my Studebaker, I scrambled up onto the road and, keeping as low as my old knees would allow, hustled to Flint's side. "Here buddy, use mine," I said, handing him my .380 and a spare magazine.

"Thanks, man," he said in relief, "I owe you big time." He slipped his thumb over the safety and flicked it off.

"Next fire run, you're buying the doughnuts," I said, laughing in spite of myself as Flint forced a grin.

It was quiet on the other side of the truck. The sound of a tractor running came to us from somewhere off across a distant field.

Flint peered around the back of the patrol car bumper and watched.

I got low and could see the feet of the two men hiding behind the pickup, then I crept alongside the patrol car. Flint saw what I was doing and nodded his head. He got a two handed grip on the pistol, ready to give covering fire as I inched up and leaned in over the seat. Pushing the release button and grabbing the shotgun from it's mounting, I eased back out, avoiding the shattered window glass. On the way out, I grabbed the radio mike and pulled it along with me as far as the cord would stretch. Flint grinned.

We were dealing with amateurs. I scrambled over and handed the shotgun to Flint, who promptly racked a shell into the chamber. I only hoped the men wouldn't do something stupid and try to rush us.

"Okay, cover me," he said, slipping the safety on and handing back my pistol.

I lay on the pavement and peered from behind the back tire of the patrol car, watching as the deputy inched along to the mike flopped on the car seat. Reaching in with one hand, he keyed the mike and called in to Central Dispatch.

The guy with the pistol popped over the bed of the pickup and fired at us, the rounds whistling over-head. I squeezed off one round from my spot, striking the pickup bed, and he ducked back down, cursing loudly.

"Yes, those were shots being fired, damnit!" I heard Flint exclaiming to the person on the other end of the radio. "Get somebody out here!" he shouted. He dropped the mike and scooted to the front of the car, behind the left front tire. "How do I get into these things?" he muttered, glancing over at me.

I grinned at him, "Damn, we're in a tight spot," I said, using one of my favorite movie lines.

"Guess it could be worse," he muttered,

shaking his head.

Shouting and scurrying sounds came to us from behind the pickup. Flint peeked cautiously over the hood of the cruiser and then stood, shotgun at the ready.

"Drop the weapons and walk slowly toward me," he barked. "That's it, keep the hands up."

I peeked around the trunk and saw the men walking around the rear of the pickup, hands thrust over their heads. What had caused their sudden change of heart? Then I saw the reason they'd given up. Hank McIntyre was walking briskly down the sun dappled road from the west. His truck was parked across the road about fifty yards back. He clutched his .45 in his right hand. From the look on his face, I thought he was intent on killing someone. I was ready to throw down my own weapon.

Hank approached the pickup and leaned against the truck bed, holding his weapon in both hands, elbows on the bed rail. He trained it on the two as they walked slowly toward Flint. He stood, stony-faced, not saying a word. I stood and pointed my pistol into the ditch. No need risking an errant shot with Hank in the way.

Flint ordered the men to separate by a couple of feet, then to face away from him, drop to their knees, and lie on the ground, arms and legs spread. Hank stepped around the truck while Flint walked slowly forward, stooping slightly to scoop up the errant magazine. I walked around the rear of the patrol car, slipping the safety on and keeping the pistol pointed down.

Flint and I met up on the other side of the car. He handed me the shotgun, ejected the spent magazine from his gun, and inserted the fresh one all in one clean motion. I don't think he ever took his eyes off the two guys on the road in front of us.

I double checked the safety, then tucked my .380 into a back pocket. I flicked on the shotgun's safety as well and, keeping my finger well away from the trigger, swung the barrel on the men laying in the road.

Behind us, a State Police Cruiser pulled up and stopped. The officer, one that I recognized from the Jonesville post, got out and hustled forward, pulling a set of handcuffs from his belt. He straddled one man and soon had his arms secured behind him. Flint had his man secure and I stepped back, directing the shotgun muzzle into the ditch.

Hank lowered his .45, looked at me and smiled that winning smile. "Tim Conway," he fairly shouted, "how nice to see you."

"Hank," I replied in greeting. I realized I was breathing heavily, and my throat was dry. I needed a bottle of water from the small cooler bag on the floor of the Studebaker. I'd get one soon. Besides, my right shoulder was starting to hurt from scrambling around in the ditch, and I needed some Motrin.

"Good work, Conway," Hank continued, glancing down at the men.

He turned and grinned at Flint and the state guy.

"Thanks, man." Flint glanced over at him. "You came along at the right time."

"Just what we needed, some more men up here," Hank paraphrased a line from a book by E.B. Sledge about Marines on Iwo Jima. "You guys were caught between a rock and a hard place."

"On the horns of a dilemma," I responded.

Hank grinned mischievously.

The state guy read the men their rights as Flint frisked them for hidden weapons. He turned their pockets, then pulled their wallets and checked their identification.

"Dillon Mark Danovitch," Flint said glancing over at the pistol shooter. "You're a long way from Nevada, kid." He waved the driver's license in front of the young man's face.

"Hey, don't we know someone from Nevada?" Hank looked at us, eyes bright with recognition.

"I'd say we've recently met someone," I said, rubbing my chin thoughtfully. We all looked at Danovitch.

"She's my sister," he said quietly while looking forlornly down at the roadway.

"Who's your sister?" Flint asked, cupping his hand to his ear and leaning forward, grinning from ear to ear. He looked like a teacher addressing a recalcitrant student.

"Claudette. Claudette's my older sister," Danovitch replied in a low voice. There was a big difference between his attitude now, and when he was walking back on me, pistol in hand.

The State Policeman escorted the driver, the one who fired the rifle, to his cruiser. Another state car had arrived and Flint walked Dillon over to a trooper who placed him in the back seat.

From behind Hank, a county patrol car stopped next to his truck and an officer got out and walked our way.

A State Command car pulled up alongside the State Police cars behind me. I looked around. The sounds of radio traffic came from the open windows of the idling cars and the light bars flashed. Policemen seemed to pop out of the woodwork.

A civilian drove up in a four-door pickup, talked to an officer, then turned his truck around and left, his wife and kids gawking in fascination.

I looked at Hank. "What are you doing out of the hospital?" I asked, while walking over to stand beside him. "I'm sure surprised to see you."

"They'd been getting me up every day to walk a little and I got tired of hanging around. So, here I am," he replied. "Besides, I only had one more day to go."

"You put some clothes on, or walk out in a hospital gown?" I asked. I could just see Hank walking down Michigan Avenue in Jackson, wearing his footies, hospital gown flapping open in the back, thumb out, looking for a ride home.

"It was all proper and legal," he said. "Though I have to admit, I'm still a little sore. Musta' pulled something hiking down from my pickup." He turned and looked back at his truck, still sitting across the road in the shade of a towering, old oak tree.

"But, how'd you end up here?" I asked, glancing around at all of the police cars huddled around Flint's patrol car.

"I was sitting in the back yard with my mom and Shonda, enjoying a cold Dr. Pepper. The police monitor was on in the background. When I heard Flint call in to Central Dispatch about tailing a white pickup truck out of Hanover, it got my attention. He said the truck was following a Studebaker. I put it all together and got my butt over here."

"A stitch in time," I said, dead pan.

"Squeaky wheel," Hank answered, grinning.

I looked over at Flint who was watching a trooper put markers near the spent shell casings. "Hey Flint, looks like I owe you one today," I said.

He grinned and wagged his head. "No problem. Mutual aid, you know."

A State Trooper whom I hadn't met before

walked up to me. "Conway?" he asked.

I nodded my head.

"I'll need your weapon," he said in a serious tone. He held out his hand.

Reaching into my back pocket, I pulled out my .380, ejected the magazine, racked the shell out of the chamber, and handed it over.

"There should be a spent .380 casing near the back of Flint's car," I pointed back to the patrol car. It was then that I really noticed the shot-out side windows and at least two holes in the front passenger door.

The officer nodded. "Got a permit?" He was going to play it by the book.

I pulled my wallet and handed over my CCW permit and my driver's license. Just in case he wanted to compare me with my photo.

He took my license, looked it over, glanced at me, then handed it back.

"It's okay, officer. Special Investigator Conway is with me," Hank said, producing his badge. He handed the I.D. wallet to the officer who took it and looked it over closely before handing it back.

Now I was a 'Special Investigator.' Where would this end up? I wondered. The wife would never believe it.

Flint had stepped over and watched carefully. I knew he was loving this.

He said, "Mr. Conway was stopped on the roadway by these individuals who probably would have killed him. We suspect they're the same ones who shot agent McIntyre, here." He pointed at Hank.

The trooper nodded thoughtfully, then handed back my CCW permit and, to my surprise, my pistol.

"I think a statement should be sufficient, today," he said with a slight nod of his head.

He still had a serious, all business, look on his face. He must have been the white, twin brother to the black Indiana State Trooper we'd met outside of Angola.

A female State Police Officer came over, carrying a note pad. She started taking our names and individual statements.

A blue van had pulled up. Two men got out and began taking pictures and measurements. One man picked up the shooter's pistol and put it in a plastic bag, labeled it, and sealed it. His partner picked up the rifle, tagged it, and placed it in a large plastic bag.

The lady State Trooper finished taking my statement, smiled and said, "You sure were lucky today."

"I know," I said. "I could have been shot."

"Well, that, too," she said. Then gestured toward the Studebaker. "Not a mark on your car," she said, still smiling.

"I hadn't thought of that," I said with relief.

"Well, that's a nice little Lark you've got there."

I looked at her, puzzled.

My grandfather drove Studebakers," she said, looking at me with bright eyes.

"From Indiana?" I raised my eyebrows questioningly.

"Kokomo," she replied.

"Muncie," I said in return.

"Good luck," she said. Giving me a pat on the arm, she turned and left.

"Thanks, officer," I called.

She waved and walked over to Flint, turned to a fresh page in her notebook, and began getting his story. If I knew Flint, he'd probably get a copy to help with filling out his own report later. Having drawn his gun, fired shots, and gotten his car shot up, he was going to have one heckuva report.

I turned to Hank. "So, did you see the parade? 'Cause I didn't see *you*," I said.

"Na, I didn't get home 'til after it started," he said. "It was enough just getting home."

"Well, as usual, I'm mighty glad to see you," I replied, extending my arm to shake his hand.

The police got everyone's statements, finished taking photos and measurements, and I was allowed to leave. When I pulled the Studebaker Lark into my driveway, my wife's quilt-club friend was just leaving in her Buick. I tapped the horn and waved. My wife would never believe my story.

I gave the little Studebaker a last inspection, then parked it in the garage.

Within minutes, I was sitting on the deck in the warm late-afternoon sun and relaying the whole story to one amazed wife. She didn't look happy.

"You could have been shot, or, or, even killed," she stammered.

"Yeah, but did you get the part about 'Special Investigator?'" I asked. Apparently she wasn't paying full attention.

"Is that what you got out of this?" she

asked incredulously. "Special Investigator, indeed!"

"Well, that's not all," I said. "The Lark wasn't damaged, so I guess all's well that ends well."

"I need a wine cooler," she said, getting up from her chair.

"Why don't you have two or three?" I asked, smirking as I watched her enter the house. "Then we can both enjoy them later," I suggestively called after her.

She stuck her head back through the slider door. "You already had your fireworks for the day, buddy."

I shook my head at her. Thirty-five years of marriage..."

Chapter Thirty-seven

I sipped my coffee from a styrofoam cup and took another bite from the thick, Amish-baked, sweet roll that Hank had brought to the fire barn. He sat across the table from me in the kitchen area, Kip at his left and Nan on his right. Schultzie and Walt were to my right, with Flint on the far end.

It was Saturday morning and no one had anywhere to be for an hour or so. Kip brought the coffee maker from his office to sit next to the one in the break room. I'd made a couple pots of coffee and Hank had paid a visit to the Amish bakery that morning, bringing in two dozen fresh doughnuts. The smell of coffee, mixing with the heady aroma of the doughnuts, put us practically in fireman's heaven.

We sat drinking coffee and eating as we talked over the case. In a way, we were celebrating. I felt a certain sense of euphoria, like we'd solved America's number one crime.

Nan put down her coffee cup, the one from Gas-N-Go, and looked around the table. "What happened to the guys from Romulus that were arrested in the traffic stop?" she asked. "How exactly were they connected?"

I'd almost forgotten about them.

"You must mean Mr. Green and Mr. Brown." Kuhlbaugh's voice came from the doorway. We all turned and looked as the detective walked into the room.

"The men have been charged with possession, distribution, and conspiracy," he said. "They're being held in the Jackson County Jail, pending trial. Because of prior felony records, bail has been set at half a million dollars each."

We let out a collective breath of amazement and looked at each other.

Nan said, "The judge must be serious."

"Have they been linked to the LaBlancs?" Walt asked.

"The two worked for a wanna-be big time dealer in Detroit and purchased meth from the LaBlancs. That's the connection," Kuhlbaugh

said.

"Sometimes they'd trade heroin for the meth," Hank added from his spot across the table. He'd taken a sip of coffee and absent-mindedly turned the mug between his large hands.

Kuhlbaugh poured himself a cup of coffee, pulled up an extra chair, and sat down at a corner of the table, next to Flint.

Hank shoved the box of doughnuts toward him.

"Thanks," he said, his face lighting up. He took a moment to decide, then selected a rather large glazed one.

Nan handed him a paper towel. He put the doughnut on it and looked around at us.

"Claudette LaBlanc had her own suppliers around the countryside," the detective said. "Mostly young people, teenagers and twenty-somethings. They kept a stream of meth coming into the organization. This not-so-little enterprise kept the kids in spending money, heroin, and of course, meth."

"So that's where the kid in the white van came in?" Nan asked, a look of concern on her face.

"Mmm, hmm," Kuhlbaugh said with a nod. He

swallowed some coffee. "The LaBlanc boys helped recruit and get the network of kids going. I guess they'd do anything for their step-mother," he said.

"Hell, who wouldn't," Flint added with a smile of delight.

The rest of us laughed somewhat guiltily at his comment while glancing over at Nan.

"How exactly was Jake involved, other than being married to the woman?" Schultz asked. "Heck," he added, "I went to school with the guy, and find it hard to believe he'd be so stupid." He looked at Kip, who'd also known the ex Maple Grove Chief since childhood. "He could be a jerk sometimes, but I couldn't imagine him being in the drug trade."

"Betraying his community like that," Kip added with a nod.

"He had his own little racket going with department funds and supplies over at Maple Grove," Kuhlbaugh said.

"When he met the lovely Mrs. LaBlanc," Flint nodded at me, "he had no idea what he was in for. She saw what was going on, had a few prior contacts and made some new ones. That's when they went big-time. The boys were quite taken with her. I guess as we all were."

"NOT I!" Nan spoke up forcefully. "The woman didn't impress me at all."

"Well, nevertheless," Flint smiled at Nan, "Mark and Mike LaBlanc soon fell under her spell and recruited friends as runners and suppliers."

"She tried to work her spell on Duke Williams," Kuhlbaugh said. "Apparently, he went along for the ride, if you get my drift, then balked at getting in too deep."

Hank met my gaze from across the table. I knew he was thinking of the time we saw LaBlanc's wife and Williams coming out of the Pulaski General Store and riding off together in that Jaguar convertible.

"Well, it ended up getting him killed for his troubles," Kip reasoned.

"When you have only one thing on your mind...," Nan offered.

Kuhlbaugh smiled. "Yes, I guess Duke had something on his mind. That's probably why he and Jake were such good drinking buddies."

"He was married, for God's sake," Nan interjected, "with kids." She flushed red.

We men looked at each other, not knowing how to answer.

"He was married and he made a bad choice,"

Flint said, looking at Nan. "But, he tried to come around and square things up. When he went to break it off with Claudette LaBlanc, she asked to see him one more time, only her two murderous friends were with her. That's how they got close, they were with Claudette under the guise of a double date."

"The two people we, I mean you, caught on the farm south-west of Reading?" I asked.

"That's right," Hank answered for him. "The two people we caught hiding in the pole barn on the farm, the same day you and I inspected the burned out hulk of Duke's pickup truck."

"Where was Duke killed?" Walt asked. We were all sitting quietly listening to the story unfold from the major players. It suddenly dawned on me that I was one of the major players.

Flint cleared his throat, "Duke was lured to a rural area not far from the pond where the boys discovered his body. His killers are finally talking and have filled us in on how they did it."

Kuhlbaugh nodded in agreement, his mouth full of glazed doughnut.

We were all turned in our seats to face

Flint, coffee cups or doughnuts in hand, eager to hear the details.

Flint continued, "The killers were walking behind Duke and Claudette. The male pulled a .22 pistol from under his shirt and shot Duke twice in the back and finished him off with a shot to the back of the head."

Kuhlbaugh leaned forward and took a refill of coffee offered by Kip. He took a sip and looked around the table at our unbelieving faces.

Nan looked shocked, her face pale.

The detective said, "The killers then used Duke's pickup to transport his body to the pond where they slid it in. Then, they used a long sapling to shove him out into the water. He must have drifted some. The next day the boys were back gigging for frogs, and well, the rest you know," he concluded.

"So," I said, "Claudette LaBlanc didn't pull the trigger, but she was a conspirator?"

"That's right," answered Flint. "She called the shots for the gang, so to speak.

And," he continued, "Claudette's brother and his buddy, who turned out to be a petty crook from Coldwater, are cooling their heels in the Jackson County Jail. They claim shooting Hank was an accident. They only meant to scare him."

Kuhlbaugh let out a snort, "Those idiots couldn't even do that right."

"Hank makes too big of a target. They couldn't miss," Flint said with a laugh.

"They did enough," Hank said. He shook his head and took up the story. "Meagan Grawn made the mistake of answering her cell when Claudette called her. Claudette made like they were old pals and all was forgiven. Under the guise of taking her to a job interview, and a new life, in Angola, the killers took Meagan to a rural area near the Ohio border and killed her by walking up behind her with the .22 pistol. She never saw it coming. They dumped the truck, with the body in it, over in Indiana and torched it."

"That's where our trail of fun began," I said, "leading to Claudette LaBlanc's arrest and the rescue of Richie Collins from certain death."

Nan blanched white. "She was killing off witnesses one by one," she said, shaking her head.

"Yes," I said, "those who weren't dying on their own from overdoses or accidents."

"Who picked the killers up on the road in Indiana?" Walt asked. "Did one of them drive the body to the clearing and the other follow?"

"I wondered the same thing," Hank said. "The killers both admitted that they rode together with the body wrapped in a tarp in the truck bed." He looked across the table at me. "That's the blue scrap that we saw in the back. They moved the body to the front seat before torching the truck," he said.

"They had it worked out with Mrs. LaBlanc to pick them up at the road, and that's how it happened," added Kuhlbaugh with a nod.

Nan asked, "But, did Jake actually know any of this was going on?"

"Jake knew something was going on," Kuhlbaugh said. "He was worried about being found out, that's why he started showing up at overdose calls and wrecks where runners had drugs on them, trying to keep things cleaned up and his wife out of trouble. I think he liked the money, and of course he liked the exotic woman in the form of Claudette LaBlanc."

Flint said, "He got involved in the delivery of drugs as a supervisor, but I'm convinced he knew nothing of the murders. He just got drawn into her little web and couldn't get out. But, like I said, look at her."

That last remark elicited a look of disgust from Nan and chuckles from us guys.

Flint said, "This has killed the talk of Jake running for township treasurer next year, that's for sure."

Kuhlbaugh sipped his coffee, then spoke. "The LaBlancs have all posted bond. Jake and the boys are restricted to the state and must wear ankle tethers." He paused and looked around the table at us, as if not knowing what to say next.

"And the Missus?" Kip prompted.

"As of this morning, can't be found," Kuhlbaugh said with a shake of his head. "She was wearing an ankle bracelet, too, that turned up sometime last night on a draft horse down by Camden."

We all looked at each other in stunned silence.

"Well, that's nice," Kip said disgustedly, sliding his chair back. He got up, rinsed his cup, and put it in the sink. "I've got a garage to start on." He shook his head in resignation.

The rest of us sat like we'd been struck dumb. My eyes met Hank's across the table.

"This is the first I've heard of it," he said with a sigh, "but if she's in southern Michigan, we'll find her."

I nodded in agreement.

John Riley and his wife, Susan, live on a small farm near Parma, in south-central Michigan. He is a retired elementary school teacher as well as a farmer and writer. Riley uses Minneapolis-Moline and Cockshutt farm equipment. His fair weather driver is a 1964 Studebaker.

Made in the USA
Charleston, SC
29 July 2016